D0298264

ALL
THEIR
MINDS
IN
TANDEM

ALL
THEIR
MINDS
IN
TANDEM

David Sanger

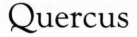

First published in Great Britain in 2016 by

Quercus Editions Ltd
Carmelite House
50 Victoria Embankment
London EC4Y 0DZ

An Hachette UK company

A CIP catalogue record for this book is available
from the British Library.

ISBN 978 1 78429 395 6 (HB)
ISBN 978 1 78429 396 3 (TPB)
ISBN 978 1 78429 397 0 (EBOOK)

For Mum and Dad
For Kat

Keep out of the Past! for its highways
Are damp with malarial gloom;
Its gardens are sere, and its forests are drear,
And everywhere moulders a tomb . . .

Ella Wheeler Wilcox

VETERANS
ARE YOU FIXING TO FORGET?

The war is done but your troubles are not.
Forget or else remember better things.
Leave word for 'the maker' at
Main St. Post Office, New Georgetown.
Fee depends on trauma.

Excerpt from the *West Virginian Oracle*,
Issue 34 (September 1879)

AUTUMN

I

October 1879

Emerson arrived and was glad for it. His heavy pack had long since begun to cut into his skin and, at seeing the fresh sign that read *Post Office*, he dropped it from his shoulders and dragged it the last few paces. Where other men tied their horses, Emerson left his pack, securing it to a wooden post. He trusted the lack of interest regarding its contents more than the men who walked by, and casually strode into the building.

A heavyset woman with greying brown hair leaned over the main desk as she sifted through a tall pile of letters. Her face was red with exertion, and a sheet of paper, possibly a letter, stuck to one of her clammy forearms. She didn't seem to notice, nor did she look up once Emerson walked in. He gazed along the sides of the post office. On the floor near a window was an upturned crate sat next to another. On the second one stood a stack of white paper, pristine and neatly ordered.

'You'll have to excuse the mess,' the woman said. 'Things have changed hands and there's plenty still to do.'

Emerson walked up to the desk and placed his hands there, pushing back the edges of envelopes with his fingertips.

'I'm here to collect some mail,' he said.

The woman smiled and looked up. She fanned her red chest with the clutch of envelopes in her hand.

'Then you're in the right place.'

She stepped back into a slight corridor lined with pigeonholes.

'Name,' she called.

'It's more a title,' Emerson began, the words soft.

'Name,' the woman called, not hearing him.

'The maker,' Emerson shouted.

'Baker?' the woman returned, tracing a finger along the italicised names below each hole.

'The maker,' Emerson repeated, looking over his shoulder to the door.

The woman looked at him and her face pushed back in the folds of her neck. A rumble came from her chest and she blew out a belch, diverting her breath as best she might. 'The maker?' she asked.

Emerson nodded, turning back to her. The woman muttered some things under her breath and took to looking over the names on the holes once more.

'As if I haven't got enough to do without some crooked-minded—'

She halted over one of the pigeonholes and peered closer, as though doubting the handwriting. With a thumbnail, she pulled the slip of card from its brass frame and studied it. Emerson watched as she wandered over and held it up to him.

'This you?' she asked.

Emerson nodded.

'My husband must have had the folly to write this down. We take names here, mister.'

4

She strode back and took a cream envelope from the pigeon-hole, tapping it against her shoulder as she went. She handed it to Emerson and then tore the label in two, all the time watching his face. Emerson pocketed the envelope and met her eyes.

'There's another. Emerson.'

'Emerson?' she asked.

'That's right.'

The woman went back and looked impatiently over the names before finding the one labelled *Emerson*. She pulled a fold of paper from this hole and handed it over.

'Any more names?' she asked him, her faced twisted with suspicion.

'No, ma'am,' Emerson said. 'And I'd appreciate it if you could keep our conversation to between us.'

The woman's eyes widened before she returned to poring over the envelopes in front of her.

'And there was me about to tell the *Gazette* all about it,' she said under her breath.

Emerson smiled and placed the fold of paper in his pocket next to the cream envelope. He took one of the dollar bills he'd gotten earlier and pushed it across the desk. The woman's eyes fixed on it like a hawk's on a mouse.

'I'd right appreciate it,' Emerson said.

The woman looked up, her fat, reddened face suddenly kinder.

'And would there be anything else I could help you with, young sir?' she said.

'This town,' Emerson began. 'It a new one?'

The woman nodded. 'Since the old one was near levelled. It's in the name too. New Georgetown. After that prancing pony, McClellan. Pretty much why I'm looking over these letters like I am. You think it's hard sending a letter to no place? Try delivering one. Another building pops up, another number does too. Then you gots yourself two "13 Chestnut Street"s. Depending on your trade, you might be able to find yourself some work.'

Emerson felt the stab of the woman's enquiries and nodded to her in thanks. Once he was outside, he drew in the cool evening air, pleased to find his pack still there. Pulling the envelope from his pocket, he tore along its edges and spilled the contents – a single white card – into his hand.

It read:

Meet me at the Long Cape tavern. Wednesday 15th, six o'clock.

The writing was finely done and gave Emerson the impression of great wealth. But he noticed the absence of a name and pondered whether to tear it up and head back the way he came. The farmer's son would most likely sell him back his horse for those same three dollars.

He looked down at the card again.

Today is Wednesday, thought Emerson.

As though the town conspired to play out the urgency of the situation, he heard the bell strike five. He twirled the card in his hand and watched as the gas lamps at the far end of the street were lit. He had not noticed the darkening blue of the sky and would have to make up his mind soon enough lest he want to sleep rough.

He read the card once more and then placed it back inside the torn envelope. Untying his pack from the post, he heaved it on to his back, the straps neatly settling in the painful grooves from before. More lights were lit as several men worked their way down the street towards him.

'I'll meet you at the Long Cape,' Emerson said in a hushed voice, as though the light might overhear his words.

2

October 1879

Like every morning before it, that one began with a memory. Despite the early hour, Kittie pushed the sheets back from her bed and walked to her parents' old room, taking a seat at her father's desk. The room sat at the front of her family's house and looked down the smooth slope of the main road leading into town. The gas lamps were lined up there like obedient fireflies. She struck a match and lit the oil lamp sitting on the desk. The warm light shone brighter and there she was in the window's reflection, intersected by the wooden hatching of the frame like a puzzle pieced together.

There's something to being up when everyone else is still, she thought.

It seemed too precious and significant a thought to let fizzle away in her sleepless mind and so she looked to write it down, searching the desk for a sheet of paper. As she did so, Kittie repeated the words aloud in her hushed, tired breath, fearing they might not care to stick around; they were beating their eager wings against the inside of her skull like a bird keen on flying away.

She pulled out the middle wooden drawer of the long desk. It squeaked in its joint and she worriedly listened for the sound of bedsprings from her sisters' rooms. No sound came though and she removed the paper, finding her father's pen too as it rolled down the tilted wooden drawer to her fingertips.

Kittie uncapped the inkwell that sat on top of the desk and lowered the pen inside. The blue liquid quivered with the movement – its first in years. She felt a tug at her conscience, something similar to betrayal, in disturbing the ink. Until that moment, the items had lain untouched, with the room only visited like a tomb. Kittie had been the one to insist it stay as such. Like a part of the past she could walk into and, in doing so, never forget.

As she moved her father's things, it was as though someone had filled her soul with warm water, the liquid washing memories free that had long stained its sides, pulling them into the potent swirl of her mind.

She wrote her earlier thought three times on the page before her –

There's something to being up when everyone else is still
There's something to being up when everyone else is still
There's something to being up when everyone else is still

– and was satisfied that would be enough.

Yet, her memory continued to scratch ardently at the door and Kittie knew she would not be able to return to her room and sleep. She instead decided to write down the things that troubled her, name those that came into her mind, hoping they would then reside on the page rather than inside her head.

Father, she wrote. And then quickly after, *Mother*.

The old walls of the room about her groaned, as if from

appreciation. The next name she waited on. The pen hovered over the page and the ink dripped until it had pooled so much she could see the nib mirrored back at her.

Shelby, she finally wrote.

August 1877

Kittie's uncle had lived in part of an old coaling station just east of the woods bordering New Georgetown. The line that ran past was a small offshoot of the Baltimore and Ohio Railroad, most notable for the views it gave as people travelled the bridge out over Honor Gorge. Tall mountain faces climbed up before them and, not being able to see from cabin windows where the train was headed, people had reason enough to worry they might plough straight into them.

Following the approach of Union troops in 1861, rebel militia burned most bridges west of Grafton, that one included. By the time Kittie's uncle inherited the place, a steam engine sat on the tracks outside and had little place to go other than straight over and down into the gorge. The wood of the bridge was blackened all the way back from the edge and the metal puckered there as though it continued to bubble in the heat of those flames.

As Kittie stepped out from the heart of the woods, her boot tapped the steel of the track that ran across her path. It was hidden beneath the clutter of nature and she brushed her foot from side to side, uncovering it. She followed its curve as it turned to point ahead of her and there, behind a veil of overhanging foliage, was the train. The locomotive was held there still as though waiting on a conductor with other intentions. Nearest to her was the welcome sight of the end carriage and the faded lettering that told her, just, that it was *Third Class*. The stones between the tracks moved against one another like giants' teeth. Weeping willows hung out over the carriage and they looked to her like the half-raised curtains of a stage.

The doors of the carriage were flung open and she grabbed onto a metal rail, pulling herself inside. The space came instantly and briefly alive as things moved into corners and spaces hitherto unseen. A mustiness hung in the carriage and misplaced weeds swung almost respectfully at her arrival. She walked down the aisle, bumping her hands along the backs of seats. Some were wet from the rainwater that crepwt through the old ceiling. The door between carriages was held fast by rot and Kittie spotted the steps that cascaded down to the ground. She had often wondered who those steps had been for. The dominant, but nevertheless fantas-tical, supposition in her mind concerned a once wealthy dowager resorting to third class in a bid to escape her watchful pursuers, her cover eventually blown by the steps and her reluctance to leap the foot and a half from the train to the ground below.

Kittie moved away from the rotted door and raised a foot over the steps, lifting her head theatrically. One arm was bent at her side while the other held an imaginary cigarette. Phantoms of newspa-permen crowded before her arrival and she smiled nonchalantly.

'Announcing Lady Kittie of Virginia,' came a voice.

Kittie straightened up out of shock and slipped on some damp on the step. She managed to catch the frame of the carriage door as she went, but still hit the floor with a bump. She squeezed her eyes closed as a sharp pain shot up from tail to tip.

'Woah, you okay there?' the voice said.

Kittie opened her eyes to see her Uncle Shelby walking along-side the carriage towards her. A barely restrained smile trembled his lips.

'I'm all good,' she said back. 'Just hurting from embarrassment.'

'Ain't that the worst,' her uncle said frankly, lifting her down from the carriage.

Kittie brushed the dirt from the back of her skirt and gave her uncle a hug. She could tell he had been out most of the day as the smell of rain was caught in the heavy fabric of his old army coat. Trails of rainwater slipped along the crown of his hat as he bent down to kiss the top of her head. His thick grey beard itched her forehead as he did so.

'Good to see you, old man,' Kittie said.

She turned to see that he was carrying two rabbit carcasses over his back. He didn't have his gun with him, as was his practice those days, so they must have been lifted from the traps he set.

'Old?' Shelby exclaimed. 'Why, who says I'm old?'

'Everyone, don't they?' Kittie returned with a laugh.

It was true that, in lighter days, the townsfolk in New George-town had affectionately named him Ol' Shelby. He rubbed at his beard as Kittie stepped back.

'You're right.' He nodded. 'But I recall at some point I used to be called Young Shelby, perhaps even *Handsome* Shelby.'

Kittie laughed again, shaking her head at her uncle's play-acting. He put his arm around her shoulder and they began to walk alongside the carriages, away from the woods and towards his cabin.

'I'm sure you were called handsome plenty,' she said, taking the rabbits from him.

'Well, now,' he said. 'No. No, I wasn't. And I'm fixing to realise that's a damned shame when a man thinks back over his years and can't recall being called handsome even the one time.'

He heaved a heavy sigh and acted wiping imaginary tears from his eyes. Kittie swung the rabbits into his belly.

'Hey, now,' he continued. 'That's dinner.'

'Then quit acting the fool,' Kittie said.

Shelby let free a wide smile that spread his beard. They eventually reached his cabin, turning from the train and walking up onto the porch, Kittie swinging the rabbits casually all the while.

'So, tell me,' Shelby said, stopping short of the door. 'How goes it?'

He looked down towards his niece's face, her expression changing as readily as loose leaves in the wind. Her mind was elsewhere.

'Fine,' she said.

Shelby waited for more but Kittie stayed silent.

'Fine,' he repeated.

Kittie looked back towards the first-class carriages. She noted the dark numbers above the windows, like shadows, where the fancy gold lettering had once been. Shelby had told her he'd seen a deer in there one time, walking softly down the aisle as though it had forgotten its luggage. In the animal kingdom, that seemed about right to Kittie. She expected they might find owls there too, perhaps a dog in second and then rats crawling over the floor of third.

Spots of rain had begun to sound on the wooden roof above them. Shelby watched as Kittie shivered and he put his arm back around her shoulder. Four years he had spent occasionally quieting the erratic minds of men shot through or about to have a limb taken from them, but now the prospect of a female with something on her mind made him draw a deep breath into his lungs.

'"Fine" won't do,' he said. 'But "fine" I can work with.'

Kittie just kept her eyes on the train.

'You hear about those doctors now? Head doctors?' he asked

as Kittie shrugged. 'By my reckoning, they do half the work for double the fee. And your luck is in, lady. Cos I'm thinking that might be my calling. And, seeing how you're my first, you can go for free.'

Kittie looked up at her uncle, a smile on her lips that trembled there unsteadily like the loose boards of a bridge. Shelby stopped walking and took his niece's face in his hands. He brushed at her warm cheeks with his thumbs and saw the beginning of tears in her eyes.

How she looks like her mother, he thought.

As though the words were spoken aloud, Kittie began to cry and he pulled her in towards him tightly.

'This don't seem like no "fine",' he said.

Kittie laughed and tightened her grip around her uncle. He reached behind them and pushed the door to his cabin wide open. As they turned to go inside, Kittie willed herself to hear a rush of steam, impossible as it was, sweeping out from under the train, the clamour of passengers taking their seats and the final whistle as the machine lurched into life.

Nothing came, though, and, as the door of the cabin fixed behind them, Kittie felt foolish at expecting something so fanciful.

Things gathered in and around Shelby's cabin as though they had no other place to go. From fallen buttons to the locomotive outside, size was no problem. He abided by placing what he could along his shelves, each and every one a treasure. The only things he could truly call his own were the numerous bottles some trinkets found themselves in.

Shelby had won the place years earlier during a card game at a Confederate camp near Richmond. The previous owner had run the coaling station and dodged the draft out of the necessity of his job. But, since the Honor Gorge Bridge had been destroyed, the recruitment officers argued – successfully, it turned out – that he might as well join in with the fighting. It only took a few weeks for the war to be on its last legs, and without fighting to occupy the man, gambling did. Soon, his keys nestled amongst coins and tobacco on a game table. Shelby had won the pot – and, with it, the cabin.

Following the end of the war and his departure from New Georgetown, Shelby used that set of keys for the first time. He could recall how the building was stilled by a curious staleness that seemed to hold in the air the smell of food the previous owner had cooked years earlier. He had left it mostly how he had found it and only opened up the windows and doors to air the place.

From the train outside he had retrieved all manner of treasures. During the years that had passed since that train had stopped in haste, people had stripped the carriages of anything that could be considered worth selling on. Shelby found plenty worth taking though. Passengers must have left in a hurry as items littered the carriages. Things were cast about the empty seats in a bid to preserve a moment when the passengers decided they had little time to gather them up and, instead, fled. He found a cane slid beneath one of the seats. At the time he had wondered why the owner had left it there and concluded perhaps they had only had a problem with walking, not running.

Out of everything, he was pleased with the number of books he had retrieved from the train. They proved a welcome companion in his times of solitude and he accrued new words along the way, finding at long last an enthusiasm for learning. Three piles were stacked against a wall in his cabin, the tallest reaching to almost head height and tottering slightly with each tread on the floorboards beneath it. One was of books he had read, another of books he intended to read. The third was of books he intended to return to. A pile of ashes in his grate accounted for those he had read and could not bear to set sight on again.

Now, as Kittie drew in the warming, sweet smell of her uncle's rabbit stew, she bent down to look over those piles of books. She moved an oil lamp along the floor, closer to one of the stacks.

'You *liked* this one?' she said, easing it free.

Shelby looked over and squinted at the title. 'It's in that pile, ain't it?'

Kittie murmured disapprovingly and returned it to the same spot. She snorted at another title and, before going further, thought better of it. Her uncle attended to the stew and she recalled how he disliked being interrupted.

The books' spines slid into shadow as her uncle hooked the oil lamp on the end of an old cane. He hung it over the stew and looked in before setting it down next to him and stirring some more with a wooden spoon. Kittie wondered if he had needed the better light or whether he just had not cared for her picking holes in his makeshift library.

Kittie stood up and walked out onto the porch. The rain hammered on the wood above her head but she welcomed the cool air around her. She found it too warm inside the cabin with both the stove and fire burning. She walked to the edge of the porch and stuck a hand out into the rain before placing the cool wet skin against the back of her neck. It was a habit she had had since childhood.

'Dinner!' came the call from inside.

Kittie turned and went back into the cabin to see her uncle setting a second chair at something hoping to pass for a table. He placed her bowl of stew down unceremoniously enough, saying, 'Fix your gums around that, kiddo.'

The rabbit was always fatty and Kittie struggled through chewing it. Some time ago she had nicked a back tooth biting down on a bullet still in the rabbit's meat. She was glad to eat freely now, knowing the rabbits had been killed by a trap instead. Her uncle barely looked up as he ate, shovelling the food in, spoonful after spoonful, as though what happened in between was all inconvenience. After a few more mouthfuls he was done and pushed his chair back from the table.

Kittie watched as he lifted a bottle of whisky from beside an old armchair and took a drink from it. He had his back to her all the while.

'So,' he said, raising his head to the ceiling, 'how's about we get to you being just fine.'

Kittie stopped eating and brushed the corners of her mouth.

'Forget it,' she said.

She stirred at her bowl, watching as the lumps of meat turned in the folds of thick brown sauce.

'Consider it forgotten then,' Shelby said, watching her. 'What's say we get some air instead? Go for a train ride? It's a fine evening, after all.'

A thunderclap sounded outside and Kittie smiled weakly.

'Ain't I a little old for that?' she said.

Kittie hunched against the old driver's seat in the cabin of the train. Her uncle sat next to her. They had pulled a blanket across them to try to block out the cold that crept through the windowless sides. Shelby had hung an oil lamp on the back wall of the cabin and now ran his old hands across the pages of a book, searching for something.

Kittie turned her head sleepily. 'Don't matter if you can't find it,' she said.

'I'll find it,' her uncle replied. 'Don't worry yourself.' He flipped a few pages more and then stuck a finger into the book, like a stamp into wet wax. 'Ha!' he exclaimed.

Shelby started to read from the book. He was wearing a pair of glasses he had fetched from some corner of the train. The way the arms splayed on his wide head told anyone who cared to notice that they were not his, but rather another token from a different time.

His mouth and the words made a good fit, like a story told before and often. Kittie listened and felt her mind loosen in the cabin, the patter of rain on the roof consistent. She had heard the story many times before, but not recently. It was set in a made-up town, far away, but Kittie turned from these details and imagined herself as the main character. A boy and a girl from opposing sides of the same town fell in love and, owing to their families' dispute, were driven apart. The young man married someone else and the girl was left on her own. Kittie realised it didn't sound much like a story capable of else but sadness, but the part she loved was the end.

Her uncle looked down to see her smile as he began the final paragraph. The girl was walking alone through the countryside and looking down at the town she lived in. She watched the house her love resided in and imagined him there with his wife. On the verge of tears, the girl became distracted at the sound of music on the wind and turned to see where it came from. The hillside was empty but for the tall grass moving shapes overland in the wind. The music continued and she found she no longer cared about the boy she had loved. She began to turn on the spot and tilted her head up to the sky. She danced on the hillside with that strange music playing.

'*How she turned,*' her uncle read. '*How she danced.*' He closed the book and patted the cover.

Kittie shifted her weight, satisfied.

'Sure you're not too old for that?' Shelby asked.

Kittie looked up at him and smiled. Her lips contorted and she closed her eyes, tears spilling down her cheeks.

'Hey,' her uncle said. 'I was just kidding; come on, now.' He pulled her closer. 'I'll be damned if you're gonna tell me this is *fine*.'

'I'm sorry,' Kittie said. She balled her fists beneath the blanket and shook her head angrily.

'You'll have plenty more to be sorry for down the line, kiddo. So don't go wasting your apologies on me.'

Shelby gave her a squeeze and then stood up as much as he could in the cabin. He unhooked the lantern from the back wall and stuck an open palm out into the night. Since it had stopped raining, he hoisted his body out and disappeared onto the roof. Kittie watched, perplexed, until she felt his hand on her opposite shoulder.

'Come on up,' he said, leaning down. 'Careful, now; it's slippery.'

He pulled Kittie out of the cabin and onto the roof. She sat down on the cold metal, feeling the rainwater soak through her skirt. The night had grown colder since the rain and she reached back down to retrieve the blanket.

Shelby sat the oil lamp behind them.

'Charles,' he said.

Kittie looked at him, confused.

'That's not it,' he said, rolling his eyes. 'Chester,' he said, satisfied.

Kittie let out a deep sigh and her uncle twisted at the oil lamp, the flame pushing at the glass. Kittie looked away from the brightness of it.

'I heard about him leaving,' Shelby said, looking at Kittie. 'I'm sorry for that. I can't say much on that matter though.'

He rubbed at his chin and Kittie brought the blanket tighter over her shoulders. Her uncle seemed to be struggling with something. His way of speaking had changed, each word having its own space as he took his time, talking with care.

'You call me old and I know some others do too. My knees are shot and my eyes can't see much these days,' he said, removing the spectacles. 'But you ain't alone in this. Heartbreak is a common thing.'

Kittie looked down and placed a hand flat against the cold of the metal roof.

'Might embarrass you to hear it, but I had someone once too.'

The words surprised Kittie and she looked at Shelby, trying to imagine it.

'She was as good as they came, kiddo. And she had as little sense as to love me back.' He seemed to be chewing on something and then the words unstuck from his mouth. 'Happiest I been.'

Kittie turned from her uncle and looked out at the light touching the tracks that spilled into the gorge. She watched things spin and drive through the night, alive from the light of the lamp. Shelby turned it up once more and Kittie winced for fear of it cracking the glass and spilling out burning oil. Instead, the light shone brighter than she had seen and Shelby pointed up ahead of them. Across the gorge their silhouettes were projected onto the cliff face. Kittie raised an arm and waved it in the air, smiling as the shape waved back.

'All that,' her uncle started, 'ended with a choice. One I go over every single day. I think of that man,' he said, pointing again, 'and whether he's happy. Different, maybe. But that's all it comes down to: thinking.'

Kittie kept her eyes fixed on her shadow across the gorge.

'You're still young and you ain't like me. If we was talking

19

about bridges, then, hell, yours is still there – strong tracks across it, brand new. You can cross it and you might have plenty of time to do as much. But I promise you, one day, some fool will blow it up. Might even be you. And then you'll be staring out at that shadow, filling your days with little else but wondering. And believe me, it ain't the choice that kills you, kiddo, it's the wondering.'

Kittie nodded to her uncle and started to sob. He pulled her close once more.

'You cry at an old fool like me? What's that make you, huh?'

Kittie let out a weak laugh and Shelby pulled the corners of the blanket up around her.

'I best head inside,' she said.

Shelby nodded and held her arm as she lowered herself down, watching her walk to the cabin. He turned the lamp down and blinked against the darkness of the night. He caught a black shape, going round and round, blocking out the stars, getting lower and lower.

A crow, he realised.

'Squawk,' he said aloud.

The crow grew bigger still and shot out across the gorge. It flapped its wings and turned back, heading towards the train. The fanciful part of him thought it might be the crow from before, back from the town. It flew right up to Shelby and fluttered its wings a yard or two from his face. He squinted against the gust of air and watched as the bird landed on the roof, tilting its head this way and that.

A moment longer and the bird took to the air again and disappeared up into the sky. Shelby watched it go, but soon its vague black shape became lost against the night, particularly to an old man's eyes filling with tears.

20

October 1879

The pool of ink had run over most of the word *Shelby* by the time
Kittie set the pen flat. She lifted the first page carefully and saw
the liquid had climbed down, dwindling its way to the bottom
of the stack, shrinking like a stain scrubbed away.

Kittie remembered her uncle telling her about the crow the
next morning. He sat near her as she was still lying in bed. She
had smiled with his storytelling, charmed by how much he treasured the event. But she soon stopped and watched as his eyes
grew more red. She had thought his face weak and weary from
drinking the night before, but now supposed him to have been
crying. Shelby crying – something Elena and Blanche would
never believe.

Later, after breakfast, Kittie had walked back to town. Her
uncle followed her further than he had ever done, making her
hopeful he might walk all the way back and things might turn
out differently at last.

As if her hope could set his legs in stone, he came to a halt.
Kittie turned and he took a handful of her curls, laying them in
his palm as though panning for gold.

'You'll be fine?' he asked her.

Kittie shrugged, feeling a weight in her throat.

'You'll be fine,' he said, convinced, and let her hair fall,
squeezing her shoulder.

'How?' she asked, her gaze dropping to her boot tips.

Shelby bent down and raised her chin so their eyes met; she
saw how clear his seemed in amongst the hatching of his weather-beaten face.

'You turn,' he said. 'You dance.'

3

October 1879

Emerson thought the Long Cape tavern a curious building in every meaning of the word. From the outside he saw the thick curtains of a foreign cloth covering each and every window of the second storey.

Fine, he thought. *Perhaps someone doesn't care for the gaze of passers-by.*

It was only after speaking with a fellow drinker that he learned the curtains had not been drawn for over a decade.

Emerson had headed straight to the tavern from the post office, deciding to spend the hour until the appointment inside and warm. A storm had gathered in the sky and now he heard it rattle the windows as it swept up off the town road and onto the porch. He perched by the bar, waiting to be served. Behind it he noticed a large mirror, misted over by age and neglect. Various shapes of bottles, each one a different colour, climbed the space there, stacked neatly like the pipes of a church organ. Emerson was wondering what sound such an instrument would make when the awkward scratching of another filled his ears. He turned in his seat to see an old man perching on a wooden chair not far from the centre of the tavern floor. Drinkers filled the place, but mostly sat in booths that pressed into the shadows, close to the walls. They watched with smiles on their faces as the old man played a violin that rested on his shoulder. He moved the bow as though he intended to slice the instrument in two and Emerson's teeth were set on edge by the screeching.

After a second more, the old man dropped the instrument into his lap and scratched at the back of his head with his bow hand. He looked up, over his shoulder towards a balcony on the second storey. Emerson followed the man's gaze and noticed another thick curtain running behind the balusters there. The old man seemed to be listening for something. A single weak clap broke out from the corner of the bar and soon the whole tavern joined in with a chorus whose weak patter could only be taken for pity. Emerson turned back to the bar, but listened still as the man was comforted by a woman's voice.

'You gave it a good try, Reuben, and that's all she asks,' she said.

A smatter of laughter broke out from one of the booths and Emerson felt sorry for the old man, hung out there in front of people like that. He wanted a drink before he was forced to think on it longer, but the bar remained empty still.

Emerson turned and saw the bear, his breath drawing in sharply as his eyes locked with the beast's own. Its paws were raised parallel with its face as though it were also growing impatient for a drink. Emerson noticed how its claws were long and gnarled, flaking away in yellow-brown pieces like glue from an old book's spine. What such a sight was doing in a tavern, only the stories held within the town could explain.

Emerson had seen bears during his travels, but none so close. Even with its heart long still and most likely elsewhere, the creature gave him a fright. He could see every detail of its face and noted how, through some skilled taxidermy, its expression contorted into a roar. Its long yellow and white teeth hung there and Emerson could tell the roof of its mouth was black like a dog's. In the absence of its tongue was curled a strip of velvet, resting against its lower teeth.

The bear wore a tile of dark fabric, awkwardly placed on its breast where the bullet likely blew a hole. As though it were a pet or an escapee from a circus, a brown leather strap wrapped itself tightly around the bear's throat and from it hung a silver bell, spinning ever so slightly in the draught that crept under the tavern's door. Emerson caught the soft glow of the tavern's light in its polished surface and thought with each spin he heard its muted ring, like some far-off town clock marking the hour.

'What's your story, friend?' Emerson asked the creature.

He looked at its long, still lips and wondered if that velvet might unfurl into life and the bear answer him, or else strike him down from his stool.

'What'll it be?' he believed the animal to ask.

Emerson squinted and his heart beat harder in his chest. 'Huh?' was all he could muster.

A finger touched him on the chin, pushing against the thick stubble he had not had occasion to shave. He flinched slightly as the finger turned his head to face forward. His eyes traced the snowy skin down an arm and saw it belonged to someone else he had not expected to encounter in a tavern that night.

Months on the road had left Emerson tenderfoot, but he could not help but drop his jaw at the woman before him. Her eyes were the darkest brown, held between smears of kohl. Her cheeks sat high, giving her features a peculiar beauty only inflamed as she looked at him, a guarded smile parting her lips. Even in the weak light of the tavern, Emerson could see how white her skin was. The bridge of her nose was dusted in faint freckles that spilled out onto those high, pronounced cheeks. All this beauty was framed by rust-coloured hair that came down over her shoulders.

'You can speak?' she asked, raising her eyebrows. Her hand dropped from his face and Emerson was sorry for losing her touch.

'Whisky,' he said, clearing his throat.

'Well, all right,' the woman remarked, smiling. 'The man *can* speak.'

She fetched a glass from the back of the bar and filled it to the brim. Emerson looked around expecting the townsfolk to be transfixed by her. They only carried on drinking, though, perhaps acquainted with such beauty. Something Emerson hoped he might never be.

'One whisky,' she said, placing the glass down.

Emerson noticed the shape of her breasts loose in her blouse, but he kept his eyes trained on hers, even as he reached inside his jacket for his wallet. She just stood there still, watching him and, he believed, trying to work things out.

'Make that two,' came a voice.

Emerson turned and saw a squat man with a thick white-grey moustache that turned up at the corners. Below his lips was another patch of hair, running to a point just below his chin. He wore a bowler and, beneath his suit, a waistcoat. A fine silver chain trailed up one side of his jacket where a pocket bulged with the promise of a watch. His clothes were free of any dirt or lint and Emerson noted how it had been years since he'd seen someone so well turned out. The man nodded to the woman serving before turning to Emerson and smiling mischievously.

He took off his bowler like a magician preparing to astound, but instead placed it on the bar top before tossing his gloves inside. The man's actions all seemed a precursor to offering his hand to Emerson, which he promptly did.

'Doctor Umbründ,' he said.

Emerson shook his hand in silence as the woman behind the bar stepped away to fill another glass. Umbründ watched Emerson's face and then squeezed his eyes shut, realising his mistake.

'But of course,' he said, bouncing a finger off his temple. He leaned in closer and looked from side to side. 'The card,' he continued. 'It's me.'

The doctor's voice came in a curious accent – the consonants exact and the vowels drawn out and prowling. Emerson wanted to hear more of it and stayed silent in waiting. The doctor's expression grew worried as the woman returned with his glass of whisky. He took a small sip and savoured the warmth of it.

'He's a shy one,' the woman said, gesturing towards Emerson.

Umbründ acknowledged this but kept his eyes trained on the man before him. The woman left and the doctor leaned in once more.

'Forgive me, my boy. Perhaps I have been mistaken. Are you not "the maker"?' He said the word as if uncomfortable with its pomposity.

Emerson swallowed hard before replying, 'I am.'

The doctor looked relieved at once and took another drink, his eyes turning to Emerson as he did so. With a sigh of satisfaction, he ran a hand along Emerson's back and patted his shoulder.

'The way you were looking at me, I thought perhaps not.'

Emerson straightened in his seat. *Shape up*, he told himself, *else you lose yourself some business.*

'My apologies,' Emerson said. 'Been a while since I've had

26

company.' He reached out to shake the doctor's hand once more. 'Doctor . . . Umbründ?' he said.

The doctor held up a finger in protest. 'Umbroooeeeeend,' he said, giving great flair to his name. Emerson watched his mouth and repeated after him.

'Exemplary,' the doctor said, spinning a hand in the air. 'I have to admit, I had my doubts about your advertisement. Such mystery, such tricks at play.'

'No tricks,' Emerson protested.

'Tell me, so long after the war and you still find business?'

Emerson nodded, not appreciating the doctor's inquisitive tone. He eyed the tavern exit.

'Wonderful,' the doctor exclaimed. 'And so there you are and here I am. And there she is.' He said this turning to watch the woman behind the bar and hummed into his glass as he took another glug.

Emerson followed the doctor's gaze and soon the woman came over. Umbründ asked for two shots of the *boisson de luxe*. Emerson considered counting himself out but didn't want to perturb the doctor so early in their meeting. Instead, he watched as the woman stepped to the back of the bar and gazed over the bottles that climbed before the mirror. Umbründ tapped his fingers on the bar like an impatient child. The woman lifted a leg up and leaned forward, reaching towards one of the bottles. As she did so, a split in her skirt showed the top of her thigh and the white skin there, hardly distinguishable from the plain colour of her stocking. Emerson looked down out of courtesy.

'My boy,' the doctor began, noticing, 'do not lower your gaze. That is the *luxe*. The *boisson* alone tastes like piss.'

He let out a wheezing laugh before bringing a finger to his lips. Emerson looked up to the mirror, catching the woman's smiling face in the reflection. He had the feeling the doctor was no stranger to her as the woman stepped back down, smiling still, and poured two shots.

This fella has dash, Emerson thought and took up his shot while the doctor slipped an extra coin into the woman's palm.

Before Emerson could set the glass back down, the doctor lifted his own drink and hopped down from his stool, taking a seat in an empty booth across the tavern. He nodded towards the hat and gloves that were still on the bar top. Emerson collected these things and walked over to join him. The wooden compartments were back to back and, to take his seat, Emerson ducked below a runner with a curtain pushed to one side.

This place and its curtains, he thought.

As he peered down the line of booths, he noted one at the end filled with men, clashing their drinks together and laughing in self-congratulation. One held the others in rapture as he told a story that fell to a whisper before they all erupted into laugher once more. His face was handsome and wide, the features devoid of any whiskers or scars. He pushed a hand back through his blonde hair and walked across the tavern. He looked over to Emerson, who quickly dropped into his seat.

'You strike me as the nervous sort,' the doctor said.

Emerson shrugged and took up his whisky. A loud clang rang out in the tavern and he jogged his glass, spilling a trail of liquid down his chin. He followed the noise to see the blonde man standing by the bear, the silver bell swinging from its collar.

'Correct diagnosis,' the doctor said, clapping a palm against the tabletop.

A thick white candle burned there and spread its wax out into a milky web. Emerson didn't appreciate the doctor's assumption and wiped roughly with his jacket sleeve to dry his chin.

'What's with the bell?' he asked, eager to avoid ridicule.

'Ah, the bell,' the doctor said, looking over. 'You strike it and you buy everyone a drink. A display of bravado, but a welcome one.'

The man who had rung the bell walked back to his booth, welcoming thanks from people as he went. The doctor raised a hand and encouraged Emerson to do the same. The man took his seat in the booth and settled into the backslapping of his companions before starting up with another muted story. Emerson was straining to catch the gist of it when an old clock, propped against the back wall, rang out. He would have failed to pay it much attention had the tavern not seemed to change. The red-haired woman came over and set their fresh glasses of whisky down before rushing past the clock and down a corridor. The clock rang again and Emerson turned to look over his shoulder, watching as people settled. Rabble died down and drinks were set softly on tabletops.

'What—?' Emerson began.

The doctor raised an urgent hand, leaning forward, his forehead almost touching Emerson's. 'Distractions,' he hushed. 'But we must abide.'

By the seventh chime, all was silent in the tavern but for soft footsteps along the unseen balcony. Emerson tried to make out the slightest of movements, but the curtain covered every bit of space behind the banister. He heard the scrape of a chair against the floorboards and wondered if the red-haired woman was up there. But she came rushing back down the corridor and took her place behind the bar. Her movements were silent and practised.

Before Emerson could enquire as to what was happening, music began to play from up on the balcony. He heard the notes from a violin as they passed through the tavern and into the welcoming ears of all who sat there. Emerson had never seen such rapt attention before, even in the skin shows he had passed through in busier towns further north. Every person was captured in some majesty and Emerson too felt his thoughts make way for the music.

Time passed and not a sound other than the violin could be heard. The froth on people's drinks fizzed and parted from being overlooked and many a mouth grew dry. Then the music drew to a close as softly as it had begun and, after a moment or two of uncertainty, the peace ruptured with the sound of applause. Emerson only became aware of joining in once his palms began to sting. He looked around, astounded at what had just taken place. The red-haired woman moved from behind the bar and darted down the corridor once more.

Emerson looked at Umbründ, who banged a hand on the table, drinking with his other.

'What was that?' he asked the doctor.

'That was the Bird,' Umbründ replied matter-of-factly.

The curtain on the balcony receded to reveal an empty wooden chair. The red-haired woman then came into view as she continued to pull the curtain back. A few whoops went up from the booth at the end and she made a small bow down to the men there.

'And now she has flown away,' Umbründ said.

'Well, I don't know much about music, but that was fine playing all right.'

The men drank their drinks as the applause finally died away.

'Doctor,' Emerson began. 'Your accent.'

The doctor smiled and bobbed his head slightly.

'Where are you from?' Emerson continued, encouraged by the drink.

The doctor leaned forward, his face suddenly serious. He tugged at the curtain by their booth and drew it shut, affording them some privacy.

'To tell you the truth, my boy,' Umbründ began, 'I don't know.'

'You don't know?' Emerson repeated instinctively.

'I hope that is where you can help,' the doctor said. 'I am not "fixing to forget" but I want ... no, I *need*, a past.'

The flicker of the candle played against the doctor's eyes as he stared at Emerson. His mouth twitched. Emerson watched as his face appeared to loosen and become slack, as though it were a mask now worn by someone else.

'Did you hear me?' the doctor asked after a moment.

'I heard,' Emerson said.

The doctor leaned closer still, the tip of his beard perilously near to the candle's flame. 'Then what now?' he hissed impatiently.

'Now?' Emerson said. 'Now we give you a birth.'

4

October 1879

Marianne House was creaking in most places and leaking in the others, but Blanche decided repainting George's portrait would come next.

She had decided to replace the loose tiles on the roof that morning, noting how rainwater had crept in during the last storm. She had trailed its brown-yellow stain on the otherwise white walls of the bath-room, eager to put a stop to it before rot set in the aged wood.

As she ascended the stairs, she stood before the portraits that decorated the wall. She considered what a curious place it was for them to reside; her sisters – she hoped – the only ones to climb the stairs and likely ever to see them.

Black and white photographs slotted together in a neat pattern, varying in shape and size. Blanche smiled as she looked over her sisters' faces, changing with age to more closely resemble those she saw every day. Set next to a photograph of her youngest sister, Kittie, was the portrait of her brother, George.

His face was missing parts. Blanche had painted it almost seven years earlier and had often returned to refresh the colours and lines of her younger brother's features. Now, his eyes were faded almost completely white with only faint circles of blue where the irises used to be. The hair was faded too, trailing over his head like brown mist. He seemed altogether a ghostly apparition.

Despite the errand at hand, Blanche lifted the frame from the wall. As she did so, the nail it hung on pulled free and a splinter of wood fell to the step below.

Another thing for the list, she noted. *How this house is growing old.*

Blanche took the portrait to her room and set it on her desk. She struggled to recall where her paints could be, stowed away someplace downstairs. After all, it had been years since they were used for anything but the portrait. She resolved to refresh George's image the moment the tiles were replaced on the roof, unable to stop her mind protesting at the futility of trying to replace what was lost forever.

Once she had climbed out onto the roof, Blanche remained there until the afternoon. The clouds softened the autumn sun and she was able to walk about, gingerly toeing the tiles to see which ones came loose.

'Found it yet?' came a voice.

Blanche turned to look over her shoulder and saw Elena leaning out from the window of their parents' old room.

'No such luck,' Blanche called back, looking about her feet.

'Want me to come out and see if I can help?' Elena called.

'Yes, I'd like that,' Blanche called back, smiling to herself.

Elena's face dropped and she rubbed a hand against her neck. 'Well, I was—'

'Don't worry yourself, El. Go back inside. I'll be down soon enough,' Blanche said, keeping her eyes trained on the roof and shaking her head.

33

Why bother asking? she thought as Elena disappeared from the window.

'El, wait!' called Blanche. 'Have you seen Kittie?'

Elena appeared again and looked back inside the house, dumbly.

'I figured she was up there with you,' Elena said, and she turned back inside once more.

Blanche nodded vaguely and walked up the side of the roof, looking down the road to town. She tried to make out Kittie's slight figure climbing that dusty path back up to the house. Nothing. She was far from being newly acquainted with this kind of disappearing act, but nevertheless trod quickly back down and across to the bath-room window.

Blanche looked in, noticing that the towels set aside for Kittie that morning were still folded neatly in the open linen closet. The bath-room was usually in a state of disarray once Kittie had done with it, but today it remained clean and ordered.

She returned her attentions to the roof and noticed some tile fragments, likely loosened by the wind. She was beginning to gather the pieces up when she heard the bell go. Her heart untightened at the idea of Kittie home once more.

Looking down, she saw a black centipede uncurling itself from beneath the tile pieces and wrapping casually about her wrist. Blanche shook her hand, gasping in disgust as the creature clung to her still. Standing upright, she flung her arm out towards the yard and the centipede let go, spilling through the air like a streamer.

She caught sight of the drop, close to where she was standing, and her legs trembled. She fell back on the roof and closed her eyes, placing her hands on her knees and slowing her breath.

George could do this, she thought. *He'd be old enough by now. He could do this while I drank iced tea.*

Her wrist throbbed with the tracks of the centipede and she

came over itchy. She was brushing at her hair and looking around her for more creatures making their way out of the roof when the bath-room window came loose in its latch and swung open. Elena looked out one way and then saw Blanche.

'You all right?' she asked, looking over her sister's hunched figure.

Blanche nodded, her head still dizzy. 'Is Kittie back?' she asked.

'Not yet. But Clay is here and I was thinking . . .' Silence filled the air and Elena bit her lip.

'Go,' Blanche said.

'You sure? I don't mind staying, if Clay can too.'

The thought turned Blanche's stomach.

'Just go,' she said. 'There's no sense having a family lunch without the whole family.'

'She'll be back soon, Bee, I know it. Don't she always pull this?'

'That's the problem,' Blanche said, raising her head up to the sky.

Elena watched her for a second and a man's voice came from down inside the house.

Blanche opened an eye. 'He inside?' she asked.

'He's on the porch,' Elena insisted.

'Sounds like he's in the house.'

'I'll be back for supper,' Elena said, ignoring her. 'You want for me to leave this open?'

Blanche nodded and raised herself on bent legs, treading inside the bath-room. Elena took her arm as she stepped down from the windowsill and breathed a sigh of relief.

'It's almost gone again, El,' Blanche said.

'What?' Elena asked, looking up to her.

'George,' Blanche said, thinking of the blank space on the wall beside the staircase.

The name halted Elena on the spot and she let out a heavy sigh.

'Perhaps it's for the best,' she said, not turning to meet Blanche's eye. 'Let it go this time, huh?'

A voice called up from downstairs again and Elena turned round to Blanche.

'I have to go,' she said to her sister.

'I know that,' Blanche replied, holding her arms as though feeling a chill.

Elena left the room and sped noisily down the wooden stairs. Blanche heard as she talked with Clay, most likely apologising.

After washing the phantom creep of the centipede from her wrist, Blanche walked downstairs, running her hand along the bannister and taking her time over the photos that hung on the wall. She traced the discoloured wallpaper where George's portrait had so recently been. From the top step to the front door she could record her own life from infant to woman, only missing the last few years.

In grey hues of dark and light she saw her family aligned in the largest of the photographs and wished George had been born to join them. Her mother sat in the centre, holding the infant Kittie, while her father stood at her back, his uniform dark and brand new. Unlike most soldiers' portraits she had seen, her father had his pistol holstered and on his opposite side. His hands lay bare on his wife's shoulder and softly in the hair of his youngest daughter. Elena held the hem of her mother's skirt bunched in her hands and looked at the photographer mischievously. Then she saw herself, standing apart from the family by a step or two but with her uncle's hand on her shoulder.

How young I look, she thought.

She was often modest but could not help, with some distant satisfaction, remarking how beautiful she looked.

Her eyes reluctantly moved to her uncle and his other hand on the butt of his holstered pistol. He was a southpaw and so wore it on the opposite side to his brother. His uniform was lighter too – the grey of the Confederates. The slight distance that separated her and Shelby from the rest of the family made it seem as though they were two separate photographs in one frame. It would have made sense, given that two men, dressed as enemies, resided in the same room.

And yet there they were. The familiar tale of two sides in one family. Blanche remembered her father leaving for war that same day, how he shook his brother's hand as though agreeing to suspend familial sense and look to killing for a while. The remembrance turned her from the photograph and down the last of the stairs.

After brewing herself some coffee, she took a seat at the kitchen table and thought on where exactly her paints could be. She heard the door but didn't turn to see who it was. She knew from the way it eased shut, hoping to be silent, that it was Kittie. Her footsteps approached and Blanche took a sip of her coffee, its earthy taste pasting the roof of her mouth.

'Well, afternoon,' Blanche said as Kittie walked past her and into the kitchen.

'Can we not get into it?' Kittie asked, her head down.

'Were you there? At the cabin?'

Kittie brushed a hand against her other wrist.

'Were you?' Blanche asked again.

'You know I was.'

'Can I ask why?'

The room was still and Blanche took another casual sip of her coffee. Her swallow rang out in the quiet.

'If you're gonna ask me every time, Blanche, then I'm

going to tell you the same thing,' Kittie said. 'Because I miss him.'

Blanche sat still, unfazed by her sister's words. She thought on something to say back, but decided otherwise, swallowing the words down with another gulp of coffee.

'You needn't go there each time,' she said eventually.

The door clicked open again and Blanche turned to see Elena walking in with a wide smile on her face. She carried a clutch of flowers in her hand. As she walked towards the kitchen she hummed a tune, swinging the flowers back and forth. She looked up, seeing Blanche and Kittie, and her smile fell away.

'Aw, hell,' she said, hoping it would lie under her breath.

She placed the flowers on top of the kitchen table and kissed Kittie's cheek as she walked to the faucet to fill a vase.

'Another one!' Kittie exclaimed. 'Who are they from this time?'

'Clay, of course,' Elena replied, beaming. 'Good to have you home, Slim.'

'I'm glad someone feels that way,' Kittie replied.

Blanche shifted in her chair. 'You know it's only because I care for you.'

'Do we have to get into this?' Elena asked.

'That's what I said,' Kittie chimed in.

'You two are always ganging up on me,' Blanche said decidedly.

Leaving her coffee on the table, she went to the back door, swinging it open and walking down the yard to the clothes hanging on the line. A breeze moved them about and Blanche tried to discern from the darkening sky whether it was fixing to rain.

'I'm ganging up on *you*?' Kittie shouted, walking out after her.

Elena moved to the side of the kitchen where she had earlier

38

laid out some cornbread and cuts of meat. She opened the oven and retrieved a ginger cake.

'I don't suppose we can just have a civilised supper,' she called, raising her head from the oven.

'We were meant to be having a civilised *lunch*,' Blanche replied from outside.

'Well, I guess not, then,' Elena said to herself.

Blanche took a sheet from the clothesline and began to fold it, setting it over her shoulder when she had finished. Kittie stood before her for a second, remonstrating in silence.

'You can help me, if you're just going to stand there,' Blanche said.

She passed the folded sheet to Kittie, who flung it to the ground.

'Pick that up, please,' Blanche said, continuing with her work.

'I will not,' Kittie protested.

'You know how immature you sound?'

Kittie bunched her fists and then picked up the sheet, brushing grass from it.

'I'm eighteen, Blanche,' she said.

'Seventeen. For a few months longer, anyway.'

'The point is, if I want to go see the cabin, I'm plenty old enough to.'

Blanche watched as Elena dressed the table outside. 'It's fixing to rain,' she called over.

Elena ignored her or else didn't hear.

'Blanche,' Kittie said, 'I miss him.'

A breeze kicked at the items on the line and Blanche looked at Kittie's face. She noted how much she looked like their mother, down to her expression when she was angry.

A beauty, thought Blanche, *not quite as obvious as Elena's, mind, and quietened through neglect.*

'Okay,' she said, reluctantly. 'Let's just forget it.'

She set down the sheet she had been folding and pulled Kittie to her.

'I don't mean to cause trouble,' Kittie said, talking into her sister's neck.

'I know you don't,' Blanche replied. 'Anyhow, the trouble was caused long ago.'

A strong breeze came again, and Blanche turned to watch it shake the tall trees at the end of their yard. They climbed high, packed tightly together like the wall of a fort. Yet the wind made them sway uncertainly and clunk into one another like drunken giants. The sky above was divided, as dark clouds met clear skies, the sun shining still. Blanche steered Kittie towards the house, where Elena set down the last plate of food.

'Supper is served,' she said, pulling out her seat and looking exhausted.

All three sisters sat around the table and set about placing food on their plates. Kittie fished a bacon rasher from a bowl and folded it whole into her mouth.

'Manners, Slim,' Elena scolded.

Kittie pulled a face at her sister and chewed noisily.

'Is it hot, or is it just me?' Elena asked. She patted her red face, as though making sure it was still there.

'It's you,' Blanche said and bit into a corner of cornbread.

'Must be that oven,' she said. 'Cooking will play havoc with a woman's complexion.'

Blanche rolled her eyes and Kittie smiled.

'Smile all you like,' Elena said, noticing. 'You'll realise soon, Slim, that beauty costs not a penny, but it can buy you the world.'

'Is that what Odell thinks?' Blanche asked.

Elena stilled her hands and tilted her head back to the sky.

'Oh, Odell,' she said. 'That boy wouldn't know beauty if it sat down next to him at that piano and played a merry tune.'

'That might be true enough,' Blanche retorted.

Kittie laughed as Elena threw a crumb at Blanche.

'Not what I meant,' she protested. 'Odell's a boy. He's not even Kittie's age.'

The wind blew harder again and a sheet came loose from the line. It rolled along the yard and caught around Kittie's chair. She bent down to pick it up and looked worriedly at the sky.

'I told you it was fixing to rain,' Blanche said.

'Nonsense, it's fixing to be a fine evening,' Elena objected. 'It'll—'

The wind swooped down the yard towards them and blew over one of the glasses, spilling water across the table.

'It might pass,' Blanche said. 'But I'm heading inside.'

Blanche lifted her dish and hurried in while Elena sat there. She and Kittie exchanged looks and, making a faint expression of apology, Kittie followed Blanche inside the house. Elena looked once more at the sky and then felt the wind push her back in her chair.

'Aw, hell,' she said and stood, collecting as much as she could carry and hopping up the steps.

Her sisters were standing there, arms folded, to greet her.

'Okay,' she said, breathlessly. 'I admit it is getting a little breezy.'

Elena set the things down on the table and the sisters watched from the kitchen door as the trees bowed and shook in the wind. Rain had begun to spatter the glass of the window and Blanche felt the compulsion to light a fire in the drawing room and wrap up warm.

As she went to turn, a red shape flitted past the kitchen window and Elena and Kittie gasped.

'Did you see that?' Kittie asked.

'I saw something,' Blanche replied. 'What, I can't tell you.'

The three of them stepped closer and the shape appeared again, red and corkscrewing towards them. It slammed against the glass and moved around there like a phantom.

'Ass!' Elena screeched, pulling on Kittie's shoulder.

The shape moved about over the glass for a second longer before dropping to the back porch. Instead of eyes, black buttons stared up from it, two legs of fabric spinning about.

'Ass?' Kittie asked, turning to her sister.

'Sorry.' Elena shrugged. 'Just came out.'

'What is it?' Blanche asked.

'What the hell do you think it is? They're my drawers,' Elena said.

'From the line?' Kittie asked.

The three of them laughed and watched as the shape swirled around the porch before being blown out of sight.

'It's finally happened,' Blanche said. 'Off they go.'

Kittie and Elena looked at each other.

'What?' Elena asked, confused.

'Your undergarments – they've gone and seceded. Off to throw themselves at men, with or without your help.'

Elena let out a stunned laugh and Kittie turned, wide-eyed, to her eldest sister. Blanche looked happy with herself and chewed on her smile, eyes fixed on the approaching storm.

'Why, Kittie,' Elena began, poking a hard finger into Blanche's shoulder, 'best alert the state archives. I do believe this is the day our sister upped and got herself a sense of humour.'

Umbründ's head swung out over the table as though hung loose in the casual grip of a puppeteer. A bead of drool had gathered on his lower lip, which threatened to fall onto the candle and likely extinguish its flame. His eyes blinked dumbly and, with a sharp whistle, he drew the saliva back into his mouth. Emerson too was weary and, in a sudden panic, turned his head to make certain the curtain was drawn shut.

'W-What?' the doctor stammered. His head swung back against the seat of the booth and he blinked with the impact. After a moment, he fixed on Emerson. 'What happened?' he asked.

Emerson raised a hand to quiet the doctor and took some deep gulps of air. He felt the doctor's hand on his and pulled it away immediately, eager to be still a moment longer.

'Do not shrug away from me,' the doctor said, offended. 'You owe me an explanation.'

Emerson met the doctor's gaze and then looked down again. The doctor went to speak once more but winced at a sharp pain just above his left ear. He touched a hand there and drew air in through his teeth. He looked up, angrier than before. 'Did it work?'

'Please,' Emerson said, running a hand over his face. Sweat stung the corners of his eyes and he felt a stranger in his skin.

Umbründ looked from him to the empty glasses on the table and clenched his teeth. 'A drunk,' he concluded. 'But of course. What am I to expect from such an advertisement?'

'I ain't no drunk,' Emerson protested feebly.

'Then you're at least a fool and so am I for thinking this could work. Whatever tricks you performed here tonight, my boy, I hope they lack any lasting effects, otherwise you'll find a marshal at your tail.'

'Where were you born, doc?' he asked softly.

The doctor continued, barely noticing the question. 'I'd expect compensation if I wasn't so certain your pockets were empty. Tell me, are you familiar with the word *charlatan*?'

43

Emerson slammed a fist down onto the table, toppling over the smaller glasses. 'Where were you born?' he repeated, planting the words one after another, like bricks in mortar.

The doctor looked at him, first frightened, then bewildered. His eyes were narrowed in contempt, but then widened as the pupils began to quiver from side to side.

'Gengenbach,' he said instinctively. A hand shot to his mouth. 'That word is new to my tongue.'

Emerson nodded and tipped the last of his whisky down his throat.

The doctor's eyes raced about in their sockets. 'I don't remember the birth.'

'Who does?' Emerson retorted.

'I remember . . .' Umbründ said, his fingers moving in the air, plucking at something. 'I remember my mother.'

'She was plenty beautiful,' Emerson said.

'Yes. But I don't remember Gengenbach, only her stories of it. We moved,' he said, the last words a revelation. He was a man caught up in conversation with himself.

'Good,' Emerson replied.

'The buildings became darker. And, my goodness, the food! The weather, too. England!'

Emerson continued to nod all the while. 'Do you remember a night in particular?' he asked.

The doctor lowered his head in concentration.

'I remember my father, in his study. He turned in his chair to speak with me, his words stern. He was dressed in black, but for a collar of white around his neck.'

The doctor fell silent and went to drink from his glass, only to find it empty. He set it down again, nonplussed.

44

'I ran, crying, to my mother and she was sitting by the fire, sewing by the light. Her dress was red.'

These last words caught in Umbründ's throat and he covered his face with his hands. Emerson watched as the doctor began to cry.

Good, he thought. *It's taking.*

The ring of the bell sounded once more and Emerson jumped in his seat, angry at its taking him by surprise a second time. He turned from Umbründ and peeked out past the curtain, seeing the blonde man from the end booth, his arm around the neck of the bear and a finger flitting the bell from side to side. The red-haired woman watched him and protested, saying the tavern was closing. The man ignored her and only rang the bell again. Each time, a small hoot went up from the drinkers left around the tavern, as they gathered their things and ambled out the door.

He watched how the red-haired woman looked at the man with a smile on her face, as she had looked at Umbründ earlier, almost encouragingly. Eventually, he accepted her decision and called over his friends from the end booth. A fat young man was first up and waved shyly to the woman as he went towards the door. Then two others tried their luck further, leaning across for a kiss goodnight. The woman laughed, but raised her hand into the air and they each kissed it softly goodnight. Emerson smiled at the show until the handsome one took his arm from the bear and walked over to the woman. He kissed her hand just like the others before, gripping her elbow tight. Tilting his eyes upwards, he licked along her forearm before stepping away, laughing.

'Come on, Clay,' the others called from out on the porch.

Clay, Emerson thought, dislike already covering that man from head to toe.

The woman shook her head and brushed a hand down her wet forearm. Suddenly, she looked over towards Emerson. They locked eyes and he dropped the corner of the curtain.

'I think it's time to go,' he said.

The doctor began to compose himself and smoothed his thinning hair back over his head. 'Of course,' he said. 'Of course.'

A knock came on the side of their booth and Emerson pushed back the curtain once more.

'We're about ready to close,' the red-haired woman said.

'Then we're about ready to leave,' Emerson replied, fetching his coat from its corner and pushing the curtain all the way open.

Umbründ took longer to gather himself and stepped awkwardly from the booth, dropping his hat and gloves onto the floor. Emerson bent down to help him up by the arm and the doctor laughed, muttering 'Gengenbach' under his breath.

'Come on, doc,' Emerson said, pulling him towards the door.

'There's so much to see now,' Umbründ remarked. 'So much to remember.'

Emerson opened the door, pushing the doctor outside. He was glad to see the men had cleared from the porch and he could hear their rabble moving off into the incomplete town.

'Mister,' he heard the woman call.

He turned and saw her holding his hat aloft.

'One second,' he said to the doctor and turned back inside. He walked over to the booth and pulled at his hat, the woman holding firm.

'Your friend, the doctor,' she said. 'I ain't never seen him like that. That man can hold his liquor. Looked as though he'd been crying.'

Emerson relaxed his grip and smiled at the woman. This was the closest they had been and he noticed once more how beautiful she was. Now they were alone in the tavern he had the compulsion to reach an arm around her waist and pull her against him. The way the doctor and Clay had been around her, it was as though she was there for the taking.

Her eyes watched him for an explanation. 'You misplace your voice again?' she asked.

'No, it's right here,' Emerson said, tapping at his mouth.

'What's your name?' she asked, smiling.

'Emerson.'

'Mine's Ora, if you'd care to know it.'

'I would,' said Emerson, thinking what a beautiful name it was.

Ora laughed and rubbed at her forearm again. Emerson looked down at it.

'You're not like the others, are you, Emerson?' she said.

Emerson paused a moment, a sad smile pulling at the edges of his mouth. 'I'm glad you said that.'

He pulled his hat from her and set it on his head, tipping the brim as he turned. He walked out onto the porch and found Umbründ facing the street, his hands on his hips as though he might be surveying a gold dig. The doctor turned as the door closed and walked over excitedly.

'Do you have somewhere to stay, my boy?' he asked.

'Sure do,' Emerson replied, pulling the folded paper from his jacket pocket. '*The Mariannes*', he read out.

'Ah, the Mariannes', the doctor repeated. 'At the top of the hill. First Ora and now the sisters. I think you'll enjoy your time in New Georgetown, my boy. Very much.'

Umbründ clapped him on the back and walked down from the porch and into the street. The doctor arched his back. Standing amidst the discs of light from the gas lamps, he looked like an actor about to recite his lines.

'Might I ask you a favour,' he said, his back still turned, 'before I leave?'

Emerson set about buttoning his jacket. 'Shoot.'

'The question from before. Would you ask me again?'

Emerson thought on what the doctor could mean, and then remembered, turning his collar up against the cool night. 'Your accent. Where are you—?'

Before Emerson could finish, the doctor spun on the spot and pointed forward with his arm outstretched.

'Gengenbach,' he shot forth. 'By way of England.'

He let out a wheezing laugh and then placed a solitary finger to his lips.

'Our next appointment,' he said, stepping forward and patting Emerson on the chest. 'We must not delay.'

'We won't,' Emerson replied.

'Good,' he said, reassured. 'Good. Then, until next time! I will send word.'

With that, the doctor walked up the road, occasionally glancing back as he did so.

'Until next time,' Emerson repeated, watching his shape disappear and reappear underneath the gas lamps.

He stepped down onto the road and saw his pack still fastened there. As he untied it he looked up and noticed Ora watching him through the glass door of the tavern. Her face was different from before – sadder, almost. She wet her lips and brushed her hand over her forehead. Emerson felt the compulsion to walk back up the steps and act on what he had failed to do earlier. He raised a hand in Ora's direction, but she seemed not to care. She only twisted her mouth and looked down.

She's looking at her reflection, Emerson realised with disappointment.

He watched as she raised her head once more before walking back into the dim light of the tavern.

Emerson swung his pack onto his shoulders and felt that now familiar pinch of pain. He would be glad to reach the Mariannes' and set his things down for a time. A shadow caught his eye, moving behind the curtains on the second storey. He stood still for a moment, thinking it could be Ora and that she might pull the curtain aside and beckon him up to her room. But the shape seemed different from hers and moved in a curiously dainty way. He watched for a while longer until the light there died away, and, with it, the shadow too.

Stepping from the porch, Emerson turned on to the street and began his walk up towards the Mariannes'. He wondered if someone would have waited up for him, and if, smelling the alcohol on his breath, they might turn him back out. He would have to come up with a story to explain and he worried for a moment he might not be believed.

He pulled the pack higher up onto his back.

'Gengenbach,' he sighed aloud, the word clumsy in his mouth. *I'll be believed*, he thought. *Telling stories is what I do.*

5

October 1879

When Blanche awoke, she was alone in the drawing room. The fire burned still and the room swelled with heat. She felt sick from it and sat up in her chair. She wondered how long she had fallen asleep for and looked about her in the darkened room. Her sisters must have gone to their beds. A blanket was curled loosely on another of the chairs and a book was resting on the arm, a folded page keeping someone's place.

The floorboards creaked above her and she realised it was Elena walking about in her bedroom. For a moment she thought she heard a voice and wondered for a fearful second if her sister didn't have Clay up there with her. Her earlier joke about Elena's promiscuity had been just that, but she had had occasion to hear tell of Clay's indiscretions, supposed and yet all too likely, to her mind. So few were the inhabitants that a place such as New Georgetown could accrue someone a reputation, whether they liked it or not, and Blanche would have preferred her sister apart from his.

After a further second of silence, Blanche concluded Elena

was alone and that she would head upstairs herself. Rain pattered softly at the bay window and she walked over, opening it slightly, eager for the cool air of night. She welcomed it in and watched the fire as the dying flames laboured in the breeze. She enjoyed those evenings of reading or else talking things over with her sisters. The feud from the afternoon had been forgotten, but still she wished Kittie might heed something from it. She wondered if her youngest sister was upstairs and decided not to think on the question anymore lest she be tangled in knots of worry.

She turned her attention back outside as she heard footsteps on the wet dirt leading up to the house. She pulled the window shut by its latch, quickly drawing the curtains and hoping whoever was out there had failed to see her. The town was still rebuilding from the war and she had read on the post office wall herself about the sheriff dying at Sharpsburg. Now she cowered behind the curtain, wishing he, or any other lawman, were casting their watchful eye up the road and towards the house.

A soft knock came at the front door and Blanche heard the blood pump in her ears. She wished they had rung the bell and woken her sisters. Then all three of them could open the door and face what was out there.

The knock came again and Blanche, fuelled by responsibility towards her sisters, stood to go and answer it. The gas lamps leading up the road threw some light onto the glass of the door and she saw a figure out there, shifting about on the porch. It seemed a curious shape.

Her mind set to thinking on her sisters finding her body splayed out on the hallway floor come morning. Another member of that photograph gone from this earth.

Quit it, Blanche urged herself.

She stepped towards the door and, as she approached, the

shadow there thinned and disappeared. She drew the bolt and opened it, peering out through the crack.

There was nothing but a large pack set down on the porch. It was a canvas bag, tightened shut at its top by a thin length of rope. Blanche opened the door fully and stood on the threshold, looking left and right. She loosened the neck of the pack and pulled it down a way. A lantern poked from the top and, next to it, a large wooden wheel, like the inside of a drum. She continued to look and spotted a reel of paper, carrying sketches across it.

Blanche tugged the paper up from the pack and held it to the light spilling out from the hallway behind her.

A tree, she noted.

Running the paper between her fingers, she started to see the subtle changes in the image. The tree's branches swayed slightly and a piece of fruit began to sprout there. In her haste to spin through the paper, she tore a part of it to the middle.

'Oh my!' she said aloud.

'Don't worry yourself,' came a voice in reply.

Blanche let out a short shriek and dropped the paper, toppling the pack over with her foot as she stepped back. The man bent forward and caught it before the lantern could smash against the porch.

'I didn't mean to look,' Blanche said, feeling the doorway at her heel. 'I heard a knock, is all.'

'Like I said, don't worry yourself.'

'It's just late, and we're not expecting anyone.'

The man lowered his pack down and pulled a fold of paper from his pocket, craning his neck to look up at the house.

'This ain't Marianne House?' he asked.

Blanche calmed herself. *The guest*, she remembered.

'Emerson?' she said tentatively.

Emerson smiled and stood up. His face was hidden in the shadow of his hat, but Blanche could see the stubble that surrounded his mouth.

'I'm glad to see it is,' he said, rubbing at his sore shoulders. He tipped the brim of his hat before taking it from his head. 'I'm sorry to trouble you so late.'

'I'm sorry to be caught searching through your things,' Blanche said with a weak laugh. He was a handsome man and Blanche felt embarrassed for noticing it. His eyes darted about the porch and he brushed his hair back across his head.

'Might I come in?' Emerson asked eventually.

'Of course,' Blanche replied. 'Please.'

Emerson followed her inside and set his pack by the door.

'My sisters are asleep, so I'd appreciate it if you could speak softly,' Blanche said, feeling better for saying it, her authority in its rightful place once more.

Emerson nodded and raised a finger to his lips.

Handsome or not, he'll be staying on our property, Blanche thought.

'Will you be wanting anything to eat?' she asked, walking down the hall into the kitchen.

Emerson reluctantly picked up his pack again and followed her. He spotted a few scraps of food on the table.

'Just some of that cornbread and bacon will do me fine,' he said.

Blanche smiled at him as she placed a few pieces of each into a napkin.

'Thank you,' he said, taking it from her.

'I'll show you to your room and then I must be getting to bed myself,' Blanche said, lighting an oil lamp and opening the kitchen door.

Emerson followed her down the yard, his feet sinking into the wet ground.

'I'm sorry for arriving so late—' he said again, but Blanche turned and raised a finger to her lips. Emerson abided in silence until they reached the end of the yard. At its base was an old shack, its wooden panels shrugging off their white paint. Blanche lit an oil lamp hanging from the porch and set about unlocking the door. The sight of a bed through the window was enough to draw a deep, unavoidable yawn from Emerson.

Inside, he put his pack down again and took in his surroundings with satisfaction. Before he spoke, he looked up at Blanche as though asking permission.

'Please,' she insisted.

'This all looks fine,' he said. 'Real fine.'

'I'm glad you think so . . . Now, is it Emerson or Mr Emerson?' she asked.

'Just plain old Emerson,' he replied.

'Then, Emerson, it's our pleasure to have you here. You can come up to the house and meet my sisters in the morning. There're three of us – Elena, Kittie and myself, Blanche.'

Blanche left a pause, expecting him to ask after their parents. No question came.

'You know, you're our first guest in some time.'

'Is that so?' Emerson said.

'Our last one was more a friend of the family, mind. You know, just then, in the house, you reminded me of him. The eyes. But now, not so much.'

'I get that a lot,' Emerson said.

'Well, how can you?' Blanche asked, confused. 'It's not like you know who I'm talking about.'

Emerson shook his head, patting his parcel of food.

'No, but you'd be surprised how often people tell me I remind them of somebody else. Sometimes it's a privilege just being myself.'

Emerson laughed and Blanche smiled back out of courtesy, although she found his words queer. Emerson seemed to notice and rubbed at his eyes.

'Sorry,' he said. 'I'm awful tired.'

Blanche smiled faintly. 'I'll be leaving you now, Emerson. If you need anything, just ring the bell. There's one hanging from the back of the house too.'

Emerson nodded and thanked her for the food. Blanche turned from the shack and walked up to the house. She looked back once to see if Emerson was still there, perhaps eager for further conversation. Instead, she caught him closing the door, his shadow's movement troubling the sliver of light at the foot of the frame.

Blanche was pleased to have someone staying with them again, as they could use the money. She was even more pleased to see he was handsome, and knew Elena would be too.

Another bouquet, she thought bitterly.

She watched the shack for a moment longer and thought, even hoped, perhaps this time it would be her turn. She shook the thought from her mind and blamed her tiredness for her mood.

'Goodnight, Emerson,' she said quietly, closing the kitchen door behind her.

6

October 1879

Kittie set the pails on the bath-room floor, the steam lifting like clouds. She liked the water as hot as possible, but this proved difficult with it already beginning to cool from the kitchen stove. Once, eager to have a hot wash, she had leaped up the stairs and, in her haste, dropped one of the pails, the water streaming down to the ground floor through the balusters. Her preferred approach was to linger by the stove, heating the water almost to a boil. Then she would bunch an old sheet about the handles to stop the heat from burning her. Such procedure meant Kittie rarely considered a bath, when heating water for something a fraction its size was trouble enough.

Despite the delay, the windows of the bath-room slowly veiled over with steam. She felt contained in that sliver of the house and hidden away from the attention of her sisters, particularly Blanche.

She dropped her robe and stood in the middle of the room, the key turned reassuringly in the lock. She lifted one of the pails and felt a pinch in her hand from its heat. She hastily poured its contents into the basin and set the pail clattering back onto the floor. The pain in her hand soon dulled to a wetness that cooled into fine dew and beaded along her palms.

Kittie used a slim bar of soap to wash under her arms and matted the hair there with lather. Sliding the bar over her body like a stone, she halted as she came down towards her hips.

Seventeen and still scared, she thought.

Shaking her head, she ran the soap over the tops of her legs and then briefly between them, refusing to be a stranger to her own skin.

She thought on how Elena behaved. How she would talk with such openness even when Blanche's eyes almost rolled themselves free of their sockets. It was no secret to Kittie that she was twenty kinds of lost in the world, and perhaps finding herself – or at least being briefly acquainted – was a fine first step.

The steam in the mirror cleared and there she was before it, more attractive than she had thought she might have been. The water had darkened her hair and its curls plastered against her neck and chest. She smiled slightly and revelled in how much older she looked. For a moment she was reminded of the photograph of her mother along the stairwell.

'Kittie!' came Blanche's voice from downstairs.

'What?' she snapped back impatiently, her grip on the moment lost.

'Are you decent? Are you planning on getting up?'

'I'm up,' Kittie replied. 'And I'll be down in a moment.'

Kittie heard a murmur from Blanche and then footsteps down the hall.

Always treating me like a child, she thought. This frustration knitted itself together with her previous coyness. *Perhaps it's Blanche, hoping to make a maid of me, just like she's done to herself.*

Spurred on by these thoughts, Kittie ran her hand down her wet hair and onto her chest. She brushed the side of her left breast and felt a lift inside her. She held her breast and felt the nipple harden beneath her fingers. She wasn't sure if it was her touch that did this or the thought of going against some unspoken rule of her own body. She moved her breast and sank her fingers gently into her flesh, trying to decipher what was pleasure and what was pain, as though both were new to her.

She heard a clunk on the roof outside and thought it might be Blanche in her room, trying to hurry her downstairs. Kittie ignored it and returned her attention to her body, moving her hands across it, running them through the condensation on her skin. She traced the turn of her ribs and hips and, inexplicably, the thought of meat-stripped bones on a plate filled her mind.

I don't like it being me, she thought.

Almost instantly, she remembered him.

Chester, she thought.

Her mind was at once blank and then filled with a dozen bursts of light catching Chester as he moved about her remembrances. She thought she heard his voice too. She gave in to the woman in the mirror – dark curls and eyes of mystery – and, more so, to that heat that flamed up and started to consume her. Her finger moved quickly, now feeling at the edges of what she recognised as pleasure.

That voice, Kittie thought, *sounds so real.*

Out of caution, she opened her eyes, her hand slowing. The steam on the mirror had all but cleared and her reflection was given no frame of fancy; there was no ambiguity about her surroundings. She saw the same bathtub behind her in which her mother had first washed her, and noticed her sisters' things stacked along the shelf above it. Then her eyes fixed on what they tried their best not to – a girl, flushed with heat, shame-fully touching inside herself to reach something that was not hers to have. Chester was nowhere to be seen and her memories of him lay bare and unprotected from the shame of what she was doing.

But then, an impossible moment of hope as the light played against the window and a shadow passed over the bath-room floor.

'It's looking fine,' a man's voice said.

Kittie's body tightened as she realised the voice was real. That same clumping sound grew louder and make-believe fell hope-lessly into truth.

'I found the ones you were talking about,' the voice came again. 'I'll be able to nail these down.'

Kittie dropped her hand and turned slowly from the basin to look out onto the roof. The windows were clear now and the room seemed to shake with its damp cold.

A man stood out on the roof, bending down to pick at the loose tiles. His shadow reached into the bath-room still and ran its dark path over Kittie's bare feet. She stepped out from it as though the man might notice her if she did not.

She moved quickly across the room to the linen closet, knocking over one of the pails in her haste. The man's head lifted with the noise, looking straight at her. Kittie froze, naked, in the middle of the room and moved her arms clumsily across her body, not having limbs enough to cover herself.

How much has he seen? Kittie asked herself.

The man dropped the tile in his hand and Kittie watched as it tumbled through his legs and out over the edge of the roof, making a faint smash on the ground below. She could hear her sisters' fussing. The man stood up to speak but just made futile attempts at forming the words, puckering away as though drawing at a pipe. Kittie noticed as his eyes shot about her body, looking everywhere at everything.

'I . . .' he began.

His foot slipped on a loose tile and he fell onto his side, rolling down the roof. Kittie shot a hand to her mouth before returning it to her body. The man seemed to bounce off the gutter and clawed desperately at the roof to hold on. He groaned and blew out a sigh of relief, smiling, as he came to a stop.

'Are you okay?' Blanche called out urgently.

Kittie seized the moment and grabbed a towel from the closet, tying it around her. She unlocked the door and the click drew the man's attention back towards her. He seemed relieved to see her someway dressed but raised a cautionary hand to his eyes anyway. Kittie questioned whether the man's consideration of her modesty mightn't have come earlier.

'All fine,' he shouted down to Blanche, keeping his eyes on Kittie.

As he climbed carefully back up the roof, he raised a hand to her, someplace between a wave and an apology. To her surprise, Kittie returned the gesture, the other hand fastening the towel across her body still.

Who are you? Kittie thought.

Kittie walked down the stairs, clutching a book to her chest. It was an idle thing she had read little of, but she felt a security in holding it close to her. It was a fine day and the last warmth of autumn shone through the windows of the house. Nevertheless, she had buttoned her blouse up to its collar and wore an old skirt of Blanche's that was so long she had to hold the bannister for fear she might trip over it.

'Did you see him?' Elena asked, appearing from round a corner.

Kittie jumped, her mind elsewhere, and caught her feet in the hem of the skirt. She steadied herself and looked angrily at her sister.

'No,' she shot back. 'Who?'

'Our gentleman guest,' Elena replied. 'He arrived late last night.'

'And Blanche let him in?' Kittie asked, shocked.

'Wait till you catch a sight of him. If he'd arrived with Satan at his back, she'd have let him in.'

Kittie thought how she had failed to consider the man's looks earlier, too drawn into the horror of her embarrassment. Then it came back to her: his freshly shaved face and longish hair, curled at the tips. But it was his eyes that held her memory firm.

'He ain't no Clay,' Elena continued, 'but he'll do for Blanche, I'm thinking.'

What makes him Blanche's? Kittie asked herself, fighting off the reason that followed quickly behind it.

'Jesus, Kittie,' Elena said, flapping her arms at her sides. 'I thought you'd be glad for the excitement, yet Blanche is the one in there spoon-feeding the pour soul and you're out here on the stairs, clutching that book to your chest like it's the Bible.'

Elena's grin faded from her face and she stared at the book, almost threatened by it.

'It's not the Bible, is it?' she asked.

'No, it's not the Bible, sister,' Kittie said, exasperated.

'Well, then, we'll make a sinner of you yet,' Elena said, pulling her down the last few steps.

Kittie felt a lurch in her stomach at the word *sinner* and recalled standing before the man naked, as though in some sickening dream. She thought how it seemed too distant, too opposed to who she knew herself to be, to have happened. Her hands began to shake slightly, thinking of meeting him now.

'Count yourself lucky he ain't dead, anyhow,' Elena said. 'At the first sign of daylight, Blanche had him up on the roof. I'm surprised he didn't break his neck; near did, one time.'

Kittie thought how that might solve the situation. If he had fallen from the roof, the sight of her would have spilled out onto the back porch as readily as his brains.

'How long's he staying for?' she asked, solemnly.

Elena pulled her sister to a stop and faced her.

'Now, what is the matter?' she asked. 'Did that storm blow all the Kittie out of you and into Blanche?'

Kittie avoided her sister's gaze, but Elena could see her hands were shaking as they clutched the book.

'Hey, now, talk to me,' she said, steadying it with her own hand.

'I feel so stupid,' Kittie began.

'Well, we know that ain't true.'

'It's just,' Kittie began with trepidation, 'he saw me, this stranger. I was getting washed.'

Kittie felt her stomach lurch again. Elena's eyes flickered over her, waiting for more to come.

'Undergarments?' she asked.

Kittie shook her head and let out a long, whimpering sigh.

'Naked!' Elena said, her voice raised.

Kittie's eyes widened and she dug her nails into her sister's hand.

'Oh, Kittie,' Elena said, smiling. 'That's not the end of the world, now, is it? Hell, it might even be the start of something if he got a look at that fine body of yours.'

'I knew you wouldn't understand,' Kittie said, turning to walk back up the stairs.

'Oh, come on, Slim,' Elena said, pulling her back and laughing softly.

Kittie thought on how her sister would likely have been happy to show the man her body. Her head throbbed with jealousy once more and she watched in a rage as the corners of her sister's mouth flickered with half-realised smiles.

'Ain't nobody seen me like that,' she said with hushed venom.

'There ain't no harm in it,' Elena said. 'Now, look, I'm your sister *and* I'm something else, and both of them don't see no harm in this thing.'

Kittie dropped her hands and Elena pulled her closer. Kittie's voice was beginning to waver as she hoped with each passing moment she would wake from some nightmare.

'It's just so goddamn embarrassing,' she said hopelessly.

'Honey, you're a woman,' Elena replied. 'Embarrassing is something you're gonna have to get used to.'

Kittie rested her head on her sister's shoulder and blew out the air in her lungs.

'He saw everything?' Elena asked.

'Uh-huh,' Kittie replied.

'And he almost fell from that roof. I'm guessing that was no accident, neither. You almost killed a man, Kittie,' Elena said jokingly.

Kittie smiled for the first time. After a moment she raised her head and asked coyly, 'Do I really have a fine body?'

'Oh, Kittie, the finest,' Elena replied.

Kittie smiled and hugged her sister again. Elena pulled her along and they walked down the hall towards the kitchen. The man was sitting there, drinking coffee and touching a flat hand into his side. He winced at the pain and Blanche looked on, helplessly.

'Don't worry about him,' Elena said. 'Just you sit next to me.'

The two sisters walked into the kitchen. Blance was telling the

63

man about the town, offering her opinion on several buildngs, for what purpose Kittie couldn't tell. For a moment, she wondered if her sister wasn't about to suggest he stay elsewhere.

'Yes, indeed,' Blanche said to him. 'That might do.'

Upon seeing Kittie and Elena, the man instantly pushed his chair back and stood up. So hasty was his movement that he troubled the pain in his side once more.

'You'll have to forgive Emerson, Kittie,' Blanche said. 'He took a tumble on our roof this morning.'

Kittie was glad to have Elena's arm still through her own. She nodded faintly to Blanche and kept her eyes on anything but the man.

Emerson, she thought, and remembered lines of poetry from school.

Emerson recovered and reached out a hand, introducing himself.

'A pleasure to meet you, miss.'

Kittie looked at the thick scar of white that ran down his palm like pith from a fruit. She drew her eyes up and went to shake his hand, pulling free from Elena. Out of some miscalculation, their hands ended up back to back before they moved awkwardly next to one another like some game.

'Oh,' Kittie let out.

Blanche watched in puzzlement while a sigh escaped from Elena's mouth. Emerson reached out with his other hand and held Kittie's arm just below the elbow. She drew her breath in sharply at his boldness, her arm so finite in his grip.

'There,' he said, and shook her hand firmly. 'Got you.'

Kittie began to blush and thought how this stranger had only seen her in shades of pink and red. She looked into Emerson's eyes once more. Something took hold of her in that moment, something not quite yearning but much more misshapen. His eyes fostered some sort of pain she wanted to pull her gaze away from. And yet she traced it in its every detail for no other reason than believing it not to be his own.

With Emerson at their table, the three sisters found conversation enough to stretch their breakfast out into the afternoon. A heavy rain had started to fall and their company drew closer with the shivering patter on the windows echoing about it.

Blanche had fried some bacon and was about to wash the pan in the sink.

'Hold it,' Emerson said, standing up.

Blanche looked at him, stunned for a moment.

'I'm sorry if I spoke out of turn, Blanche. Do you mean to pour that grease away?'

Blanche looked dumbly at the pan in her hand and the specks of bacon held in the thick, yellow fat.

'Why, I wasn't planning on drinking it,' she said.

Kittie and Elena laughed and watched as Emerson took the pan from their older sister and, with a spoon, eased the grease into his empty bowl.

'Do you?' Blanche asked, not entirely in jest.

Emerson grinned as he scooped the last of the grease into the bowl and tapped the spoon on its side.

'Not quite,' he said. 'I recall the time when you might be shot for pouring such away. But you throw some cornmeal in there and you got yourself cush.'

'Cush?' Blanche asked, her eyes fixed still on the grease.

'I know cush,' Kittie spoke up. 'Our uncle used to make it.'

'He a soldier?' Emerson asked, looking at Kittie.

'He was,' she replied, shrinking under his attention.

65

'Were you a soldier, Emerson?' Blanche asked, trying her best to move the conversation along.

'I was,' he replied.

'You couldn't have been older than—'

'I was thirteen,' Emerson said, letting go another brief smile. 'But there were plenty younger.'

Blanche took this information in as an awkward silence filled the room. Emerson set his bowl of grease on the side carefully as though it were brimming with gold.

'I hear you gave my sister a real fright,' Elena said.

Kittie twitched in her chair and shot her a look of horror.

'Blanche!' Elena shouted, realising the ambiguity of her words. 'I meant Blanche.'

Blanche looked at her sisters in confusion and caught a glance between the two of them, once more a stranger in her own kitchen.

'You gave Blanche a fright?' Kittie asked, half to herself and half to Emerson.

Emerson ran a hand across his chin and, not finding any hair there, dropped it to his side. 'I'm afraid I did,' he said, apologetically. 'You see, yesterday, I left an appointment late, and there are chimes but no clock face in this town.'

'That's Horace,' Elena sighed. 'He's been fixing that clock for near on a month now. It chimes, like you say, but, unless you're about on the hour, you'll never know what time it is.'

'What kind of appointment?' Kittie asked.

'Kittie!' Blanche snapped, shooting her sister a stern look. 'You'll have to forgive my youngest sister, Emerson. She does not mean to be rude.'

'Oh, she ain't being rude,' Emerson said. 'I'm your guest, so ask me what you want.'

Blanche smiled at his reply before staring at Kittie again.

'So, what kind of appointment?' Elena asked, leaning forward in her chair.

Emerson laughed. 'Well,' he began, 'I tell stories is about the whole of it.'

Blanche let out a sigh while Kittie swallowed hard, thinking of the nights she spent listening to her uncle reading aloud in the train.

'About the war and such?' Elena asked.

'No,' Emerson said, shaking his head. 'Absolutely not.'

Now Blanche's curiosity betrayed her courtesy. 'Then what about?' she asked.

Kittie and Elena exchanged satisfied smiles.

'It's hard to say,' Emerson began. 'Easier to show. You got a room you can make plenty dark?'

Blanche nodded, saying, 'Our drawing room might do.'

'Then, if you all have the time, I'll fetch my pack and tell you a story.'

With the heavy curtains pulled, the only light that came into the drawing room was from the hall. Emerson could be heard rooting through his things while the sisters sat in an orderly fashion on three chairs, all in a row.

'That poor man and your questions,' Blanche muttered.

'Oh, hush,' Elena replied. 'You want to see what it is he does as much as we do.'

'A storyteller?' Kittie asked. 'Doesn't that sound kind of old fashioned to you?'

'Kittie,' Blanche said. 'He's our guest, and after all those questions we'll be listening to whatever it is he says.' She shifted about in her chair and looked over her shoulder cautiously, towards the door. 'But, yes,' she continued to her sisters, 'old fashioned is right.'

Emerson came back into the room, his arms filled with apparatus. He set the various pieces down by the fireplace and spread them out.

'It's best you face the other way,' he said to the sisters, making a circle in the air with his finger.

The sisters moved their chairs around.

'Might I take down that painting?' he asked.

Blanche stood and pulled it from its hook. It was a watercolour of the town during winter.

'My sister painted that,' Elena said, turning to Emerson.

'It's a fine painting,' he replied distractedly.

Blanche blushed and set the picture down, against the wall. As she turned, she looked at Elena reproachfully.

Kittie looked over the back of her chair and gazed at what Emerson was doing. From his pack he pulled a large wheel-like object, about the width of his shoulders, then a brass contraption that looked like the pedal from a bicycle. Kittie's eyes moved over the objects, trying to place their function.

A black book had tumbled from the pack, its pages loose and held in only by a length of string. Kittie thought how it might be a manual for such a curious instrument, but it also had a look about it similar to a journal. Emerson quickly replaced this in the pack and looked up at Kittie. He smiled in the low light of the room and she turned back to face forward, embarrassed.

As much as she tried, Kittie could not keep herself from turning round once more. Emerson had almost completed putting his device together. It resembled a plate camera, set atop a tripod. Instead of a wooden box, though, the lens was fixed to the drum. Emerson was in the process of feeding the decorated paper into this, turning a handle at its side until the paper took. His care meant he failed to notice Kittie watching.

68

After a moment, Emerson checked over the tripod, twisting at the locks that held it in place. Kittie stared, uninhibited, and she jumped when Blanche squeezed her knee.

'What?' she asked, turning to face her.

'Don't spy,' Blanche said, reproachfully, her eyes twitching back themselves.

'I think that about does it,' Emerson said finally.

A match struck behind the sisters and its faint glow spread shadows across the floor. The light grew as Kittie imagined Emerson lighting the oil lamp. Blanche gasped and Kittie looked up to see an image projected onto the bare wall. It was a black tree. The drawing was simple and had little else to it. A faint whirring started up and the image flickered. The branches moved, at first disjointedly and then smoothly, as though living on their wall.

Kittie wondered how Emerson was doing this, imagining that the paper must carry the drawings and, one after the other, they must slip before the light of the oil lamp. But her busy mind gave way to the show in front of her. The edges of the projection flickered slightly before settling, as if it were a sheet pulled tight on the line.

Soundless moments crept by. Even the rain against the windows seemed to die down out of respect for Emerson's show. The sisters felt drawn into the shape on the wall and a heaviness spread over them. Their attention remained rapt, but their bodies became strangely limp and redundant.

From one of the tree's branches sprouted a red apple. It grew there and bobbled about with the sway of the tree in the wind. A scatter of fragile black shapes moved against the sky and Kittie swore to herself she heard birdcalls. Before she could think on that any longer, a green line spread across the base of the tree and over its edge came two figures. One was a man dressed in a simple white cape, while the other, a woman, was dressed in black. The figures held one another for a moment before the man raised a hand and pointed off into the distance, touching the woman's waist with the other. The woman looked to where the man's arm pointed and lowered her head in what was unmistakably sorrow.

Out of the distance came a vague grey shape that fixed into something more certain as though moving from behind a veil of low clouds. It was a black castle. As soon as it became clear, another castle, this one white, appeared on the opposite side of the tree.

The woman turned to face the man and he pulled the apple from the tree. The man proffered it to the woman, who reluctantly took a bite before he did the same. The man then held the apple back up to the branch, which took it in its grasp and curled back in on itself like a witch's finger.

The man and the woman kissed softly and then embraced. Their shapes folded into one another and they moved down onto their knees, resting their heads on each other's shoulder to form a smooth curve, their colours mixing to grey. The shape stilled and Kittie recognised the outline of a gravestone.

Two figures came from each side of the tree: one pair, a king and queen cloaked in black; the other, a king and queen cloaked in white. Each looked over the gravestone and bowed their heads in sorrow. As another scatter of birds moved across the sky, they looked up to see the tree's branch unfurl once more and proffer a red apple that hung there like a jewel.

The edges of the frame began to tremble and Kittie heard that faint whirring sound of Emerson's contraption. The sisters all blinked as though waking from a dream.

'Bravo!' Blanche said, eventually breaking the silence.

She turned to watch as Emerson blew out the lantern. Elena stood and pulled open the curtains.

'That was a hell of a show,' she said.

Emerson smiled at their praise, before turning to look at Kittie. 'What did you think?' he asked her.

Kittie recalled the story her uncle had read to her all those years earlier – the girl dancing on the hill as her love married another. She could not help but see the likeness between that and what she had just witnessed.

'Kittie?' Blanche prompted, knocking her knee.

'It was fine,' Kittie said.

'You are not one to varnish your opinion,' Emerson said, laughing as he removed the lantern from inside the drum.

'It was truly wonderful,' Blanche reiterated, looking disapprovingly at her sister.

Emerson took the device apart with routine care: the paper from the drum, the drum from the lens, the lens from the tripod. Soon it lay before the fireplace in its component parts once more.

Elena looked at the now blank space on the wall and shook her head in disbelief. 'How did you manage that?' she asked Emerson. 'And where did you get such a thing?'

'I made it,' he said, gathering up the apparatus. 'As for how I did it – someone taught me.'

Elena narrowed her eyes at Emerson. 'You're a secret kind of fella, aren't you?'

Emerson nodded.

'Fine,' Elena said. 'See if we care about your secrets. We'll get it out of you. Not three sisters who can work out a man's secret like us Mariannes.'

'Elena,' Blanche said, embarrassed. 'What must you make us sound like?'

Kittie seemed to come to, and turned in her seat. Emerson met her eyes.

'So that's what you do?' she asked.

'Yes, it is,' he answered guardedly.

A sound came from outside and Elena walked into the hall as the bell rang.

'You tell stories?' Kittie asked.

'Kittie,' Blanche interjected, 'the man just said that's what he does. And he gave us a fine demonstration too.'

Elena came back into the room holding a cream envelope. She stood close to Emerson, tapping it against his chest before he took it.

'Millicent from Doc Umbründ's place came with this,' she said. 'Now, what business does the doctor have with you?'

Emerson ignored her probing question and tore open the envelope, spilling a white card into his hand. Elena watched him as he did so, toying with her hair.

A flirt don't cover it, thought Kittie.

'It's for another appointment,' Emerson said.

Elena stood back, bumping into a side table. She looked at Emerson as though he was suddenly contagious. 'For what?' she asked with a grimace.

Emerson laughed as Blanche shook her head.

'It ain't like that,' he said, assuring her. 'He's the one making the appointment.'

'You tell stories to him?' Kittie asked.

'In a way,' Emerson replied, holding her gaze.

'More secrets,' Kittie said.

Her tone lacked the playfulness of Elena's, and Emerson's face grew serious as he looked at her. He chewed the corner of his mouth and Kittie grew uncomfortable from his stare.

'Now, if you'll excuse me,' Emerson began, lifting his pack, 'I think I'll have a lie-down. Blanche, tomorrow, might you still show me the place we talked about?'

Blanche moved forward, eager to smooth over Kittie's rudeness. 'Of course,' she said. 'And will you be joining us for supper tonight, Emerson?'

As he walked from the room, Emerson turned and took another look at Kittie.

Stop those eyes, Kittie thought, *from looking on me*.

'You're forgetting,' Emerson began, 'I've got my cush. But thanks all the same.'

With that, Emerson left. The three sisters watched him as he walked from the frame of the door, like one of his stories slipping off the page.

When she heard the back door close, Blanche turned to Kittie, gripping her by the arm.

'Will you stop trying to get at him?' she asked.

'I'm not,' Kittie said, reproachfully. 'Where are you taking him tomorrow, anyhow?'

'It is no business of yours, Kittie. No business at all.'

Blanche shook her head and left the room with Elena.

Kittie picked her book up from her chair and held it close to her chest. She thought of the black book Emerson had unintentionally spilled from his pack.

What I'd give, she thought, *to read the secrets in it*.

7

October 1879

'It's a theatre,' Blanche said, turning to look over her shoulder.

Emerson followed her through the door leading into the auditorium. Motes of dust shifted dreamily in the light as though the air were thick like water. Blanche had brought a lantern with her. She needn't have though as the boards that once covered the windows had slipped in their fittings, or otherwise been pulled down by someone attempting to bring some light back into the space.

Emerson looked around him and nodded happily at the scene.

'Will it do?' Blanche asked.

'It will,' he replied.

'I mean to say, it's not good enough for a show. Most of the seats were torn free and the stage is pocked with holes . . .'

She meant to go on, but Emerson stopped her with a hand on the shoulder.

'It is just what I need, Blanche,' he said.

Blanche smiled, pleased, and tried not to look at his hand on her shoulder. She stilled as though a bird had landed there and she was loath to scare it away.

He moved down between the rows of seats and leaned on the edge of the upper circle balcony. Blanche drew in a breath as the old wood creaked beneath his hands.

'Careful,' she said, trying her best not to sound like an over-anxious mother.

Emerson looked down into the stalls and saw Blanche had been right. Most of the seats had been torn free, as though a blast had gone off. The metal brackets that once held the seats in place were sticking up out of the floor at awkward angles. Even in the weak light, Emerson could see how the floor was lighter and unstained where the seats once were.

Like the opposite of a shadow, he thought, *whatever that might be.*

'Does anyone come here?' he asked. 'Will I be disturbed?'

Blanche joined him at the edge of the balcony and shook her head.

'No one's come here for a long while,' she said. 'I used to come sometimes with my students from school. Just to show them what a theatre was like. The nearest one is still a journey away and most of them don't seem to realise we have one.'

'When was the last show?'

Blanche thought back to the talks she'd given the schoolchildren.

'Around 1865, I think,' she said, uneasy with her affected vagueness.

'So it survived the war?' Emerson asked.

'It did. Then, after Lincoln was shot, some fools took to tearing the place apart. It does not reflect well on our history that those men considered the theatre to be as implicated in our President's death as Wilkes Booth.'

Emerson laughed. 'People do strange things,' he said.

Blanche waited for the thought to continue, but Emerson only walked back up between the chairs to the staircase.

'Mind if we look downstairs?' he asked.

Blanche enjoyed showing him the theatre. In some ways she felt like an archivist of sorts. Despite it reminding her she was now past thirty years of age, she relished the history she had lived through. As the town prepared for new residents, she believed it was her responsibility to uphold its history – or at least remind folks it had one.

After seeing Emerson's show the night before, her imagination came alive with the possibility of him performing for the whole town. She would of course say, to anyone who cared to listen, that she and her sisters were the first to witness Emerson's unique talent, that she had been the one to answer his request for lodging and that she had encouraged him to perform for the benefit of everyone else.

Already, Blanche felt a purchase on Emerson. She believed him someone worth keeping close and someone she cared to carry association with. What other thoughts she had about him were kept at bay, held back by a sternness ushered in with the loss of girlhood and unfortunate experience. A reluctance, perhaps, to dabble in the possibility of happiness when it had evaded her so readily before.

The two of them exited the staircase and walked out into the middle of the stalls. It struck Emerson as odd that the chairs had been ripped up in such a number. It added a strange sensation to the place. As though, far from being on stage, the show was out amongst them. Or, at least, it had been.

He took the lantern from her and twisted it brighter. He held it out towards the stage and a golden glow grew on a white screen at its back.

'That's one thing they left untouched,' Blanche said.

Emerson walked towards the stage and set the lantern down on its edge. He pulled himself up onto it and walked towards the screen. He smoothed a hand across it, loosening clusters of dust and cobwebs.

'You are in the spotlight, Emerson,' Blanche called.

Emerson turned and saw himself glowing from the lantern. He smiled at Blanche's words but stepped aside from centre stage and walked to the side curtain.

'What's back here?' he called.

'Just empty space,' Blanche answered, 'where the actors used to wait to go on. There are some props back there, I believe. Old things.'

Emerson nodded and, with one eye on the curtain, stepped towards the front of the stage once more.

'Watch your step—' Blanche began, when Emerson's foot fell through a hole in the stage.

'Shit!' he cursed and fell on his other knee.

'Are you okay?' Blanche came rushing towards him.

'I am.' Emerson smiled, lifting his leg out and tearing the trouser fabric on the splintered wood. 'As you can see, I am acquainted with accident. Roof or stage, I'll find a way to injure myself.'

'This town does not mean to kill Emerson, I assure you.'

Blanche's tone was playful, but Emerson moved quickly to shrug off her words.

'What's down there?' he asked, looking at the space from where he'd pulled his leg.

'That's where the musicians used to sit. It was too small to have them in front of the stage and we never had a full orchestra, anyhow, so they used to sit beneath and play music up past the actors' feet.'

Emerson enjoyed this image and lay face down on the stage, cupping his hands over the hole and looking in.

'Can you get in there still?' he asked, his voice muffled.

'You don't mean to rehearse down there, do you?' Blanche smiled.

Emerson didn't answer.

'You can,' Blanche eventually replied, 'from backstage, where some of the old instruments still are.'

Emerson stood and feebly brushed the thick coat of dust from his clothes. He saw he'd left footprints and the vague shape of his body on the boards, pressed into the layer of dust. His gaze drifted towards the back of the stage where he noticed lines like a railroad.

'You look to me like the ghost from *Hamlet*,' Blanche said.

Emerson rubbed something from his eye and looked at Blanche in such a way that she failed to recognise whether he had understood her.

'So, Emerson,' she said, keen to move on, 'will it do to rehearse?'

Emerson looked around him, along the rows of seat still remaining in the circle and the balcony.

'It will,' he said. 'I'll fetch my things and return this afternoon.'

'So soon?' Blanche asked.

But Emerson did not answer, and only stepped down from the stage.

'Where do you suppose they are?' asked Elena.

Her face was concentrating on the sewing in her lap. Kittie looked up at her but still she kept her eyes down.

'I don't know,' Kittie said, trying her best to sound uninterested. 'Walking through the fields? Him reciting poetry all the while?' She snorted, trying to force a laugh, but Elena remained silent.

'I think that unlikely,' Elena said eventually.

Kittie sat with a book on her lap and had read the same page at least five times over. The words refused to settle over her curiosity concerning Emerson. She had hoped the book, a fantastical thing, might by contrast convince her their guest wasn't worth thinking on. Instead, her mind's determination only served to make him more of a problem.

'Could they have gone far?' Elena asked.

Kittie closed the book with a clap. Elena looked up.

'I don't know, El!'

'Okay, Slim, I was only asking. What's gotten into you?'

Kittie turned the book over in her hands and then saw Elena's gaze return swiftly to her sewing. She had misread her sister. She had assumed Elena was asking because of what she'd divulged earlier about Emerson having seen her through the window. Instead, Elena was, of course, only thinking on one thing. Or, rather, one man.

'I won't tell,' Kittie said softly.

'Hmm?' Elena hummed, eyes down.

'Go see him, El; I won't tell.'

Elena looked up, eyes brimming with protest. Kittie's smile did away with that, though, and she tossed her sewing to the side.

'Oh, thank you, Kittie. I won't be long, should Blanche return. Tell her ...'

Elena moved to the mirror above the fireplace and began looping strands of loose hair behind an ear.

'I'll tell her something,' Kittie said.

'That's right, tell her something.'

Elena's words were muffled as they worked their way around a hairpin she held between her lips. She twisted her hair behind her head and turned from side to side before the mirror.

Kittie smiled, yet felt a strange pride in her sister's vanity. 'Just tell him to hurry up and propose,' she said, 'for I can't bear this sneaking about any longer.'

Elena smiled and the hairpin dropped to the floor and bounced towards Kittie. Elena cursed. 'Ah, I'll wear my hair down, anyway,' she said, and nodded decidedly to her own reflection.

She walked over to Kittie and squeezed her shoulders, kissing the top of her sister's head.

'Thanks, Slim.'

Elena skipped from the room and out of the house. The door slammed behind her and Kittie almost felt grateful her sister had had occasion to open it rather than leave an Elena-shaped hole in the front of the house, such was her enthusiasm to see Clay.

Kittie bent down to pick up the hairpin and looked over its design. It had been one of their mother's. The pin was a fine slip of silver and the end a portrait of a bird of some kind. Kittie stroked the bird's wings with her thumb, trying to reach for some memory of her mother that wasn't, nor had ever been, there.

She recalled how, years earlier, her Uncle Shelby had once pulled a pin from Blanche's hair when he had needed to unlock Marianne House. He had locked the four of them outside and left the key someplace. Despite Blanche's protestations, he'd pulled the pin from her hair and used the occasion as an opportunity to talk of the war.

'A man can learn plenty from war,' he'd said, lowering himself painfully to his knees and peering into the door's keyhole.

It had been a heavy lock and yet he'd prised it open. Kittie had been impressed, while her sisters had merely stepped inside, Blanche pulling the pin from his hand as she went.

'Will you show me how?' Kittie had asked.

She considered the skill now, turning her mother's pin over in her hand. She looked on Elena's sewing, discarded on the sofa, and wondered if she wouldn't be better placed knowing fine needlework.

Kittie felt adrift. She was younger in years than her sisters but still she felt apart from them. Having been denied the years of parenting they had received, she was raised more under the guidance of her uncle. She wondered if that didn't make her part of a separate family altogether.

The thought saddened her and she suddenly became fearful she might lose her sisters. The senseless thought was not helped by their absence and she cursed Clay and Emerson for their role in this whim – however instant, however prolonged.

Emerson's mystery lent itself to every possibility in Kittie's mind. He could well be there in their town to find a wife. He could well have thought them rich, for Marianne House was the biggest in New Georgetown. Her opinion of him began to darken as it rolled about in the dirt of her accusations. Suddenly it was no longer a matter of curiosity; in Kittie's mind it was a necessity that she uncover his intentions.

Brandishing the hairpin, she left the house and walked down the yard towards the shack where Emerson was staying. Her heart beat quickly, as though to interrupt her determination and question, stammering so, her intentions.

She came to the porch and stepped up towards the door. At once, Blanche or Elena returning was something she both longed for and dreaded. It would stop her from crossing a line in her mind that she thought far off. It would also stop her from knowing what Emerson intended.

Kittie set the pin in the keyhole to the shack and knelt down as her uncle might have. Staring along the gap between the door and the frame, she saw it was already unlocked and twisted the handle, spilling the door into the room.

She stood hastily.

'Emerson?' she called, fearful he might have returned without her noticing. 'Are you here?'

Had a reply come, Kittie would not have known what to say.

It had been years since Kittie had been inside the shack. She had avoided it and felt now the tide of the past lapping at her mind. She wavered and put out a hand to steady herself. Her fingers pushed into a layer of dust on a dresser and she brushed hastily at the mark.

Emerson's belongings were few. The pack he had arrived with was gone and only a damp shirt hanging from a clothesline strung across the room told her someone was staying there. Even the bed seemed undisturbed.

There was a desk pushed towards the window. Kittie recognised it as one from her old school. Blanche must have brought it home to add something more to the room. She noted how the foot of one of the legs was broken off and a pile of coverless books had been propped underneath to steady it, their pages pressed downwards, the words contorted.

On the desk were rolls of paper that resembled those Emerson had fed into his strange contraption. Kittie unfurled them greedily, but saw they were blank.

She drew in the surroundings, eager for some hitherto unseen explanation, as though Emerson's life might be scrawled out on one of the walls.

If only pasts were that easy to get at, Kittie thought.

She sat on the bed and felt something underneath her. Pulling the covers back, she saw it to be a coverless book like those beneath the table leg. She flapped the pages from side to side, trying to discern what manner of book it was.

Struck by a thought, Kittie looked over to the table and saw one of the pile holding it steady was black. She ran over and, lifting the leg, eased the book free. It was Emerson's journal.

She set the table back down, limping on the depleted pile, and tossed the coverless book aside. She sat cross-legged on the floor, as she always did when pulled into a world of words she was eager to enter. The open door to the shack, the thoughts of her sisters' or Emerson's premature return, all slipped from her mind.

Opening the cover and looking over the scrawl, her ears were filled with the sound of her quickening blood.

Even as she began to read, Kittie thought what things Emerson would have noted down over time. It would stretch back years, maybe even to the war. And yet she knew that, even with all that man's mystery detailed before her, the page she would read first would be that of the morning before – to look for any mention of herself.

8

October 1879

Odell felt his arms sting as he pushed the piano from backstage. He had done as much two nights previous and forgotten how heavy it was. His body lurched into its side and he eventually felt it give and begin to lumber forward. What muscles he had in his arms still ached.

He had started visiting the theatre after his mother died. Why he did it the first time, he couldn't say. Perhaps urged on by some childish willingness to trespass. When he had found the piano backstage, though, he knew he had been right to go there. He felt his delinquency had been rewarded and therefore excused. He still worried his father might realise where he had been and scold him for it. Reason was never the thing that lit his father's anger, only something to be added to the flames later on.

Odell reached the side of the stage and moved the piano onto the small lift. He was relieved to let the pulley do the work as he wound the piano upwards, ready to push it out through the curtains. He had played beneath the stage earlier on, but desired to hear the notes ring out into the theatre's auditorium. Despite his initial worry about being seen, he soon realised that if he were to go out there before the stalls there would be no audience to greet him.

The first time he'd seen the theatre was when he was in Miss Marianne's class. She'd taken him, Chester and Kittie along soon after it was vandalised. He recalled chasing Chester across the stage, imaginary guns drawn. He longed for the theatre to reopen and play a show. His sister had told him of the ones she'd seen in New York before the family had moved. She always apologised to Odell for remembering so little, but her descriptions were rich to his ears and he relished each and every word, his back straightening at the most minute of new details.

Once the piano was level with the stage, Odell pushed it out through the side curtain. At hearing a strange sound, he thought he'd pressed on the keys by accident before he realised it came from elsewhere. He ducked down behind the piano and sat in the dust, listening.

It was a whirring sound, not unlike that of his father's clocks as he wound them. He pictured what could be on the other side of the piano and worked on an excuse to have ready. But he became distracted as the white screen that climbed the stage before him lit up with images.

In silence, he watched as figures moved before him. It was unlike anything Odell had seen before. He blinked dumbly as a man stood in the street of a town. He was dressed in white and wearing a Stetson. The image was simply drawn but moved as smooth as life. Odell could not unstick his gaze as another man, this one dressed in black, entered the scene and drew his gun.

A shoot-out, Odell thought excitedly.

The newly appeared figure twitched as the other shot him. His black-clad body crumpled to the ground. The backdrop came alive with waving arms and floating, joyous mouths, which Odell took to be a crowd in celebration. He watched the man in white, charmed.

A figure came together from the vagueness of the crowd and walked towards the man in white. It was a woman with a red dress. Odell was embarrassed to find his heart beat faster at this phoney image before him. The woman embraced the man and they kissed. He turned her around in his arms and then straightened like a bolt. Odell's eyes widened and he saw the crumpled man in black had lifted his gun and fired one last shot into the man in white's back.

He watched as the man in white fell, the woman cradling his head. Odell was suddenly aware of the images fitting together more crudely. He watched as the scene became boxed in by a flickering light before he found himself able to look away.

Curious to see where the show had come from, he looked cautiously around the side of the piano and saw a camera on a tripod in the stalls. He squinted to make out the finer details and saw he was alone in the theatre. Nevertheless, he trod carefully as he walked towards the camera.

It was making the whirring noise still and Odell saw it had spilled a ream of paper out onto the floor. He lifted it, noticing how the images he'd seen on the screen followed one after the other. He picked up the end of the paper and began to look over the story's beginning, which he had missed.

The paper came free from the tripod and a clicking sound started up. Odell worried he had broken whatever it was, and made to run back to the stage. Then he noticed a slot where the paper had come out and, on the adjacent side, another. Without thinking, he fed the paper into this and was relieved as it was taken from his grasp and pulled inside.

The screen in front of him came alive once more and Odell recognised the town. He smiled widely and watched the show, his heart twitching at the arrival of the man in black and the inevitable outcome.

Once it had finished, Odell fed the paper in once more and hopped back onto the stage. Taken with the images, he sat at the piano and began to play along, adding sound to the scene. He enjoyed playing his part in the show and the way he pounded the keys to bring the gunfire to life. To finish the performance, he played a piece of music his mother had taught him, which he thought fitting for the man in white's tragedy.

As he relaxed into the piece, he raised his eyes to the white screen and looked on the woman in red, holding her love's face. The contraption's whirring stopped and her image stilled. A faint recognition had bothered Odell before and now he realised why she had seemed so familiar.

Elena, he thought.

He arched his head back in frustration, squeezing his eyes shut tight so that they might spill the thought out to be wiped away.

'Damn it!' he said aloud. 'Always Elena.'

He longed to forget her, to be able to move on and think on someone else, or, better still, no one at all. And yet she stuck in his mind like crushed glass, impossible to extract amidst the folds and pulp of his memories, fantasies and dreams.

Odell began to play again, but now found his mind elsewhere. He started over once more, but his playing became distracted and he forgot the path of the piece several times. The image of the woman was fixed on the screen and Odell wished it to disappear.

Eventually, he stood and pushed the piano off stage. He lowered it on the lift and replaced it back among the other instruments.

He found a cruel symmetry between Elena's likeness on the

screen and how he remained part of the audience. The thought gave birth to more rumination as he imagined Clay as the man in black. He fantasised how one day he might be the man in white, able to put his adversary down on the ground. The images reaped relevance from Odell's mind and he became assured the man in black was the woman's previous beau, there to seek revenge.

Odell thought on the story some more, aware that it had affected him in a far greater way than he expected. Rather than a show, he felt he was waking from a dream. Yet the impossibility of Elena made her presence in his mind a discomfort and he left the theatre, hopeful the bright afternoon light might wipe his mind clean.

As he walked down towards his father's shop and home, a change crept into his posture and he fancied himself one part more a man in white.

'He's gone,' Emerson said, walking under the stage. He looked up out of the hole his foot had made earlier that day and moved about to make certain the boy was not hidden from view.

Umbründ breathed a sigh of relief and pressed his moustache flat against his upper lip.

'We must find somewhere else,' the doctor said.

'Blanche swore to me this place was deserted.'

Emerson thought on where to continue their appointments. The tavern, now the theatre . . . Both had either drawn suspicion or were close to doing so.

'Why the show?' Umbründ asked, interrupting Emerson's thoughts. 'Each time – your contraption. Why?'

'Anyone turns up, I have a reason to be here. Plus, Blanche knows I came here to rehearse. She walks in and the place is empty, she'll grow suspicious.'

Umbründ nodded. 'Such caution,' he said approvingly.

'Carelessness makes for a bad trade,' Emerson said.

Umbründ reached inside his jacket and pulled several dollar bills out. He pressed them into Emerson's hand and patted him on the arm. Emerson was still unfamiliar with the paper money. He felt it was somehow fake and it lacked the certainty the weight of coin dollars gave.

'We done for today?' Emerson asked as Umbründ pulled on his coat.

'Yes, my boy, I think so.'

Umbründ seemed flushed from having been so nearly discovered.

'He was only a kid, doctor,' Emerson said, trying to reassure him. 'It would not have mattered—'

'It would have mattered,' Umbründ interrupted sharply. He cleared his throat and drew Emerson out from under the stage. 'A good deal,' he said, finishing the thought.

Emerson walked Umbründ to the theatre exit and watched as he eased the door open and peered out into the side street. Emerson had worked with people who harboured all kinds of dark things in their minds. He had pulled them out of the rough earth of memory, and had occasion to be troubled by some since. Yet, all the while, he had not seen one of them as nervous as the doctor was. It seemed to Emerson he had more to fear in remembering than the others had in forgetting.

'Stay here a while,' Umbründ said.

'I plan to,' Emerson replied.

He contemplated whether to encourage the doctor to stay, but did not want to dissuade him from further appointments.

'I—' Umbründ began.

'—will send word,' Emerson finished.

The two men smiled.

'We share a thought,' Umbründ said. 'And not for the first time.'

He stepped out into the side street and pulled the door closed behind him, leaving Emerson alone in the theatre.

Emerson listened as the doctor's footsteps receded down the alleyway. Soon, the clatter of hammers on wood and men calling out to one another buried Umbründ's retreat.

Emerson sighed and hit his palm into the wall, frustrated. An old theatre poster came away, stuck to his palm. It was aged paper and fell from his skin like dried leaves. He longed for the privacy to carry out his appointments and thought on how it had never before been such a problem.

During the war, his first appointments had happened a stone's throw from campsites or else on the march to someplace else. Nevertheless, there was always seclusion there when he had wanted it.

In New Georgetown, it seemed, despite everybody's supposed privacy, they each of them wormed their way from one place to another, moving silently, eyes down. So intent were the townsfolk on keeping secrets that they kept constantly on the move – the perpetual dance of the covert.

Emerson went back to the main auditorium and gathered his things. He felt the ream of paper he'd chosen had left an impression on the boy. He and Umbründ had listened as the boy had dallied over the piano, playing music and watching it a second time.

Even in an empty theatre, the boy seemed to find an unwelcome audience and had cursed himself.

'What is happening?' Umbründ had asked.

Emerson had raised a hand to quieten him and continued to

watch the boy. He was drawn into whatever trouble the young man had encountered and wished he could step out from beneath the stage and look into his mind.

Now alone, Emerson walked on the stage and fixed his feet over the boy's footprints. They overlapped in the dust as he trod around, lost in the steps the piano player had taken, wishing that he might somehow know more about him by doing so.

9

October 1879

Odell had dwelled for too long in the old theatre, drawn in by that curious show. Upon leaving, he had quickened his pace as he walked home, though eager not to break into a run and draw the gaze of those around him. When he had finally stepped inside, he was happy to see he had arrived before his father, and sat down immediately at the piano.

Despite seeing fit to marry a pianist, Horace Patch had never been one for his son's piano playing. In Odell's mind, he lacked the patience for such things. Odell recalled how, after his mother had passed, he had set to playing her sheet music. He had practised for weeks and weeks while his father spent nights drinking or gambling. He remembered how he had sat at the piano and played for his father, believing it to be one of his finest performances. He had hoped it would be a fitting tribute to his mother, a way to show that she remained in some way, at least. He turned to gauge his father's reaction – expecting, at the most, tears, and, at the least, an approving nod. Instead he saw a face contorted with confusion. Standing from his chair, Odell's father pushed him aside, opening up the instrument, convinced the tuning pin was out of sorts. It was then that Odell realised his father, the clockmaker, was a man of mechanics. He didn't hear music; he only heard the sound caused by strings and keys. To Odell that was like being told your heart was only there to pump blood, not to love.

Horace Patch had known his tragedies; that could not be denied. But they bubbled beneath the surface and rarely did he ever talk about them. He had few quarrels with the world, but, out of some cruel twist of life, those he did have perfectly mirrored the habits of Odell.

Odell recalled how one of his oldest friends, Chester, had a father who liked to pull a cork and throw a punch. Time would be when Chester came to school with a new bruise almost every day, his green eyes folded up painfully between two puckered welts. It wasn't unknown for a man to turn his hands on a wife or child, but, in its infancy, New Georgetown decided against going bad so quickly. One morning, when Chester arrived at school with a broken arm, he was placed in the care of the schoolmistress and the people made it known to the boy's father that he was no longer welcome in town. The man turned heel like he was leaving little else behind than a favourite shirt.

Odell knew Chester like a brother, but couldn't help but think that, given the choice, he would rather the physical bruises from a father who didn't care to the unseen bruises from a father who refused to understand him. After all, the bruises were still there, just deep inside, along the walls of unseen things.

The dark centre that all these thoughts spun around was one Odell cared not to think on. For he knew that, if his father had died and his mother were alive, he would doubtless be happier. His piano playing would be encouraged and, as his mind raced along a more favourable scenario, he would be more confident, perhaps even daring enough to speak with Elena. In this scenario he housed all kinds of fancy.

Guilt-ridden from his thoughts, Odell stood from the piano and moved to get a drink of water.

'Odell!' he heard.

He froze on the spot. The voice was drawn out and desperate. Odell looked up, out of the window, but saw nothing. He drank from a glass, thinking it must just be his imagination playing tricks.

'Odell!' he heard again.

This time he set the glass down in the sink and turned fearfully to face the door. He recalled a show that had come through New Georgetown, about an old man's conscience and three ghosts eager to pick at it. He feared the surface of the door would be drawn in scratches from the chains of some transparent ghoul. He reluctantly checked and saw the wood was the same as always. Regardless, Odell made a promise never to see a show again.

'Help me, son!' the voice said.

Odell felt his palms dampen and the pinch of sweat as he rubbed awkwardly at his eyes.

Mother, he thought.

He decided in that moment that the dead could read the minds of the living like a book, and now expected his mother to deliver some spectral scolding about his earlier thoughts, where he'd wished his father dead.

Then he realised: *Father*.

He raced to the door and swung it open. Looking down the steps he noticed his father, crumpled at their bottom.

'Where in the hell have you been?' Horace asked, looking up awkwardly.

Odell clambered down the steps, racing to think of something to say.

'Here,' was all he could muster.

'Not out someplace? I stepped out once and didn't see no light on.'

Horace's words slipped about in the air, loose and out of tune. *Drunk*, thought Odell.

'I might have gone out for a while,' admitted Odell.

'I thought I told you ...' Horace began, before letting out a rumbling sigh. He reached down to his left knee, the trouser leg hanging empty over the steps.

'Where's your leg?' Odell asked.

Horace let out a wheezing laugh. 'Fredericksburg, I believe. Up some rebel's ass.' He laughed again and reached for the bannister, missing it.

'I meant the wooden one,' Odell said.

Horace's face quietened and his wet eyes blinked up to the night sky.

'Help me up,' he said, seriously.

Odell hooked his arms under his father's shoulders and lifted him.

'Help me up, damn it!' Horace shouted.

'I'm trying,' Odell rebuffed.

Horace hopped on his one leg and steadied himself against the side of the house. He looked at Odell as though recalling he was his son.

'You wouldn't have lasted five minutes on the field,' he said, swallowing something down. 'Plenty didn't, neither.'

Odell stared at Horace's chest, avoiding his eyes.

'Now help me up,' he said, hooking his arm around Odell's shoulder.

Odell carried his father up the steps and set him down on a wooden chair. Horace wheezed like he had done the carrying and then pulled his left trouser leg all the way up to his thigh. He rubbed the skin there. Odell noted how the flesh folded inwards, and turned away to fetch his father a glass of water.

'It hurt?' Odell asked over his shoulder.

'When don't it?' Horace spat back.

Odell handed his father the glass and noticed his hand was bloodied.

'I fell,' Horace said. He set the glass down and Odell looked at the patches of blood painted onto it.

'Since you were sleeping, best you go back,' Horace said, taking long blinks of his heavy eyes. 'Right now.'

Odell went into his room and closed the door behind him. His thoughts about his father being dead flared up again and this time he relished them.

I wish you were dead and rotting, he thought, daring not to speak aloud.

He lay on his bed, trying to calm his anger in the best way he knew how. He pulled a scrap of newspaper out from under the mattress and unfolded it. It was a cutting from the *West Virginian Oracle* about Memorial Day and Miss New Georgetown. Elena's eyes stared back at him and he wished she were there with him.

He wondered if his spite towards Horace might shock Elena, perhaps even disgust her, given how he was showing a disregard for having a father – something he was sure Elena longed to have again.

Odell's eyes were drawn to the light around the frame of his door. It died away and he heard his father retire to his bedroom. His walk was loud and sloppy: single footsteps more like the hammering of a post into the ground.

Pity always followed in the wake of his anger and Odell, clutching the picture of Elena between his fingertips, couldn't help but think of his mother and what it must have been like for Horace to lose her. His heart was upturned at the thought.

He stood from his bed to listen at the wall between their rooms. His conscience itched still from his earlier anger and so he now smothered his actions in care for his father, eager to prove to himself he was better than he had been. He remembered his sister listening at the wall whenever their parents made love, her giggling face twitching all the while, hands spread across the partition, as though divining something.

Now, years later, Odell pressed his ear to the same wall and heard his father sobbing. He had never once seen his father cry, even after his mother's death; this made Odell listen more keenly, hearing something he had never imagined possible. The deep and muffled sob pressed against the partition like the beat of a human heart.

Odell woke with the early morning light spread out across his chest. His dreams had been troubled. It took him a moment after waking to pick actual events out from what he remembered. His father's moans on the outside steps had drawn a crowd, and they'd all laughed at him, lying there without his wooden leg. Odell had come out onto the porch and looked down at him. The crowd turned their faces up and laughed at him too, pointing and screaming with hilarity such as he had never seen before. Elena was there amongst them, hiding her smile beneath a raised hand. The dream left him almost certain his family's secrets had been drawn out and laid bare before the town's eyes.

He stretched for a moment and then heard the whistle of the kettle from the stove. He was shocked to hear his father up and he quickly dressed.

'Mornin'', his father said, as Odell walked from his room.

'Mornin', sir,' Odell replied.

'You want me to fix you something to eat?'

Odell took a piece of bread from the side and spread some honey across it. 'I'm fine,' he said, noticing that his father had shaved and his hair was slick back over his head.

As Odell ate, trails of honey sticking to his chin, he watched his father itch at his stump. 'Want me to fetch the doctor?' he asked.

Horace looked up. He stopped scratching and spread his hands flat on the table. 'I'll go see him myself,' he replied.

Odell nodded and wiped at his chin.

'Last night,' Horace began reluctantly. 'I'm sorry if I spoke out of turn. I asked you to stay inside the house, is all.'

'I know,' Odell replied. 'Sorry, sir.'

'Would you stop that "sir" shit,' Horace snapped, clapping a hand on the table.

Odell nodded and set the crust of bread on the side. He rubbed at his arm, not knowing what to say or where to look. His father raised his arms and then let them fall again.

'I try to apologise, Odell, and you tie me in knots.'

What have I done to you, thought Odell, *to tie you in knots?*

Horace pushed his chair back and lifted his jacket from it. It was still streaked with the mud from the steps and he brushed at it, frustrated. He put it on, cursing at the effort, and lifted a crutch that rested against the table. With some difficulty, he moved across the floor towards his son. Odell flinched as Horace laid a hand on his head.

'You need to see a barber,' Horace said, attempting a smile.

Odell shrunk away as though his father's hand were pushing him down through the floorboards.

'It's tonight, isn't it?' Horace said.

Odell nodded.

'Thought I'd forgot, didn't you?'

Odell didn't move.

Horace took his hand from his son's head and brushed a thumb across the boy's upper lip. 'Seen more hair on a hen's beak,' he said. 'But I guess you're growing up.'

For a moment, Horace looked past Odell and out of the window. He breathed in and blew his breath out so Odell caught the smell of coffee.

'Well, okay,' Horace said. 'I'd best be going. And you might as well play for a longer time. Seeing as it's tonight.'

Odell met Horace's eyes. It was the first time he could recall his father encouraging him to play.

'Just keep it soft, son. The more you practise, the more likely it is you don't embarrass us. We don't need the attention, though, so play it soft.'

Horace ruffled Odell's hair and turned to leave, the knock of his crutch echoing around the half-empty room. His father paused at the open door before leaving, down the steps. Once the knock of the crutch on the steps stopped, Odell let out a sigh of relief.

Embarrass us, he thought.

He turned to look out the window as his father walked towards the doctor's, holding a hand up to a man on a horse, bidding him to wait until he had crossed the muddied road. The man's horse shifted about, keen not to stand still.

Bolt, wished Odell, before turning to play the piano.

10

October 1879

Kittie untied the string that held Emerson's journal together and the cover sprang open encouragingly, splaying the pages like a fan. She moved their edges subtly with her fingertips. One page was filled with fine illustrations – the workings of Emerson's contraption, she supposed – while maps and names crowded others.

Her heart beat faster for this trespass and she looked up through the window of the shack, towards the house.

If I see any sign of Emerson, she vowed to herself, *I will hide it away once more.*

A scatter of birds flew from one side of the yard to the other and tempted her resolve. Yet, after a moment of silence and calm, she returned to the journal. Its opening pages lay creased and incomplete – strips torn away in places – while the paper that remained was covered in handwriting both smudged and illegible.

Then, a few pages further on, the words were temptingly crowded before her, promising at least some insight into the man she strove to understand.

Orderlies and nurses running about. All these rooms. Being in this hospital reminds me of the first time I visited a hotel.

My daddy was on the road, as was his profession - travelling salesman. He carried with him a large leather medical bag filled with all kinds of things - nothing as useful as medicine, mind. Whenever we pitched up on someone's doorstep, I'd catch a look inside and see all sorts in there. I recall once seeing a series of buttons, all different shapes and sizes, held out on a piece of string. I thought my daddy a proper sort at the time, but I could not think who might buy buttons from such a man.

He liked to walk into the big hotels that towns sometimes had - the ones that reached over three storeys and had handsome signs with the finest lettering. The man behind the desk would fix his eyes on us as soon as we walked through the door. Maybe he recognised my daddy, or else the sort he was. I sometimes think he only took me along so he wouldn't be turned out onto the street with a few teeth less.

Regardless of these looks, my daddy strode right up and placed a hand on the counter, as though he had money enough to rent plenty of rooms. Instead, he asked for just the one. He'd persuade the man behind the desk he was waiting on an associate of his to arrive later that evening with his share of their business's profits. At this point, the man behind the desk, no matter what man or what desk, would narrow his eyes to better fix on what my daddy was. My daddy would just smile throughout, happy to have the conversation. He said if the man didn't believe him then he'd leave something of his in the man's care until it be replaced by the money. He sometimes joked about leaving me and ruffled my hair as he said it. The man behind the desk would sometimes look down and laugh, or sometimes look at me as though he didn't quite believe I was there. Then my daddy would reluctantly pull a watch from his pocket and hand it over. In the best cases, he'd lead the man behind the desk to asking for it.

'Worth more than a room for a whole week, that watch,' he'd say.

The man would look over it doubtfully, but then he'd see an engraving on the case - To my dear R, with love.

'That's me,' my daddy would say, pushing a thumb into his own chest. 'R.'

Nothing but a letter, was what I thought. The man was always taken with it. By the time he'd stopped doing such, we must have visited over sixteen hotels and not once did we get turned away. The man behind the desk would reach to the back wall and lift a key from the hooks there. I always liked how each one was numbered and belonging in its place. I told myself as I grew older, one day I'd like to stay in such a hotel. I'd like to be a man to have a key from one of those hooks and feel good about it, not fearful of lying as my daddy must have been.

From the moment he set his things down in the room, my daddy would shave and make himself presentable. He'd change into a fine suit and, rather than that old medical bag, he'd carry his things about in a folded pouch of calfskin. If you were that man on the front desk, you might not recognise him.

My daddy would ask me to stay in the room and then he'd be gone for a long old time. Sometimes he didn't return until it was long dark and I lay curled, sleeping on a corner of the bed. I recall when I was older - say, on hotel number twelve of those sixteen - I looked inside the near empty medical bag and found a half dozen of those watches, all engraved with the same message - To my dear R, with love.

Once, my daddy came back up to the room in quite the state. He had his shirt torn about his neck and told me to get my things together quicker than was possible. We left that particular hotel in the most curious way - crawling down a steep-sided roof, before hanging from a gutter and turning our ankles with the drop. I never once heard gunfire, though. I heard plenty else - names called that were blunt and somehow already alarming to my young ears.

We ran around the building and headed in any direction that was away from town. Before we did as much, though, my daddy stopped at the hitching post. With a laugh, he untied the horses there and sent them running with a clap on their hides. All but one - a brown colt that moved around on the spot as though it were treading the last steps of a weary journey. It looked troubled and had a cut below its eye that crawled with life. I felt sorry for it there, troubled by something I couldn't solve. My daddy told me to hurry and, when I stayed fixed, he ran off. I reached out to touch the horse, but it flinched from me and its eye wept some more. I ran to catch my daddy up and, before I turned the corner, saw the horse return to its troubled movements, trying to shake the flies from its cut.

I know now that horse was dying. But at the time I didn't know squat.

That might sound a harsh memory, but the last hotel I visited was plenty harsher.

I worked and worked, plying my trade across the country. I was a man then too; I'd paid to be as much. Women of disrepute had taken my coin and turned it into the movement of flesh. I don't quite know if it helps, but after each time I felt guilty. It settled a soul's debt, only to be replaced soon after by another. It made me want to settle down with a wife and perhaps even a child. Whether because of this, or maybe it was headed in my direction anyhow, I met a whore and stayed for a while. The man *of the house had asked me to help her and afterwards she and I fell into something you might call love.*

Now I don't need to be the one to tell you that loving a whore is a fool's game. Soon enough all things grew weary and I left. Turns out that guilt from before weren't so bad compared to the other kind. Weren't till you walked in here that I knew my and her time together didn't just stop at the two of us. I swear to you now, I did not know before.

I don't know what you've seen. But I hope you've seen enough for what follows not to sound like folly. Maybe I shouldn't wish such sights on my own son. Feels strange, that - son. Do you mind me calling you that?

We all heard stories about the hospitals. Some said they'd sooner be killed than injured and taken off for curing. I caught a piece of branch blown from a tree in my left leg years before and I sure was scared. All came to nothing, though, and I could walk good as new after that. But this was different. This time they'd have to open me up and take those bullets out of me. Once they'd set me down in a room with a dozen others, I wished I'd died. Wished for something peaceful

Kittie searched for the following page, but found it missing. She read the next written words, but they belonged to the story later on. Holding the book flat before her eyes, she saw the flakes of torn pages, stuck upright like scales. She supposed they might have been removed after a mistake had been made. And yet the thought was turned away by the more loaded assumption that they had been removed on purpose.

Regardless, she started to read the first words that followed, hopeful her mind might be able to surmise what was missing.

left. The nurses and other staff went too. I guess they was worried they might be seen as the enemy, if they was curing them. Like I said before, things in that hospital weren't right. I ain't no doctor, but I knew plenty enough that my arm should have healed by then.

Ain't nowhere in the world where stories don't exist. That place was the same. We heard terrifying things. Things not welcome to the ears of the injured and the fearful. Worst of all, they had a home there. Words gave way to truths and, sure enough, we all started seeing them. Perhaps they were there all along? Perhaps sometimes truths need stories to be seen?

You'll learn that. The opposite too. Now that you're here with me, you'll learn it all. Judging by the look of you, I'm thinking you've already seen more than you'd hoped.

Shit, look at me. Some sight, huh? But it ain't from being here now, being somewhere safe, thank the Lord. It ain't even from remembering the horror of that other place. It's from having you here, son.

I I

October 1879

The itching had begun to bother Horace. He sat up on the examining table, his trouser leg rolled up over the stump, and he rubbed at the skin roughly. He traced a finger along the deep groove and turn of his scarred flesh.

'Does it hurt?' Umbründ asked.

'Always,' Horace replied bluntly.

'And your leg?' Umbründ enquired. 'The wooden one?'

Horace looked up at him, thinking he was making a joke. But Umbründ's face was serious and his anger fizzed back down. He ran through some ways of explaining in his mind, but failed to reach an outcome that did not sound even faintly ridiculous.

'I lost it,' he said simply.

Umbründ leaned back in the chair behind his desk. The wood creaked and he looked up to a corner of the room, as though preparing a diagnosis.

'And how does one lose a leg?' he asked. 'A wooden one.'

Horace breathed in deeply and gripped the edge of the table. 'A card game.'

Umbründ closed his eyes for a long time before taking a pen from its inkwell. Horace could not make out if the doctor's face showed disappointment or just plain fascination.

'Can it be retrieved?' the doctor asked.

'I'm guessing not,' Horace mumbled.

'And if you were to think, rather than guess?'

Horace watched the eyes of Umbründ; they were like glass ones from a stuffed animal, small and shiny.

'No,' he said decidedly.

Umbründ jotted this down and exhaled in a tuneful manner. It skipped about as he wrote, as though the movements of his pen were those of a conductor's baton. He opened one of the drawers in his desk and pulled out a sheet of paper. From his top pocket, he unfolded a pair of spectacles.

'It was three dollars before,' Horace said.

'I have five,' Umbründ replied, tapping at the invoice. 'Yes, five dollars.'

'Well, it was three,' Horace said, turning his head.

Umbründ looked up and lifted the invoice in his direction. 'Would you like to look?'

Horace slowly shook his head, biting the side of his tongue. Umbründ set the paper down again and began to fill it out.

After a moment, Horace got down from the table and fixed his crutch beneath his arm. 'Forget the leg, doc,' he said.

Umbründ stopped writing and looked up.

'I can't afford it, anyhow. Just give me the morphine.'

Umbründ replaced the invoice in the drawer and shoved his pen expertly into the inkwell.

'And you can afford that?' he asked, anger creeping into his words.

Horace didn't reply and instead fished two dollar notes from his trouser pocket. He walked over to the desk and put them down.

'This is not a chemist,' Umbründ said. 'I cannot just hand out drugs.'

'Sure you can,' Horace replied.

He stared down at Umbründ relentlessly and the doctor seemed to shrivel under his gaze. Horace was a tall man and whatever authority Umbründ believed he had in that room began to slip away. Before the moment could be drawn out any longer, the doctor pushed back his chair and went to a cabinet hanging on the back wall. From it he pulled a bottle of morphine. It was enough to kill Horace and he thought fitfully over the likelihood.

'How do I know this won't come back to me?' he asked Horace.

'What's that?'

'If you take it all?'

Horace laughed. 'Take it all? Listen here. There ain't nothing to live for, but there ain't nothing to die for, neither.'

Umbründ's mouth twitched at the horrid poetry in Horace's words. He set the bottle down on the desk beside the dollar bills and took the money as Horace pushed the bottle into his jacket pocket. The deal was done. Umbründ felt Horace's eyes on him, but looked up to see he was gazing over his shoulder. As if unfamiliar with his surroundings, Umbründ turned to see that Horace was looking at the painting on the wall.

'You know,' Horace said, 'this room, all this — it ain't like no doctor's office I ever seen before. This painting, that desk, these . . . trinkets . . .' With that last word, Horace pointed at items arranged on a shelf across from the examining table.

'Are you judging me on a matter of personal decoration?' Umbründ asked.

'I'm judging you on plenty else,' Horace said and turned towards the door.

'And what am I to take from that?' Umbründ called out eagerly.

Horace walked out of the office and slammed the door behind him. The echo reverberated around the soft furnishing of the room and Umbründ felt helpless behind his desk.

What does he know? he asked himself.

His moustache twitched and he smoothed it out with his fingers. He sat down in his seat again and thought as far back as he could. He recalled arriving in New Georgetown and meeting Horace and his family.

But what if, he asked himself, *that man knew me from before?*

A knock came at the door and Umbründ straightened up in his chair.

'Yes,' he called out.

His secretary, Millicent, timidly crept in. She had a wholesome look to her round face that only made Umbründ feel more sorry for her. She was misplaced in that part of the world and slunk deep into the shadows cast by women of more note.

'Your next appointment is here,' she said uneasily.

Umbründ looked down at his appointment ledger, confused.

'A Mr Emerson,' Millicent said, looking worriedly back at the reception room.

Umbründ continued to hunch over his desk, but lifted his eyes. 'Of course,' he said. 'Show him in, show him in.'

Millicent nodded and slipped away, leaving the door open. Umbründ recalled how her manner had become so hesitant since the time she had caught him pleasuring himself on top of the examining table. She had walked in unannounced, carrying folders in her arms, and looked up to see his britches round his ankles, his ecstatic, huffing face turned to the ceiling. She had dropped the folders and run from the building. To his surprise, though, she'd returned later that afternoon – only changed.

Umbründ thought how, if she had not been so dull looking, he might have asked her to assist.

The doctor heard a murmur from outside the door and Emerson stepped into his office, taking the hat from his head. Umbründ raised himself from behind his desk and strode towards him emphatically, hand outstretched and a studious bend still in his back.

'My boy,' he said, taking Emerson's hand.

Emerson remained silent, smiling.

'Thank you for coming so quickly,' the doctor continued.

'Not a problem,' Emerson replied, setting his hat down on the examining table.

Umbründ considered telling him to move it elsewhere, but carried on instead. He walked across his office to the shelf of items Horace had commented on. Next to it was a large wooden cross. The doctor stood before it and smiled distantly.

'That new?' Emerson asked.

'It is,' Umbründ replied, keeping his eyes on the cross. 'Just like my memory of him.'

Emerson watched him for a while. 'Your father?' he asked.

'Indeed,' said Umbründ, as though he were looking on a photograph of the man himself. 'Indeed.'

He turned from the cross and gestured for Emerson to sit down. Emerson lifted himself up onto the examining table and felt uncomfortable for it. He thought of Elena's reaction the day before, when learning of his appointment with the doctor, and wondered now whether he was the patient, after all.

'I trust this does not interfere,' the doctor said, pointing to the cross as he sat back behind his desk. 'I couldn't resist.'

'Were you a religious man before we met?' Emerson asked, looking over at the cross.

Umbründ ran a finger along his moustache. 'No, I could not say I was,' he replied.

Emerson shifted on the table. 'Don't rush it,' he said. 'You remember why I'm here?'

The doctor nodded.

'Then you've no memories yet. What you have now, I guess you could call dreams. They seem real, but they're stuck to the outside of your mind – tacked on, but not yet set. One shake and they'll fall away. It takes time. Once it's a memory, you won't need to go out and buy some memento. You'll just remember it and, if you want to buy a cross, you'll go buy one.'

Umbründ felt embarrassed for his mistake. He looked at the cross again. 'So many rules,' he said, almost to himself.

'Just a few,' Emerson said. 'But they're important.'

He could see Umbründ's mood dipping and so started up again.

'After all, if you just remembered it like anything else, straightaway, then who's to say I get paid? You'd recall our meeting, but you'd think it curious and that's the end of it. Other side of things is I tell you everything you remember is down to me and, if you believe it, you pay me a small fortune. By the time you call what I did a memory, I'll be long gone and you'll think on me as little else than a stranger you met with. Once your last memory has taken, I'll brush my boot prints from your mind.'

The doctor tapped a finger on his desk. 'And what of the advert?' he said. 'I remember that and then I start to wonder.'

'There is no way your mind would allow it.' Emerson smiled. 'A man giving you memories? It's too fanciful to be believed. Otherwise, if you're unsure, I can get rid of that for you for a few dollars more.'

Umbründ stopped his tapping and leaned across his desk. 'How do you do it?' he asked. 'How did you even learn?'

Emerson hopped down from the table and walked across to the shelf opposite. He picked up item after item, turning them in his hand before placing them back.

'I don't know how I do it,' he said distractedly. 'It's a talent, I guess. But the details of my business I'd sooner not discuss.'

Umbründ sighed and sat back in his chair.

'And you?' Emerson asked. 'How did you get like this, anyhow? Why can't you remember back then?'

'I don't know,' Umbründ said. 'Perhaps we met before. And now you are back for more of my money, yes?'

The doctor laughed and Emerson smiled, turning a small mirror in his hand, the light playing across his face.

'No, that wouldn't work,' he said, a vague smile on his lips. 'I considered it in the early days, believe me. But if I took something, you'd know about it. Navigating somebody's mind's a difficult thing. I could try and do it right now, get double my fee, but you'd know about it. You'd shake me free and have a gun on me before I could take one step.'

'I can kick you out?' Umbründ asked.

'Sure you can. See it like your home. I can walk around there from room to room. I make enough noise, though, or wander someplace you don't want me to go, and I'll be turned out.'

'Fascinating,' Umbründ said.

Emerson set the mirror back on the shelf and walked to the front of the doctor's desk. It was a curious piece of furniture. The legs were bulbous and heavy, reminding him of flesh.

'It can be,' he said. 'Can be dangerous too, though.'

Umbründ's face paled. 'Dangerous?'

'Not for you,' Emerson said, smiling. 'For me.'

'It can't hurt you, surely?'

'Not in the way you're thinking. And, anyway, people find out about it, they'll start wanting it for free. There's plenty to forget, after all.'

Umbründ nodded slowly. 'Your secret is safe with me,' he said. 'After all, I owe you so much already. You've no idea what it means to have a past.'

Emerson nodded courteously, eager to avoid the doctor's praise. 'I see you got the objects,' he said, turning to the shelf of items.

'Of course,' Umbründ replied.

'Then let's start.'

Umbründ called for Millicent. She entered as hesitantly as before and looked suspiciously at Emerson, who seemed not to notice.

'Millicent, my dear, Emerson and I have some business, some private business, to attend to and I wondered if you would be so good as to leave us undisturbed for an hour or so. I believe my schedule is clear?'

Millicent nodded.

'Wonderful. Perhaps treat yourself to an afternoon stroll.'

Millicent took one last look at Emerson before shutting the door behind her. As Emerson rolled up his shirtsleeves, Umbründ thought on his plain-looking secretary and how her mind was most likely fraught with conspiracy.

Given what she's seen in here with one man, he thought, *what must she think is about to happen with two?*

Umbründ felt his head swell. His hands touched his temples and he was glad to find it remained the normal size. His teeth were clenched and he moved his jaw uncomfortably, pushing with his hands left to right, right to left.

I haven't ground my teeth since I was a child, he recalled.

The thought was like a warm pool forming on the inside of his skull. He straightened up and looked at Emerson, who stood before him.

'Wait,' Umbründ said. 'The teeth grinding?'

Even in his rapture, the doctor noticed how exhausted Emerson looked. His hair stuck in strands to his forehead and his face was grey.

'Are you all right?' the doctor asked him.

Emerson nodded and the doctor took a handkerchief from his waistcoat pocket. He looked it over, making sure it was clean, before he handed it to Emerson. Emerson thanked him and wiped at his forehead.

'Teeth,' the doctor said, disappointed. 'I admit I was expecting something more, my boy.'

Emerson handed the handkerchief back to Umbründ, who dropped it onto a small table. He walked across the room and lifted himself onto the examining table once more. His movements were slow and heavy, as though he drew himself through water.

'What of the memories from before?' Umbründ asked. He was growing impatient and noticed some saliva clinging to the hair on his chin. He wiped it away with disgust.

'Before was –' Emerson paused, taking a deep breath – 'an audition.'

Umbründ twisted his mouth in anger and then rubbed at his jaw painfully. 'So now it is all plainness? Why toothache? Why not the memory of a trip to the latrine?' he asked in a gathering rage.

'Remember the house?' Emerson asked, staring at the floor. 'You can't know I've been there. I put a –' he looked around the room – 'a painting on the wall, that's fine. I put a steamboat there instead? You're gonna know something ain't right.'

'But you said it takes,' the doctor continued in a fitful rage. 'You leave and I believe it.'

'But it has to be believable. Say I tell you you're Napoleon. You think you are and maybe you walk outside expecting to see France. But all you see is Virginia. Then you tell yourself you're not Napoleon and that memory gets kicked out, same as I might. Or else you think it's a dream instead, stuck on the outside, remember?'

'But toothache . . . ?' the doctor said pathetically.

'Is believable,' Emerson countered.

'Nevertheless,' the doctor said, rubbing at his sore face.

Emerson stood up, faltering as he did so. His colour had returned and his breath steadied. 'Look,' he said, reaching to the shelf. He took the small mirror and gave it to Umbründ. 'Tell me about this,' he said.

The doctor turned it over in his hands as though it were little more than a trinket. Slowly, realisation settled in his eyes like snow on the ground. Emerson watched with care.

'It was hers,' the doctor said. 'Lucinda's. She broke my heart.'

'Good,' Emerson said, patting the doctor on the shoulder. 'What else?'

'It was in a carriage of her father's. She used to meet me in it by the bridge nearest to home.' The doctor's voice cracked on this last word. 'The colours, the feel, there's so much . . .'

Emerson took the mirror from the doctor, having to pry it from his fingers. 'Don't think on it too hard,' he said.

'She . . . Lucinda had told me she didn't love me anymore. I was heartbroken. I wanted her to stay and pulled at the sleeve of her dress, tearing it. She left in such a hurry her mirror spilled from a pocket in her shawl.'

Emerson smiled. 'Good.'

The doctor shook his head and reached out for the mirror. Emerson pulled it back and stepped away from him.

'No, not good,' Umbründ said. 'You have given me toothache and now heartache? What torture is this?'

Emerson raised a hand for the doctor's shoulder, but he swatted it away.

'No!' the doctor shouted. 'You think this is what I wanted? Pain and suffering?'

'Lower your voice,' Emerson said, looking to the door of the office.

'Why stop there? Why not a rape? Why not a murder? I wanted happiness!' Umbründ hissed.

'Then you wanted a fantasy,' Emerson returned calmly. 'And what you are paying me for is a past.'

The doctor was shaking and sat in a nearby seat, sobbing quietly. 'To have this,' he said hopelessly. 'To go through this now.'

Umbründ collapsed into sobs and Emerson turned to give him a moment. He looked at the curious painting behind the doctor's desk. Emerson had not seen its like before. It was a scene of people looking at a bird trapped within a glass prison. The vessel ballooned around its shape as it lay on one side, possibly dying. People watched, or else turned away, while the man in the centre looked straight out from the painting. Emerson searched for a title or the painter's name, but could not find a thing.

'I know it's difficult,' he said. 'But a past is a patchwork. What man can look back on his own life and claim no hurt, no disappointment?'

Umbründ stayed silent.

Emerson turned from the painting and looked at the doctor. 'You quitting on me?' he asked.

Umbründ wiped his eyes. 'I, of all people, know that steps to a cure can be painful,' he said.

Emerson turned the thought over in his mind. He'd never considered it a cure before.

'Is there much worse left?' the doctor asked him.

Emerson folded his arms. 'Some worse, but some far better.'

Umbründ ran a hand over the back of his neck and stood. 'Then we shall continue,' he said.

Emerson stepped away from Umbründ and felt his mind rise from its swamp. His throat bulged with a sick feeling and he took a seat beside the doctor.

He's got some mind, Emerson thought, *to take on so much, so quickly.*

Umbründ's hands twitched and his eyes unglued themselves. He swayed forward and Emerson put a hand against his chest, fearing he might topple over. The doctor looked at Emerson, resting a hand on his shoulder.

'Each time,' he said, 'is like being pulled from water.'

Emerson nodded. When the doctor regained his strength, he pointed to the items lining the shelf. Umbründ looked them over, picking some up to examine more closely. A while earlier, the shelf had been filled with nothing but junk. Now it detailed the doctor's life from moment to moment. Umbründ opened his mouth to speak, a dozen things racing to be said and, at the same time, discovered.

Emerson raised a hand. 'Not this time,' he said, before tapping at his temple. 'Keep it up here.'

The doctor nodded slightly and the chaos that lay behind his eyes settled, the lights dying down calmly.

Emerson took a box from the floor and began to put away each item from the shelf.

'What are you doing?' Umbründ asked.

'You can't have these lying out all together. Put them about your home. Or else hide them away. Your memories will decide as much.'

The last item Emerson placed inside the box was the mirror he still held from before.

'That I will hide away,' Umbründ said.

Emerson nodded. 'I've got some hidden mirrors of my own.'

Umbründ took the box from Emerson and placed it beneath his desk. He sat in the chair and blew out an exhausted sigh. Emerson pulled on his jacket and noticed the cold damp of sweat soaking his shirt.

'You're leaving?' Umbründ asked, raising his head.

'Sure am,' Emerson said, nodding. 'You've had enough for now.'

Umbründ looked as though he was about to protest, but then, flinching at a pain above his left ear, nodded. He frowned, but reluctantly thanked Emerson, who came over to the desk. The two men shook hands.

'I apologise for before,' the doctor said.

'No need,' Emerson said. 'It happens. Had a man pull a gun on me in Deer Isle once.'

'I would like to hear these stories,' Umbründ said eagerly.

'Best you concentrate on your own for now,' Emerson replied, retrieving his hat from the table.

A knock came at the door and Umbründ called for Millicent to come in, sighing deeply as he did so. The door opened slightly but Millicent remained out of sight.

'Your next patient is here,' she said from behind the door.

'What?' Umbründ called out. 'I cannot hear you if you stay hidden.'

Emerson walked over to the door and opened it fully. Millicent stepped back, gasping. Standing behind her was the barmaid from the Long Cape. Emerson was struck anew by how beautiful she was. He made no gesture of greeting and instead looked her over. She was wearing her hair up and her blouse was fastened at the neck by a piece of frilled lace.

'And are you the doctor today?' she asked Emerson.

'You might say that,' Emerson replied.

Ora tilted her head in puzzlement and went to speak again, but before she could say a word, the doctor had moved across his office and stepped between them, ushering Emerson out and Ora in.

'Thank you, my boy,' Umbründ said, and shut the door.

Emerson stepped back and looked to Millicent for some explanation. She just kept her eyes trained on the paperwork before her and smiled at one of the waiting patients sat on a chair. Feeling his gaze, Millicent opened a drawer in her desk and handed Emerson a thick envelope.

'Thank you,' Emerson said, pushing the envelope inside his jacket.

Millicent remained silent and Emerson took that as a sign to leave. The sight of Ora with her hair up and dressed so smartly had left a stamp on his mind. He cursed Umbründ for shutting that door between them and hoped he might have reason to visit the tavern again.

I am here for other things, though, he thought. *Plus, the betting is she'd just be another hidden mirror.*

He smiled at the thought – mirrors from women tumbling over a box's edge in some imaginary attic.

Stepping out onto the porch, the chilled air surrounded him and he pulled the collar of his jacket close about his neck. It was near to supper time and he decided tonight he would join the

Marianne sisters. They were pleasant enough company, but he thought on Kittie and the way she had spoken to him the day before. Emerson was taken by surprise at how his heart snagged on something. He recalled seeing her naked through the bathroom window and again his heart twitched as readily as a restless limb. He pushed the thoughts to the back of his mind, blaming them on tiredness.

He raised his eyes to the street and saw the skeletons of buildings that filled the town. Work was halting for the day as the light faded. He listened with strange comfort to the last sounds of hammer falls and boards being stacked in piles. He hoped for a saloon that had as yet gone unnoticed – the balcony all filled with frill and flirtation – so he could make use of the money in his jacket.

After all, he told himself, *it's been too long when you're thinking on a girl not yet eighteen.*

12

October 1879

Shaking someone from your mind, thought Ora, *is about the hardest thing to do.*

She was dwelling on Emerson as she sat at her dressing table, readying herself for work, and wondered if the stranger would linger in the town. He wasn't quite what she would call handsome; however, her encounters with him so far stuck in her mind like a barberry twig.

Since she had been a girl, she had always welcomed a man into her thoughts by imagining herself as his wife. She would see fat men on the street and even fatter ones propped up against her bar – all of them, at one point or another, dressed in top and tails, holding her hand before a congregation of the misty faces of half-realised guests. Given that this was always inevitable, it was usually how long these men dwelt in her mind that revealed to Ora how she felt. And by her count, this was the sixth time since the previous night she had held Emerson's hand. Some of those faces seemed clear, too, and the smile grew on her imagined face at their envy and cursed missed chances as they watched her wed the stranger – glorious and iridescent in his mystery.

She stood up from the mirror and turned down the oil lamp sitting by the door. The room flickered into darkness and, as always, she took that as a sign to leave what lay there to rest. Her most intimate moments – and, indeed, the Ora she kept hidden – resided there, as though it were a locked room deep inside the bowels of a hotel. She only ever sent her shadow out to tend the drinks at the Long Cape.

The building was a curious one. She was aware what the rooms surrounding hers had once been used for. From time to time, as the building moved, restless in changing weather, she assigned a thump, a creak, a bang to the whores and their clients who had long since concluded their business. It was a tomb to the sinful; but, nevertheless, it was her home.

Her room had been the only one that was fit to sleep in when she arrived. The Bird herself must have decorated it, for the bar had long been shut up, and its shabby arrangement and half-handled hospitality fitted the stories she had heard before and during her time there.

Her mind often flitted back to her interview and, to date, the only instance of her ever speaking with the Bird. She sifted through the memories of that meeting again in the hope of finding more detail and perhaps something to dispel her fear and uneasiness with working for someone she had never laid eyes on. Town gossip made the Bird into a monster, and Ora the captive. Her only reason for staying was because she was fleeing something far worse, the horror of which she was all too familiar with.

She reached the sanctuary of the bar and looked around at the vacant booths, wondering who might fill them that night. As her imagination ran wild, she tried her best to ignore the sad truth:

she already knew exactly the kind, even the names, of each man who would sit there.

The gas lamps hummed and began to glow, softening what had moments before been charmless. She took an old, weathered box of white candles from behind the bar and noticed how few were left.

The old clock rang out and quivered against the tavern walls. Ora ran the base of each candle over a lantern's flame and fixed one in the centre of every table, lighting them as she went. By the time the sixth chime sounded, the tavern existed in a half glow. Along with the old haunted sound of the clock, the place seemed at once newly alive and long dead – residing in the corners of the world most frequented by phantoms and glimpsed lives.

The front door of the bar shook in its frame and the doorknob twisted. Ora rolled her eyes and walked over to see who it was.

'Drunks,' she predicted. 'Just wait thirty goddamn minutes.'

She pulled the curtain back from the window and saw Odell standing there. He coyly raised his hand and waved. The soft light from the bar bumped along his pubescent skin and wisps of facial hair. Ora tugged the curtain back into place against the glass and fished the key from a pocket in her dress.

Pulling the door open, it struck Ora how cold the nights had begun to get. She recalled how, not long before, she had walked through town with the afternoon sun warm and reassuring on her face and neck. Now a gust of wind blew across the porch and some golden leaves cartwheeled their way into the tavern, as though seeking shelter.

Odell stepped in, holding his hat to his chest. It was a wide-brimmed hat such as a pastor might wear. The boy's shape was loose with the absence of adulthood and his clothes hung from him crudely. The hat did nothing to help and Ora was glad he carried it with him anywhere but on his head.

'Evening, Ora,' he said, walking into the tavern with a wide smile on his face. He shuffled about awkwardly and seemed unable to decide where to stand, stepping from place to place after a second's stillness.

'Odell,' Ora replied weakly. 'Cold evening, isn't it?'

'Why, yes, I suppose it is,' he said, looking back dully at the curtain against the glass. 'I mean, I've only been outside for a moment or two, and this coat sure is warm. Well, that's to say, I'm sure it's cold, I just didn't . . .'

Odell watched Ora walk away and the last of his words melted like snow on a warm palm. As the boy was prone to in such nervous situations, he squinted his eyes shut tightly, as if the dust from the road had kicked up into them.

Moving off to another table, Ora looked back at him, his figure awkwardly separate from the surroundings of the tavern.

'So how you feeling about tonight?' she asked. 'About playing for the Bird?'

A smile broke across Odell's face again and Ora noticed how pleasant a smile he had when there was occasion to share it.

'I still can't quite believe it,' he said, scratching the back of his head and staring at the floor.

'Well, you'd best start,' she said.

Odell's smile fell from his face and his mouth was wide open. 'No, I mean, I do believe it, Ora. I've been practising and all.'

Ora rolled her eyes at him and walked over to the bear at the end of the bar, resting a hand on the animal's high shoulder. 'Odell?' she said. 'I'm hardly serious. Anyways, if you didn't practise for this here audition, I'll smack you upside the head.' She accentuated this with a slap on the head of the bear. 'Sorry, brown bear,' she said, pursing her lips affectionately.

Odell moved towards the bar and climbed onto a stool. He spread his hands before him and examined them, as though making sure each finger and thumb was present. Ora watched and thought on how the boy had talent and whether she would trade for the same, getting in return those awkward ways he had about him.

She moved behind the bar and tugged a cloth free from its knot. The place was already clean, but she felt a compulsion to wipe over the surfaces again so she could remain close to the boy.

'Want something for the nerves?' she asked him.

Odell looked up and laughed. 'No, thank you.'

'You laugh,' Ora began, 'but I've seen it help. Turn a boy into a fighter; turn a maid into a lover.'

Odell shifted on his stool at these words and squinted hard. Things passed between them unheard but no less deafening. An ocean bed of memory disturbed and kicked upwards, dirt clouding the otherwise pristine.

Odell closed his eyes and moved his fingers across the bar, practising. Ora watched and willed him to open his eyes once more – to assure her he wasn't thinking what she feared, or in the hope of stopping her saying the words she held in her mouth.

She stepped forward and stilled his hands with her own. His fingers ceased their moving and spread flat on the wood. 'How's your daddy?' she asked.

Odell opened his eyes and looked up at her. 'I'm trying to practise, Ora,' he said somewhat impatiently.

'And I'm just asking a simple question.'

'There ain't nothing simple about it,' Odell snapped back.

Ora took her hands from him and let out a long breath through her nostrils.

'Why don't you go ask him, then?' Odell kept on.

'You know why,' Ora said with a calm force.

'And stop calling him "your daddy". Don't think I'm as dumb as the rest of this town.'

'How about "your loving father" instead?'

'How's about,' Odell said with a heat to his words, '"*our* loving father"?'

Odell had raised himself from his stool and only now, in the stillness that followed his words, did it become an embarrassment to sit back down. Ora watched him do so, patiently.

'You little cunt,' she said calmly.

Odell jumped with the word and then straightened up in his seat, trying to affect the look of someone familiar with it. He knew he had to say something back, but could not think of anything and, besides, did not want to. He wasn't yet blooded in the ways of combat, verbal or otherwise, and, after one scuffle, sought a truce with his sister.

Ora watched the fire die in his eyes and let out a little laugh, turning to organise the bottles climbing their way up behind the bar.

The words *I'm sorry* were edging ever closer to being formed in Odell's mouth and yet they did not come. Ora watched his reflection in the mirror behind the bottles and narrowed her eyes like an animal smelling blood.

'Oh, and Elena said you've been bothering her again,' she said, watching his face.

Odell squinted and felt the skin of his throat draw tight. The humiliation hit him deep in the heart and he was half tempted to run from the bar.

Forget the audition, he thought. *Then maybe Ora will feel bad for once. Maybe she'll realise what it is she's said.*

Ora turned and wrapped the cloth about the fingers of her left hand, smoothing it out with the fingers of the right. 'Says you're always looking at her,' she continued. 'She and her sisters come down into town and there you are, gawping away. Eyes wide, pockets fidgeting—'

'Okay!' Odell yelled, his fight gone. 'Okay. Jesus!' He pulled roughly at the corners of his eyes and kicked the outside of the bar. 'I'm sorry I brought it up. He's fine – the old man. Still comes home drunk. Last night was a bad one. He don't ask after you, but that don't mean he's not thinking about you. I sometimes see him looking off across Main Street. Looking at nothing in particular, but then I reckon he's thinking on something for certain – you.'

'That right?' Ora asked, loosening the cloth about her hand.

'Yeah, that's right. You think I'm lying?'

Ora shrugged. 'He still hard on you?'

'Yep.' Odell laughed. 'Must run in the family, huh?'

'Quit it, Odell. I mean it.'

'Fine. It's done been quit. Now leave me alone to practise.'

Odell closed his eyes and the last of his tears squeezed out. He impatiently wiped them away and took to playing across the bar top.

'You got it,' Ora said and traipsed off down the bar.

'And Ora,' Odell said, shouting after her, 'I never been fidgeting my pockets.'

Ora spun round and flicked the cloth in his direction, smiling. 'Odell, you dope. I made the whole thing up.'

By the time the clock rang out seven chimes, the tavern was filled with townsfolk. Odell sat at the bar, patiently answering as just about every customer asked wasn't he a little young to be drinking, or did his daddy know he was there. He shrank in on himself at the bar and tried to move his fingers there, silently and perfectly. The truth was he had not managed it perfectly once – not even aptly – since he had arrived.

Past the shoulders and thrown-back heads of revelling drinkers, Odell saw the corridor of rooms, one of which he had hoped he might practise in. He wondered if Ora had intended that before their heated exchange. Once the bar had started to fill up he had said as much to her, yet her returned words were final: 'I don't want you going into those rooms.'

'Odell!'

The boy felt a thump on his back that knocked the air from his lungs. He knew the voice and reluctantly turned to see Clay.

'What the hell are you doing here?' Clay asked, slapping the boy's back once more. He moved Odell about like a man looking over a game bird for slaughter, setting his large hands on his shoulders, a few inches away from a strangle.

'Nothing,' Odell said, squinting.

'Clear and concise as always, Odell,' Clay said with a laugh and squinted back as though it were a joke they shared. 'You sat here keeping an eye on Ora for me? Making sure none of these dogs gets too frisky around her?'

Upon hearing Clay's voice, Ora moved down the bar past the outstretched hands of impatient drinkers. A smile crept free despite her finest attempts to hide it. Odell knocked Clay's hand away from his jacket, watching the man look over his sister hungrily.

'What'll it be?' she asked.

'Now, that . . . that is the question,' Clay replied, slamming a fist onto the bar. 'Listen up, Patch. Your man, Clay, is about to show you how to woo a beautiful woman.'

'Leave him alone,' Ora said, swishing a hand nowhere near to Clay. Her eyes set on pity when looking at Odell, this phantom brother of hers.

'The usual,' Clay said to Ora, watching her figure as she turned to reach for a glass, the shape of her body visible through the tight pull of her clothes.

Ora was the kind of woman for whom nothing was accidental. Each turn of her hips, each brush of hair from her face – it all worked towards something. Odell recalled how he had watched the faces of men turn from indifference to intrigue over the years the Patches had walked through upstate New York and, later, New Georgetown. He had been jealous at first, then angry – an anger which now burned strongly within him.

'So you here on an errand, Odell?' Clay asked. 'Here to fetch your daddy another bottle to crawl into?'

Odell noted Ora's shoulders tense and her raised glance caught in the glass. He recognised the look as one of pity, but also of begging – to keep their secret and not invite the past into the Long Cape.

'Huh?' Clay blurted, tugging at the back of Odell's jacket. 'I'm talking to you, boy.'

'I'm here—'

'You're here?' Clay interrupted.

Ora turned to face them and planted Clay's drink in front of him with a slam that quickly fizzled away in the hubbub of the tavern.

'He's here to see the Bird,' she tried her best to whisper.

Clay looked from Ora to Odell, blinking dumbly. He curled a finger and beckoned Ora closer, taking a moment, Odell noted, to look down the gaping neckline of her dress.

'Bullshit,' he said.

'It's true,' she said.

'Ain't nobody seen the Bird. You telling me this green bean gone and got a meeting with her?'

Ora leaned back, a playful smile on her face. 'I'm telling you what I been told,' she said. 'But keep it to yourself.'

'You think I'm about to risk my reputation and go telling people that? Think again, darling. I'm more likely to tell them ...' Clay narrowed his eyes, the effort of trying to find something apt to say visible on his face.

Odell could not help but smile, which made Ora twist her mouth in an effort to keep her own hidden.

'It's fiction,' Clay said with heat in his words, and he took a long drink from the glass before him.

Ora shrugged, refusing to be drawn into convincing Clay of Odell's audition. Clay appeared disappointed by this, but took another long drink to hide his expression.

Ora returned to serving the impatient men, more of whom had gathered to place their orders. One of them had a crudely painted whore between him and the bar, and Ora wondered where he had brought her from. She looked young and held her arms as though to shut out a shrill wind. The man kissed the bare skin on her shoulders and she tugged a shawl to cover up. He seemed to think it a game and laughed drunkenly to the men around him. All the while, he tapped a silver coin on the bar top.

Clay turned to face Odell, who tried his best to ignore him but felt as trapped as the whore, his figure dwarfed beneath Clay's.

'How the hell you swing that, boy?'

'Swing what?' Odell said.

'You know what and I ain't looking to tell you again.'

'Ora helped,' Odell said, and turned his head away, his limp hair swinging to hide his face.

'She helped, did she?' Clay looked back over at her.

'She's a kind soul,' Odell said, picking at a nail until it turned red at the edge.

Clay let out a laugh that momentarily quietened those around him. 'A kind soul,' he said with pomp. 'A soul. Now, there's a handsome notion.'

'Same again?' Ora had come over to them once more and set about refilling Clay's glass.

'There you are, sweetheart. Always where I need you.'

Ora blushed and shook her head as though the colour might shake free.

Clay glanced down at Odell and then took Ora's hand as she placed the full glass back in front of him.

'You know what?' he said.

'What?'

'You're a kind soul.'

Odell's head shot up; he was aggrieved to hear his words in that man's mouth, all bent out of shape and misappropriated. He turned to Ora, anxious for her reaction.

'What's gotten into you?' she asked, almost trembling.

Clay smiled in reply and patted her hand. 'Thanks for the drink,' he said finally.

Ora walked down the bar, looking back all the while.

Clay began to laugh and snaked his arm across Odell's shoulders.

'They weren't your words to use,' Odell said bitterly.

'You think you own those words?' Clay asked. 'Boy, you don't have a clue. She's your sister, but that don't make her just yours.'

Odell looked at those around them, pleased to see Clay's words had failed to take root in idle ears.

'Oh, shit,' Clay said, noticing Odell's nervousness but caring little. 'I forgot the game.' He stepped away from the bar and raised his voice in affected worry. 'Whatever did I mean?' he asked. 'Why, she's not your sister!'

'Quit it,' Odell said, worry running across his face.

Clay's smile fell and he came closer, gripping the boy's side so hard Odell felt his ribs might moan like bowed wood.

'Don't you ever tell me what to do,' Clay said. 'You want to pretend? Sure, let's.'

Clay turned Odell towards the bar and pointed at Ora, who was facing away from them.

'What do you think of her, Odell? Fine ass, wouldn't you agree?'

Odell struggled away before Clay brought him back to the bar, all the while laughing as though they were friends.

'Know why I used your words, Odell? See, you want to mount something like that? Words will get her wetter than Newton Lake.'

Odell shrugged him off and turned away as much as he could.

'You keep turning, Odell. Round on that stool until you're facing me once more. I'll be here. Oh, and good luck with the audition. Try not to fuck it up like you done with the rest of your life.'

Clay stood there for a moment longer, his full glass before his lips. He watched the back of Odell's head for a glimmer, anything he could react to. But there was nothing. The boy, as he had done so often before, remained quiet and frightened. Clay shook his head and moved off to the corner of the tavern.

Odell reluctantly turned to watch Clay regaling his friends with a story, some of them looking over in his direction and laughing.

'You ready?'

Odell looked up and Ora was there, her face flushed and smiling at him.

'Now?' he asked, as though he thought the time might never come.

'Now.' She nodded.

More out of relief than eagerness, Odell collected his things from the bar and moved through the crowd, Ora leading the way. Keeping his head bowed as they passed Clay's table, they at last came to the corridor that led to the back of the tavern.

'You nervous?' Ora asked.

'Yep,' Odell replied immediately, his mouth dry.

'There's no need,' Ora said, taking his hands in hers.

Odell's lips cracked open to say something and then shut again. Ora noticed one of his legs trembling within his thick trousers.

'What is it?' she asked.

'Can you come with me?' Odell asked feebly.

Ora sighed through her nose and ran a hand across his cheek. 'I got to get back to the bar, Odell. I weren't even meant to come this far.'

Odell nodded quickly. 'I know,' he said. 'I'm sure I know.'

Ora felt a sadness tug at her insides. Seeing Odell scared reminded her of him as a boy and a rush of warmth came over her. She wanted to protect him in that moment, but she knew it would be the beginning of something – something she once swore herself off. Family.

'You'll be fine; I know it.' She pulled her hand away from him and straightened up. 'Now, you go on up and knock twice on the door there,' she said, pointing.

Odell followed the direction of her arm to the dimly lit landing with several doors along its edge, one of which had a glowing lantern outside.

'Now, listen. The Bird – you heard the stories, right? Well, forget them. How I remember it, she keeps hidden. You can't see so much as her toes, so don't go worrying about her face.'

'How long ago was that?' Odell asked eagerly.

'Four years, maybe,' she replied.

Odell let out a long sigh. 'What if things have changed? What if I go in there and she's in plain sight?'

'She won't be,' Ora said.

'You don't know that,' Odell said.

'You're right. I don't. But quit worrying about it. You go in there and be brilliant. Don't think about nothing but that music, Odell. You do that and you'll be fine.'

Odell felt his throat smart. He missed his sister and he wanted her back in this moment. His mind raced to say something to her, to ask her the impossible, but she just pulled him close and hugged him. She kissed the side of his head and brushed his ear with her lips. It reminded him so much of his mother's kiss that he thought he might burst into tears.

Ora turned and hurried away down the corridor and into the bar. As the door closed behind her, Odell felt himself missing the hubbub of conversation and drunken laughter.

With his hand drawn into a fist and mere inches from the door, he found himself looking at the lantern. It was unlike those hanging downstairs and standing outside the other doors on the landing. The metal was heavier and more rusted, the glass weather-beaten into a cloudy grey.

It's a ship's, he realised.

He tried to look for the name of the vessel but the rust had only spared a few engraved shapes. He had always dreamed of the sea and so found himself compelled further to enter the room.

Remembering Ora's words, he knocked twice on the door.

After a moment's silence he feared his knock had been too quiet and was drawing back his hand again when the answer came.

'Please. Come in.'

Odell remarked how the words were struggling against something and seemed oddly slurred. His mind's eye painted a dozen horrid images of what could be missing from the Bird's face to cause those words to tumble out that way.

He turned the doorknob and pushed it open a foot. Red light spilled out from the room and onto the toes of his boots.

'Please. Come in,' the voice repeated.

Odell opened the door further and stepped inside. His eyes were dulled by the soft red of the room. He steeled himself and looked around, hoping for that drape Ora had spoken of. But instead his eyes danced to the wonder of the room.

Fabric seemed to hang everywhere. It was embroidered in gold and held colours Odell had only seen in the gallery of the natural world.

His gaze was feverish. It flitted from one thing to the next as though the scene might disappear at once. He greedily snatched at the room's quirks. But then he noticed an elegant and finely carved chair. On top of it was a cushion made from the same fabric that decorated the room. And on top of that was a violin. And next to that was an upright piano.

'Please. Shut the door,' came the voice again.

Odell raised his boot heel to push the door shut behind him and then thought better of it. He turned courteously and twisted the knob so the latch slipped back into place, not disturbing the mood of the room. As he turned back, he realised that, in his appraisal of all that surrounded him, he had failed to notice the source of the voice. So wondrous was the decoration that the fears he'd had out on the landing disappeared quite completely.

A drape of the deepest crimson hung from a gold rail and pooled on the floor of the room. Odell made out shapes behind it, but he failed to discern anything that struck him as familiar.

'Please, sit,' the voice said.

Odell moved across the room, careful of where he stepped, keen to avoid the tails of fabric. Eventually he reached the chair with the violin. The object quivered slightly in the soft light and Odell's fingers flickered with the impulse to move it and take a seat. Instead, he was thankful to see a stool tucked beneath the piano, which he pulled out and sat upon.

'Thank you for agreeing to listen to me, ma'am,' Odell said.

His own voice took him by surprise. Silence filled the room again like a bottle being corked. Odell felt his ears hum with it. A thick plume of smoke wrapped its way around his face and he broke it apart with a shake of his head. On top of the piano were several sticks of incense, all alight. The smell was too sweet for Odell and his eyes began to sting. He pinched either side of his nose, eager not to have this distraction.

A match was struck behind the curtain and Odell caught more of the shape there. He hurriedly rubbed at his eyes again, trying his best to focus. The distinction slipped away and all he could make out for sure was the golden tip of what he assumed was another stick of incense. Shapes moved about on the fabric like kites against a greying sky, subtle and majestic. For a moment Odell imagined that if he pierced the drape, whatever queerness rested behind it would flow out, pooling on the floor amidst the books and cloth. As he leaned closer to look, he thought he could see a hand holding a piece of paper.

His heart hitched up in his chest and the stool beneath him let out a loud creak. The shape behind the curtain turned from the paper and, he assumed, looked straight at him. He sat upright.

'O-dell-a,' said the voice behind the drape.

It took Odell a moment to recognise his own name. The *O* was given such ceremony it sounded like the first note of a song, the *a* like an afterthought, a breath that escaped, as though the speaker wanted more from the word. The voice was strange and again Odell wondered what could be causing it to sound that way. He had heard a dozen stories and seen several sketches of the Bird, and any of the portraits could serve to explain it. The one that came back to him in that instant was a particularly grotesque effort, with the Bird's mouth contorted into a fleshy beak, black feathers fanned out across the face, each quill piercing the beak's lips like a threaded needle.

'Yes, ma'am,' Odell replied, unsure what to say in response.

'Ora,' the voice said. The mouth was fighting to straighten out the word on its tongue. 'She said you play the piano.' The voice stopped, cleared its throat. 'I heard you once. Across the street.'

Odell concentrated hard on the voice, looking down at the toes of his boots. He found it difficult to follow and, to make matters worse, kept picturing the feather-faced woman in his mind, the puckered holes where the feathers pushed through flexing and twisting as the words came out.

He swallowed audibly, choking down that sickening image; the swill of the smoke in his nostrils was not helping matters.

'She said,' Odell blurted out. 'Ora, I mean. She said about you hearing me.'

'Which house?' the voice asked, the pitter-patter of surplus vowels scattering the air.

'I live above Patch Clockworks,' Odell replied. 'Live there with my daddy.' He looked up at the sound of more shuffling paper.

'Ah, yes,' the Bird said after a long pause. 'Your name is Patch.'

Odell looked at a pile of books in front of him. On top of

them was a small glazed figure of a rabbit. It could not have been bigger than his thumb, but glinted in the room's hum on account of the amber stones set for its eyes.

'Do you have a sister?' the voice said. 'Brother?'

Odell, eyes still on the figurine, almost said about Ora before remembering their secret.

'No,' he rushed out. 'Just me.'

A long sigh of realisation slipped beneath the curtain. 'Your parents,' the Bird said finally. 'They expect . . .'

For an instant, Odell thought the Bird mad. So short were her sentences that the boy struggled to interpret them. Furthermore, he willed her to speak for longer so he could more closely scrutinise the strange speech her quick words only hinted at.

'They expect,' she said again, 'a lot of you.'

'Oh,' Odell sighed with realisation. 'Yes, ma'am. A lot.'

Odell found himself adopting the Bird's stilted speech. Suddenly fearful she might think him poking fun at her, he continued, 'My daddy – he wants what's best for me, sure.'

'And is music,' the Bird said, 'good with him?'

'Music is good?' Odell said, puzzled. 'He don't play, ma'am.'

'No,' the Bird said, followed by a scattered murmur of frustration. 'Is he happy with your music, your playing?'

'Oh, I get you!' Odell said with all the self-congratulation of solving a riddle. 'No, ma'am. He likes music about as much as I like clocks.'

The work of figuring out the Bird's speech had loosened Odell's reserve and he slouched back on the stool, at once at home in the curious red room.

'Clocks is what he does,' Odell said. 'The only music he likes is tick-tock, tick-tock.' He let out a shrill laugh that made no secret of his youth. The sound rippled off the walls and he was silent all of a sudden. He felt awkward and cursed himself for taking his mind off the audition. Then came the most glorious sound he thought his young ears had ever heard: a youthful laugh in return, which hopped its way across the air, not disturbing a thing. The Bird, even in her great mystery, grew younger in his mind's eye.

'My father,' the Bird said, her laughter dying away, 'he was the same. He would always want me to read and to study. Never to play. "Piano is a waste of time for such as you."' The latter words carried the gruffer tone of an impersonation.

Odell laughed aloud, relieved he had not sabotaged his audition. 'That sounds familiar,' he said himself and continued to laugh.

After a moment, the laughter ceased and Odell swelled with the importance of the appointment. He again found himself conversing with his heart, untethered from his head.

'I heard you playing once, ma'am,' he said. 'It was the most beautiful playing I've ever heard. I feel I need to say that. And I don't mean to colour your opinion of me to the positive. More because, if I don't . . . Well, I just have to.'

'Thank you,' the Bird said after a pause. 'Please play.'

Odell turned round on the stool and the blood thrummed in his ears. The audition was now all he could think of. The smoke from the incense sticks appeared to grow thicker and choke him, his eyes weeping hot tears. He thought about asking the Bird if he could move the sticks, but then worried about compromising the gentleness of their company thus far.

He squeezed his eyes tight and felt tears well up along their creases. With his hands cupped in his shirtsleeves, he wiped them decidedly and then pulled his sheet music from inside his jacket.

The piano before him was in beautiful condition and Odell noticed how well the wood was cared for as he lifted the cover from the keys. He placed his hands on the cool ivory and watched them shake.

You know the piece, he told himself. *You know it.* But still his hands quivered.

He heard the Bird move behind the drape and he grew more nervous with her impatience. He imagined Ora's disappointment when he reached the bottom of the stairs, eager to escape unnoticed into the night. He thought how she would be glad he was no longer a brother to her. His father would be angry, that was for certain.

Then Odell thought of his mother, her image frozen where the others were filled with colour and life. Her smile as she watched him, the sound of her playing. He imagined his mother's hands on his shoulders, the reassuring knead before they spread to comfort him, to tell him, wordlessly, *You'll be fine, my love.*

Odell's heart slowed and he began to play.

The piece started to flow from him with ease. Where before he had worried about remembering each note in sequence, now they came together as though one. Odell believed he flourished in the strangeness of the situation – the room, the veiled woman, her manner of speech – and, in doing so, took more liberty with his mother's music. He had played it so often before, but never dared, never even thought he might be able to turn it into something else – something better.

He was in rapture with the piece. He felt a closeness to the music, and a unity between his playing and his heart.

Odell finished playing and let the final note reach on, his foot pressed down onto the pedal. He opened his eyes and lifted his head, almost breathless. Everything caught up with him in the silence and he half thought about playing something else to delay the Bird's verdict.

He wet his lips and his hands started to shake again. He was reaching up to the sheet music to select another piece when a gentle clapping came from behind the curtain.

Odell looked over, his breath tight and anticipatory in his chest. 'You liked it?' he said.

'Very much,' the Bird said. 'Very much, O-dell-a.'

Odell shut the door tightly behind him and stood there for a moment, staring dumbly up at the ship's lantern.

'We play together,' she had said. And then it was over.

He wanted to let free a whoop of excitement and race down into the tavern, making the announcement. He was imagining how Ora might react when, walking down the last few steps, he heard her laugh.

She must have heard the news, he thought, a smile breaking out on his face. *But how?*

Anything seemed possible in that moment, so freshly born from the strange dwelling of the Bird.

Ora's laugh came again, followed by a groan. Odell stopped dead on the spot and, standing in the unlit space before the long corridor, he pulled his jacket closer about him. There was something familiar about that noise, which laid the foundations of his fear. It reminded him of his mother. The voice of a spectre seemed to penetrate the walls of the tavern and, rather than his mother coming here to congratulate him, it seemed maddened as it laughed and groaned.

He was quick to move towards the tavern, although it meant passing the doors of all those rooms, each one hiding the possibility of abhorrence. The feather-faced woman was no longer the Bird in his mind, but she stalked him. She hid in the rooms waiting to scratch his face with the twisted bone and untidy wound of her mouth.

At the end of the corridor, one of the doors was open. The glow of an oil lamp cleaved the darkness of the corridor and Odell stepped towards it. As he did so, the curious noises grew. It sounded like a steam engine of human components, lurching and grunting with the creak of metal and wood. He stepped into the slice of light and squinted against the scene of the room.

As his eyes focused, he saw Clay, his shirt tails loose behind him and his trousers below the knee. In that feverish moment, Odell took in the scene with the same unstoppable hunger as he had done upstairs.

Clay's braces hung from his shoulders in the crooks of his arms as he jolted forwards and backwards furiously. Odell's shame was that he felt a sense of arousal from watching this primitive act. He knew the history of those rooms and how whores had been treated with contempt, which, in that moment, he could not deny was enticing.

Odell pressed his face closer to the gap in the door and watched as Clay turned his body to get a better purchase on the mattress beneath his knees. The woman's hair was tussled free and wild, and its copper colour held the light like firewood. Odell's curiosity turned to venom.

Ora was bent over on the bed, her hands splayed out, pulling at the sheets. Like Clay, she was only partially in a state of undress. Her face was reflected in the mirror atop a table. Odell stepped back. Her expression was contorted in ways new to him. Like an animal, she bit at her lower lip and groaned encouragement. And, at once, her eyes opened, wild. She didn't see Odell. She only looked at Clay's reflection and smiled before being drawn back into her groaning laughter.

One of her breasts freed itself from her blouse and Clay's hand shot round and grabbed it as though it might fall. His touch was so rough it looked like he was trying to pull it from her body, like pulp from a ripe fruit. Ora's mouth opened but she was silent. She pushed back into Clay, drawing a long and deeply mined sigh from his body. He slowed and made long, drawn-out movements.

Ora seemed about to cry. Odell thought it the most curious thing he had ever seen. Clay bent over and heaved his breath out over Ora's back. He patted her side like a horse and then ran his palm back over her body and onto her behind. Just below his hand, Odell saw a starling – a tattoo he never realised his sister had. It was finely done and inked to fly away from the back of her thigh. He noticed how it was rubbed red, angry on her skin. The sight made him sick.

Odell turned from the room and walked back along the corridor, no longer fearful of the feather-faced woman waiting in the darkness. He unlatched the side door and skirted the edge of the building, ducking low beneath the window ledges and into the street.

His ears hummed and his throat grew sore. Without thinking on it, he walked across to his father's shop and climbed the stairs to their home. His movements were quiet and practised and, by the time he lay in bed, the house was as still as when he had met it.

13

October 1879

When Emerson returned to his shack, he lay on the bed for a while, tilting his head to look out of the window. He watched as Marianne House dimmed in the fading evening light and finally, as the lamps warmed the windows, he allowed his head to drop back onto the bed.

He wondered if he couldn't bring the doctor to the shack for the next appointment. Blanche was often occupied with something, while Elena seemed intent on charming the male population of the town at all times. It was the youngest sister that worried Emerson.

Kittie was one never to remain still – her mind, too. Emerson knew that if she saw the doctor visit him, privacy would be the last thing they got. If it was to be done, it would have to happen at night, when she was asleep. Emerson wondered if that was the only time her limbs lay still; but, he supposed, they'd likely jerk through the night at the behest of eager dreams.

Nevertheless, he decided to send word to the doctor that their next meeting should be at his shack. He sat up and walked over to his desk to pen the note, keen not to waste any time. Umbründ's anxiety earlier had worried Emerson and he was keen for their acquaintance, and the appointments, to continue.

He tore the end from one of the reams of blank paper. As he set to writing, the table tilted and he just caught the oil lamp as it slid towards the edge.

Emerson looked down to check the short leg and saw a space between the stump and the pile of books. He wondered if more of the table leg had broken off but could see no evidence of such a thing. He bent down and lowered the oil lamp to look closer. He was relieved to see his black journal there still.

Struck by a thought, he strode back to the bed and reached beneath the sheets for the book he had been reading. He ran his thumb to midway and saw it was a different story. Denying it could be possible, he flicked back and forth, convinced he would find the passage he had read the night before.

Reluctantly, he returned to the pile beneath the table leg, and there instead he found the book he sought. He held both volumes before him, in the impossible hope that they might explain what had caused them to change places.

Is it possible, Emerson thought, *I am being watched?*

A day or so before, he had noticed a trespass in the dust covering one of the dressers. It had seemed innocent enough and he had assumed either he had brushed it when leaving the shack in haste, or else it was one of the sisters' half-hearted attempts at cleaning. Now, though, with the switched books, it became something else.

Emerson remembered the pages he had torn from the journal. At the time, he had embarrassed himself with his caution. Only now did it seem the most sensible thing he might have done.

His mind raced with the question of who could have been

there. Might it have been Umbründ? Or else one of the sisters, intent on finding out more about their guest? Emerson decided to remove the chance of it happening again and lit a fire in the shack's stove.

Once the fire was going, and with no small reluctance, he placed the journal inside. He closed the door and watched as the flames began to eat away at the pages, melting the fine black cover into something resembling oil.

He tried not to think on what things in there he had now lost. Instead, he sat once more at the desk and again took up the note to Umbründ, now steadier and increasingly urgent.

14

October 1879

As Blanche took the washing from the line, her mind dwelled on Emerson and the theatre. She had often thought about the morning she'd shown him around and, to her embarrassment, still recalled his touch on her shoulder. It seemed to linger there, like a warm patch of sunlight.

Blanche set the last sheet atop the pile and put her hands on her hips, smiling and looking towards the shack. She had been alone in the house before and had hoped Emerson might return so they could sit together and talk, apart from her sisters. Blanche had only taken the sheets from the line in order to better discern whether Emerson was in his shack. Finding herself out there and unsure if he was watching her, she had started to fold them, despite their dampness.

When she returned indoors, she lit a fire and hung the heavier bed sheets before it. The steam rose from them and crept like grey moss over the mirror above the fireplace. The smaller items were dry and she took them upstairs.

Passing the photographs on the staircase, she paused once more before the one of her family all together. She wondered if she didn't favour it because George was missing and the memory of his loss was therefore not easily encouraged. She felt the lightness to her mood dissipate and was reminded of her little brother's portrait she had promised to look to. It lay in her room still, untouched since she had taken it from its place on the wall.

The finer clothes in the pile she placed on Elena's bed – cloth decorated with delicate needlework and running in alluring colours. She wondered how much Clay must spend on her sister, ensuring no item in her possession was without flourish. Kittie's things seemed so plain in comparison that Blanche removed a fine ribbon from Elena's, likely not intended to be washed, and placed it in amongst Kittie's pile.

In her youngest sister's room, she placed the items on top of the bed. The ribbon stood out, spilling from the plain folds like an exuberant tongue. She worried Elena would think Kittie had stolen it and so decided to hide the item – to be uncovered and treasured at a later time. She opened the top drawer in her sister's cabinet and decided to place it beneath the dresses folded there.

The thought that Kittie might wear it in her hair brought a smile to Blanche's face. The idea that the town might soon be filled with suitors, that Kittie might meet a boy, warmed her heart.

As she tucked the ribbon away, she felt the edges of an envelope and, for a moment, wondered if such a courtship hadn't already happened. With little thought, Blanche pulled the item free and saw it was a letter addressed to Kittie. She could see it was open and well worn. Only the faintest of hesitancies made protest to the curiosities of an older sister as her fingers unfolded the pages.

Dear Kittie,

I find the best place to start a letter is with a curiosity. Something to keep a man interested. Or, in this case, a niece. Did I ever tell you about Tallahassee? I don't think I did. I'm glad for that, because now's its time.

During the war, we were fighting there and made camp near some swamp. The men were more spooked by the gators that splashed about in the night than the Union troops we knew to be nearby. I remember getting out of bed to piss and almost sticking another soldier with a knife. He'd been creeping through the swamp, the water up to his chest. I called out to him in a hiss and then recognised his face in the moonlight. He stood there, perplexed, the ripples going out to shore from his body. 'What are you doing?' I asked him. 'I'm making to see the woman on the island,' he said back. He replied as though it were the most obvious thing. Since we'd made camp, another troop of southern boys had passed us and told tale of the island lady. Through the swamps there was a clearing and the only way of making this out was the single beam of light that came from there. The place was cocooned in weeds during the day, but at night you could see that beam and know where to head. They told us fools there was an old shack in amongst those weeds and the lady who lived there could tell you where and when you'd die. A few of the men threw in that she was a belle too, while others said she was more man than woman. The claim passed across our tongues like wildfire, but I didn't think anyone would believe it. Now I saw this fool – Mettison, I recall his name being – wading out to hear how he might die. I questioned whether to tell anyone, but just went back to sleep. An hour before sunrise we heard the Union was close by and we left everything but horses and ammunition in that swamp. I didn't mention Mettison to anyone and, sure enough, he wasn't there when we'd finished our long march north. I do find myself wondering about that man. Out of all the war, all the terrible things and the glory, he's the one who sticks. I find that strange.

I must take respite from this letter to first congratulate myself for getting

149

so far. Such were the hours and days, weeks and months I had written to you, and now, finally, I am able to get this far without littering the floor of my cabin with paper scraps. Secondly, as you might have guessed, I must take a drink to steel my nerves. For they are weak and frayed from sights no man should see.

I guess, when an old man starts to confess, he starts to see the end. That's about as much poetry as you'll get from this old fool, half drunk or otherwise. You know, Kittie, I keep looking up from this page and hoping to catch sight of you walking across those tracks and raising an arm. The sight of your pale freckled skin in the moonlight, like the best ghost I could hope for. Instead, I'm troubled by others. You know all too well what led me here those years back. It ain't like I wanted you to believe it; more that I didn't, not once, entertain the possibility you wouldn't. Families are bound by blood, and so they are bound by secrets. The same one that binds your sister and me, led me here.

Even now, the fingers of one hand curl the edges of this page, about to tear it in two. But still I write. That must mean something, huh? That must mean that finally this secret needs to be told.

I'm guessing you know what I might have done in the war. For a country so preoccupied with it for so long, we don't often talk about it. Especially us who lost it. I was a solider to a man named Nathan Bedford Forrest. Those three names might mean something to you. They meant something to us, sure as that. We who took the grey would have followed that mad man into hell and not troubled him to question it. Twice, or maybe three times, you could call it hell where we went to and what we did. We were his devils, Kittie. One April, at Fort Pillow, I recall the cuffs of my coat were damp and twisted brown with the blood of men I did not know. You come to realise in the maddened fever of war how much it takes for someone to raise their hands and tell you they're done with fighting. The shame and resistance, to defy what it is they'd been doing for near on three years. You know what curious thought returns to me now? The light colour of a Negro's palm. Ain't that something? I saw plenty of them that day, held up as we walked past, our guns drawn and some boys cawing their rebel yell still. That yell, Kittie. It could scare the feathers off a buzzard. Scared me plenty for the first year. Then you grow used to it. You hear it so often it becomes a sort of anthem, a hellish trumpet sound signalling something plenty awful.

I digress. Fort Pillow isn't something I am inclined to mention. But to say I've done bad things and not allow you to ignore that, I must talk about it. We killed prisoners. Plainly, that's it. We murdered them, Kittie. We spared some, but that came down to the colour of their skin. I remember the Negro boys were terrified. Perhaps they knew what was coming. Perhaps they knew we'd never let them surrender. How horror sticks in my mind! I recall setting alight a row of hospital tents. The doctors ran out, of course, but those laid out plenty injured burned. I saw men without limbs claw their way from burning tents, half on fire. Like I said before, it was hell.

Forrest favoured a scalp. His granddad was scalped and you could say he took a liking to it. I'd watched men scalped before, but never once had I done it. Fort Pillow was the first time. Mine was a coloured boy about the same age as you are now. That very fact turns my stomach some. The springiness of his hair surprised me. I'd never touched a Negro before I killed one. You don't need to know the detail of that. And, please God, don't make me recount it.

I caught Forrest's eye some time later. My hands would not still from what I'd done and my heart shot around my chest like a cork from a fancy bottle. I moved into new skin that morning. I became someone else and I supposed, no matter what followed, I'd never go back. It's a one-way journey, that well-worn path to hell. As Forrest came riding by, his eyes were ablaze. He saw all before him and took great pleasure in it. He hated the coloured boys and, next to their hickory colour, the worst was the Union blue. He was the devil at the helm and we were going about his work. Horrors swilled about him and blood pooled in the ever-sinking earth, and he rode through the scene, a man content.

I never paid for what I did that day. None of us did, as far as I can tell. If a man later received a gunshot to the gut, would the afternoon it took him to die equate to what he'd done? Who can make such judgements? What scales can make sense of the decisions of men?

The closest I believe I've come was the day I left New Georgetown, or at least when my exodus began. Your sister had asked me to walk with her and the clockmaker's wife, Lori. I don't need to tell you that George came too. Blanche was preparing to take her class up the mountain and through the woods. She planned to teach them about the surrounding nature and wanted some lessons from me, after my war years of living off the land and such. I'd pull a leaf free and show it to her, relaying all I'd learned and maybe adding some dash for her to impress her students, come the day. I enjoyed it when she made such use of me. Of the three of you, Blanche was the one I struggled the most with. I don't mean to colour your opinion of her, but there's a coldness there. I saw this day as an opportunity to change that.

I'd brought my gun along to do some shooting too. It was a Burnside carbine I might have shown you once or twice. I liked the look of the thing and, during peacetime, I'd taken to shooting animals up in the hills. I planned to show George and maybe have him fire off a round himself – set the boy on the path to manhood. Growing up with three women can soften a boy.

In earlier times, I'd shown Blanche how to load such a weapon and she'd seemed interested too. Now, though, she disapproved of the gun. The clockmaker's wife, on the other hand, seemed relieved by it. Did you ever meet Lori Patch? Perhaps you were too young. I bet you know her son, though, the awkward fella? Lori was an odd woman. She stuck close to me and, whenever my head turned to some curious sound, she followed my gaze, at once scared but expectant. Some people have a familiarity with shadows and she was one of them. I'd be damned if she didn't walk out into those woods with us, knowing she was about to die.

Not halfway up the mountain, we turned to look down towards the town and I held George aloft in my arms. He squealed, as he could make out the peak of Marianne House. When I set him down, we turned from the path to walk into the woods. I took point and made sure the trail was clear, although the ground was uneven and I near turned my ankle a few times. The jaunt reminded me of days with Forrest and, for that, I started to feel queer. The butt of the Burnside carbine bumped into the back of my leg the same way my old Springfield had, and as simple a sensation as that took me back near thirteen years.

The path twisted off into nothing and I looked about, seeing if it didn't pick up a few yards off, someplace else. All was a mess, though. Trees and branches fell in on one another as though placed there to form a shelter. I was aware then how silent the woods had become. I say 'become', Kittie, because back with the girls the noises had been as you'd expect – bird calls, the snap of something under a fox's paw. But here it was silent. Out of some instinct, I swung the Burnside from my shoulder and checked the barrel was filled. I nestled the butt into my shoulder and felt better for it. I walked forward a few paces, placing my feet in amongst the woodland mess, hoping the path would still be there. Then I saw it up ahead: a building, overgrown and resembling a ruin. I looked from window to window, but all was bare. I heard a tapping come from the building; it was close enough that I could hear that much. I raised the rifle and set the sight on the door, but there was nothing there. Soon, I felt the cool beginnings of rain on my face. The sky was dark too, clouds pulling heavy overhead, closing out the late afternoon sun. As I turned, I heard that tapping again, from deep within the ruin. I swear to you I did. I write this down because, after years of thinking on it, I believe that's where it came from.

I'd worked my way back to Blanche and saw her, Lori and George huddled tightly beneath a tree. I told them we'd be heading back and come up another day. The ruin had changed me somewhat. I felt ill at ease and Lori Patch, with her curious nature, didn't improve that feeling. She'd grown pale and was shivering plenty. Even George wasn't that bad. Blanche asked if we might stay now that the rain was coming down harder, but I told her we were leaving right then. It might as well have been night for the clouds above our

153

heads and they were rumbling with impatience. Blanche lifted George into her arms and began to walk back, but Lori stood fixed beneath the tree, her breathing heavy. I asked if she was all right, but she just looked up at the dark sky and – I swear to you, my dear – began to weep. A flash filled the air and she whimpered more and more, turning in on herself, against the wet bark. I couldn't hear what she was saying for the rain against the leaves. I saw it was making George scared and so I gripped Lori's arm and pulled her out from the tree. She leaped forward and took me in her arms like an animal. The rifle pushed tightly against my gut and I was worried it might go off. With my arms pinned against my chest, I struggled to push her away and turned in a panic to Blanche, who looked confused by it all. The thunder rumbled up and cracked overhead like cannon fire. Lori's face was close to mine, wild and white. She looked at me with a madness in her eyes when I finally shook her free. 'They come out in the dark,' she said. She turned to Blanche and said in a small voice, 'I'm sorry about your brother.' Blanche held George tighter and asked what she meant. When Lori didn't answer, Blanche shouted at her. I shared her anger with Lori; that woman talking of the boy's death as though it were close. However right she was, it was a cruel thing to say.

Blanche began to walk away with George in her arms. I told her to stay but she only moved away quicker. The sky lit up again and Lori turned and ran back where I had come from. I called to her but she was already out of sight. So too was Blanche. I checked the Burnside once more and went after Blanche, racing along the path like a younger man might. When I reached the mountain road, she was nowhere to be seen. I could make out fifty, maybe seventy yards down the trail and knew I'd see her if she was there, but she must have gotten lost. I turned and heard Lori scream. It was difficult to tell it was her, and I only know now that it must have been.

I ran, Kittie – deep into the woods, on the path and off. I fired a round or two, looking to scare whatever it was hurting Lori. I called out to Blanche and George until my throat was torn. I can't remember ever being so scared. I expect you'll look to the drink to explain what I'm about to say next, but I saw things in them woods that reminded me of the war. I have tried to tell myself it was the fear, taking me back some years. But eager as my mind is to believe that explanation, I know I saw something. One man, maybe two. Wearing uniform still, or at least snatches of it. Like soldiers crawled from the grave. I turned from them, fearing they were spectres of men I might have killed – corpses from Fort Pillow looking to claim me.

I ran and ran until I saw her – your sister – walking from the trees to the sliver of path. She looked as though she had dragged herself through the rain-tossed earth, her face and arms covered in mud. I ran to her and brushed it from her. Her shoulders shuddered and she looked at me, all the girl gone away. Her eyes turned down to my hand and she wept silently. I held it up to my gaze and saw blood. Looking over her dress I could see it now, the blood having turned the fabric brown. 'My dear,' I said, 'are you hurt?' She shivered more and more. 'It's not mine,' slipped from her mouth like bile.

Is it cruel to tell you these things? There have been times, sat on the old engine, when I've been sorely tempted. But I don't care for family feuds and I worry these words might not be the same ones your sister has said. I know she blames me. The town does, too. You might also read these pages and see only fancy in this old man's account. It takes more and more, these days, to hang a man. But the town seemed plenty happy to know just the facts – that I went into the woods with three and came out with one; that I was a drunk, and still am some; and that whatever killed my nephew and Lori Patch wouldn't have if it'd been someone else up there on the mountain. I didn't fight it. I took the judgement as something owing to me from Fort Pillow. I've served my sentence beyond the town, Kittie, and I'm sick of staring out over that gorge. If the town won't hang me, then this old man will. Your visits are about all the life I have left, but soon they'll go. I just need an end. I feel that maybe I'd have been better filling these pages with ways in which I'll miss you. But you should know, Kittie. Dear God, you should know.

Without realising it, Kittie, you are what I fought for. You are my dearest and I will miss you. Oh Lord, will I miss you.

15

October 1879

Odell had waited for two days before returning to the Long Cape. Finally, he decided he would not allow Clay to rob him of his success with the Bird, although he still fretted that Clay might arrive at the same time, hoping to meet Ora once more.

Fearful, he walked up onto the porch of the tavern. The oil lamps out front were unlit. Odell worried he had left it too long and the Bird had, for some unknown reason, closed the tavern. Then he spotted a shadow moving inside and rapped gently on the window. The shape stopped and walked over, a solitary match illuminating his beard.

Odell recognised the figure as Hammond. He lived on a farm not far from New Georgetown and was built as someone raised on long days of work. Much to the disdain of his family, who needed him back on the farm, he would sometimes work at the tavern, often lending his strength to the cryptic instructions of the Bird.

'What do you want?' he said through the glass door.

'Where's Ora?' Odell replied.

Hammond turned to go, 'Not here, that's for sure. I been called in, like I live just down the road, don't I? My daddy is furious, that's what.'

'She didn't come in for work?' Odell asked again.

'Didn't I just say that?'

Odell stood in silence and Hammond reeled as the match burned his fingertips and went out. He lit another and held it with suspicion.

'I got work to be doing, Odell,' he said.

'No, wait,' Odell said as Hammond went to leave. 'There's something else. I'm here to meet with the Bird.'

He noticed the shadow of a grin stretch out on Hammond's face.

'Now, there's a new one,' he said.

'It's true.'

'Oh, sure it is. Why don't you come on in? I'll fetch her down and we'll have ourselves a tea party.' Hammond laughed and moved to turn away from the door once more.

'Hey!' Odell said, twisting the handle of the door and moving it against the lock. 'Go ask her.'

Instead, Hammond pulled a piece of paper from his back trouser pocket and unfolded it. He looked down at the list before him. Odell tried to look as best he could and saw that the writing was scratchy and the letters varied in size and shape like that of a child's.

'Don't say nothing about you seeing the Bird.'

'It has to,' Odell said, anxiously thinking on those days he had waited.

'Hold it! Well, I'll be . . . You're right,' Hammond said. 'Now, what in hell are you doing seeing the Bird? Says here you're to proceed upwards and not be disturbed until playing time. As much as I can make out, anyhow.'

'Then can you unlock this door?' Odell asked.

'I guess I ought to,' Hammond said, still looking at the paper in amazement. 'This ain't a trick?'

'How could it be?' Odell said, pushing at the door once more. 'I write that list and put it in your back pocket?'

'It is unlikely,' Hammond said, reaching behind him as though rehearsing the possibility.

Finally he replaced the paper in his back pocket and, with the keys on his belt, unlocked the door. Odell shuffled in out of the cold and was glad to slip away from the attentions of passers-by.

By way of apology, Hammond offered to take Odell's hat and coat, but he refused and instead walked up towards the back of the tavern.

'You know I would have let you in anyway, right?' Hammond called after Odell, who just continued walking. 'Right?'

The ship's lantern was lit, but something halted Odell in his tracks. He struggled to remember the Bird's kind words that had so shortly before been tinder to his passion's fire; what he had seen after had picked away at their sincerity. He asked himself if he had misunderstood that evening and if she had merely praised his talent rather than invited him to take the job. His mind con-spired against him until he recalled the paper Hammond had been given.

Before any further hesitation could creep in, he knocked twice, hard on the door.

'Come in,' came the Bird's voice. Her strange way of speaking was something he was gladdened to hear again.

He pushed the door open and stepped inside. The room was much like it had been the night of the audition, except now there were different books lying open on the floor and different sheets of music scattered about the furniture.

One disarray is much like another, thought Odell.

He had hoped, despite his earlier fears, that the curtain would be drawn aside. Instead, it was held in place, betraying its delicacy with immovability.

'Afternoon,' Odell said and quickly removed the hat from his head.

'Good afternoon, O-dell-a.' The familiar voice worked hard to say his name. 'Please sit.'

Odell took the same seat before the piano and faced the curtain. A quivering silence filled the room.

'Are you well?' he asked, his lips running away with the idea of courtesy. He couldn't think of anything else to say and cursed himself for sounding so awkward.

To his relief, her voice spoke out from behind the curtain. 'I am well. How are you?' The words had that same delicacy to them.

'Fine,' he said. 'Just fine.'

Odell rested his hands on his thighs and looked around the room, his fingers drumming on his corduroy trousers.

'Hammond will set up for us,' the Bird said after a moment.

Odell nodded politely and turned back to the piano. He fixed on the sheet music before him. It was similar to that which his mother had played. He noticed some familiar looking names, most of them too fancy for his tongue. The paper was delicate and Odell handled it like porcelain, worried it would crack and splinter to the ground at any moment. It had not been cared for and Odell wished he had brought his own music – all held together in a fancy-looking file his mother had insisted on.

He recalled how, once, before he could play, he had left the sheets splayed out on the floor around the piano stool at home.

When his mother returned from the school, she just picked up each sheet with care and replaced them all snugly in the folder. She put the folder on top of the piano and said to Odell, her hand on his small shoulder, 'Music needs to be cared for.'

Odell felt a greater compulsion to be careful from that one sentence than from all the stern glances and quick slaps his father had bestowed on him put together.

A mother's power, he thought, *is a quiet one.*

Odell shuffled the papers into about as neat a stack as he could manage and replaced them on the piano. Remembering his mother had brought on a sudden sadness. His body became closed off to the room, head bowed, arms folded. Reluctantly, he found himself retreating further into the past, the red room swelling about him like the inside of a dream.

March 1872

In the days that followed his mother's death, Odell's father had told him to remain at home, away from school. Odell had reacted gleefully, as any child might, but found his mood misplaced in a world of glances and hushed weeping in the corners of their house.

At times, Ora would scream at him or watch, red-eyed, as he played at the piano. Other times, she would pull him close and hold him for longer than she usually would.

Their father was hardly there. So soon after the war, he was adjusting still to his new form. He would curse a lot more and think the world conspired to make him a fool. If he reached out to steady himself and toppled a plate to the floor, he would curse the plate.

He was in his workshop a lot more or sat in his old chair, staring off into someplace else, long ago. But when the news came about Lori, he disappeared. Odell would ask Ora where he went but she only grew angry at the mention of his name. Over those first weeks, Ora grew into the responsibility of looking after Odell, and then, one day, she insisted they walk into town together.

Ora marched his young, tired legs up through the street, pushing anyone who cared to open their mouth aside. The crowds dissipated and he soon realised they were on their way to Marianne House.

Odell sat on the porch swing, kicking his boots. He peered down into town and noticed the small figures of people moving about like ants. To his mind, he could still make out the expressions on their faces and that spiked the fear in his belly. He wondered what could have happened to cause those looks. Was it pity they felt at a boy and girl deserted by their parents? Or something worse?

Before his sister had gone inside to talk with Blanche, she made Odell swear not to follow her in. Since the clock tower had been lost in the war, he had no way of telling how long he had been sitting on the porch, but guessed it might be an hour.

'Or two,' he said aloud.

'Two what?' came an echoed voice.

Odell jumped from the porch swing and felt something underneath his foot.

'Hey!' came a sharp shout of pain.

Odell looked beneath him and saw movement between the slats of the porch.

'Kittie?' he asked.

'That's right!' she shot back. 'You damn near broke my finger!'

'What are you doing under the porch?'

'Spying,' she said simply.

'On me?' he asked.

'No, Odell,' she laughed. 'Not on you.'

Odell paced about, trying to get a better look at her as she shifted around on the wet leaves and dirt beneath the porch, like an animal.

'Well, there ain't nobody else here!'

'Sure there is,' Kittie said. She moved out from under the porch, sucking her hurt finger.

She waved him over and they both crouched down low, squeezing through a loosened slat in the porch. Odell's hands sank into the mulch.

'Yuk!' he exclaimed.

'Shhh!' Kittie snapped. 'You want to be a spy or not?'

Odell obliged and followed her as they crawled forward, weaving in and out of the beams that held the house upright. It was like some maze, but Kittie knew it well and soon Odell heard the patter of voices above their heads.

'Who is that?' he asked.

Kittie turned and pressed a hand against his mouth. She leaned in and whispered in his ear, 'Your sister and mine.'

'We shouldn't listen,' Odell said, but the words were lost, muffled against her palm.

Kittie stood up and craned her neck so her ear pressed against the wood, shaking a subtle rainfall of dust from the slats.

'What are they saying?' Odell asked.

'It's about Clay,' Kittie said, flapping a hand at him to hush. 'He's going to hunt the bear!' Kittie said excitedly.

Odell squinted hard. 'Who is?' he asked.

'Clay!' Kittie snapped before clasping a hand to her own mouth.

'But ...' Odell rubbed at his eyes, the dust stinging them. 'What bear?'

Kittie's excitement propelled the words from her mouth, words she would think on often: 'The bear that killed your mamma.'

Odell sat there silently beneath the house. Kittie looked over at him and realised from his stilled expression that he had not known his mother was dead before. His face held in time the way someone's does when their life changes forever. Before she could think of the words to say, or else decide they were not there to be found, Odell crawled away from her towards the porch.

As he sat back on the swing, Ora burst from the front door. She was followed by Blanche and Elena.

'He didn't kill them, Ora,' Elena said.

'He might as well have,' Ora spat back, her eyes red.

'What was he meant to have done?' Elena pleaded.

Ora looked from Elena to Blanche. 'Ask her,' she said, pointing at Blanche. 'Tell us. What was he meant to have done?'

'Bee,' Elena pleaded softly. 'Please don't think this.'

'What was he meant to have done?' Ora said again, sobbing. 'What was—?'

'Save them,' Blanche said suddenly. Her face shook at the words.

Elena raised her hands to her mouth and Ora nodded, her face in a grimace. She turned and pulled Odell up from the porch swing, marching down the steps and along the road.

'What are you going to do?' Elena called out after them.

Odell turned to look over his shoulder and, for the first time in his life, found Elena's gaze on him unwelcome. He turned back quickly and watched his sister.

'Why are we angry at them?' he asked.

'Their uncle killed our mother,' Ora said.

'Kittie said it was a bear,' Odell said, confused.

'It's more complicated than that, Odell,' Ora said, sounding like their father.

'Where are we going?'

'Clay's.'

At first, Ora had told Odell to sit on the porch of the timber shop, but, given the stares of the passers-by, he refused. Ora dragged him inside and all but threw him downstairs into the workshop. He had gone to protest, but Ora was already up the stairs, talking with Clay. Odell sat with a friend of Clay's called Ellsworth, whose large shape eclipsed the light of the forge. When Ellsworth turned, Odell saw features much softer than expected. He smiled at the boy and beckoned him over.

'You know what we do here?' he asked.

Odell shook his head and Ellsworth laughed.

'Well, we ... You see ...' He stopped for a moment and scratched at his unkempt beard. 'Well, look at that. I'm not sure, neither.'

They both smiled and Ellsworth took to showing him the different kinds of timber that were used in the workshop. He set the boy in front of him, directing him with care so that he didn't brush up against the hot metal or snag on any tools that were littered about the place.

Despite Ellsworth's best efforts, Odell's head swam with everything that had happened that day and the boy wished for the safety of his home, where everything had been normal, or what he recalled normal to be, only a few hours earlier.

After a time, Ora called down to him and he ran up the steps, waving to Ellsworth as he went. Clay watched them from a window as they crossed the street.

'What did you ask Clay?' Odell asked.

'How do you know I asked him anything?'

'He looked like he might have an answer, is all.'

Ora paused, folding her shawl, and rested a hand on Odell's hair.

'You're a curious thing,' she said.

'What did you ask him?'

'To hunt the bear,' she said. Still, Odell looked at her and she heaved a heavy sigh. 'And to speak with Elena's uncle.'

'Will he kill him?' Odell asked. 'The uncle?'

'No,' Ora said, turning away with disappointment. 'He won't do that. He'll keep him where he is, though – away from us and not about to return, neither.'

'What about Kittie and Elena? And Miss Marianne?' Odell asked, following her into their house. 'His family?'

Ora turned and crouched down to face her brother.

'He'll be fine without one,' she said.

Even to that day, in the tavern, Odell wished those words had been written down – just so he could know for sure whether she had said 'he' or 'I'. The next morning, after losing his mother and father, Odell lost his sister. She lodged at the Long Cape and she stopped being a Patch. People's pity forged her new identity and, as the years passed, so her old life died away. People obliged her secret and, as with the truth, so died the sorrow of those days.

Odell remembered watching Clay and Ellsworth and some others walk through town towards the mountain pass and the forest there. They carried with them all sorts of traps and rifles slung over their shoulders like they were soldiers. Most of them had been, but not Clay.

After four nights' camping, the men returned, carrying the body of a bear, as wide as Ellsworth and several feet taller, on an old army stretcher. Townsfolk cheered as they walked past, as though they had brought Lori Patch and George Marianne back to life. Odell had watched the scene from the dust-coated windows of his home. For by then it was his alone – nobody else to claim it and no one to care for it.

Clay delivered the bear to the door of the tavern, as though it were a trophy for Ora. Odell couldn't see her accept such a gift. Truth be told, he tried not to see his sister much. His mother was gone and so too, it seemed, was his father. His sister, though, was right there – a walking glass negative, reminding him his family was all gone.

Odell never knew what Clay had said to Shelby, the Mariannes' uncle. He was living in an abandoned stationmaster's cabin now and seemed likely to stay there. When thinking on Clay, Odell reckoned him to be just the man to tell Shelby to get out of town more than a month after he had done as much. Odell would have liked to have seen Shelby's face, staring down Clay's threats. He had always liked the Marianne uncle and, to this day, that had not changed. He refused to blame him for things. At the time, it seemed all men had made bad choices. Such is the price of having someone to protect.

October 1879

'O-dell-a?'

Odell lifted his head and remembered where he was. He felt laboured in the room as though weights were tied to his every part. He stood and clumsily fell back onto the keys of the piano.

'I feel I need to get some air,' he said.

'O-dell-a,' the Bird said with concern.

Odell moved across the floor and knocked a pile of books

over as he went. He felt tearful and didn't want the Bird to see him as such.

'O-dell-a,' she repeated.

He had a sudden dislike for the backwards way she said his name. He almost turned to tell her as much but reined the impulse in.

'I'm sorry,' he said. 'I should leave.'

'We must play together,' she said.

'I can't,' he said.

'This is not ...' the Bird reprimanded, searching for a word.

'I know it ain't,' Odell said and continued to walk away. He heard the swish of the curtain behind him but couldn't bear to turn around, frightened by the idea of that mutated face, which must look angry, now, as well.

'O-dell-a!' the Bird called. 'Face me!'

The heat of the words, rather than sounding intimidating, brought out the youth of the voice. Odell halted and put his hands over his face.

'I can't do this, ma'am,' he said. 'The music. It reminds me of ...'

His voice froze at the touch of a hand on his shoulder. It felt like any other hand, but stories once heard fought to replace the likely with horrors.

'Face me,' the voice said once more, this time more softly.

Odell turned and drew in a deep breath. What he saw astounded him.

'You can't be the Bird,' he said.

'I am called Kyoko,' she replied.

'Kyoko,' he repeated, the word like sugar on his tongue.

16

October 1879

Blanche folded the letter in two and returned it to its envelope. She'd felt Shelby come back to her as clear as though he'd stood beside her in the room, talking aloud. She was disturbed by the return of that which she'd considered herself parted from forever – his whistling Southern voice, the long-drawn-out vowels and gentle contemplation that wouldn't be rushed.

She had once longed for that voice. When her parents had been alive, she would hear him downstairs in conversation with her father. Her father, who had been better educated than Shelby and spent time in the company of finer men, resorted to his own Southern ways when his brother was there and Blanche wondered at this. It was as though the rest of the time he was hiding behind something, and only with Shelby about was he himself.

Yet, in the years that had passed since her father's death, Blanche had grown to hate that voice. It reminded her of his attempts to console, insisting he would look after them when all she wanted was for her father to come back.

Blanche soon sought to rewrite Shelby in her mind. She

wanted to poison his character in her past, twisting every stubborn fibre of her own self to replace love with hate, to turn up the earth of her youthful memories and substitute the recollections buried there.

The letter provided yet more justification for her doing so. Shelby, even as he was about to leave the earth like a coward might, refused to admit that it was he who was responsible for the deaths of George and Lori. And, worse still, his last act seemed to be to turn Kittie against her eldest sister, to throw doubt on the events of that day and make it seem that Blanche's account was made from little else but spite.

Blanche felt an unwelcome doubt in the back of her mind. She clutched the letter before her, eager not to damage it in her angry grip, but already she was thinking on how much she remembered from that day – how much she was certain took place and how much was made whole from the component parts of tragedy and hatred.

She shook the doubt from her mind, convincing herself that, even if things had not been entirely as she'd told them, her uncle was nevertheless deserving of his end. After all, what man chose a different side in a war, against his own brother? What man would prefer to defend the land he called home than stand beside his own blood at Gettysburg and perhaps keep him from dying? Yet that was what Shelby chose – to divide the family in colours of grey and blue. Just one brother returned from that war and, however unwelcome, a victory was made by her uncle.

Blanche walked towards Elena's room to replace the ribbon, the letter still in her hand. She struggled to ignore how the note had undone the past, realising Kittie would know what she had said wasn't true and that there had been some colour added to her account.

More unwelcome than his poisoning of Kittie, though, was the effect the letter had on Blanche. It unsettled her conviction of him that had been so steadfast moments earlier.

On occasion, she would remember things about the day. Things that her mind had sought to protect her from. Two years ago, she had been taken ill and had been unable to eat or drink for nearly a week. During that time, she struggled to tell the difference between a dream and the waking world. Her existence during those days was a terrifying pantomime of shadows and horrors.

She remembered running after her brother through the rain-soaked woods and an awful scream filling the air. The next thing, falling over a stray branch and onto a tattered dress belonging to Lori, the back torn away and covered in blood.

Sometimes Blanche would think she had seen the bear. Each time, its hulking figure would shrink and quiver like a candle's flame about the wick, and what she knew to be true would come sharp in her mind: that instead of pelt it was a uniform, and instead of a beast it was a man.

It was only by her condemnation of Shelby that she was able to forge the day in her and the town's mind. All that remained unexplained slipped away in the face of his negligence. The town needed its villain and she gave it to them – a Confederate who had fought against his Union brother and drank to excess.

Blanche stopped outside her room, swaying at the potency of such things long buried. She held the ribbon tightly in one hand, the letter in the other.

Stepping inside her room, she took a drink from a glass of water beside her bed and saw the portrait of George on her dresser. Her paints were lined up beside it, a freshly pumped jar of water next to them. She walked over to the likeness, feeling her heart lurch at seeing his face. It was all that she could remember him by now; all, that is, apart from the horrors and the tragedies.

Hatred aside, she knew that, had Shelby been sober that day, George and Lori would have stood a better chance of living. How, free of alcohol, he might have steeled himself to take a more accurate shot with that rifle of his he so treasured. Instead they had died, and even from death he protested – appealing sentences long since passed, and urging Kittie to rebel against her eldest sister.

How can I banish this man? Blanche asked herself. *Will I never be rid of him?*

A crazed thought entered Blanche's mind. Rain had started to spatter against the front of the house and droplets hung on the windows like pearls. By craning her head back, she could see the darkening sky, but couldn't tell if the rainstorm had passed over or was about to.

Blanche looked to the portrait of George, as though expecting an answer from her brother. Despite the silence, her mind was made up. She tossed the letter and the ribbon onto her bed and went into the hallway to fetch an oil lamp, before setting off down the road to the cabin.

Blanche had not walked to Shelby's cabin in near on four years, but she remembered its twisting path like an old childhood rhyme.

The rain had become heavy as Blanche passed through town. She thought about going back, but explained to herself that however swift her pace in returning to the house, her clothes would be soaked through anyway. She was burning so brightly with determination that she did not feel the bite of the cold wind as it swept between the buildings and into her increasingly wet clothes. She attracted a few curious looks as people rushed to take shelter beneath storefronts or hurried back to their homes. She only huddled herself against their looks and held the lantern further outwards, as though it would bring the still–distant cabin into view.

The sound of men's laughter caused her to lower the lamp, out of sight. She feared she was being laughed at and her schoolmistress's intuition prompted her to send forth a scolding look. Her heart stopped, though, when she saw from where it had come.

Patch Clockworks hummed in the cold and wet as light spilled out onto the porch from an open door. The laughter had come from within and Blanche was relieved not to see a gaggle of men standing there, laughing at the half–mad schoolmistress.

But one person did stand there, a shadow against the warm light from within. Blanche studied the figure and noted how it perched on a single leg. As much as she tried to stop it, her mind reasoned it was Horace standing there before her.

As though to confirm as much, a lit match made his features glow in the darkening afternoon. His forehead creased as he stubbornly tried to light his pipe against the weather lashing its way up onto the porch.

Horace puffed more vigorously at the pipe and Blanche watched the tobacco pulse orange like dragon's breath. Horace held the match away and the wind blew out the flame almost instantly. Another smattering of laughter came from within and Horace turned to go inside, the pipe pulled into the corner of his mouth.

Now is the time to leave, Blanche thought to herself, *and be glad for it.*

As she stepped to walk away, her foot came loose, lifting free from her boot. She swayed for a second before righting herself, the lantern swinging about in her flailing arms. The sky above erupted in a flash of blue lightning, and Horace's form turned to see her in the road.

'Who's there?' she heard Horace cry, his voice hoarse with the tobacco.

Blanche said not a word and lowered the lantern once more, her bare foot sinking into the mire beneath.

'Who's there, God damn it?' Horace's voice came again.

Blanche tried to move her other leg but found her boot stuck in the earth.

'I've got a gun!' Horace shouted.

At once, Blanche swung the lantern out and held it up to her face. 'It's me,' she called dumbly.

'You'd best be more specific, less you're likely to get shot,' Horace shouted.

A light flashed the sky blue and Blanche winced.

'It's Blanche,' she called out as Horace lit the oil lamp hanging from the porch.

'Blanche?' he called back, squinting pink-eyed against the new light. 'What in the—'

Suddenly a clap of thunder rang out. Blanche was sure it moved the earth beneath her and, in her shock, dropped the lantern, which rolled to a stop before dying in the mud.

Horace looked upwards inquisitively at the sky. Another blue flash came and lit the scene before them like a photographer's plate. Blanche shivered on the spot and leaped again as the sky crashed and rolled with thunder once more. She dreamed of the safety of Marianne House and the warmth of the hearth she had deserted.

She heard Horace call something out and his face filled her with dread. It had aged since last she had seen him, the thick lines and greying hair about the edges of his beard and head making him seem much older. His features held in a grimace as another shock of blue light filled the earth. She noticed that his lips were moving.

'What?' she called out as the thunder deafened her once more.

She thought she caught the word 'fear', and then, like a blade shaving at her heart's meat, 'Lori'.

'Lori?' she called back, unsure if the word even left her mouth.

'What?' she heard him call.

The afternoon was now as dark as night and the sky pulsed like a black heart.

'Lori,' she repeated, this time whispering to herself. Her feet were aching so sharply in the cold of the earth.

Despite his savage expression, Horace raised the pipe casually to his mouth and drew long on it, blowing out smoke that was quickly whipped away down the street. His eyes watched Blanche unblinkingly and she felt them push to her core.

Lori, Blanche thought. *Does he blame me?*

Horace sucked on his pipe once again and, to Blanche's surprise, took a seat on the porch bench behind him. He leaned forward, elbows on knees, and watched her intently, as though the storm raging about them was entirely in her mind.

'Do you blame me?' she called out.

Horace blinked and then pointed the stem of his pipe at her, his words carried up the road as easily as the tobacco smoke.

'Why?' Blanche asked desperately.

Her heart swelled with injustice. She imagined Horace siding with Kittie, and the town sifting through the whole ordeal with a mind intent on finding a new villain.

'Can I speak with you?' she called.

The words rushed from her awkwardly, predetermined from

174

long ago when she had imagined seeing Horace about town or, in her worst nightmares, at Marianne House having sought her out.

Horace stood wearily from the bench and, with an outstretched arm, rapped the pipe against the porch. With the other, he doused the flame in the oil lamp. He looked at Blanche for a moment and then down at the ground, before turning and slipping inside the house.

In an instant, Blanche was in darkness again. Only the now occasional blue flashes of the retreating storm served to show her where she stood: in a partial river from the unrelenting rain, dumbly separate from her boots a few paces away. She leaned over and tried to tug them free, but her hands slipped on the leather and she toppled backwards into the mud, the shock of cold running up her spine.

Feeling humiliated, she began to sob and pounded a fist against the sodden ground. She spun round onto all fours like an animal and cursed loudly into the night. Her words would be lost, she knew it, as nobody was there to hear them, not even her own wind-whipped ears.

She pushed herself up from the mud, her body aching with the cold and her mind aflame.

17

October 1879

'What the hell are you doing?' Clay asked, his eyes still on his cards.

Horace stood awkwardly, resting a hand on the back of his chair. 'Just a minute,' he said wearily.

'You stand up from this table,' Clay said, 'you pay for the privilege.'

Horace glanced down at his dwindling pile of money and tossed a few coins into the centre. 'That do?' he asked Clay, turning away before he could hear the answer. He knew Clay didn't care about the amount, more he wanted to show the others his power over Horace. Ellsworth nodded along to his friend's protestations while a fourth player, Jenkinson, was merely glad to see someone's money other than his own added to the pile.

Horace left the table and picked his way through his workshop, careful not to trip up on any of the larger pieces of wood and swarf scattered about the floor. The players who were still gathered around the table began to talk and the hushed murmur told him he was the subject of their conversation. As he approached the door of the shop, the men let out a sudden burst of laughter that caused him to ball his fists.

'Be quick about it,' Clay shouted. 'I'd be grateful for the money.'

Horace swung the door open onto the porch. The wind tore the handle from his grasp and the door sprang against its hinges. The night was wild and he hesitated a moment on the threshold, wondering if he should not stay inside, but thinking on Clay sitting at that table only made him step out more determinedly.

December 1862

Nature had always held sanctuary for Horace. Even during the most raw moments of the fighting, he would find a childlike solace in an approaching storm, the darkening sky moving in with the far-off patter that soon thumped on the brim of his hat and the surrounding trees.

A pastor once exhorted that the rain turned the blue coats darker while the grey would go to black and that it was God's way of showing the world – or so far as Virginia, at least – that all men were equal and should lay down their arms. To Horace's recollection, that same pastor drowned during a pontoon crossing, letting forth such a smattering of curses that some of the men laughed, even under the threat of their own death. Horace wondered what God's plan was in that moment, drawing filthy water and grit into the lungs of one of his most dedicated followers.

Horace was part of the 20th Maine who fought at Fredericksburg. It was here that he first dallied in the realm of superstition. War did as much to a man; encouraging him to turn from a brutal reality and instead place faith in the random. In their preparations for battle, he would witness men who would untie and then retie their bootlaces a certain number of times before moving on; while others would refuse to look in a mirror on the day, fearing Death would stare back at them from over their shoulder.

When Horace saw those same men alive the next day, he started to do the same. Witnessing so many soldiers carrying lockets about their necks, Horace took to it also, purchasing a cheap silver imitation from a roadside merchant. He wore it empty, not having had the foresight to ask Lori for a portrait. Even so, he held it open before battle, as others did, clasping it through the fighting, as though it might persuade a bullet from its path.

'That your sweetheart?' a man asked.

Horace hastily tucked the pendant back inside his collar.

'Oh, come on, now,' the man said. 'I'll give you a peek at mine. I loves me a sweetheart.'

The man was tall, even by Horace's standards, but tottered uneasily. His limbs seemed ill attached to his body and his teeth were all at angles, as though hastily set in his gums. Because of this, he occasionally whistled as he spoke. His lips would shut tight each time, perhaps self-consciously or perhaps to stop the spittle that fell from his loose mouth.

He gestured again to Horace's locket. Seeing no change on Horace's face, the man drew a portrait from his own. It was printed on newspaper and folded tightly several times over. He unwrapped it, occasionally glancing up at Horace's face.

'You ready to cast your eyes over the most beautiful woman you ever saw?' he asked Horace, holding the paper flat against his chest like a giant playing card.

Horace tried to ignore the man, but his eyes wouldn't leave him. Finally he relented, nodding, and turned to see the portrait. The man unveiled the page and Horace saw it to be an obscene photograph showing a woman crouching above the ground, lifting her skirt above her knees.

Surprised at his own coyness, Horace turned away. The man laughed heartily and pushed the paper further into Horace's view.

'Ain't she a belle?' he said. 'She'll be my wife once I'm home and safe.'

Horace gripped the man's outstretched arms, bringing them down.

'Do you know her?' he asked.

'Know her?' The man looked shocked. 'Of course I do. What do you mean, "know her"?' He seemed to take offence and was quick about folding the paper back up. 'Let me see yours,' he said, the glee replaced on his animal-like face.

Horace clutched at his collar as though by mere association such obscenity would slip inside his locket.

'Come on now,' the man said. 'We had a deal.'

'We had no such thing,' Horace replied bluntly.

The man cursed and in doing so spilled a foamy line of spit down his chin. 'If you ain't about the worst Yankee I ever met,' he said, watching still.

Horace began to busy himself looking over his rifle and was glad to hear a private call-out to say the pontoon had arrived and they would be crossing the Rappahannock into Fredericksburg that morning.

The next time Horace saw the man, he learned his name.

'Hey,' Horace heard a voice call out. 'Hey, fella, it's your old pal, Cloyce.'

Horace looked about, recognising the whistle to the man's speech.

It had been three days since they had crossed the Rappahannock. They were slumped at the foot of Marye's Heights, a hill it would trouble no man to climb, but, as the last days had proven, would trouble thousands of men to take.

This was the first serious fighting Horace had seen. He traced his time spent at war by what he had seen and done, recalling how, once, seeing a man kill another had been the darkest moment of the conflict. This measure was soon reset when he took up a dead officer's pistol and shot a charging rebel in the throat, the man's yell spilling silently to the ground with an arc of blood.

Now, Fredericksburg had reset it once more. The things he had seen over the last few days were enough to fill the volumes of war from the ancient Greeks. Men were strewn all about him, some whole and others in the most curious formations, detached from what it seemed to be human.

'You owe me four dollars,' Cloyce called out.

A smattering of hushed voices followed, telling whomever it was to keep the noise down. Horace lay on his back but looked up and over at the sideways world and saw the man from the pontoon crouching against a stone wall that ran along the foot of the hill.

Cloyce shot back some cautionary words to those men and their voices died away.

'You'd best go over there,' a soldier beside Horace said to him, 'or else he'll never shut up.'

Horace made to protest, but saw a group of soldiers all urging him forward with their eyes.

'We don't want to draw more rebel fire,' the soldier said, taking a bite out of some tobacco.

'Why don't you go over there?' Horace asked.

'He's your friend, ain't he?' the man replied smartly, passing the tobacco behind him to the other soldiers.

Horace wove his way to Cloyce around the dead bodies on the ground, murmuring 'He sure as hell is not' to himself.

'You can sit up, friend,' Cloyce said. His eyes were wild and his face filthy, much like Horace imagined his own to be. He shifted uncomfortably against the wall and Horace noticed that he kept his hand at his side. It was difficult to see in the dying light, but he figured Cloyce had been shot there.

'You got my four dollars?' Cloyce asked, offering Horace a cigarette.

Horace stared at it, thinking of how Lori would protest. Regardless, he drew it from Cloyce's dirty hand and stuck it to his dry lips.

'What four dollars?' Horace asked distractedly, shielding the flame from Cloyce's match.

'"What four dollars?" he says.' Cloyce laughed. 'You're certainly city folk, ain't you? "What four dollars"!'

Horace felt his lungs smart with the smoke and let his head drop back against the wall. 'I don't know what you're talking about,' he said plainly.

Cloyce shifted against the wall and, glancing sideways, Horace could see he was bleeding heavily from his side. Without his hand pushing his uniform onto the wound, he imagined he might have died already.

'Remember the boy?' Cloyce asked.

'No, I do not,' Horace said, taking a long pull on the cigarette.

'You do; I know you do. He was proud as a cockerel. It was the first – no, second night here. He climbed over that wall and ran up to the line. An Irish, I think?'

Horace tried to ignore Cloyce's words.

'Anyhow, he looks about thirteen, this boy. All pale, skin like milk. So curious we were, we looked over the wall's edge, remember?'

Horace began to protest, but just shook his head softly.

'Then – *bang*,' Cloyce said, clapping his hands together with a puff of his own blood. 'He takes a shot full in the face. Must have been a cannon shot, from the mess it made. Took him apart.'

Horace thought of Lori and the child she was carrying.

'Why are you telling me this?' he asked Cloyce, refusing to look at him.

Cloyce patted him on the shoulder. 'Because I said to you that I bet you four dollars that boy was so young I wouldn't be able to find a single hair on the jaw that flew some from his face.'

Horace turned and looked to Cloyce, barely able to make out his features in the dark. 'You did not make that bet with me,' he said sternly.

'I did, and, boy, I went and won it!'

Some men called for Cloyce to quiet down again, which he ignored.

Horace was still for a moment, taking in what Cloyce had said.

'You went over this wall?' he asked. 'And searched for that poor boy's face for a bet?'

'What of it?' Cloyce asked. 'I'm four dollars richer.'

Horace wondered if that was how Cloyce had been shot.

'Best smoke up,' Cloyce told him. 'It's dark and you don't want some reb sharpshooter on you.'

Horace pushed the cigarette into the ground by his side. His mind stuck on the image of Cloyce, over the wall and in the body-strewn field beyond, crouched and searching on hands and knees, as if for treasure.

Throughout the previous day, they'd heard names being called from over the wall. Men were dying there, cut through by shrapnel or gunfire, and, with the temperature dropping and darkness cloaking the field, they were calling out to their comrades with ever more desperation. Horace tried to hunch his shoulders against his ears, but their words still found a way to him.

'What name was that?' Cloyce asked. 'Did he say "Morag"?'

Horace tried not to turn to look at him.

'Hey, fella, he called out "Morag", I'm sure of it,' he said with a laugh. 'You think that fella's belle is Morag?' He laughed again, whistling as he did. It seemed even louder than before, echoing out across the freezing night.

'Why don't you go over there and bring him back?' Horace found himself asking.

'What's that now?'

'Same as you did for that kid. Go over there and bring him back.'

Cloyce twisted with some pain and peered through a hole in the wall. 'Shit, I might if you give me six dollars.'

Horace could do nothing but smile at Cloyce, trying as he was to make a business of war and all the chaos that surrounded him.

As the moon passed over the field, the men were lit up in the palest blue. Even the pools of blood that swam about corpses were beautifully alive, like quicksilver. The light would come and go as heavy snow clouds passed before the moon, lighting and unveiling the men as though flares went up into the night sky.

After a prolonged moment of darkness, a soldier named Pate hurried down the line and pulled Horace out. Horace knew him to be a career man, inviting of war and the opportunity to add more braid to his uniform. He said that their officer himself, Joshua Chamberlain, intended to bury the men and that Horace had just volunteered to help.

'Are you mad?' Cloyce interrupted. 'They'll still be dead when the battle is over.'

He received a stern rebuke from the soldier, but for one damning moment Horace happened to agree with him.

His foray into that field was about the worst moment of the war. He was told not to stray too far, in case the moon came out again and he was lit up for the rebs to pick away. This meant that he was far more likely to pull dead bodies back over the wall for burial than bring back the live soldiers calling out names only a few more yards ahead of them.

In case anything might shine in the moonlight, Horace had reluctantly left his wedding band with Pate, back at the wall. At removing his bayonet, he had been told to keep it, lest the enemy sneak up on him and he not want to get burned by his own gunfire. He stuffed the blade into his trouser leg, occasionally pulling it up as it slipped like a soldier's garter.

Horace watched the moon worriedly. He could see its weak beams veiled by the snow clouds each time he ventured out, heart pounding, to bring another body back. Each time, he assured himself that it would be the last. Chamberlain himself was watching and Horace reasoned that this repeated act of bravery might result in him escaping the line for a few days' rest.

Then, in one terrifying moment, the night sky came alive. He was staring a man in the face, trying to surmise if he was dead or not. He'd ventured a few steps further than he liked to imagine was his limit, reasoning that bringing back someone still breathing would guarantee his rest from the line.

The eyes of the man came alive in divine clarity. Colours of amber and blue swirled where his pupils had been and his skin glowed warmly. Horace thought for a certain moment that he was looking upon a soul.

He heard the hushed voices of Union soldiers before he heard the gunfire. 'Horace!' they called out over and over so that it sounded like crow calls. A crack of gunfire snapped him out of his trance and he leaped away from the body, running back to the wall as more shots rang out. He saw, to his right, another soldier take a shot in the back and fall down on the shallow grass where he had lifted a body not moments earlier.

Horace stared at the glowing ground before him, wondering if the sun had not come up three hours too early. Gunshots picked up and he realised that with each man that fell, he became a more likely target. The wall in front of him, just steps away now, sizzled with bullets on brick.

In one moment of delirium, Horace leaped over the wall and stretched himself out mid-air, prostrate, as though to jump straight into a grave. That he almost did, too, as his arm landed in one of the shallow holes the soldiers had been scraping into the frozen earth.

Men's hands clapped down on his body in camaraderie while he heard a voice, which he liked to imagine was Chamberlain's, say over and over, 'There's a man; there's a man.'

As he rolled onto his back, he became aware of a strange pull in his left leg, as though the skin had tightened and the muscle had come alive in the slow cold of the night. He let out a yelp and, embarrassed, turned to look at the faces still smiling in congratulation. His head fell back against the ground and his breathing quickened, a more intense agony worming its way into his heart and head. He clapped a palm to his own mouth and the men's faces changed. New men took their place and the field medic rushed over.

As Horace opened his mouth to scream, the medic slipped in a shell casing, which tasted bitter, like blood. He bit down hard and felt something crack. Whether this was metal or tooth, he couldn't tell.

He tilted his head in confusion and saw the doctor rip open his left trouser leg in urgency; all the while the other soldiers were keeping his head down beneath the line of sight over the wall. Horace saw his bayonet pressed deep, almost to the hilt, into his calf muscle, the bloody silver peak parting the skin on the opposite side.

He let out a prolonged groan, even then feeling the weight of his stupidity for jumping over the wall like that. The doctor worked urgently and touched the handle of the knife, figuring how best to pull it free.

'Can we move?' he heard him ask.

There was a general murmur of indecision before he heard someone rush down the line of the wall. Horace followed the medic's worried look to see an officer shaking his head and pulling at the end of his beard in thought.

'Then we do it here,' the medic said. He was a young man, who blinked furiously. He wore an apron tied tightly across him, which Horace found curious given they were miles away from the nearest field hospital. He noticed Horace's look.

'It's so they don't shoot me,' he said with a charming smile, before looking down at the leg once more.

It was only then that Horace realised he had stopped screaming. The bullet casing nestled along a row of his teeth and a line of drool fell down to his chest.

'What are you going to do?' he asked, embarrassed at the lightness in his own voice.

'Take the knife out,' the medic said.

'It's called a bayonet,' Horace heard another voice say.

The medic looked at one of the men with weariness before turning back to Horace.

'What's your name?' he asked.

'Horace.'

'Well, Horace, my name is Odell. It's in my opinion that a man should always be acquainted with another before he causes him pain – which goes against this whole damn war, I know.'

Horace watched as Odell wiped his forehead with a rag, a soldier pressing his head down angrily. Odell folded the rag carefully and then tilted his eyes up at Horace.

'This will hurt, friend,' he said plainly. 'If you've a loved one in that locket, best think of her now.'

It was Lori he had thought of: her blonde-brown hair and the way it looked on the pillow as she slept. He thought of her at every moment and afterwards believed it had gotten him through the ordeal better than all else might.

October 1879

A burst of wind blew rain into Horace's face. He drew his pipe from the inside of his jacket and shielded it against his chest to light the tobacco.

The pipe was one thing he picked up from the war; the other was the taste for morphine.

Not long after Horace had fallen on his bayonet, they had retreated. Back through the ruin of Fredericksburg – one of their own making. Back across the water.

Horace had been taken to a hospital along the march. By this time his leg was rotting. He recalled how, as the nurse lifted his torn trouser leg, his skin had come away with it, causing her to faint and be laid in the bed next to his.

The doctor had taken one half-glance before telling Horace his leg would have to be amputated below the knee. He had barely registered the idea when they pulled a curtain closed around him and slid the morphine into his arm.

Even then, on the porch, in the rain, he felt the ache of the limb he once had – as though it stood there still, somehow otherworldly and still that of a younger man. He was scratching at the folded flesh when a light swung out before him.

He steadied himself all of a sudden and called out a warning. The memories of the war had unnerved him.

'It's me,' a voice called back.

He called back in answer, not quite believing the voice to be real. He lit the oil lamp on the porch, eager to disturb the demons in the darkness.

'It's Blanche.'

'Blanche,' he shot back instinctively.

The storm still raged and he watched as the lantern fell from the air and rolled to a stop at the porch's edge. The sky lit up blue and Horace looked out, amazed at the scene.

When it happened again, he saw Blanche there in the road, barefoot and soaked through.

'Are you all right?' he called out.

'What?' she called back.

'You look a sorry state,' he said.

Her eyes widened in the blue flashes of the sky.

'Lori,' she replied, although Horace was sure he misheard.

'What?'

His mind piqued with anger at the sound of his wife's name from Blanche's mouth. He turned to take a seat on the bench behind him, aware he would have to return to the game if he wasn't to forfeit everything to Clay and the others.

Blanche said something more and Horace pointed his pipe at her. 'I can't hear a damned word. Come up on the porch and speak to me.'

He could see Blanche's face contort in the storm as though phantom hands pulled at the flesh there. Her eyes were pushed out on their stalks and Horace had grown tired of looking at her.

He doused the oil lamp and slipped inside. He was glad to close the door against the night, not because of the storm but because of the memories it had whipped up and driven into his mind like a fence post through a barn door.

As much as he tried, Horace failed to stop that day coming back to him: the knock at the door and Blanche's face, blank and utterly terrified at the same time.

The sorrow had consumed him. He had fallen down in the hall after Blanche had left, and dug his fingernails into the wood of the floorboards, calling Lori's name throughout the house. He'd stretched out on the floor and screamed over and over, never once giving a care for who might hear him, only ever wanting her to answer.

It had been several hours before he'd summoned the strength to stand. He had trouble remembering those moments, feeling as he supposed a spectre to feel: formless and wrongly housed in the world of the living.

Horace had been convinced he would never live again and so he left town. He supposed that any delay in leaving might lead to further consideration and so gave in to the impulse. He pocketed what money he had about the house and pulled his jacket from the back of a chair in his workshop. He had hung it there only that morning, when his world had seemed entire. Already it struck him as cruel to even think on the past – when things had been so different and so comparatively complete.

Stumbling into the light of the day, he'd concluded that he and Blanche were the only ones to know. Not one person showed him pity. One man had said good afternoon to him and Horace felt the compulsion to loosen his teeth with his fist.

He'd spotted a carriage outside the post office and hobbled over as quickly as he could.

'Where are you headed?' he asked, his throat sore.

'Underwood and then a way further,' the man called down.

'Can I hitch a ride?'

'No,' the man declared, fastening a rope over the bulk of the carriage. 'Unless you want to mail yourself someplace.'

'Look,' Horace said and set his hand on the man's arm.

'Listen, mister, we needn't go down this path. Now remove your hand.'

Horace took a breath and his exhale shivered from him. He pushed the wet from his face with his palm.

'I just need to leave this town,' he said. 'Please.'

The man looked Horace over and, after a moment more, told him to climb on board. 'You'll be leaving before Underwood, though. I don't want no one to see me taking passengers.'

Horace rode with the man until early evening, when he said that would do. He knew he might find solace in a whisky bottle and thought about arguing his passage on until Underwood. There, he could drink and whore his way to numbness. Even the consideration of such a thing seemed to skin his soul.

How is betraying her the right thing for me to do? he asked himself.

The postal worker implored Horace to remain with him at least until they passed somewhere he might stay the night. Instead, Horace walked away from the road and down a bank towards a river. He watched the water until he heard the carriage pull away and the road fell silent once more.

Walking alongside the river, the uneven earth ground Horace's artificial leg into his stump like a pestle. After little more than a mile, he removed it and saw the skin there red and flaking. He dipped it into the river water and gasped at the relief. The sun was almost down and yet he was met by no caution or fear. He half hoped he might be bitten by a snake and not live to see the new day.

He was not proud to say he never once thought of Ora or Odell, but only of himself and his late wife. To his ravaged mind and heart, he was the one who had suffered. He had lost his Lori and, in doing so, lost everything.

Horace didn't return home for two weeks. Much of the town supposed him either dead or stalking the woods, trying to find the bear that killed his wife. Instead, he did neither. Finding nothing, no vice capable of eclipsing his pain, he only walked on and on, never finding the snake that might sink its fangs into his good leg.

Tired and half starved, he eventually returned to New George-town, not to check in on his children or return to his life but to look on a portrait of Lori. In his haste to leave, he had forgotten to take her with him and, to his alarm, on the thirteenth night, had begun to lose the sharpness of her likeness in his mind.

When he returned home, Ora had left and Odell remained. He could not leave the boy there alone. He saw Lori in him and he could not turn from such a thing.

As Horace walked back into the workshop, Clay looked up from the table.

'Well, look who it is,' he said. 'Any cards hidden up your sleeves, Patch?'

'None that I know of,' Horace replied glumly.

'Maybe we ought to check?'

'You go right on ahead,' he said back. 'So long as I can check yours too.'

Clay laughed and clapped Ellsworth on the back. 'We're all fair

191

men. It's just that some of us . . . well, we're more fair than others.'
He laid out his hand of cards, drawing a chorus of groans from
the table. He laughed like a fool and clawed the money towards
him.

'I'm beat,' Horace said and tossed his cards into the middle of
the table, unsettling some coins there.

'Then have some coffee,' Clay shot back, not lifting his eyes.

'I'm not tired,' Horace replied, although he was. 'I mean, I'm
beat; I'm out of money.'

'You mean you're broke?' Clay said, picking at his bottom lip.

Horace considered the word and wondered if Clay was toying
with him in some way.

'I mean I'm not playing any—'

Before Horace could finish, Clay let out a sharp hiss as he tore
a strip of skin from his lip. Blood welled up and he drew the lip
into his mouth, holding the scrap of skin accusingly.

'We can play on, Clay,' Horace said, 'but I'm telling you I've no
money left. You win, don't expect to see anything on that table.'

Clay was sucking at his lip still while he rolled the strip of skin
into a ball between his thumb and forefinger. The cold wind
whistled through the cracks in the house, turning the back of
Horace's neck to gooseflesh. Through the rain's steady patter, he
made out of the muffled din of music.

Clay did, too, and he flicked away the mottled ball of bloodied
skin as if to confirm as much.

'That your boy?' he said.

'Sounds like it,' Horace replied, wary of Clay's intentions.

'He's playing with the Bird, ain't he?'

Horace nodded and pushed his chair back from the table.

'Sit down, Patch,' Clay said plainly.

'Clay, I mean it when I say I've nothing left to bet.'

'And yet,' Clay said, raising a finger to his ear.

Horace felt a dawning like a hammer to his chest.

'You still got your piano?' Clay asked.

'No,' Horace shot back bluntly.

'You lie, Patch,' Clay laughed. 'Everyone hears your boy playing it.'

'It's a no, and I'd appreciate it if you left.'

'Fine,' Clay said, standing. 'If that's what you want, then I'll leave.'

He shuffled the money on the table together and folded the wad into a pocket.

'My father said you were a fine man, Patch. One of the finest clockmakers around. I guess that's why he brought you here. He said you could make a timepiece from the shavings on a work-shop floor.'

Clay fixed his hat on his head, walked round the table and pointed a hard finger into Horace's chest.

'I never did understand why he liked you so much, though. Was it just that? I can't convince myself it was friendship.'

Horace drew a deep breath that rattled inside of him.

'But whatever it was, I can't abide the rates he gave you. I can't abide generosity when it steps on the toes of business.'

'You took up the rates once already,' Horace said.

'And I'm about to take them up again. That is, unless you play.'

Horace took a long look at Clay and thought for a moment about taking a swing at him. Instead, he watched the blood gather on his lip, weeping from the raw skin.

'What poisoned you?' he asked. 'Can't you just leave me alone?'

'How you gonna make these clocks without any wood?' Clay said, ignoring him.

'What in this world made you so cruel?' Horace said, his blood rising.

Clay walked around Horace and opened the door into the night, scrunching his face against the cold and the wet.

'Cruel?' he said. 'I'm giving you an opportunity to win some money, Patch.'

'I win and you keep the rates the same as they are?'

'And I give you some money too.'

'And if I lose?'

'Then I get the music.'

Of all the things that might have come into Horace's mind at that moment, it was Blanche, standing there in the rain, wide-eyed and white as a sheet, staring his way. Not his wife, nor his son. Not even the daughter he had lost to another life. But a stranger, cast in the cold solitude of a rainy night.

He pushed past Clay and shut the door against the storm.

'Fine,' he said.

18

October 1879

Kittie's arm was slight and yet she pulled Emerson through the woods with little trouble. Her small frame and youth betrayed a clandestine strength. Emerson remembered hearing during the war that Virginia girls were tough.

'Like jackrabbits,' he recalled someone saying. 'Don't go thinking they're pushovers, boys; they ain't. Beneath those buttoned-up dresses are more muscles than anything else. You try it on with them – they'll pull your pecker free and use it for a bayonet.'

Where else but war was such talk common? He struggled to recall the instance further, but his mind was clouded against those days and he was glad for it. It was crowded with roads he would like best never to walk down again.

'It's just along here,' Kittie said, turning back and tugging at Emerson's wrist.

He noticed that her face was flushed. Her cheeks were bright red, as though coloured in a back-room mirror.

Emerson was still uncomfortable with the way he thought of

this girl. For that was what she was – a girl. No more than seventeen, he was guessing. He had known men, particularly when he was a boy, who favoured the young with their devastating lust. He had thought them evil and, because of that, considered himself immune to their weaknesses. But it could not be denied in that moment, that if Kittie had turned in her tracks and kissed him on the mouth, he would have been lost to reason.

His heart quickened at the thought. He dropped her hand instinctively and, unbalanced, toppled forward into the mud. He managed to slow his fall by catching a branch as he went down, before finally sinking to his knees in a pool of rainwater and dirt.

'Are you all right?' she said, turning back to help him up.

'I am,' Emerson said. He caught his breath as he knelt in the water, recalling the warmth of his shack.

'We have to hurry,' Kittie said. She stepped back towards him tentatively, encouraging him to stand. She reached out her hand but Emerson only waved her on; he was suddenly exhausted.

If Kittie had turned from him, too eager to find Blanche, he supposed he would have been relieved. If she left his company, so would those thoughts he'd sooner not have to deal with – a distraction from the task at hand, and something he could not understand well enough to want to be acquainted with. He wished he could place his thoughts about her in that same prison he did the war, before wondering if that prison were nearing full capacity, so many shameful thoughts did it now contain.

When Kittie had fetched him in her search for Blanche, he was embarrassed to say he'd thought her there for other reasons, supposing, for a moment, her attraction mirrored his own. Yet when he examined the likelihood of such a thing, he struggled to find any clarity. This was not from her vagueness so much as from his own; the contents of his mind, when it concerned Kittie, at least, were draped in a curious shroud and he could not discern what lay beneath.

Emerson had been holding an appointment with the doctor in his shack when she'd called. His frustration at yet another interruption died away as he saw the Marianne girl there, in her nightdress, a heavy coat slumped over her shoulders and his own boots on her two feet.

He had looked down at them but she failed to notice his gaze. Bringing his head up, he couldn't help but see the transparency with which the night's soft rain had peppered her nightdress. Even in his shame, he lingered for a moment to see dark shapes which moved him from the inside.

'My sister is missing,' she had said.

'Which one?' Emerson asked dumbly, as though it changed the matter at hand.

Despite his protestations, Kittie stepped inside and casually glanced around, taking in the cabin's details and, Emerson thought, some of the items the doctor had brought with him that night. He was relieved to see that the brief delay in letting Kittie enter had allowed Umbründ enough time to hide. He quickly scanned the room, but could not see where he might be.

Kittie's frantic need to locate her sister contrasted with Emerson's own slovenly mind, so recently separated from the doctor's, and he struggled to talk to her. This time had been different from the others. The doctor had asked him to remove rather than place. He had spent the last portion of that evening poring over amputations and surgeries from Sudley Church after the Second Battle of Bull Run. He was clammy with the blood and bare organs that had hitherto filled the doctor's mind.

He moved across the room to clear away the doctor's items.

'Will you help me?' Kittie asked, her gaze on him.

Emerson looked over his shoulder at her. 'Help you do what?' he asked.

'Find her,' she snapped back impatiently.

'Kittie,' Emerson began, 'I'm in the middle of something.'

Kittie looked at him in silence. Emerson noticed the freckle she had on her lower lip – it sat there like an inkblot, darker than the rest around her face. When he had first met her, he'd almost reached out to rub it away.

'Please, Emerson,' she said.

The way he was beholden to her never ceased to grow in its mystery. He knew it was in part due to his attraction to her, but there was something else there too. He wanted to please her and to make her happy; he wanted to care for her.

'Give me a moment,' he said, watching as she left the shack and returned to the house. He closed the door behind her.

'What is the matter?' the doctor asked, pulling himself out from under the bed, his black suit patterned with dust.

'I'll be damned if I know,' Emerson replied angrily, helping Umbründ up. 'Something about her sister. I have to leave.'

'We are finished, anyway?'

'For now,' Emerson replied, before insisting, 'Still, we should meet again. I've something more in mind.'

Umbründ nodded, brushing his suit clean.

'I'm sorry to leave it like this,' Emerson said.

'Do not worry,' Umbründ returned, looking at his pocket watch. 'I have an appointment also.'

Emerson dulled the oil lamp and told the doctor to wait until he and Kittie had gone. He pulled on his boots and marched up to the house, finding Kittie pacing the kitchen. Emerson had intended to tell her he could not suffer any further interruptions, but on seeing her face, any anger within him soon fell away. He was greeted by that familiar shortening of his breath, something he had hoped, ever since the first time he'd seen her, would cease. Without saying anything else, he told her he would help and they readied themselves quickly. So lost was he in agreeing to go with her, Emerson didn't even ask where they were headed.

'This has to be where she came,' Kittie said now, looking around the woods.

Emerson wondered whether she was speaking to him or rather assuring herself. Her eyes darted around the darkening scene. Emerson raised himself from the water and squeezed the wet from his trousers as best he could. Kittie waited only a moment before setting off ahead of him once more.

The cold wind now cut through the damp clothes to his skin. Emerson believed such a night should only ever be appreciated from the warmth of one's home, and yet he was entering its icy heart.

If Kittie had had her way, she might have left without even an oil lamp. Emerson had snatched the one from the porch as they left Marianne House, already running to catch her up. He had then hoped she might tire, yet she raced forward into the night with little regard for anything other than Blanche.

Emerson willed her to slow down, the light from the lamp only kissing the hem of her dress before him. Their journey had been so fast paced, so without hesitation, that he worried she was leading them anywhere rather than somewhere in particular.

'Kittie!' Emerson called out, his voice rasping in his chest.

He caught no sight of her and worried his voice had slipped beneath the far-off thunderclaps.

'Kittie!' he called out again, angrily. He watched as she came back into view, her face riven with frustration. She walked over to him and beckoned him on like a stubborn mule.

'Tell me,' Emerson said calmly, 'what's happening?'

As Kittie walked away, Emerson reached out and grabbed her by the wrist. He was keen not to hurt her and only swung her back to face him, as though caught in a dance.

Kittie breathed on the spot and looked at Emerson. 'She's gone to Shelby's old cabin,' she said.

'Who's Shelby?' Emerson asked.

'Please, Emerson, we don't—'

'Who is he?'

Emerson was not keen to meet yet another individual who was likely to ask him questions.

'He's my uncle,' Kittie replied.

'Jesus, Kittie, won't she be safe with him?' Emerson asked.

Kittie shook her head and, for the first time since the cabin, he held her full attention.

'He's dead,' she said.

Emerson released her wrist and tried to align the situation in his mind.

'It's not a safe place,' Kittie continued, stepping closer to him. 'Not for her.'

When they found Blanche, she was lying in a pool of rainwater a few steps from the edge of the cabin's porch. Her dress was splayed out around her and coated dark. Her skin though was as white as the flashes of lightning above them, and Emerson couldn't help but fear she was dead.

He saw her before Kittie and ran towards her, his boots sliding across the wet ground. He lifted her head and found her eyes quivering beneath their lids. She was muttering something and Emerson pressed his ear against her lips but failed to make out anything that made sense to him. He knew he had to get her inside if she was to stand a chance of surviving.

He tried to lift her on his own, but she was too heavy with her sodden clothes. He searched for Kittie and saw her looking at Blanche and shaking on the spot. Emerson called her name but she refused to take her eyes away from her sister, fear rupturing her face.

'Kittie!' he shouted. 'Help me lift her.'

She stood there, still, until Emerson tried moving Blanche on his own. Watching her sister being pulled from the water spurred her into action and she lifted Blanche's legs, as cold and white as a doll's.

They carried her into the old cabin and set her down on the floor before the empty fire. Emerson looked about him, searching for dry firewood. He could find none and so dragged in a chair from the porch, relieved to find it dry enough to burn. He smashed it underfoot and piled the scraps into the grate.

'I need a light,' he said, urgently searching around the fireplace.

Kittie ran to a drawer by the stove and tossed him a pack of matches. His hands were shaking, but finally he struck one and set to lighting the fire. The wicker seat of the chair went up like kindling and his hands itched from the sudden heat.

'We need blankets,' he said and strode towards the bedroom. The door was closed but, as he gripped the handle, Kittie shouted in protest.

Emerson froze. 'What?' he asked her.

'Not in there,' she said, her face aflame with emotion.

'She needs to get warm,' Emerson said.

'Please,' Kittie said, tears welling in her eyes.

Emerson spied a blanket pulled over an old bench and nodded towards it. Kittie lifted it free and Emerson crouched back over

Blanche, tearing at the neck of her dress, exposing her corset beneath. Kittie looked as though she had been slapped across the face.

'What are you doing?' she asked.

'She needs to get warm,' Emerson repeated. 'She can't stay in these clothes.'

Kittie moved him aside and took over undressing her sister. Emerson stood, at first infuriated, but then he realised what he had been about to do. Decorum overcame the urgency of the situation and he stepped apart from the two sisters.

Treading backwards, he felt something underfoot and saw it was an old Burnside carbine. He bent down to pick it up and pushed back at the memories that accompanied the feeling of a gun in his hands after all these years.

He supposed it belonged to the uncle, but felt the barrel still warm from the flare of being shot. He swung out the loading lever and found an empty cartridge in the breech, then noticed others sprinkled around the floor. Gradually, he started to take in the scene and realised there were bullet holes everywhere. He felt a breeze on his neck that came from a shattered pane of glass, and he tugged at a curtain to cover it.

Still holding the rifle, Emerson walked across to the bookshelf and found the shredded remains of pages blown out from books shot apart.

What happened here? he thought.

He looked over the carbine and saw even that had not been spared; the butt was cracked as though swung against a wall. Emerson thought it a shame, as the weapon was a beautiful thing, despite its purpose.

He looked to Kittie for an answer, but saw that, having undressed her sister, she was now winding the blanket about her like a cocoon. He turned away out of courtesy and decided to stand on the porch.

The storm still raged, yet Emerson found it strangely peaceful for all that had gone before. He sat on the remaining chair and set the carbine by his side, curiously comforted by its presence. He blinked his tired eyes and looked out before him, only then noticing the locomotive a few yards from the cabin. He followed the line of carriages with his eyes until the track beneath it spun out over the gorge. Despite the ache in his limbs telling him otherwise, he was certain he was already in the grip of a dream.

February 1863

The building where Emerson grew up was an old townhouse that creaked and swung out into the street. It had been a part of the landscape since the last century, or at least that was what his father had told him. Only his father wasn't his father, and in this curious house Emerson had many mothers, while any siblings were unwelcome and buried out back.

As he grew older, Emerson drew the ire of the father. A potential reason for this he listened to intently, but disbelieved, was that he was becoming a man and so a threat. When he was but a baby, the other mothers had cooed at his arrival and the father would watch distastefully from the doorway, appeased by the fact that a happy whore was a profiting whore.

But now he had grown long and gangly and was on the cusp of what one might call manhood. He had an awkward shade of dark on his upper lip and his joints seemed to jut out strangely, as though he were pieced together from those buried in the yard – their limbs having grown there like any other life in the dirt.

The other mothers began to watch him. He was by no means a handsome young man, but perhaps they felt beholden to him, having seen him almost every day for fourteen years. Some whores had left, some had come back and some had stayed the whole time. It was strange, the consistency in sin.

And all the time, Emerson was watched. He felt the eyes on him as he bent to scrub the stairs or empty the bedpans in their rooms. Occasionally, he would stumble upon one of the other mothers mid-act. He had seen the most curious things in the half-realised light of the brothel. And all the while he was encouraged to watch by the other mothers. They made an audience of him, whether he had bought a ticket or not.

He had not been versed in the facts of life, but still his body responded to those acts as though he knew the enticement they held. They were often industrious – repetitive motions drawing gasps from older men. The whores' expressions were blank all the while, occasionally twitching into a gasp, or their mouths forming perfect Os as the customers' faces turned upwards from the ruffle of sheets.

Then, one afternoon, he was plucked. There was a dark-skinned whore by the name of Esmeralda. Emerson knew this to be a fancy name given by the father, but he liked the work it made his mouth do and it complemented her exotic look.

Much because of the father's insistence, she always wore a brightly coloured shawl that draped over her shoulders and trailed along the floor. Beneath this, she wore a deeply cut tunic that revealed the swell of her breasts and the paintbrush fleck of marks she had below the nape of her neck. She wore large gold hoops through her ears and everything about her made Emerson ache.

The other mothers were jealous. They knew, as much as

everyone else, that she was about as French as they. She was Cherokee, but the father's apparel belied her heritage, and it was no embarrassment to recognise her as an Esmeralda.

Emerson would have been happy to recall some flirtation that drew his and Esmeralda's bodies together. Instead, it was little more than a moment in the house cellar, as unexpected as it was brief, the memory of which only grew in excitement as the years passed. Once it was over, Esmeralda stood and kissed him softly on the cheek. The next morning she was gone.

'Don't I know you whores did something to her!' shouted the father.

They were gathered about the kitchen table, like the bastard family they were. Emerson's mother was sick and he felt exposed without her there.

'What did you say?' the father snapped at one of the other mothers. 'Speak up, girl!'

'I said, we didn't do nothing to her.'

The father slapped her across the face, knocking her from her chair. Some of the others gasped, while most kept their heads down. Mary, the oldest to Emerson's thinking, and the madam, nodded.

'Well, she's gone. My prize cuck is gone!' the father said.

'Ask Emerson,' Mary said.

The father spun round. 'Who said that?'

Emerson looked at Mary and shook his head in a bid to dissuade her.

'I did,' she said. 'And I said, ask Emerson.'

'Girl, I will break you in two if you don't start talking.'

The father's words knocked her somewhat and she straightened sheepishly.

'I saw them in the larder.'

The father turned to Emerson. 'Saw them do what?' he seemed to ask the boy.

Mary stood, saying, 'Come on, girls.'

The question hung in the air as the other mothers followed her from the room. The father stood with his hands spread on the table. Emerson shifted and tried not to meet his eye.

'That true?' the father asked.

'I didn't ask her to,' Emerson replied meekly.

The father walked round to the other side of the table. He took a seat and poured himself a mug of coffee from the pot. Emerson and the others had been in the middle of eating breakfast when he had noticed Esmeralda's room was bare. The table was littered with scraps of rind and quietly steaming drinks.

The father picked a tail of fat from the plate in front of him and squeezed it between his forefinger and thumb. 'You know your mother's dying?' he said, looking away from the fat.

Emerson met the father's eye and, instead of anger, saw understanding. The depth of the boy's hurt confirmed just how long he had known about his mother, but sought to believe otherwise.

'She'll be dead within the fortnight, I reckon.'

'Are you saying this to upset me?' Emerson asked, his voice cracking.

'I'm not, no. I'm saying it because by the time she croaks, you'd best be gone.'

Emerson thought about protesting, but knew from the calm on the father's face that there was no choice to be had.

'Where do I go?' he asked.

'There's a war on. You'd best go there.'

October 1879

'Emerson?' Kittie said.

She had tugged back the curtain covering the window and spoke to him through the broken pane. Emerson turned to look over his shoulder and she waved for him to step inside.

When he entered, he saw Blanche before the fire, wrapped in more blankets and glowing from the flames' reflection in her pale skin. He walked across and pulled vaguely at the blankets, making sure Blanche had room enough to breathe.

'That'll do fine,' he said.

'I'm glad to have pleased you,' Kittie replied sourly, not having sought his approval. She soon softened, though, finding the night unwelcoming of such a tone.

'Are you all right?' Emerson asked. 'Seeing a thing like that . . .'

Kittie nodded rapidly and brushed her hair behind her ear. Emerson noted the paleness of her skin and how the mark on her lip stood out more because of it. He felt the temptation to lean forward and kiss it, but quickly shook the thought away.

'You should warm up too,' he said, and moved towards the makeshift kitchen to see about boiling some water.

'Here,' Kittie said, and reached under a bench for a bottle of bourbon.

Emerson frowned, but Kittie pulled the cap free with her teeth, unaware of his disapproval. She took a glug from the bottle and coughed into her full mouth, passing it to Emerson.

His heart quickened at the idea of drinking from the same bottle as her. And, once more, he chastised himself for having so immature a thought. He drank heartily, as though to bury it deep.

The alcohol made his head spin and his gaze flare. Black dots, like flies, swarmed in the corners of his eyes, as though something rotten lingered there.

'Your eyes,' Kittie said, taking the bottle from him. 'They are so familiar to me.'

'Your sister said the same,' Emerson replied.

Kittie began to say something more, but Emerson interrupted, 'We'll wait till first light and then move her.'

'Can't the doctor come here?' Kittie asked.

'That fire won't last,' Emerson said, shaking his head. 'And without it, neither will she.'

He took a drink from the bottle again before he noticed Kittie's worry.

'I'm sorry,' he said, thinking back over his words.

'It's not that,' she said and blinked stubbornly against her upset.

Despite the better judgement that pervaded his heart, he reached out and brought her close to him. She seemed surprised at first, before stretching her arms across his back. Convention had no place in that cabin that night, and she pressed her cheek against his chest.

'What was Blanche doing here?' he asked her, fearing she might feel his quickening heart.

'I don't know,' Kittie replied, her voice muffled.

'She's shot the place up.'

Kittie began to sob and Emerson tightened his grip around her.

'She'll be fine,' he said, not knowing if there was any truth to his words.

Kittie looked up from his chest and smiled sweetly, moving away from him.

'You should try and sleep,' he said to her. 'I'll wait outside. Once the worst of the storm passes, we'll head back.'

Emerson turned to go and prayed he might make it to the

door. He had been pleased by his actions that night and did not wish to undo such work now by making a fool of himself with this girl.

'Emerson,' Kittie said, as though not believing the name.

He turned and she moved towards him.

'Thank you,' she said and kissed him on the cheek.

That was all that was needed. He had fought it for so long, but now something like a cage door opened within him and what came free was longing – longing for this girl he hardly knew.

19

October 1879

Odell was aware of how long the silence had lasted. It stretched out before him and yet he could think of nothing to say. In between long gazes, he squinted heavily, as though the image might sharpen before his eyes. Yet it was more from nerves than necessity. Truth be told, Odell would have gone without averting his gaze, even for the slightest of moments, if he could.

In the plainest of language, the Bird was beautiful. She was also Japanese.

Odell had seen two men from China once. They had passed through New Georgetown, sizing up the town with the aim of selling opiate. But they saw little opportunity there, believing it a place too young to foster addiction, and soon took their trade elsewhere.

Odell recalled how people had stood dumb in the streets – mainly children, but some adults too – looking on as if a betrayal of something natural had occurred, as though they had been assured what humans looked like, only to find themselves proved wrong all of a sudden. Compared to those men, Odell noticed how much softer the Bird's features seemed. Her eyes were round, like glass orbs set in her face, the pupils dark like ink. Her lips were upturned slightly and he glimpsed perfectly set white teeth beneath. Her hair was black and flowed smoothly, as if not one strand quite intended to become wrapped with another. It was pinned in a bun atop her head, with two wooden spears setting it in place. What Odell noticed the most, though, was that she blushed.

No old spinster sat before him. Instead, she could only have been a few years older than he. There was no half-face or lolling tongue. Instead, there was a beautiful woman. The town's grotesque portrait of her had encouraged the idea of an old hag, but in that moment all stories fell apart before his eyes. In their place, he was offered something equally beguiling, yet playing to a tune of wonderment, not fear.

'Thank you,' she said.

Thank you for what? he wondered. Then he remembered his words a moment earlier: 'You're beautiful,' he had said.

He raced to retract his words before realising he wasn't quite prepared to. He had never been so forthright in his thoughts and he blamed it on the strangeness of the room, having lowered his guard in awe of its oddities.

'I meant no offence,' he said quickly.

The Bird stepped out from where she had sat, brushing the curtain as she passed.

'You are not angry?' she asked.

'Me angry at you?' Odell instinctively shot back. 'How could I be?'

The Bird nodded and smiled, revealing more of the teeth below. The red of her cheeks throbbed in the half-light and she moved across the room towards him.

'Miss . . .' Odell began.

'Kyoko,' she replied.

'Key-oo-o,' Odell said clumsily, struggling to repeat the name as before.

The Bird laughed and covered her upturned mouth with her fingers.

Odell scratched the back of his head and his long hair stuck up in a curious thatch. 'I need help with the particulars,' he said.

The Bird continued over to him, until their toes were almost touching on the wooden floor. They were about the same height, Odell's boots affording him a small advantage over her.

She took his hands, as though she intended to teach him a card trick. He wished away the wetness beading on his palms, but Kyoko seemed not to notice.

Suddenly aware of how close she was, he became hesitant in his every instinct. His breath shortened and pulsed irregularly; he swayed on the spot, as though his balance were offset by a strong wind. All the while, his opinion of her as beautiful grew inside him, spreading shoots and finally flowers into each corner of his being.

'Kee-o-KO,' she said. 'Slower. You must not rush a name.'

Odell said it once more and felt the word come alive in his mouth. It was no longer disconnected sounds, but a name, just like Kyoko spoke it. It was music and his tongue an instrument.

He repeated it again in glee, this time giving flourish to the word and pronouncing it with a rounded mouth, as she did.

The Bird smiled and returned Odell's hands to his sides once more. He instantly regretted the speed at which he'd accomplished saying her name; wishing he might continue to try, only to prolong her touch.

'Now what?' he asked with genuine curiosity.

She smiled at him, taking his forgetfulness for a jest.

'We perform, O–dell–a.'

Odell was glad of the curtain. It ran along the balcony that over-looked the bar and booths below, meaning Odell was unseen as he took his seat at the piano. He was squinting hard from his nerves and was relieved at the comfort of the piano stool, as though he'd found something to cling onto amidst a shipwreck.

Peering through the curtain, Odell could make out the figures of the people below, moving across the tavern floor like ghosts.

Kyoko stepped out onto the balcony, carrying her violin. Odell was glad of their brief separation, as it meant he could see her anew once more.

He turned on the piano stool and she smiled faintly at him. Gentleman's impulse prompted him to give up his seat and he almost did, his legs twitching. She stood there, solid, her body a statue from neck to foot. The violin hung by her side and her head was bowed, as though she were praying.

From below, the tavern's decrepit clock struck eight o'clock. Odell's heart beat faster with each chime and he went through his curious routine of placing his fingers on the piano keys before returning them to his sides and swallowing. His nerves made a chaos of his actions, telling him that this insignificant ritual would have more effect on his performance than any amount of practice or skill.

Odell felt Kyoko's hand on his shoulder. He turned to see her smile softly, breaking her statuesque preamble to their performance.

'I'm fine,' Odell replied warmly.

At this, Kyoko removed her hand, and Odell wished it were

back on his shoulder at once – half out of encouragement and half because it was there. As the eighth chime wavered out into the tavern, Kyoko took up the violin and set the bow on the strings.

Odell replaced his hands on the keys and waited for a second, his mind suddenly awash with determination – determination to play and to be heard, not least by Kyoko. He looked up at her one more time and she nodded, somewhat impatiently. Odell pressed down and the balcony, the tavern, the town, his whole world was filled with glorious sound.

Odell let out a yell as he stepped into the room, tossing his jacket onto the floor. His shirt was soaked through and he felt the cold of the room smooth over his skin like pomade.

'Well, damn!' he said, unbelieving.

Kyoko walked in after him and replaced her violin in its case. She turned to face him, her hands clasped together.

The performance had gone perfectly. Yet that word seemed somehow ill-fitting, for their playing was unrehearsed and surprised him at each turn. The word 'perfect' suggested it had been practised and refined, and therefore lacked the spontaneity of true music. It was more apt to say their playing had been true.

'Didn't you hear them?' Odell asked, looking at the Bird's motionless form. She stood there, hands clasped like a statue. 'They loved us!'

With each thing Odell said, Kyoko nodded, taking his words in and counting them off in the subtle tilts of her head.

Odell moved towards her, wanting to hold her hands – or, better still, embrace her. The nervousness he had felt beforehand had turned into a kind of delirium. It was only his awareness of how much he had perspired during the performance that stopped him from touching her.

He paused for a moment and wondered why she wasn't celebrating with him. The realisation that she was a performer by nature was like smelling salts to Odell. He squinted, aware that he was adrift in his hysterics. For the first time, the Bird seemed suddenly very strange to him.

'Are you happy?' he asked her.

Her head dipped in a sodden nod. 'Of course.'

'I find it hard to tell, miss.'

'Kyoko,' she replied meekly.

Worry spread in Odell's heart as she continued to remain stoic.

'Aren't you happy with the way I played?' he asked, squinting hard.

He watched her fingertips tap-tap as she looked at him thoughtfully.

'Very happy,' she said finally. 'But we can be better.'

Odell's head swam. He had been certain Kyoko would be as happy as he and that they would revel together in the success of their performance. At once, he wanted to be far away from her. He wished to leave the room and hide his playing again, away from the Bird's sight and her assumption that they could 'be better'. He felt his father creep into his mind for the first time since their performance.

Two knocks came at the door – Hammond's signal that the bar was empty and he was leaving for the night.

'I should go,' Odell said, retrieving his coat from the floor. As he did so, he knocked something over with his heel.

'Damn!' he said, turning to lift it up.

'Do not—' Kyoko began.

'I want to,' Odell snapped back.

He saw it to be the lantern that usually hung outside the room. He picked it up quickly, as though his haste might spare it any damage already caused. He was relieved to see it was intact, though, and made of sturdier glass than his heel might break.

He held it before him, as one might look out from a deck.

'Where did you get this from?' he asked Kyoko.

No answer came, but Odell felt her hand on his outstretched arm. He flinched in his grip on the metal handle. He turned to face Kyoko, but she only gazed deeply at the lantern.

'Stay here,' she said to him, their faces inches apart, 'and I will tell you.'

Odell nodded, his mouth dry.

Kyoko took the lantern from his hands and set it on the floor. She then sat back on her heels beside it and Odell accepted the wordless invitation to do the same. He took his eyes from her for a moment and looked at the lantern. As she spoke, Kyoko's words began to fill his vision, brighter than any flame he might have found flickering behind the glass.

20

October 1879

'This town . . .' Elena began.

The rest of her words were carried soundlessly in a hot breath against the cool glass before her. She was facing the window of Blanche's room, an old blanket slung about her shoulders. It had grown colder the night before and the windows were draped in a light frost. Elena pushed this away from the glass with her thumbnail, watching as the icy shavings fell to the windowsill like dried wax. Her skin was red from the cold and she wrapped herself in the folds of the blanket to take away the sting.

Emerson felt a pinprick of pain in his own skin just from looking at Elena's. He was standing, leaning against Blanche's dresser. He cast his eyes over what was set out there – the disassembled parts of a picture frame and paints and brushes. There was a portrait he supposed her to have painted. He did not recognise the face and only saw that it was an old thing, the paper brown and curled from another time.

Looking across at Blanche, he was reminded of how ghostly she appeared, her face pale to the point of transparency. Blue lines ran beneath her skin, like a network of secret tunnels. Her eyelids quivered, lowered against the dull light. Elena had insisted on having the oil lamps turned down so that she might rest deeper. But Emerson felt it was too much like a crypt, and longed for a brighter room, or else one without a dying woman in it.

'You hear me?' Elena asked, her head turned to look over her shoulder.

Emerson straightened himself up.

'It ain't fair on that poor girl.' Her eyes began to mist over and she turned back to her strange practice with the frost.

Emerson took one more glance at the portrait before stepping towards her, the floorboards creaking beneath his feet.

Elena turned to him, a cautionary arm raised. 'Don't,' she said. 'Don't, Emerson.'

He had a will to comfort her. He had done as much to Kittie in her uncle's cabin and, he hoped, had gone some way to saving Blanche's life. Offering some consolation to Elena now would give him the curious pleasure of completing a full set. The need for such a thing bothered Emerson and he moved his head sharply to prevent the thought lodging in his mind for any longer.

'I can't understand it,' Elena said.

'What?' Emerson asked.

'Why she went there.' After a moment, Elena turned and looked at Emerson. 'What did you see?'

Emerson bowed his head and wondered how much to tell her. He wished for Kittie to return and for himself to be disentangled from whatever fine thread bound this family together in such a precarious way.

'Emerson,' Elena said. 'Please.'

'She ...' Emerson began. 'The place was a mess. She'd fired his gun in there, shot out the windows, turned it on the books.'

'What?' Elena asked, disbelieving.

Emerson noticed he was chewing on the side of his tongue and stopped. He was unsure whether to continue.

'When Kittie was putting the dried clothes back on Blanche, just before we left, I saw lamp oil on the floor.'

Elena shrugged.

'It hadn't been dropped there, Elena. She wanted that place gone. Shot up, burned – just gone.'

'Jesus,' Elena said.

'We found her outside, sunk into the earth.'

Emerson held his hands before him.

'Looked like she was heading to the engine to fetch something. Matches, fuel – Lord knows. Either way, she didn't plan on leaving with that cabin still standing upright.'

Elena put her head in her hands and began to sob quietly. Emerson thought back over his words, eager not to find the indelicacy he often did.

'What you must think of us,' Elena said.

'It's fine.' Emerson smiled.

'It ain't,' she croaked. 'You're meant to be our guest.'

'I don't mind whatever it is I am,' Emerson said. 'But I can leave if you'd prefer it.'

'No,' Elena said. 'The others wouldn't want that.'

The only other Emerson thought of was Kittie. He wanted Elena to go on, to speak to his heart's tune and say her younger sister wanted him to stay. Instead, she leaned forward and laid a hand on Blanche's forehead, drawing a sharp breath at how cold it was.

'Oh, Bee,' she said.

Emerson turned from them and took Elena's place at the window. Through the hatching left from Elena's thumbnail, he saw the path that passed into town, delicate with frost. He was lingering on the gas lamps when one of them broke loose. It swung out into the road and Emerson watched, intrigued, as it started to climb the dark path towards the house. The glow was suddenly independent in the darkness, a disc all the brighter for its solitude.

Emerson narrowed his eyes as the light from the house showed a figure holding the lamp. He was aware of Elena talking in the background, but focused on the approaching shape, blocking out her voice.

Realisation flooded his mind and his chest moved with his quickly beating heart. His blood fizzed like powder in the barrel.

'Umbründ's here,' he said aloud.

Emerson heated some water on the stove. He watched as the steam cast a shadow on the painted wall. For a doubtful moment, he questioned how such a thing, not quite whole, might possess a shadow. It seemed a cheat, to him. He waved his hand in the steam and watched for the return gesture in the shadow, reluctantly satisfied.

Kittie sat at the kitchen table behind him and drew invisible shapes on the wood with a finger. They were both at a loss for what to do and had again found themselves in one another's company.

When he'd arrived, Umbründ had done so in a frenzy. The bedroom door had swung open and near hit Elena. Instead of focusing on Blanche, the doctor had stridden across the room and taken Emerson's hand, tearful at the relief in seeing him. For a fearful moment, Emerson worried he might have reduced Umbründ to this by some miscalculation in his work.

Emerson had tried to wordlessly persuade Umbründ from

his unusual behaviour, uncomfortable with the attention it was drawing – the sisters' gaze was melting its way into Emerson's flesh like hot coals in the snow. He'd gestured the doctor over towards Blanche, noting how red-faced he was, sweat darkening his shirt collar even in the cold.

Once the water had boiled, Emerson made himself and Kittie some coffee. The sun was still far from rising and he was sure the day ahead would be a long one. His body ached from the rain-laden walks to and from the cabin in the woods and the cold had set into his bones like a poison. He relished a hot pot of coffee to wash it out.

He set a cup before Kittie, who smiled and lifted it in her shaking hands.

'Did the doctor not seem strange to you?' she asked.

Emerson failed to answer and she looked up at him. Seeing her face, he was quite ready to tell Kittie everything.

'What is it you do for the doctor?' she asked.

'I told you before,' Emerson replied, too eager. 'I tell stories—'

'I know what you said before,' Kittie interrupted. 'But I'm asking for the truth. Not some lie.'

Emerson kept his back to Kittie as he poured his own coffee and brushed at his face with a rough hand. In the reflection in the kitchen window, he could see Kittie still watching him. He felt her easing beneath his skin, unsure whether to be terrified or glad of the sensation.

Her eyes stayed on him and he awkwardly drank the too hot liquid, burning his tongue. Numbness pulled loosely across his mouth and throat.

'Emerson,' Kittie said.

Her voice plunged something deep inside him, snagging memories as it went, before pressing almost fatally into his heart.

'Emerson, tell me something,' she continued.

As Emerson thought on her, his mind was awash with something. As though drugged, he swayed and the coffee in his cup spilled over its edge. He was convinced he would collapse onto the floor, but he sparked back into life, glad to come round, and yet he did not feel entirely himself. He felt intruded upon. But whether it was by Kittie, he couldn't say.

'What?' he snapped at her. 'What do you want to know?'

Kittie was taken aback. She had risen from her seat to steady him, but stopped dead. Emerson too was shocked at the words, but couldn't halt more from coming forth, as though he was a spectator of his own will.

'Can't I keep some things mine?' he continued. 'Just some?'

'Of course,' Kittie began hurriedly.

Her softness and fear broke Emerson's heart, but he could no more control himself than a wild horse, loose and flailing from some unbidden rage. His mind approached an apology, only to find itself far off dictating anything. Everything he thought of as himself was pushed aside by this fearful intention to shout her down.

'You're like a thief,' he spat.

These final words moved him. They came so freely and he was afraid of their ferocity.

Kittie looked at Emerson, her eyes wide. She was trembling. The room stilled and Emerson felt something rise in his throat. He felt as if someone might be standing beside him, but found the anger in Kittie's eyes was for him alone.

'Why do you say that?' she asked him. 'In that way?'

He saw a hurt in her eyes that ran deeper than offence.

'I'm sorry,' he said, moving towards her. He was glad to hear the words he intended to say come from his mouth.

'Why did you use those words?' Kittie asked. 'A thief? Who are you to call me that?'

'I don't know why I said as much. Please, Kittie, I can explain this,' Emerson said, knowing full well he could not and would not.

He moved forward again and Kittie stood from the table to leave the room. Emerson gripped her hand and pulled her back, eager to have her at least hear his apology.

'Wait,' he said.

'Let me go,' she snapped, standing close to him.

Her hand wriggled in his and he moved his body to stop her getting free. He twisted her arm around her back, bending her over the table. She let out a light yelp of pain and continued to struggle.

'Let me go!' she said more forcefully.

He moved his face towards hers and she swung a boot heavily into the bone of his shin. Emerson cried out and let go of her arm. She slid from him and moved a few paces away.

The situation came to rest in Emerson's mind and he was both terrified of his actions and entirely convinced of them. Where he sought remorse, he only found something spurring him on. Where he hoped he might blame whatever had taken him over before, he knew he could not.

'What are you?' she asked.

The words coincided with Emerson's own line of questioning. The two of them were breathing heavily as heat swam in their blood.

Kittie felt spun out of place and was half excited, half terrified by what was happening in the kitchen of the house where her sister lay dying. She looked at Emerson and saw something she again struggled to explain.

Without dwelling on why, she moved back towards him, stepping into footprints that already lay there before her. She spread her hands out on his chest and, without thinking any further, kissed him. She pressed her lips lightly onto his and parted them. His warm breath ran into her mouth and her hands tightened to grip his shirt. Emerson brought his arms round to the small of her back and pulled her against him.

His heart raced and he remembered that morning a few days before, when he had seen her standing naked in the middle of the bath-room. Those same breasts and that same waist were now pressed firm against him.

They were both of them lost in a moment not of its time and not quite their own. They kissed with familiarity and Emerson was surprised at Kittie's assuredness, a girl just seventeen.

Their bodies swayed as one and came to tilt over the table. This time though, Kittie's hands ran up into Emerson's hair and pulled his face hungrily into her own.

Spurred on by this, Emerson hitched the fabric of her skirt up until he felt the warmth beneath. The touch thrilled him until Kittie seized his wrist. He stopped, astounded and suddenly aware of what he was doing. Kittie held his wrist firm as their breathing heaved in stalemate.

She opened her eyes and her face twitched into something new. She slowly let go of his wrist, as though it were a bird about to take flight, and pushed against his shoulders, moving him back from her.

'No,' she said.

At this, Emerson looked at her and noted her change. He stopped and pulled away.

'No,' Kittie said again, fixing her skirt.

She took one last look at Emerson and ran from him.

The room was silent and Emerson stood abandoned, his heart slowing its heated thump. He tried to explain to himself what had just happened. The ramifications of what he had done began to take shape in his mind and he waited silently for Kittie to call out to the doctor and her sister. He would be thrown out of town, maybe worse. Since the townsfolk decreed the law, he could find himself hanging from a gas lamp by sunrise. He thought of what had brought him to the town and felt it undone by lustful instinct.

He continued to wait, but the call didn't come. He heard Umbründ and Elena shift about in Blanche's room before the door of Kittie's opened and shut and her footsteps sounded above him. He wanted to go upstairs and see her, but an apology was far from his mind.

What she does to me knows no bounds, he thought.

In that moment, Emerson confronted how he felt about her. He accepted her into his heart and yet it felt uneasy somehow, as though, at the same moment, his love for her was neither private nor certain. He felt a quiet war within himself, painfully unable to hold his affection firm when all he wanted to do was shackle it before himself and declare it his.

He could not assign all this to love. It was something else, something impossible to understand or to resist. With Kittie's footsteps coming to rest, the strange company Emerson's mind kept lined the room and looked inwards, regarding the scene. And among them Emerson Limeflower was watching too, a stranger to himself and to all else.

21

October 1879

'Won't you go on?' Odell asked as Kyoko took the lantern in her hands.

Her story had brought Odell as far as the coast of San Francisco. As though words might be trod upon like the boards of a ship, she had given him passage. She did not seek to discuss her life from its beginning and dally in that foreign world that fascinated Odell. But rather she began with her life's rupture, an event that replaced her family with the crew of a ship.

Odell was privy to a tale of a voyage bound for a distant land, a Japanese emissary and a storm. It was told in halting English and yet Odell was transfixed. Throughout the story, Kyoko looked on the lantern and Odell realised it must be the one from the very ship she was describing.

He could not believe such a fanciful story to be someone's to tell. It all seemed too fantastical to belong outside the pages of fiction. Only when he saw the deep furrows of sorrow and loss across Kyoko's face did he understand it was her own story.

The frequency of their meetings had brought about an

intimacy he was ever thankful for. In stepping from behind the curtain, she had revealed to him her most potent secret, and now she began to explain the conditions by which she arrived in New Georgetown.

Odell had found a curious home in the tavern, one that contradicted the monotony of his father's house. His usual drab surroundings were redressed in wonderful red, the silence filled with stories from another land.

'What happened next?' Odell asked, recalling the start of the storm.

'That is where the story ends,' Kyoko replied, running a palm over the misted glass of the lamp. 'This is all the truth I have.'

'Do you not still wonder?' Odell asked, unfolding his stiff legs.

'O-dell-a,' Kyoko began, 'I do little else.'

Odell opened his mouth to speak again but just nodded, thinking it an occasion where no words might offer more comfort than some.

'I learned things from elsewhere. Tragedies are often overheard from whispers,' she said. 'The storm worsening. My father raising my mother to the ship deck before the waves took him. A shipwreck in the night.'

'I'm sorry,' Odell offered.

Kyoko dipped her head, appreciative.

'There was nothing but wreckage left. A scatter of papers lifted from the sea, and this lantern. Words and light.'

Odell shifted on the spot, suddenly aware of the stiffness in his legs. Kyoko gestured towards a chair. He was grateful for it and sat as she continued to kneel.

'What of your mother?' he asked tentatively.

'She died,' Kyoko explained, her face coming to terms with the words after they were spoken. 'I was born and she died.'

'You were born at sea?' Odell asked, his sensitivity betrayed by curiosity.

Kyoko nodded and stood with the lantern hanging at her side. 'After my father died, my mother gave birth to me. And then she returned to his side.'

Odell resisted asking further questions. He was bewitched by her mystery; her sobering account had shown him a young woman born at, and orphaned to, the sea, forced to continue a journey her parents never would. Nevertheless, his hunger at her story made him shift guiltily in his seat.

'I lost my mother too,' he offered up. 'It's just me and my daddy.'

Kyoko turned to him. 'Then perhaps you will tell me that story,' she said. 'One day. But not now. Now, I am tired.'

Odell stood abruptly, feeling as though he had overstayed his welcome. A part of him felt cheated by not knowing immediately what happened next in Kyoko's life to lift her from the San Francisco pier to a tavern in West Virginia. Yet his wish that she not be further upset cast a shadow across his enthusiasm to hear more.

'I'm sorry,' he said, 'to take up so much of your time.'

'I will see you tomorrow,' Kyoko said.

She moved across the room and walked out onto the balcony. Odell watched as she rehung the lantern outside the room, like a wreath.

'Don't we perform the day after tomorrow?' Odell asked, catching up with her words.

'Tomorrow we practise,' she said, coming back inside.

Odell hummed in understanding. He stepped from the room and Kyoko closed the door behind him. He walked solemnly downstairs and found the early morning sun creeping across the tavern's floor. The dust moved about, drowsy in the golden light.

So taken up in the rapture of their performance and the Bird's words was he that Odell thought not once about his father and the scolding he might receive upon going home so late.

If only I could know, he thought greedily, *the rest of that woman's secrets.*

Odell had quickly become enraptured by her, and by the mysteries that lay behind her beauty. And the excitement of knowing about the Bird, of most likely being the only one to know about her, pulsed through his mind.

He stood for a moment in the empty tavern and moved a dirty glass about on the bar top. He wondered if Ora knew the secret of the Long Cape. But soon the thought only served to make him angry at her continued absence. Especially now that he had things he wished to share with someone.

Odell unlatched the side door of the tavern and stepped out into the fresh morning. As he closed the door behind him, he caught a shadow sweeping across the bright early-winter sun and felt a tooth loosen in his mouth as he crumpled into the crisp, frosty mud.

'Where's Ora?' Clay asked. 'What's she told you?'

Odell's hands shot to his jaw, which already seemed to be growing in size.

'What?' he gasped.

Clay sank to his haunches and placed a thick hand about Odell's throat.

'I have to ask again? I'll take the eyes from your head.'

Odell moaned and turned his head painfully to the road. He could make out the sounds of work beginning in the town, but the pair of them were too concealed to be noticed.

Clay squeezed and Odell let a spittle of blood free from his mouth. He could feel the tooth Clay had knocked loose pushing painfully into the meat of his tongue.

'Okay,' Odell gasped urgently. 'I ain't seen her.'

'Bullshit!' Clay rebuffed. 'Then where is she?'

'I don't know!' Odell said, desperate. 'How should I?'

'You weren't talking to her up there?'

'No!'

'Keep your goddamn voice down!' Clay spat, looking sideways to the street. 'Then who were you talking to?'

Odell winced at the pain and squeezed his eyes shut tight. Clay squeezed harder and Odell whimpered.

'Ky—' he began.

'What?'

The importance of the secret welled up inside Odell and he swallowed it down.

'The Bird! The Bird, all right? I was talking to the Bird.'

Clay turned his head upwards, bemused.

'You were up there talking and laughing with the Bird, all cosy, like?'

Odell nodded and Clay laughed aloud, letting him loose. Odell looked down the alley again but the way was empty.

'You got a friend, Odell?' Clay said, eyes narrowing.

Odell touched his hands to his reddened neck.

'Well, now, I heard the stories,' Clay began, 'and I know she's about as ugly as you, but I wouldn't have thought she'd be as fucking desperate for human company.' He slapped a hand on his thigh and laughed again. 'Sweet Jesus!' he said.

Odell looked up at him hatefully. He thought of Kyoko and her story, and how it was likely someone like Clay who had spread the tales of her being scarred and marked in some grotesque way.

Clay fixed his gaze on Odell, his laughter petering out.

'You got something to say, Odell?' he asked. 'If that's the case, you'd best say it.'

Odell felt his anger unfurl into something otherwise, slithering its way free of his grasp.

'Why you looking for Ora?' he said, his words free. 'You looking to buy her cunt again?'

Odell shrivelled at the sound of the word in his own mouth. The smile fell from Clay's face.

'What did you say?'

'You heard me,' Odell said, surprising himself with his own boldness.

'I don't know that I did,' Clay said.

'I saw you,' Odell croaked.

'You saw me?' Clay asked. 'You saw me, huh?'

Odell nodded.

'So, now what?' Clay asked. 'You planning on telling someone? Elena, maybe?'

'I figure I could,' Odell said, clutching at Clay's suggestion.

'You figure you could, huh?' Clay mused. 'So what? You want your piano back?'

Odell's resolve broke and his face clouded over with confusion.

'My piano?'

Clay studied his face, his smile returning. 'Aw shit, and you was doing so well,' he said. 'God damn, your daddy is one son of a bitch. He didn't tell you about the piano?'

Odell's mind raced, trying to think what Clay could mean. He questioned what his father could have done and then found the answer before him with a dread too familiar to not accompany the truth. His throat burned and swelled and his insides made way for dire realisation to sink clean through. His father had bet the piano away.

'That's right,' Clay said, watching him. 'It's mine now, kid.'

'No, it ain't,' Odell spluttered.

231

Clay just nodded, a hand on Odell's shoulder.

'I'll tell Elena,' Odell said, panicked. 'Give me the piano and I'll stay quiet. Else she'll quit you.'

'No. No, you won't,' Clay replied calmly, squeezing Odell's shoulder. 'If you say one damn word to her, I'll chop that thing up into firewood and then I'll burn your fucking daddy's shop down. Now, how's that for a deal?'

Clay stood and smoothed out his clothes with the flats of his hands.

'What you said before,' he began, distracted. 'You think I paid for her?'

Odell shifted on the ground, fearful of Clay's looming stance.

'That cunt fell into my lap as freely as leaves in fall,' Clay said. Odell's head swayed and Clay clicked his fingers at him, bringing his attention back round.

'You see Ora, you tell her I'm looking for her. You see Elena, you keep your mouth shut. Understand?'

Odell nodded.

'Attaboy,' Clay said. 'You know, Odell? I've beaten your daddy plenty. At poker, mind. But each time there's been that look. The same as the one I'm seeing now. The look of a Patch, you might call it. A losing look. And it's looking on it that makes me certain, no matter how many pricks your dead mother took in her before that bear's, that one-legged pile of horse shit is your blood.'

Odell begin to whimper and Clay grinned, pushing his body down with his boot.

'I'd best leave 'fore I kill you, Odell. You just remember my words.'

Clay brought his heel down hard into Odell's chest and the boy tasted blood at the back of his tongue. His mind receding to someplace else as Clay's flickering shadow dipped out of the alleyway and into the current of town.

22

October 1879

Kittie was having trouble sleeping. Her head swam with remembrances of Emerson and the kitchen. The covers on her bed, newly replaced on account of the cold, seemed to press her against the mattress, suffocating her.

The words of Emerson's journal were first in her mind, even before her own. They were irremovable, as though inked into her skin. When she had gone to her room earlier that night, they had returned clearer than ever – the passage about his son swathing her actions in guilt.

She heaved the bed sheets free and lay there, her skin and nightdress damp with sweat and cold against her goose-pimpled skin. She tossed her head from side to side, hopelessly restless and wishing that sleep would take her and pull her into that dark carnival dreamworld where she need not account for her actions or true thoughts.

Instead, she tried to account for everything, her insides doing a loop-the-loop, like starlings in springtime. And all the while the dull heat between her legs that refused to leave her; that reminded her of a frontier crossed and now forever traversable.

Kittie thought on what Elena had said about her body and wondered if she wasn't the temptress of the Marianne sisters. She had been the one naked for him to see when he was fixing the roof. She had pulled him from his lodgings in search of her sister, when she knew there were plenty of others to choose from. And then, in the kitchen, she had kissed him.

The memory of the kiss was still hot in her mind. Not yet formed enough for her to reflect upon, it had been a moment so heady and elusive of reason that it summoned her body as much as her memory. She twisted busily underneath her sheets again, hopeful sleep would soon claim her.

Kittie looked up at the door expectantly. She knew now that if Emerson walked in, she wouldn't fight him. Even with all that had happened over the past night, Blanche's plight and the memories of her uncle, she would welcome him into her bed. Even knowing, for her, it would mean a stain, unseen and yet impossible to scrub free. She would be lost to one man and yet her heart raced with the idea. She placed a flat hand against her chest, as though she might still it.

A knock came at the door and she turned her head, unbelieving. She stood and glanced at her reflection in the mirror over her shoulder, smoothing her hair's wildness and adjusting her nightdress to cover all she might want to.

Yet when she opened it, her sister Elena stood there.

'Umbründ is leaving,' she said.

'Oh,' Kittie replied dumbly.

'He says Blanche ...' her voice halted in her throat and she paused for a couple of breaths. 'He says Blanche will be fine. She's going to live, Kittie.'

Kittie said nothing, but hung about her sister's neck and half-laughed into her shoulder.

'She's a stubborn one,' Elena said, turning to kiss her sister's head. 'Not even this could keep her down.'

'Thank the Lord,' Kittie said, surprised at her words.

'Thank Emerson,' Elena replied. 'Umbründ said that without him, she'd not have made it.'

Kittie pulled apart from her sister and wiped the tears from her eyes.

'You okay?' Elena asked, running a hand against her sister's cheek.

'I'm—'

'You've a fever?' Elena interrupted, panicked.

'I'm fine,' Kittie replied, taking her sister's hand. 'I can't sleep, is all.'

Elena put her free hand against Kittie's forehead and Kittie moved away from her touch.

'I'm fine,' she insisted.

'You were out there too, Kittie. You were out there in the rain.'

'Not for half as long,' Kittie replied. 'I'm fine.'

'I should fetch the doctor back up here.'

'El, I'm fine!'

The two of them turned at a murmuring. The kitchen furniture moved below them and the murmur grew as Umbründ and Emerson came into the hallway.

'Is Emerson going with the doctor?' Kittie asked.

'Seems like it,' Elena replied. 'Didn't you think the doctor curious when he arrived? The way he spoke to Emerson?'

Kittie remained silent, thinking how Emerson had reacted when she had asked him about his work.

'Kittie?' Elena asked.

'Huh?'

'I'm fetching the doctor,' Elena insisted, half turning.

'El, would you listen to me?' Kittie said, snatching at her sister's wrist. 'I'm fine.'

Elena took a long look at her sister.

Can she know, Kittie wondered, *what dark things swarm my mind?*

'It's been a long night,' Elena said, before reaching inside her dress for a brown bottle. 'Here.'

'What's this?' Kittie asked.

'To help you sleep.'

'What is it?'

'A tonic,' Elena said, unsure. 'Umbründ gave it to me. It quiets the mind. A few drops in a drink of water and you'll sleep, forgetting all this. For the meanwhile, anyhow.'

'Is it safe?' Kittie asked, holding the bottle to the light.

'He's a doctor, ain't he?' Elena retorted.

The front door of the house opened and closed. Kittie's chest grew empty at the thought of Emerson leaving them, even for the length of an appointment. His absence made folly of her fantasies and she grew to question whether their embrace had happened at all, without the likelihood of more to encourage it. The embers of whatever lay between them were already beginning to die away, all the while hungry for encouragement.

'You want to sleep in with me and Blanche?' Elena asked.

Kittie shook her head. 'I'll be fine,' she said, holding the tonic aloft.

'No more than a few drops, remember?' Elena said.

'You going to sleep?'

'I'm going to try. I feel I need to watch Blanche.'

'Want me to, for now?' Kittie asked.

'No, you've done enough, Slim,' Elena replied softly. 'Sleep.

I'll be fine. It's been a while since Bee and I have spent time together, anyhow.'

Kittie smiled at her sister.

'And I might even get a word in, this time,' Elena continued.

The sisters embraced and Elena closed the door of Kittie's room.

Soon after, Kittie walked across the landing to her parents' room. She looked from the window to the faint white road leading into town, and caught sight of Emerson and Umbründ. She thought how the nondescript figure she gazed down on befitted Emerson. He was someone whose nature frustrated Kittie, as it persisted in eluding her understanding. Yet despite this, or perhaps because of it, her heart raced for further time spent in his company.

Eager not to think on him, she returned to her room and pulled open the brown bottle Elena had given her and, lacking a glass of water, swallowed the equivelant of a few drops from it. The liquid was thick and coated her throat pleasingly. She then tidied her bed and lay on top of the sheets.

She tilted her head and felt the tonic quieten her blood. Her nightdress ceased twitching over her chest and soon her head fell back into the soft hold of the pillow.

She left herself standing at one end of a long room, retreating further from Marianne House. Moments from her past began to unbox – one after another, after another. And, within them, a recently familiar gaze and yet a face long unseen.

August 1877

Kittie moved the hand shielding her face, letting the sun spill out over her skin. The stark whiteness brought tears to her eyes, even closed. The warmth of the afternoon had wet the small of her back, which tacked to her dress.

'You awake,' Chester said, not quite a question.

'I am,' Kittie replied.

'It sure is hot, huh?' Odell added.

Kittie sighed at the sound of his voice, having hoped he would have had occasion to leave while she drifted in and out of sleep in the warm sunshine. She brushed a bug from the nape of her neck.

Fingers interlinked with her other hand.

'Say, Odell,' Chester said. 'How about you go get us something to eat?'

Kittie smiled at this plan, while Odell began to protest, uncertain.

'Please,' Chester said, teasing out the word.

'Fine,' Odell replied. 'But give me some money this time; I ain't paying again.'

Shadows moved across Kittie's closed eyes and she heard the clink of coins before Odell's footsteps walked away on the hot ground.

'Alone at last,' Chester said.

Kittie laughed and then felt his hand in hers once more. She turned to face him and he kissed her, making her young heart race. She recalled the first time they had kissed, two months before that day.

Chester was lodging at Marianne House, in the shack at the bottom of their yard. At Blanche's request, Kittie and Chester had been cleaning the room, something Kittie in truth never took to. She would think moving a thing out of sight a reasonable enough way of cleaning it.

She had always felt something for Chester. But having never experienced feelings like this before, she was unaware both of their importance and of what to do with them. She only knew that something moved her in a curious way. It existed in snatched glances across the schoolroom or their hands meeting in a school-yard game – meeting for a beat too long, and yet never long enough.

They had talked to one another on only a few occasions, and mainly with the audience you never lose when you're young. Schoolchildren clustered about them, eager to tease, eager to interrupt. When Blanche told her sisters that Chester would be staying with them on account of his father leaving town, Kittie was ashamed at how grateful she was to that cruel man.

It was Blanche who had first brought them together. In the early months of that summer she heard of the boy's situation and had encouraged her youngest sister to speak with him. She hoped this would give him friendship and better memories than the ones he had.

'A friend is what that boy needs,' Blanche had said. 'God knows it.'

Kittie was sweeping the shack, merely shifting the dust from the floorboards up onto her skirt. Chester watched her from where he was cleaning the windows and she caught him smiling.

'Something funny?' she asked.

He shook his head, squeezing a wet cloth damp.

'You're making a mess of that floor,' he said eventually.

'Well, those windows aren't much better,' Kittie replied. 'I can't see the glass for the streaks pasted over them.'

Chester smiled and ran the cloth down the glass with a squeak. 'Your sister said to do a job. She didn't say to do it well.'

'What kind of fool thing is that to say?' Kittie asked after a pause. She could not deny being further fascinated by Chester's words, stupid or otherwise.

Chester failed to reply and the next hour passed in silence. Kittie swept a plume of dust in his direction, but he failed to engage with it and only concentrated on his windows.

At the supper call from Elena, Kittie was moving towards the door when Chester blocked her way.

'Didn't you hear?' she asked.

He nodded.

'Then why are you standing in my way?'

He was close to her and Kittie's heart began to beat faster.

'I wish to give us both something better to remember this day by,' he said, and planted a kiss on Kittie's lips.

Kittie stood still for a second before flinching apart. She noticed Chester's cocksure smile, but saw hesitation and worry trembling its edges. She thought about cursing him, pushing him aside and telling her sisters. In her young mind, it might have been enough for them to tell him to leave. Instead she only set her broom against the wall and motioned him aside, before opening the door wider.

Before she trod up the grass towards the house, she turned to him.

'You may do that again one day, if you wish.'

She recalled how the smile had stayed on Chester's face until the very next morning.

Since then, they'd snatched moments when they could. Whenever Blanche and Elena left the room, they would hastily lean across the table and press their lips together. Its clumsiness somehow lent itself to their young affection, which unspooled more and more each day.

Once, in her determination to meet Clay, Elena had left the two of them alone in the house. She had pulled Kittie aside and asked if she would be okay, alluding in that word to any worries she had but would not speak aloud. Kittie replied that they would be fine.

As soon as Elena had gone, Kittie and Chester held one another and kissed. They cherished the moment, not urged to part by either Blanche cherished hastily re-entering the room.

'Kittie, you have never shown me your room,' Chester said, his face against her neck.

Kittie remained silent.

'Might you now?' he asked, looking her in the eye.

'Chester . . .' she said, hoping he might admit to some playfulness.

'What?' he asked her. And then, assured, 'I am fifteen.'

She was disappointed to see how serious he was being.

'I am *only* fifteen,' she replied, almost apologetic.

She brushed her hands over his shoulders and kissed him once more. Chester went to speak again, a smile readying persuasive words.

The turn of Blanche's key in the door at that moment was a sound Kittie had never thought she'd be grateful for. Chester stepped back from her and took his seat once more, as though stepping backwards through time.

There had been one more occasion since, Chester having visited Kittie in her room. He had called up to her from the yard and she had told him he was a fool and asked him to go back to the shack. Instead, he had entered the house and made his way to her room. He had spoken to her sweetly that night, telling her he loved her and that she was his soul's mate. Despite her heart swelling with those words, she'd asked him to leave, which he did, showing only a moment's hesitation before he finally slipped soundlessly from the house.

Now, almost a month later, she was glad they were alone, Odell having left for town. The sun beat down on them and Kittie listened to Chester breathe out with satisfaction.

'It's looking a fine day,' he said.

Kittie brought his hand up to her face and kissed the back of it.

Moments stretched out before them as they only have occasion to do on hot summer afternoons.

'You ever think you'll leave this town?' he asked.

Kittie laughed. 'I sure as hell hope so. You?'

'Yep. It's no home for me.'

A blade of grass tickled Kittie's nostril and she flung out an arm. 'Quit it!'

He laughed and Kittie was surprised, as always, at how high-pitched it was. She turned to look at him, as though to make sure it was him who sat next to her. She was reminded of how handsome he was and smiled.

'I'll never forget your eyes,' she said, 'for I love them so.'

Chester blinked and tossed a handful of torn grass to the wind.

'I like your freckles in the sunshine,' he said to her, before tugging softly at her lip. 'Especially this one.'

'Don't nobody like my freckles,' she said.

'Didn't I just say as much?'

She smiled again and he leaned forward to kiss her.

'You don't have to, you know,' Kittie said.

'What?'

'Leave.'

His face changed and he tossed away a flower stem he had been twisting in the air. Kittie reached over and took his hand again.

'There's more to this town than him,' she said. 'More to it than memories.'

Chester said nothing.

'I know you still think about him.'

He turned to Kittie, who tightened her grasp on his hand, knowing full well he was about to throw it off.

'Can't I keep some things mine?' Chester said. 'Just some?'

He sat up and shook his head idly.

'You're like . . .' he began, searching for the word. 'You're like a thief.'

Kittie straightened, hurt by his words.

'I'm trying to know you,' she said.

'You're prying,' he said. 'Just like your sisters. This whole god-damn town is prying.'

'We're trying to help you,' she said.

'Help me how? By tossing my daddy out of this place? Sure, that helped me. Now I'm an orphan living with three frigid old maids.'

Kittie looked away, wishing he would stop here and know he already owed an apology. Instead he carried on, running off the heat of his own temper.

'Actually, make that two frigid old maids. I must be fair on your sister Elena.'

'Stop it,' Kittie said, barely a whisper.

'You want to help me?' he said. 'Lie on your back and be more like her. That'd help me some.'

Kittie felt her throat sting, but she looked away still, eager for him not to see her face.

'Tell me you're smiling, Kittie,' he continued. 'Tell me today is the day, because Lord knows I'm sick of waiting.'

Kittie stood and brushed the grass from her dress.

'You go too far, Chester,' she said, turning. 'You shouldn't talk to me like that.'

Chester noticed the tears on her face and stammered in his anger. 'God damn it!' he said, hitting his palm against the ground.

Kittie brushed her face dry.

'I'm sorry,' he said. 'I'm sorry I said those things.'

He pushed himself up onto his feet and walked towards her, hands bared in surrender.

'I'm sorry,' he said again.

He put his arms around her and, at her lack of protest, drew her into an embrace. She put her head on his shoulder and stared out at the sunshine on the distant hills.

'I don't mean to, Kittie,' Chester said.

He moved his hands to her waist and she willed him to stop. She stayed silent, though, and kept her eyes trained on the distance.

'Only you tease me so,' he said, and placed a hand clumsily on her breast.

'Chester,' she said, her head still resting on his shoulder.

'Kittie,' he replied matter-of-factly.

She wondered in that moment whether to allow him this.

Is it so dear to him? she wondered. *Is it his take on our affection?*

Chester squeezed her breast awkwardly and tried to move his other hand down between her legs.

'Please don't,' she said, all the while thinking whether to gift him this and end his wait.

Chester didn't listen and set about his intentions with more determination.

'Chester,' Kittie said, lifting her head from his shoulder and pushing his arms away. They came back as though sprung and, with little consideration needed, she slapped him across the face.

He yelped and, when he looked back at her, a fine cut ran beneath his left eye. He touched his face and held his bloodied fingertips out to her accusingly. She went to apologise, but no words formed in her mouth.

'Maybe you is a whore,' Chester snapped. 'Teasing me all this time. And what do we have from it? Nothing.'

Kittie felt the air taken from her lungs.

Please God, she thought, *allow me strength enough for the next six words.*

'This was not nothing to me,' she said and began to march away.

'Kittie!' he called after her. 'You know I didn't mean it that way. Kittie!'

She remembered she had left her shawl, and contemplated returning for it, but she continued to walk, attempting to shrug Chester from her thoughts.

'You take, Kittie,' he shouted, angrier now, 'but what do you give, huh?'

She quickened her pace, wishing the wind would pick up and carry his words away. She tried to imagine when this feud might resolve itself, but she could not find an answer. Something had been torn and she ached all the more for it.

Despite the temptation to forgive, to turn back and lie on the grass again, she knew she owed it to herself to leave.

'Like I said,' Chester shouted, spurred on by her retreat, 'a thief!'

She broke into a run, aware of how ridiculous she must look, not being practised in doing so. She heard no laughter though, only Chester's words carried about in a summer's gust, as though nature felt some kinship in her heartbreak.

Is this the end of us, she asked herself, *or else another, harder moment in love?*

'Goodbye, Chester,' Kittie said, tears filling her eyes.

October 1879

'He'll be back.'

Kittie turned fitfully, breaking from sleep at the sound of her sister's voice.

'He'll be back, you fool,' Elena continued, holding her sister's shoulders.

Kittie sat up sharply. 'What?' she asked, her face slick with sweat.

'Didn't I just know you had a fever?' Elena said. 'I'm calling for the doctor.'

'He's left,' Kittie said. She drew her hands down her face, hoping to pull the sleep free from her mind.

'And he'll be back,' Elena said, smiling as her sister's fitfulness stilled.

'Who will be?' Kittie caught sight of the brown bottle by her bedside and her skull throbbed.

'Kittie, you've been calling out to yourself these past moments. "Goodbye, Emerson!" you called. "Goodbye, Emerson!" Even from downstairs I heard you.'

'"Goodbye, Chester,"' Kittie protested. 'I was saying, "Goodbye, Chester."' Her heart raced, thinking back over the dream.

'Oh, Slim,' Elena said, rubbing her sister's arms. 'You're about as confused as anyone in love has a right to be.'

Kittie caught her breath and tried for a moment to still her mind.

'Didn't I know it, though?' Elena continued. 'He came here, and there was me thinking him right for Blanche when all the while, you were busy falling in love with him.'

Kittie stared at her sister, astonished at her assumption.

'Ain't there no use pretending,' Elena said. 'I've an eye for these things.'

Kittie looked out in front of her and only then noticed the dipping light of an autumn dusk. She had slept through the whole day.

'He's older than could be called suitable, mind. But so long as he's decent, that shouldn't matter.'

246

'El,' Kittie said.

Her sister noted her mood and patted her leg. 'Fine,' she said. 'I'll leave you now, Slim; now that your nightmares have passed. Take a moment and then come down to the kitchen. I'll fix you something.'

Elena left the room and Kittie rifled through her memories of the day.

I am sure it was Chester, she thought to herself. *His hair, his face.*

She stepped from her bed and walked to her parents' room once more.

A heavy snow had fallen and coated the town in white. The road from the house through town was flecked with boot prints, showing the dark ground beneath. Workers shovelled snow from the unroofed frames of their buildings, while black birds swam in the bloated clouds, as though seeking to mirror the boot prints beneath them.

Kittie recalled Chester's face, her heart stinging for not having seen it in so long. She debated whether it might have been better never to have seen it again; the heartache was as fresh as she remembered it being on the day.

In a moment, she was shaken from heart to soul. A spark lit up her mind's confusion and all became clear, even in its impossibility and betrayal. As much as she tried to deny it, she knew she had seen Chester since – not an impersonation of him, but his true light, shining out in eyes and voice. Her mind knew as much, but, greater than that, her heart knew it too and its curious beating confirmed it. She placed her palm flat against it and willed it to still. Yet, as she sought an answer that did not concern Chester, she knew there was no fooling a heart.

23

October 1879

Umbründ took a lantern from his pack and struck a match to light it. His hands were shaking and it took him several attempts to summon a flame. Such nervousness had plagued Umbründ since the house. Emerson knew the doctor to possess a calmness by which he orchestrated his life, and its absence that night had begun to worry him.

The doctor had always talked with a brazen casualness and the only real signs alluding to something beneath the surface showed when Emerson placed memories for him to find. Yet, even then, there was a type of ecstasy, a joy the doctor shared at accruing a past. This seemed different, but not entirely.

Emerson hit on the similarity in that moment. Stunned, he realised this was the first time he had witnessed the doctor remembering something. All else had been whimsy or the determination to have memories. Now, not only did Umbründ remember, but he seemed troubled by his ability to do so.

'Excuse an old man,' the doctor said, laughing nervously and finally lighting the lantern.

In its weak glow, Emerson noted how old and tired Umbründ looked. In contrast to the man he'd met with in town, this doctor was grey of skin and sweating into his collar, the starch there blooming yellow like a fungus.

'Where are we headed?' Emerson asked. He tried to hide the impatience in his voice but this was betrayed by the silence of the night that followed.

'Somewhere safe,' Umbründ said. 'Somewhere far away. Away from the interruptions.'

Emerson had recognised snatches of the path from when he and Kittie had gone in search of Blanche. Instead of continuing on to the cabin, though, the doctor had led him away from the railway line and up onto a winding path that snaked its way under the thick plume of trees. It was only after nearly an hour's walking that their path broke from its cover and Emerson saw how high they were, how distant from everything he knew and could call safe.

A few lights shone in New Georgetown, like pinpricks in a curtain drawn against the day. Emerson gazed back at them and, before he could turn to the doctor, Umbründ had set off again up the road. Emerson jogged to catch up with him and tugged at the back of his coat.

'Where are we headed to? Please, doc.'

This plea fell on deaf ears as Umbründ climbed further up the road. The doctor was wheezing as he pushed on, higher and higher, but he moved with such speed, it was as if a spirit inhabited his tired form.

The woods were quiet around them and all Emerson could hear was the occasional ring of the doctor's shoe buckles, loose in their leather straps. Not long after they had left town, an animal call rang out, harsh and fearful. Umbründ's hand had moved to his hip before he smiled casually at Emerson and made to brush a leaf from his coat.

'Why did you bring the gun?' Emerson asked.

It was then that Umbründ finally stopped. He spread his feet apart and breathed heavily, head bowed, before turning to look over his shoulder. The lantern was on the other side of him and Emerson could only see his face where the light chose to nestle – the lines of age ablaze.

'These woods ...' Umbründ started. 'They are filled with things I would not like to meet unarmed.'

Emerson looked around him and narrowed his eyes against the darkness, hoping to focus on the deep layers of trees and what lay within them.

'Like what?' he asked.

'You've heard the stories?'

'I can't say I have.'

'Then that's for the best.'

Umbründ faced forward again and pushed on up the hill. Emerson took one more look about him and then, as the doctor's lantern light receded, quickened his pace.

At a turn in the road, Emerson noted a cluster of old trees. Their trunks had curved in on one another and little space was left between them, as though they were conspiratorial in their closeness.

As the doctor turned the corner, Emerson reached out and touched the sticky bark. The trees still held their leaves, even so close to winter. He tried to brush the sugary sap from his hand, but it only bunched up the fabric of his trouser leg.

'Come on, my boy,' he heard the doctor call. His voice was a distant echo.

January 1863

'Drink your tea, Emerson,' his mother said.

She stood in the doorway, a handkerchief pressed to her mouth, arms folded as though against a cold night. Yet it was warm, the stove in the corner of their room glowing bright. Emerson's forehead was beaded in sweat, but each time he complained, his mother only threw on another blanket.

'Emerson,' she said, snatching his mind back from someplace else. 'Concentrate.'

'Yes, Mother,' he answered.

He lifted the tea to his lips and blew softly over the surface of the liquid. The steam wafted away from him and he imagined it blowing all the way to his mother. She seemed to realise this and smiled softly, reaching out her hands to clutch the absent cloud. She laughed and he did too.

The murmurs of the house made him feel uncomfortable. He enjoyed the moments of quiet between the two of them, as if they were a family like any other. Yet they were often hounded by calls: the wails of the father and the other mothers running throughout the house. The cellar beneath them was constantly raucous with idle gossip and the washing of clothes.

His mother came into the room, watching the landing worriedly as she did so. If the father caught her checking in on her boy and not out on the porch, he would give her a black eye.

'Has it passed?' she asked as she sat on the side of the bed, placing a hand against his wet skin.

Emerson shook his head and he noticed the sadness in her eyes. He had suffered such nightmares those past nights: demons padding through the cellar of an old building, limbs in strange configurations and a madman cutting into all flesh. He had kept half the house up with his screams. Although the horrors had died away, he saw things still. His fever was another world, in which he hated to dwell. And his mother, like him, was beginning to understand that his condition, unlike his fever, would never pass.

'Tell me of the last one, Emerson,' she said. 'The lesser ones, if it eases your heart. Steer clear of the horrors.'

He hunched further into the blankets.

'If you speak of it, it may pass,' his mother urged.

Emerson reluctantly thought back to the night before and the most recent memories that had carried over. They pressed keenly at his mind and by inviting one in, others followed, spilling out. Hazy-faced men were crouched about campfires, one at the centre of their conversation. This man held their attention, counting coins as he promised things, like a travelling showman. Emerson recognised him as his father, and yet had only seen him from the inside of his own mind.

'She'll be pretty,' his father said.

'She'd better be,' his client replied.

'Real, too. She exists, is my meaning.'

'So I can choose anyone?'

'So long as I seen 'em. It's mine, then it's yours.'

'Can I describe her to you first?'

His father smiled. 'That'll work fine.'

The client's smile was drawn up tightly by a smooth young scar.

'Emerson?' his mother said.

Emerson surfaced from his memory, returning to the room.

'I'm looking,' he replied.

He went back again, this time to a more intimate meeting. His father sat up in a hospital bed, his side and arm bandaged. This dream was closer to the horrors.

'It helps you forget?' the clouded client asked.

'It don't just help, it makes you forget.'

'Forgive me if I'm a little pessimistic.'

'I don't care for fancy words.'

'How much?'

'Fee depends on trauma.'

The client drew a fine leather wallet from his white coat. Emerson marked the banknotes, fancier than coins; a greater fee surely meant a greater trauma.

'Was that it?' his mother asked.

Emerson leaned to his side and let free a long, rattling cough. 'It was.' He nodded.

'Did you see him?'

Emerson nodded again, weary of her line of questioning. She smiled and edged closer to him on the bed.

'How is he? Is he alive?'

'He is,' Emerson replied. He did not seek to mention the bandages.

'When was this? Recent?'

'Mother, I don't want to.'

She placed her hand against Emerson's brow again. 'Think, Emerson.'

'It was last week.'

She sucked in a sharp breath and drew her hand away from his forehead, her fingernail scratching the skin as she did so. Emerson gasped weakly.

'I'm sorry, Emerson,' she said, rubbing a fleck of skin from her nail. 'I didn't mean to.'

A noise came from the doorway and she turned. It was one of the other mothers. Emerson knew her as Phebe. She was older than most and her character seemed to slump in the loosely dipping folds of her skin.

'He's making his rounds,' she said.

His mother turned back to Emerson and brushed the scratch on his forehead.

'Can you think for me, son?'

He was reluctant to do so again. He closed his eyes and hoped his mother was unable to tell the difference.

'Now, think real hard,' she said.

He moved his eyes beneath his lids to give the impression.

'He asks for you. What you want for me to tell him?' Phebe called from the doorway.

'Tell him, go hang,' his mother spat.

'I'll get to telling him you're in the latrine,' Phebe said, and moved away.

Emerson could feel his mother's gaze on him. Her hand tightened around his.

Why does she care for him, he asked himself, *when all he did was leave her?*

After long enough had passed, he opened his eyes and saw his mother's desperate face.

'Now be quick, son,' she said. 'Was it recent? Was he well?'

She moved still closer towards him, his hand twisted uncomfortably in her grasp.

'Was he coming back to me? Was he coming back to us?'

Emerson blinked dumbly at his mother. Her face was drawn out in a vacant smile, as if all her happiness rested on the answer to that sole question.

'He's well,' Emerson lied. 'He's coming back, Mother.'

Emerson's mother sobbed and pressed her hand urgently against her trembling lips. 'I knew he would,' she said. 'I knew he would.'

She stood from the bed and dropped his hand.

'I have to go, Emerson,' she said, moving to the door. 'Before the father comes looking for me. You understand?'

Emerson nodded and she hurried back over to him.

'Oh. my boy,' she said. 'Oh, my boys. You were his gift to me, Emerson. He came and changed me. He took away the evil and left you for me.'

Emerson started to grow fearful of the father coming near the room.

His mother moved to the door to check the father wasn't there. Then she turned and stood as she had done before.

'You'll be a good man, Emerson. A good man, like your father.' She slipped away from the room, pulling the door closed behind her.

Emerson felt a void open up inside him, his father's hands creeping through to knead the present.

He closed his eyes and listened to the soft clank of wooden chimes in the yard, toying with one another in the summer's evening. His mind grew heavy and he slid into sleep.

Less than two weeks along, Emerson was the one standing by the bedside. He watched his mother, pale with tuberculosis. She was weak, but he remained hopeful she would live. He was alone in this hope, however; the other mothers and the father walked past the room as though it were a tomb they did not wish to dwell on.

'I have something to tell you, Mother,' Emerson said.

She opened her eyes with great effort. 'Emerson?'

He walked closer to the bed and took her outstretched hand.

'What is it, son?'

Emerson felt the words tread cowardly back from the edge of his mouth before the guilt rushed them forward.

'He is not coming.'

His mother stared at him blankly. 'Who do you mean? The doctor?'

'No, Mother,' Emerson said. 'The doctor is here. I mean my father.'

Emerson's mother began to weep.

'Mother, please,' Emerson said, trying to calm her.

'Why?' she asked him. 'Does he not love me?'

'No, Mother. He's . . .'

Emerson wondered whether the truth might only serve to make her final moments worse. Yet he couldn't watch his mother, so enmeshed in her love for one man, believe him to not care for her.

'He's hurt,' Emerson said.

Watching her tearful, reddened eyes, Emerson felt his own begin to sting. She made a noise and Emerson leaned closer.

'You will be a good man, Emerson,' she said.

He recalled these words from before and felt relieved to hear them again now.

'Thank you, Mother,' he said.

She smiled faintly, blood staining her lips. 'Find him.'

Emerson froze at her words.

'Emerson,' his mother said, turning her feeble gaze upon him. 'Find your father. For me.'

That night, Emerson slept on a cot pushed to the side of his mother's room. He watched her until his eyes could stay open no longer. Her words refused to leave him, but he did his best to explain the impossibility of the task. He wished to believe his father dead, yet he couldn't argue with the visions he continued to have – the carry-over from his father's mind; sign enough that he lived still.

When eventually Emerson found sleep, his dream took him

back to the appointment – the leather wallet open and the notes folded into his father's bloodied hand. The face of the client remained hazy.

'Will this convince you?'

'That it will.'

The client's hand gripped his father's. 'These memories are troubling,' he said.

'They often are.'

'No,' the client insisted. 'These are horrors unbound.'

'I care not,' his father said, counting the notes.

'Good. Good.'

'Can I ask you a question though, friend?' said his father. 'Before we begin. Might sound funny.'

'Please.'

'Your accent. Where you from?'

October 1879

As they came to the top of the hill, Emerson caught sight of a building off to their right, which nestled among the tall trees. There was something troubling about it. It was true that, in the night, little looked welcoming, but still there was something about this place that twisted at Emerson's insides – not entirely because of its instant horror and strangeness, but because he could swear to having been there before.

'This a hotel?' he asked.

'It was. And then a hospital. But, alas, no more,' the doctor replied.

'And what is it now?' Emerson asked.

'A prison,' Umbründ breathed before drawing his gun.

Emerson looked at the weapon, too large in the doctor's grasp and glorious like a cannon. The light from the lantern's flame ran down the finely polished barrel and Emerson thought on whether the weapon had ever been used before.

The doctor twitched the gun in the air, motioning for Emerson to step forward.

'Should I raise my hands too, doc?' he asked.

The doctor looked at the gun and let his hand fall harmlessly by his side. He let out a shrill, forced laugh, which echoed around them and, through some haunting trajectory, seemed to sound from within the building before them.

'You are not my prisoner, my boy,' he said.

Emerson walked ahead of him, feeling the hardness of stone beneath his boots.

In front of them, one of the two doors at the entrance lay ajar. The light crept in and Emerson could make out a fancy floor pattern of black and white tiles. Leaves and old, indistinct items littered the place.

As they stepped inside, Emerson noted the concierge's desk and a rusted bell, trying its best to shake off the decay. The hooks were filled with room keys and Emerson felt a strange tug at his insides.

A trespassing thought, he surmised. *That can't be mine.*

A grand staircase rose up before them, its carpet held in place by brass rods. Emerson could feel the doctor at his back. The hotel orbited about them in the lantern's light. It all seemed familiar to Emerson, and he had not frequented hotels enough for that to be a coincidence.

As he looked about him, he noticed a shape on the floor in front of the stairs. He stepped towards it and heard Umbründ follow. As the light grew stronger the shape became obvious, but Emerson avoided naming it until the very last moment.

'Someone's been here before us,' he said, staring at the footprint.

A small hand in Emerson's back pushed him towards the staircase. He stood rigid and longed for the chill of the night, its freshness and clarity a month's ride from the stench and wicked ether that filled the hotel.

The hand pushed him again and Emerson turned. 'Where have you brought . . . ?'

He halted in his words and looked down at his chest, where the long, glittering barrel of the doctor's pistol pointed.

'Now, Emerson,' Umbründ said. 'Now you are my prisoner.'

24

October 1879

Kyoko smiled at Odell as his eyes creaked open. The room settled. He returned the smile, his lips cracking like a statue breaking its pose. He murmured and lifted a hand to his face.

At least I'm alive, he thought.

Clay's kick had felt hard enough to cave in his chest like a rotted tree.

'O—' Kyoko began, before her voice faltered. She brought a small, delicate hand to her mouth and hushed herself.

Odell reached out and a sharp shout escaped his mouth at the pain he felt in his chest. He breathed in and it was like drawing spines into the flesh of his throat and lungs.

He lay in a room on the ground floor of the tavern. A dish was by his bedside, the water marbled pink. A single tooth sat in the middle of it, like some ivory island.

Kyoko brought a drink of water to his lips. He lifted himself again, tentatively. It took her hand around the nape of his neck to bring him forward enough to touch the glass's edge.

'Who did this?' she asked as he drank.

Odell considered sharing Clay's name with Kyoko, but thought on the hell he had promised, how he would likely deliver on destroying the piano and burning his father's shop. In a way that went against all that seemed right, Odell would have to keep Clay's secret from Kyoko, just as he had kept Kyoko's from Clay.

'I don't know,' he said finally.

Kyoko shifted in her seat.

'I'm sorry,' Odell said, on the verge of tears. 'For being a burden.'

Kyoko ran a hand across his cheek.

Leave it there, Odell pleaded in his mind, *forever*.

'You are never a burden,' Kyoko said. 'I care for you.'

Odell was unsure whether she meant she was caring for him or cared for him by way of her heart. Her manner of speech clouded the fact. He intended to ask her, but she stepped away from his side.

When Kyoko returned, he recognised the lantern in her grasp and his heart grew as a flame inside it might.

'There's more?' he asked her.

She nodded. 'Are you well enough to listen?'

Odell nodded and lay back in bed as Kyoko began to talk.

'The first American I met,' she said, 'bought me.

'After the sea took my father, the ship was little more than a wreck. An American ship was sent to accompany us.'

Kyoko paused for a moment while Odell coughed uneasily.

'By the time we arrived in San Francisco,' she continued, 'the crew considered me a bad omen. They blamed the storm on me and said I had killed my mother. This I learned later, from my master.'

'Your master?' Odell asked.

'Yes,' she replied. 'The crew were worried I would endanger

the treaty and that they would sink making their return. So they sold me.'

'Sold?' Odell whispered, fighting the tug of sleep.

'I would fetch a good price. But they wanted quick money and carried me around the harbour, as if touting a mule for sale.'

March 1860

'How much for the Chink?' Hasel asked.

'No Chink,' one of the crew replied. 'Japanese.'

Hasel pushed his hat back and scratched his head. 'No fooling?'

'No fooling,' another of the crew replied.

Hasel looked about the crowded harbour behind him, widening his shoulders as though to conceal the entire group. He was a wide man and this was not an entirely impossible idea.

'Then how much for the Japanese?' he asked, lowering his voice.

'Two hundred,' a third crew member offered.

'Sweet Christ, boy,' he said. 'That's enough to buy the whole stinking island.'

'No deal!' the man huffed, angry at Hasel's reaction, and he turned the baby from him.

'Now, hold on,' Hasel said. 'That's not what I'm saying.'

Hasel walked from the group and looked about him, between the ships and cargo. He waved away an approaching boy and then walked back to the Japanese crew.

'I'll give you one hundred dollars,' he said finally, pulling the money from the inside of his jacket.

'Deal,' the first crew member said.

'No deal,' said the third, holding Kyoko.

'Now, which is it?' Hasel asked.

The men argued in Japanese and Hasel looked about him, disliking the sound of their language. Finally, the men seemed to reach some agreement, with the first crew member holding some sort of rank over the third. The second only kept his eyes trained on the money.

'Hand it over,' Hasel urged.

The third crew member handed Kyoko over and Hasel wrapped her in his thick arms.

'What a beauty!' he said. 'A fine little thing.'

One of the crew pulled the money from Hasel's fingers.

'Her name is Kyoko,' the first crew member said plainly.

'Well, now, this is a fine piece of business for an otherwise indifferent afternoon,' he said, jostling the baby in his arms. 'You boys ...'

The men were walking away, the first crew member occasionally looking back while the others padded along determinedly. At the first turn of the harbour, they disappeared from sight and Hasel looked down at Kyoko.

'It's as quick as that,' he said. 'And now you're mine.'

Hasel M'Closky was a Virginian and had been in San Francisco with an eye to buying a new ship. He had travelled there alone, while his wife remained in Virginia. She was fearful of her husband's foolishness with a dollar, and was right to be, as, with one hundred dollars less, he began his journey home with a young Japanese child and no ship in harbour.

Hasel paid for a trader from San Francisco's Chinatown to accompany them back to Virginia. She had lately given birth to a baby without air enough in its lungs, and so she wept from her teat for no more than a ghost.

Figuring a Chinese woman to be much like a Japanese, Hasel expected her to care for the child. And, more from the promise of money than any maternal instinct, she did. She sang her lullabies in her native tongue and, as the weeks passed, took to wrapping the baby in clothes of her own when Kyoko's were soiled beyond use. The woman cradled Kyoko all the way to Virginia and was by then more of a mother than the child had ever had.

'What hell is this you've brought to our doorstep?' Esther M'Closky had asked, seeing the Chinese woman and the Asian babe in her arms.

Hasel had hastily explained that she wasn't his. Esther had quizzed her husband regardless, questioning why he deemed a Japanese child a more worthy purchase than the boat he had set out for.

Through an inconceivable understanding that only marriage can abide, Hasel brought Kyoko into the home and she was raised as his own. Esther made no allowance for a second mother, though, and the Chinese woman was turned away – cast free in a strange state, prejudice being the only constant from San Francisco.

Hasel was eager that his new daughter be embraced by his wife. Their house was remote enough for the new addition not to attract attention, but Esther hid her away like a stolen treasure each time their door shook with the unexpected calling of a visitor.

Soon enough, Hasel surpassed whatever patience Esther had been graced with. No more than a year later, he returned home having once more neglected to purchase a boat. Instead, he had bought a tavern over in the nearest town.

'It will make twice the money any ship would have!'

Esther looked on her husband with disdain, a deeper determination forming in the depths of her eyes.

'Our crew will pour drinks now. You shall see, it is a fine plan.'

But Esther decided never to see this plan come to fruition. By the next time Hasel returned home, all that remained was Kyoko, crying and filthy, sitting on the floor in the unsettled dust from the departed furniture.

Hasel left the house, too, deciding to live in his new tavern with his bastard babe, in Scottsbluff. As the years passed, Kyoko grew tall enough to look from its windows, down into the streets full of gazes she would best avoid.

'Now, Kyoko,' Hasel would say, pulling her back. 'You know you can't be seen.'

He spoke English to her and taught her enough to reply. Yet, eager to keep her otherness intact, he kept her from becoming fluent. Instead, he encouraged her to learn the language of her home – to afford her a retrospective heritage. He purchased, at great expense, books that contained Japanese words, and he instructed her to read from them. Her language was built around the principles of trade – that being the key interaction Americans sought to have with Japan.

With nothing else to fill her days, and unable to escape the tavern, Kyoko pored over the pages, setting foot in Japan for the first time, albeit through language. Yet the happenings of the town always drew her curiosity. She would neglect her learning and stare out at the faces, hopeful of spotting one like her own.

Hasel would tug the curtain shut before replacing her at the windowsill.

'You can look through,' he'd say. 'Didn't I buy the thin kind so you could?'

Kyoko nodded and returned, cautiously, to the fabric's edge.

'These people won't take kindly to foreign beauty. They ain't accustomed to it. You is like a bird, your feathers too bright for their eyes.'

Kyoko nodded all the while, heeding her father's words as he moved to fetch something from an old trunk.

'Now, look at this,' he said, pacing excitedly back towards her.

In his arms, he carried an object wrapped in a muddied sheet. Kyoko tilted her head at the package and, as instructed, sat back on her heels on the floor.

'It's for you, my Kyoko,' Hasel said, handing it over. 'My bird.'

Kyoko unwrapped the sheet and gasped at what she found.

'A lantern,' she said.

'Yes, my dear.' Hasel beamed. 'A lantern. But not just that. *The* lantern. From your ship. Look here.' He ran a finger along the Japanese characters etched into the metal.

'Nagasaki,' Kyoko said.

'Good,' Hasel replied. 'You know it. I knew you would. You read and you read. It's important a person knows the tongue from where they came.'

'Nagasaki,' Kyoko repeated. 'Is it home?'

Hasel frowned. 'Scottsbluff is home, my dear. But this is where you came from.'

Kyoko nodded.

'You know what it means?' Hasel asked eagerly. 'I found out by chance. Asked a learned man, and didn't he know? It means "long cape". Those Japs know some tricks, don't they? Hidden words in all their names.'

'Long cape,' Kyoko tried.

'And, with that, I done decided on the name of the tavern. This here is the Long Cape. It's a tribute to you, my Kyoko.'

Kyoko nodded and ran her finger across the characters again.

'Nagasaki,' she said.

'The Long Cape,' Hasel replied, looking about the room.

October 1879

'A year later, he was dead.'

'How?' Odell asked.

'The war,' Kyoko replied plainly. 'He found a ship, eventually, and died on it.'

'I'm sorry,' Odell said.

Kyoko shifted on the bed's edge and her eyes darted to Odell.

'Do you think I mourned him?' she asked.

'I don't know,' Odell replied, confused. 'He was sort of your daddy, weren't he?'

'I was his prisoner,' Kyoko said. 'I was glad to hear he died. I remember leaving here at night to look at names on the town hall door. And then one time I saw his.'

'What then?' Odell asked hungrily.

'Scottsbluff turned to New Georgetown. He left me the tavern. His wife was lost to him. And so it fell to his daughter.'

Odell felt a strong will to still Kyoko's remembering, watching the pain spread across her face.

'So you were here all along?' Odell asked. 'The Bird.'

'Yes, the Bird,' Kyoko replied. 'Like a ghost.'

She reached across and took Odell's hand.

'That is, until you came, Odell. Now I am Kyoko again.'

Odell smiled and his heart warmed at how easily she now spoke his name, the sound as natural to her mouth as it was to his own. He dwelled on her words and delighted in the responsibility of making her happy.

He went to tell her as much, but his lips would not move. A heavy breath escaped them and his injuries grew numb. Exhaustion worked alongside his happiness in that moment to claim his body and send him into a deep sleep, populated by kinder things than his waking life.

When he awoke, the room was empty. His head swam, thoughts flailing around to remember where he was. He felt sick at the stale smell in the room and shifted painfully from the bed.

He tried to open the window, but it was fixed too tight in the latch and his ribs ached from trying.

Odell left his room and walked across the tavern floor. He picked up the keys from where Hammond had left them on the bar top and unlocked the door, stepping out into the cool night. The most hesitant snowfall had started and Odell stretched out his arms to catch the flakes in the hair on his skin.

I've never seen snow, he realised.

The gas lamps along the street's edge hummed quietly and Odell watched the snow flit across their slices of light. One blazed brightly and Odell feared it might explode. He shielded his eyes, but no sound came. Peering through his fingers, he saw how it shone stronger than the others, like a star set on the end of an iron post.

'What in the hell?' he said aloud.

The light gradually faded and, as Odell focused, he saw a figure standing beneath it. He strained to make out who it was, but the image wriggled against his efforts, changing in its loose shape in the light as though a mirage.

He stepped down from the porch and tried to shield his eyes from the glare of the lamp so he could better make out the figure. The bottom of the gas lamp's bulb was caked in rust-like burns where the wick had run too close to the glass. Odell watched in astonishment as this began to drop from the lamp, like honey from a hive.

The red-brown liquid fell down, only to be caught in mid air and frame a person's face. Instantly, Odell recognised who it was.

'Ora,' he said. 'Ora!' This time he spoke louder, calling her.

She raised her head to look at him and stepped from under the lamp and on up the road, becoming incomplete and half-lit as she crossed over into the shadow between gas lamps.

'Ora!' he called again.

With difficulty he walked further into the road, searching for her all the while. Another streetlamp, halfway towards Marianne House, glowed fiercely and underneath it stood Ora once more.

With his head still rattling from Clay's beating, Odell was aware that what he was looking at was not entirely to be trusted. He rubbed at his eyes and thought on how he missed his sister, wondering perhaps if confronting the thought might do away with whatever fantasy was forming in front of him.

Yet she remained. Odell saw her as clearly as though she were real.

He ran up the road, calling out, hushing his voice as best he could lest someone might hear. Ora moved further on and broke into a gentle run herself. She glanced over her shoulder and looked at Odell, laughing. He laughed back and remembered how they had played at such games when they were a family.

Odell pulled to a halt, out of breath and his body aching like never before. He spat and felt sick rise in his throat, the pain in his stomach unbearable. He stared down at the mess and noted how it was marbled with blood. He wanted to show someone. He wanted to show Chester.

He raised his head and saw Ora continuing up the road and climbing the gentle hill. Odell spat again and carried on after her.

Where is she leading me? he wondered.

Just before Marianne House, Ora stood in the middle of the path. Odell could see her clearly now. She smiled at him, but this was somehow different – a sadder smile; a smile goodbye.

Odell walked towards her, reaching out an arm.

'Stay,' he said.

But where he had expected his hand to meet Ora, it broke apart her image like smoke and he was alone once more.

'Ora?' he called out.

He stared about him, calling aloud again, wondering if it wasn't some trick. He was reminded of the contraption in the theatre – a thing that seemed to conjure stories out of light. He wondered if the same thing wasn't at play now. He turned round on the spot, looking for conspirators in such a trick.

Facing down towards town, a pool of light stretched out before him, spilling his shadow across the ground like a rug.

'Odell?' he heard. 'What the hell? Jesus, are you okay?'

Odell turned and saw Elena standing in the doorway.

'Did you see Ora?' he asked.

'What?' Elena replied.

'I've got so much to tell her,' he continued.

Elena stared at him, dumbfounded.

'She's been here the whole time,' Odell continued. 'I knew she was okay.'

Odell stumbled about on the spot and felt the sick rise in his throat again. He swallowed it down and steadied himself on the steps that ran up to the door.

'Are you drunk?' Elena asked.

Odell laughed.

'I want to see my sister. Will you get her? I've got to tell her – about Hasel and the audition. About her.'

'Odell,' Elena said, irritated, thinking on Blanche trying to rest upstairs.

'Fine. Then I gotta tell you something. It's only right.'

'Odell, please. Go home. These games have to stop.'

'Huh? What games? Before I go, I gotta tell you something.' Odell clapped his hands together, trying to get his words out.

'I said, go home, Odell,' Elena snapped. 'This isn't the time!'

'I've got to tell you!' Odell shouted, insistent.

'Odell, you goddamn idiot! What the hell are you doing here? Don't you know when a thing is done?'

Elena turned to close the door, but then spun back, angrier still.

'My sister could be dying,' she said. 'And you pay me a visit in the early hours? Risk waking her up?'

'Whose sister? My sister isn't dead,' Odell insisted, mishearing her.

He smiled at the crazed thought. Then it dropped from his face as quick as the weight in his heart. He pictured her in the street and realised what he had seen, her smile goodbye as much confirmation as the otherworldly could offer.

'Not your sister, you fool,' Elena said. 'My sister!'

'Kittie's dying?' Odell asked, looking back towards town, only half hearing her.

Elena shook on the spot. She came down from the doorway and seized Odell by his collar. She turned him towards her.

'I don't know how this happened to you,' she said, looking over his wounds. 'But I can only hope whoever done it knocked some goddamn sense into you. And seeing as it's the day for it, Odell, you can have some from me too. I would rather court your ass of a father than you. Hell, I'd rather his horse than you, Odell. You are nothing! You are some weed that's grown out of the ground and nobody wants around, but can't nobody be bothered to pull you out, you're so insignificant.'

Odell stood there, stunned.

'I'm sorry,' was all he could say.

'Sorry? Go hang, Odell.'

'I ...' he began.

Elena welled up in anger and pushed him onto the ground. She towered over him.

'You. Are. Nothing to me,' she hissed.

Instead of saying those words, Elena might as well have dug her fingers into his heart. He kicked away from under her and stood, treading tentatively backwards as though out onto a precipice, before turning to run back into town and to the tavern.

Elena's heart raced, and only after Odell had gone did she realise what she had said.

Who am I, she thought, *to crush that boy's heart?*

When she returned to her room, Clay had begun to get dressed.

'What's happening?' he asked.

'You're leaving?' she said, moving closer so as to keep their voices down.

'I was about to come down. Was that Odell?'

Elena nodded and Clay stung with fear.

'What did he want?' he asked, reaching out to her tentatively.

She pressed herself against him, linking her arms around his wide back. 'Something about Ora. He was hurt. Made no sense. Not a bit.'

'Ora, huh?' Clay asked.

'He needed to tell me something. Only I told him something first. Damn, Clay, I was hard on him.'

'What about Ora? Did he say where she was?'

'Clay, I don't know,' Elena said. 'He was all nonsense. Please, can we go back to bed?'

Clay ran a hand over Elena's hair and took to undressing again. He cradled her in his arms, stroking her slim back.

'I was hard on him, Clay. Cruel, even.'

Clay kissed her cheek and sighed heavily into her neck. 'Whatever you said to him, that boy needed to hear it.'

Elena nodded and took Clay's hand in her own. 'Still, I needn't have been so cruel,' she said.

Clay's heart beat quicker and he decided then what had to be done.

I'll not lose everything, he thought to himself.

25

October 1879

Emerson kept his head low as he watched his snow-speckled boots tread through the hotel's corridors. He still felt agitated by his familiarity with the place, unable to distinguish between the memories lodged in his skull and decide whether this recognition belonged to a phantom or himself. He stared at what passed beneath his muddied boots, afraid that by looking up he might meet an unwelcome memory as easily as a hotel guest stepping from their room.

Broken glass was scattered all about the floor. The lantern's light spun within the fragments, gold and pulsing, as though each piece promised a window's view of the hell that raged below. Finally, they came to a room like any other.

'Stop now,' Umbründ said.

Emerson stopped and looked over his shoulder cautiously.

'In here,' Umbründ continued.

The door was ajar, and pushing it open more fully, Emerson was met by a cloud of pungent rot. He reeled backwards, knocking into the doctor, who reacted quickly and clipped the formidable butt of his pistol across Emerson's skull.

Emerson fell onto a knee and propped himself up with one hand, while the other clasped to stop the stench winding its way down his throat.

'Up! Up!' Umbründ said, as though training an animal.

Emerson stood, feeling the warm run of blood from where the doctor had hit him. He stepped inside the room and saw a line of hospital beds on either side. The frames were rusted and Emerson supposed they had been here since the war. Some of the mattresses were torn open, while others were unrecognisable for their decay and caved in on themselves in the blackest of tones. The window was boarded up and Emerson was glad such a room was kept from the outside world.

In the middle of the room were two chairs, facing one another. The doctor seemed unaffected by the smell and marched Emerson towards them. Umbründ pulled Emerson by the shoulder and brought him to a stop. The doctor's fancy shoes clipped their way back towards the door and Emerson felt the compulsion to turn.

'Sit,' Umbründ said.

Emerson turned tentatively.

'Sit,' Umbründ repeated.

Emerson still felt nauseous and was glad to sit down. The chair creaked under his weight and he sat there, hands on his legs like an obedient schoolboy. He traced the continual run of blood beside his eye, from where Umbründ had hit him with the gun. He wanted to wipe at it, but dared not make a sudden move with the pistol trained on him still.

The doctor sat down opposite him and rested the gun on his thigh. Emerson stared at it and watched as Umbründ's hand flitted awkwardly across its shape. The doctor appeared to be unfamiliar with holding a weapon, which only deepened Emerson's fear.

Emerson expected the confrontation to end with his own

death and, to a degree, could comprehend that. What he could not think on, though, was urging the doctor into a hasty shot and spending a long night dying with a hole in his stomach pumping black blood out onto the floor.

'Coincidence is a wonder, is it not?' Umbründ said.

Emerson tried to ignore his words, but could not help but be drawn into the temptation of fate. The image of his father, sitting with Umbründ all those years before, sat flush over the present.

'Is that why I'm here?' he asked.

Umbründ stared at Emerson a moment. 'You look like him,' he said.

'And how the hell would you know that?' Emerson said.

'He didn't remove as much as he thought,' Umbründ replied. 'He was weak. Perhaps not at his best. I remember too much, or else you'd be safe.'

Emerson remained silent.

'I can see that is a comparison you do not wish to hear,' Umbründ went on.

The blood on Emerson's face had run beside his mouth. He licked at it with his tongue. Why, he couldn't say.

'I need your help one last time,' Umbründ said. 'Something to remove. You do this and I'll allow you to live.'

Emerson refused to speak and Umbründ grew uncomfortable, shifting in his chair.

'Something happened,' the doctor said, 'with the girl.'

His words were ghostly in their meaning. Emerson thought on them and his heart quickened for thinking of Kittie.

'What's your meaning?' he asked.

'She's dead.'

Emerson clenched every fibre in his body. 'How?' he asked.

'We will come to that.'

'Right now is when we'll come to it.'

Umbründ patted the gun resting on his thigh. 'Be mindful of your position,' he said.

Emerson took a moment to think on what the doctor was saying. They had left Kittie at home with her sisters. She had to be well. The doctor could only mean Blanche, her fever having worsened, but how would he know if she had died?

'What girl, doctor?' he asked.

'The girl from the tavern. You met once, twice perhaps. Ora.'

Emerson remembered her and her red hair. 'How did she die?' he asked.

'I said, we'll come to that.' Umbründ was beginning to lose patience and turned the gun over in his hands. 'You can remove something so recent?' he asked.

'I can.'

'You'll take this from me. You'll take her from me and leave me with something else.'

Emerson felt sickened by the ease with which Umbründ dealt with his own mind, the way he believed himself free to pull memories out so readily and without recourse to his conscience. All the while, Emerson knew he and his father had enabled this; their trade created such possibilities; men could become acquainted with horror, knowing it need not bother them for long.

'I should have killed you back in town,' Emerson said.

Umbründ was ruffled by this. He stretched his arm out and pressed the barrel of the gun to Emerson's head. 'Then why didn't you?' he asked.

'I had to be sure,' Emerson replied. 'I'm not in the habit of killing.'

Umbründ felt the accusation in Emerson's words. 'When were you sure?'

Emerson delayed answering, so Umbründ pushed the barrel harder against his head.

'My shack. The third appointment,' Emerson said.

'How?'

'He left a sign.'

'Who did?'

'Amos.'

'Your father? What sign?'

'A mark. Something to tell me it was you. He knew you'd kill him, or else leave him to die. I suppose he wasn't as weak as you imag—'

'What was the sign? What was the mark?'

Umbründ's thumb teased the hammer of the pistol.

'My mother. He left her in your mind, where she had no right to be.'

The doctor thought on this.

'She's here?' he asked, tapping his head. 'Like a note from father to son?'

Emerson closed his eyes, expecting the shot.

'You can remove her, also. Take it all from me.'

Emerson nodded.

'So tell me,' Umbründ asked. 'What stopped you? We were in your shack, no? You could have killed me easily enough.'

'I came close,' Emerson said. 'But then . . .' He trailed off.

The doctor moved his eyes with remembering. 'Ah,' he laughed, thinking on Kittie's interruption. 'But she intervened. You were too love-struck to kill me and flee, weren't you? Too busy saving the Marianne sisters.'

'When did you know?' Emerson asked the doctor.

'From the beginning,' the doctor bragged. 'Such a unique talent. You would have to have known him. Or else be of his blood. You had too much faith in your father, Emerson, to think he removed all traces of himself. He only took the horrors.'

'And I can see you've found new ones. I think you flatter yourself,' Emerson said. 'If you had known, you would have fled or killed me sooner.'

'Or perhaps I needed you to remove everything,' the doctor said, 'and to finish what your father did not.'

Emerson said nothing.

'I have one more question for you, Emerson, before we begin.'

'How did I know you'd bite?' Emerson proffered. 'Fine. I have more memories of yours than you do. I am more Umbründ than you. I know you to be a man of dark intent. I placed that advertisement to draw a snake from its hole. I got to thinking that whatever you asked my father to clean up was likely to get messy again. You can be rid the crimes, doctor, but not the man. After all, we're each of us a devil on a carousel.'

Distant sounds echoed through the bowels of the hotel.

'Why did you bring me here?' Emerson asked.

'It is a place where secrets disappear easily, my boy. I discovered it some months ago.'

For the first time, Emerson indulged the tug of a memory in the place. He looked about him with that phantom recollection and realised it was not his memory, after all, but that of his father.

'You claim to remember,' Emerson said. 'But you don't remember as much as you think.'

'What do you speak of?' Umbründ asked, reluctantly breaking from his rehearsed behaviour.

'You found this place, doctor,' Emerson said. 'But not months ago – years.'

'What?' Umbründ spat.

'You were here before,' Emerson said. 'You and my father. During the war. This is where it happened.'

Umbründ looked firmly at Emerson. As much as he tried, the doctor could only recall Emerson's father, nothing of where they had been. He grew frustrated at the patchiness of his own mind, reluctantly realising the younger man knew more of his past than he.

Umbründ pushed the barrel of the gun painfully into Emerson's eye. He held it there and watched as Emerson raised his hands, jerking at the pain.

'Enough!' the doctor said.

He retracted the gun and Emerson sighed with relief. His eye throbbed as Umbründ stood before him. The swill of the past lapped over into the present and Emerson recalled leaving Amos in the state hospital those fourteen years ago, his father's plea to kill Umbründ still ringing in his ears.

26

October 1879

Clay stood in the road before the Long Cape, breathing deeply into the silent night. He carried with him a timber bag from the wood shop, the smell of kerosene slicing through the cold air.

He turned his head as Ellsworth ran up from an alleyway towards him, hunched close to the ground.

'Ain't nobody gonna see you,' Clay said.

Ellsworth stopped and straightened himself up, embarrassed.

'How are you planning on getting him out?'

'First, I'm gonna set the place alight.'

Ellsworth motioned to speak.

'Second,' Clay continued, raising a cautionary hand, 'you're gonna cry "fire" and wake the town up. Not before I've pulled Odell free, though.'

Ellsworth was silent for a moment.

'And the Bird?' he asked.

'Fuck the Bird,' Clay snapped back. 'What do you care about that degenerate, anyhow? This is about Odell and me, not the Bird.'

'So you pull him out and I shout "fire"?'

'That's right. Just allow me time enough to get him to the wood shop.'

'Then what?' Ellsworth asked.

'Then people are watching the tavern burn while I'm watching Odell. You do a fine enough job and people will think him dead in the flames, or otherwise coward enough to flee. You wait, you help, and then you come to me.'

'What are you gonna do to him?'

'Nothing you'll care to know right now,' Clay said. 'Now, go hide yourself nearby.'

Ellsworth hesitated a moment before retreating into the night. Clay watched him go.

He strode up to the tavern door and bunched a sheet about his wrist to punch through the glass. As he wound the fabric, he thought of the side door. If Odell had returned that night, drunk, he wouldn't have had sense to lock it.

Clay walked around the side of the building and tried the door. It pushed open and he smiled, satisfied at his stealth. He took one look around him before pouring the kerosene over the bar top and flinging it at the bottles stacked behind. He moved across the floor and wound the liquid around the space.

When the can was empty, he moved down the corridor, first taking occasion to look in on Ora's old room. It was empty, as it had been for some time. He didn't know whether he was relieved or pained she wasn't there. She was a threat to him, an embodiment of his betrayal of Elena, and yet he lusted after her still.

In the room opposite, he found Odell. The boy was sleeping, curled on the bed with the sheet tucked awkwardly between his limbs. His face had bloomed in an ugly fashion from Clay's beating and his hair hung limp and greasy across his features.

Clay walked out of the room in a fever and struck a match. The next moment, the tavern floor was ablaze. He staggered back, astonished at the speed of it. He rushed into Odell's room and, as the boy began to stir, hit him twice in the face. Odell whimpered as Clay dragged him from the bed and out of the room. As he pulled him past the bar and out of the side door, he heard the bottles beginning to pop and crack in the flames.

'Fire!' he heard Ellsworth call. 'Fire at the Long Cape!'

'Not yet, you fool!' Clay cursed to himself.

He heard a shift in the floorboards above him and imagined the Bird waking up with the calls. For a moment he was tempted to stay, steadfast in the flames, to see what the mystery was, what kind of ghoul resided in the tavern's nest of rooms.

'Kyoko,' Odell said.

Clay looked at him. 'What you say?'

'Kyoko!'

Odell struggled from Clay's grip, continuing to shout and clawing his way to the stairs. Clay pulled Odell's head up and brought it down onto the first step in a dull thud. Odell whimpered and was out. Clay tossed him over his shoulder and sped around the back of the buildings. As he went, he heard the town come alive in sound. Half-built buildings pulsed as lamplight was hurriedly carried through their bones. Store shutters were drawn back far too early for trading.

The calls of 'fire' began, and when Clay reached the wood shop his hands shook as he unlatched the loading door, for fear he would be noticed. He slipped Odell through the half-open hatch and his limp body tumbled down the steps. Clay followed, lowering himself in. Before he closed the hatch, he watched the orange hue from the Long Cape reach up, as though to warm the black sky.

February 1869

'How did he die?' Clay had asked.

'A hero,' came the reply.

Clay had wondered whether August had known that much or whether it was merely what a father overabundant with pride might say.

They had never discussed his brother William's death. Clay had been out of town when William's name was added to the post office wall, four years earlier. Clay had heard that, upon hearing of his eldest son's death, August had collapsed at the news, flat out in the hall of their house, the servants rushing about him as he wailed into the fine oiled wood of the floor.

August had never recovered from the shock of losing William and his torment lingered, keeping him to his bed. Clay stood in August's bedroom, looking on the old man, who was aged by grief. He had been standing in the room for most of the morning, but struggled now to find a reason why he should remain. He willed his father's grief to turn to sickness so that he might leave his side all the quicker. He would then have the keys to the Virginian home he had grown up in and would look ahead to living in it. To inherit such a home, such a fortune, at the age of seventeen thrilled his adolescent mind.

August made a sound, which Clay leaned closer to hear. His father was no older than sixty, but his loss saw him impersonating a man past ninety. His voice rattled in his throat; the folds of grey skin on his neck were like morbid drapes.

'Sorry, Pop?'

'Do you know what a hero is?' August repeated.

The question struck Clay as strange. He kneaded the back of

his own neck with his fingers, impatient at his father's grasp on life.

'Someone who does great things?' he said.

To his embarrassment, August laughed.

'Did I fail you?' Clay asked, perturbed.

'That you did,' August replied.

He coughed and tried to clear a nest of phlegm from his throat.

'A hero,' he began, taking a sip of water, 'is someone who fights for the great things. Who confronts great difficulties.'

'Am I to suppose you mean me not a hero?'

'You will never be one, Clay. That was your brother's calling. Yours, I urge you, is just to be a good man.'

Clay's temper flared and he swallowed his words in thought: *Where did being a hero get William? Dead and half eaten by worms.*

'I worry about you,' August said.

Clay stood by the window seat and pulled a thread loose from its pattern on the cushion. 'You needn't.'

'All these great things,' August said, moving his arms apart. 'To give them to you might be a fool thing to do.'

This made Clay turn to face him.

'Do you know what I thought?' August asked, adrift in the last swells of his mind.

Clay shook his head.

'I lay there after I heard about William—'

'And you hoped it was me?' Clay interjected. 'You did, didn't you?'

August shook his head as wildly as he could.

'I would never wish that,' he said. 'I only hoped that you might have gone with him.'

'To die?' Clay asked.

'To fight.'

'Pop, I am not yet eighteen. William was older. He—'

'He would not have cared. He would have fought.'

Clay found he had walked to the bed and loomed over his father.

'You wished to send me to die.'

'Clay,' August moaned. 'You will go on about me wishing you to die. My son, I only want you to live. To be a man. To do as William might.'

'I am not his ghost,' Clay said, a hand gripping the bedpost.

'You would do well to be so,' August replied.

That May, August died. The conversation proved to be the last Clay would have when his father was of sound mind. In the last weeks, August screamed and hollered and talked about Mexicans trying to rob him of his fortune. Clay knew him to have had dealings down there, but failed to document his fevers.

Clay buried his father in the family plot between his grandparents and his brother. Although dead, his mother was absent. In the words of his father, she had 'suffered from madness' and had died in a psychiatric hospital far away from their home. Her body had been returned to them, but August insisted she be buried elsewhere, as though madness might travel through the soil and pass into the others long since laid to rest.

Clay recalled the morbid pronouncement from the undertaker that he would need to extend the cemetery if Clay were to be buried there too. It was this that led him to his father's lawyer's office, where he came to understand his father as a man of hard learning.

August had promised the house to an hotelier friend. The lawyer had said how the man intended to raze the building, keeping only the cemetery, due to his father's stipulation, which was to remain in a shaded spot.

'My father would not have wanted that,' Clay had shouted.

'Mr Welston, he insisted upon it.'

August, then, would rather have seen his house destroyed than his son left idle in its halls.

Clay had been left the timber business in the newly christened New Georgetown. With little choice, he lived above the office while the men still in his employ worked in the cellar.

If my father wills it, he thought, *I shall build an empire greater than his.*

A crucial step, he decided, would be forming a courtship with Elena Marianne and, in doing so, shaking off the attentions of Ora Patch. He concluded that a finer match was needed for a finer man. The town would surely respect him more if he carried the hand of a maid in his own, and distanced himself from New Georgetown's own Jezebel. It was a calculation made by a man's ambition rather than his affection.

While other men his age were victim to follies of the heart, Clay's beat only to his plan. He could not arrive at the door of Elena Marianne the very next day. He would have to work on himself first, to build up the character and reputation his father had considered lacking. The irony of the situation eluded Clay as he would begin to take the business and himself seriously in a bid to prove his father wrong, rather than proud.

As the months passed, his opinions of Ora grew sharper in his determination to marry Elena. In talking with her, he did not remove himself entirely from her portrait as a loose woman, nor did he accept blame for it. He merely concluded that he had his desires and Ora had been a fool to go along with them. Simply put, and in an image Clay was certain his father would approve of, he saw their dealings as a partnership that was now at a close.

Having made his decision, Clay worked hard for Elena. He set her image in his eye and strove relentlessly towards it. Whenever Ora's tears troubled his mind, he explained to his weaker self that it was all the past and not worth thinking on. When he felt his good character was confirmed enough, Clay visited Elena's family and, in the absence of her parents, made pleasant with her older sister. His dedication took effect and he wondered if it wasn't the easiest of tasks to win the affections of someone such as her.

Then, once he had Elena's promise, the affection dulled. He was a man who favoured the chase and while Elena was a woman he deemed worthy to call his wife, his hunter's eye strayed elsewhere. He convinced himself he could be two men in one, satisfying the heat of his desire and the practicality of his ambition. The heart had no place in either of these two bodies.

The talk of an engagement stalled, other than in his glib promises to Elena when she sought to assure herself Clay had not changed his mind. He would talk of wanting to provide for her properly and to concentrate on his business first.

'I want to buy you a house, Elena,' he would say. 'One big enough for all our children. We will marry when I have a fine threshold to carry you over.'

After Clay had separated from Ora, a term followed where she felt both rejected and betrayed. She knew his reasons for choosing Elena as much as he – he had cruelly explained the majority of them. Ora felt misused and yet unable to speak to others of her treatment. Her troubles were confined to herself and soon, with no voice to the contrary, Clay's accusations set. Ora became who he deemed her to be and eventually she returned to him. His engagement to Elena was given life through the heat from another. The ease with which it happened only inflamed Clay's desire. He couldn't understand why Ora would want him still;

only that she had given her body to him and now was no one else's to have.

October 1879

Clay paced about the workshop floor, idly turning wood and tools over in his hands. He feared someone might have watched him enter the tavern or else have seen him escape towards the timber shop with Odell. Yet nobody came.

As the bustle from those trying to extinguish the fire died away, he listened to the smouldering whisper and the floorboards shifting above from the heat. He had propped Odell up in a chair and tied him to it with rope. Sawdust stuck to the blood on his face and his head hung limp. The boy's previous wounds had reopened like some ungodly bloom.

'You alive?' Clay asked aloud.

His heart beat hard in his chest as the silence stretched out.

'Odell!' he barked. 'You alive?'

Odell's body twitched awake before he hung limp once more. Clay rested against one of the workbenches, relieved. He dwelled in that strange mist where anger and consequence swept about, each as potent and yet intangible as the other.

The double doors to the workshop strained against the latch. Clay straightened, fearful.

'Clay,' he heard from above.

He moved over to the ladder and listened again, ready to pull it away. Beyond that, his plan was unformed.

'It's me – Ellsworth,' came the voice.

Clay leaped up the ladder and pulled the bolt free. The doors opened up and Ellsworth clambered down, locking them in.

'You took your fine time,' Clay said, walking back to Odell.

'I couldn't leave,' Ellsworth said. 'They were fighting the fire. I had to stay and help.'

'Is it burned to the ground?'

Ellsworth shook his head. His face and forearms were streaked black and red, covered in smoke yet flushed with heat. He was breathless and paced about, brushing ash from his clothes.

'What remains?' Clay asked.

'It stands, if that's what you're asking,' Ellsworth returned.

Clay nodded to himself and his eyes fixed on Odell once more.

'Clay, I care to know,' Ellsworth said. 'I care to know now, please.'

Clay ignored Ellsworth's gaze as his friend looked on him in desperation.

'Know what?' he said.

'What you mean to do to Odell. You said you'd tell me, didn't you?'

'You worry too much,' Clay said. 'All I mean to do is teach the boy a lesson.'

With this, Odell stirred.

'Rise and shine,' Clay called out.

His boldness was spurred on by Ellsworth's hesitation. As though, by Ellsworth's questioning of the very act, Clay became further convinced of its necessity.

Odell opened his one good eye and let a whimper free of his beaten body. 'What?' he said.

Clay bent down and proffered his ear. 'Say again, Odell.'

'What?' Odell repeated. 'What have you done?'

'Exactly what I said I'd do,' Clay replied. 'Didn't I warn you? Ain't we been here before? I told you not to go talking to Elena and I told you to forget about Ora.'

Odell shook his head as though escaping the attentions of a fly.

'Don't lie to me, Odell,' Clay insisted. 'Don't you fucking dare. I do not have the patience for you.'

'The Long Cape?' Odell asked.

Ellsworth shifted in his seat.

'You think you're smart, don't you? You think I wouldn't see you? This town's a skeleton, Odell, and don't nobody not notice a rat running through its bones.'

'What?' Odell asked. 'What are you saying?'

'What I meant to say, Odell, is that I fucking saw you – talking to Elena and mentioning Ora. Drunk as a skunk, she says.'

Odell took a moment and then, struck by the realisation of what Clay recalled, shook about in the chair. The sudden horror of why he was there flooded through him.

'No,' he said, breathing deeply and painfully. 'I didn't go up there to tell her.'

'Didn't I say about lying to me?' Clay shouted.

'I went there because of Ora,' Odell said. 'I saw her. I saw her walking up there. I was following her.'

This caught Clay's attention and he put a hand on Odell's shoulder. Ellsworth continued to watch with great interest.

'You saw her?' Clay asked.

Odell nodded.

'And she was staying up at the Marianne house?'

'Must have been,' Odell panted. 'Must have. That's where she was headed. I followed her from town. Please, Clay. What's happened to the Long Cape?'

'That so?' Clay replied, ignoring his question about the tavern.

'Yes,' Odell wept. 'I swear.'

'You swear?' Clay asked, looking at Ellsworth.

'Yeah, I swear,' Odell repeated. 'On my life.'

Clay clicked his fingers and made a whoop. He moved across to the fire and thrust at the coals with a small metal shovel.

'Clay?' Ellsworth asked tentatively. 'I'm thinking he knows. He knows not to say anything.'

'You stay out of this,' Clay said, not looking away from the fire. 'Stay way out of it.'

He turned from the fire and walked behind Odell, his hands on the back of the chair. Odell twitched and squinted hard, trying to turn to see Clay.

'You know who else was up there at the Marianne House? Me. And I don't recall seeing Ora. In fact, neither does Elena.'

Odell slumped forward in his chair. 'I saw her,' he spat. 'I saw her, Clay. I swear.'

'You swear, Odell. You swear. But that don't change the past. It don't make what you think you saw true.'

Clay clicked his fingers at Ellsworth and pointed towards a rack of tanned leather. 'Bring me one of those,' he said.

Ellsworth obliged and handed across the strip. Without warning, he slapped it across Odell's face, cutting into his lip. Ellsworth turned away.

'So try again,' Clay said.

'Clay—' Ellsworth began.

'Shut the hell up!' Clay shot at him, pointing the leather.

'She wasn't there?' Odell asked, his lips quivering.

'You play these games, Odell, I swear to God I'll kill you.'

Odell tucked his head into his chest and began to sob.

'Clay,' Ellsworth said, head tilted. 'I think you should stop now.'

Clay ignored him and brought the leather up across Odell's face, narrowly missing his eye.

'Tell me what you swear, Odell. Tell me what you recall.'

'Clay, he's a kid,' Ellsworth pleaded.

'You piece of shit,' Clay continued. 'You two-bit cocksucker. The Long Cape? Burned to the ground is what that is. And the deformed bitch too.'

Odell threw his body against the ropes keeping him tied to the chair. 'God fucking damn you!' he said.

Clay pulled the strap taut against Odell's throat. The boy's good eye bulged.

Poison took the place of blood in Clay's veins and he twisted the strap.

'I swear,' Odell croaked out of his sliver of open throat.

'You swear what?' Clay asked, furious.

'I swear,' Odell repeated, his face contorted and red.

Clay relaxed his grip on the strap.

'I swear, Clay,' Odell coughed. 'I went there after Ora. But when you let me out, I swear I'll go back. I swear I'll tell Elena.'

'Shut up, kid,' Ellsworth said, moving over to the two of them.

'You fucking say that again to me, Odell,' Clay demanded.

'You let me go, I'll tell her. I swear to God. I'll tell her and you'll have nothing then. No wife and no fucking war still – no war to pansy out of, you yella' son of a bitch. So you'd best fucking kill me now.'

Clay rose up and punched Odell across the jaw. He drew a knife from a table and cut the ropes from him, hurling his body to the ground and kicking him in the throat.

'You remember this, Odell,' Clay said, his hands pressing into his skull. 'You remember that you drew this from me.'

He tied the leather strap tightly around Odell's wrists, pulling him up from the floor and over to the fire.

'Clay?' Ellsworth asked.

'You best come over here, Ellsworth, lest I put the whole of him in.'

Odell looked up at the fire and unbound horror filled his mind.

'Hold him,' Clay told Ellsworth. He dug the shovel into the coals and lifted it up. The undersides of the stones were white and Clay felt the heat pocketed there, lapping against his face.

Ellsworth moved him closer, and with his other arm Clay thrust Odell's hands underneath the shovel onto the hot base of the forge. Odell screamed and his hands writhed from the surface, balling up and then arching away. Clay held them firm. Odell's screams shot through Clay, who hesitated for a moment before pulling the shovel free, allowing the coals to fall and bury the boy's hands.

Odell fell silent, his face contorted in horror. His teeth were bared and there began a short patter of gasps from him. After a second longer, they erupted into a scream that brought tears to Ellsworth's eyes.

'Shut him up,' Clay said.

Ellsworth covered Odell's mouth with his hands and looked at the floor of the workshop, shaking the sound from his head.

Clay stared at Odell's good eye, which looked ready to push free from his skull. The cry that came from the boy was so infantile and so raw it reminded Clay of all the hurts he'd had as a child. He had been so convinced in hurting Odell, but now wanted an end to it. He willed to go back, having merely shown him what would happen. Instead, his nostrils filled with the fetid burning of human flesh.

Clay had never fought in the war and so had never been privy to the horrors of what one man could do to another. But now he saw it, all ablaze before him like an aperture to hell.

27

October 1879

Kittie breathed in the smell of the shack. It felt vaguely stale, yet it reminded her of Emerson. He had already been with the doctor for some time, but she was determined to find what she needed while he was gone.

Emerson was a man of few possessions and so it took her no time at all to find what she was looking for. She searched the items Emerson would have no trouble in keeping close to his person, tracing their shape with her hands to locate that which did not belong. Her success could be owed to this as well as to her skill in finding the most carefully hidden items in a room – a skill that came naturally to one raised in the company of sisters.

The sheets of paper were rolled tightly and pushed into the lining of Emerson's heavy coat – the coat he had not time enough to fetch before Umbründ had rushed him away. Kittie eased them free and unfurled them, noting the torn edges. She looked towards the pile of books beneath the table leg to match them to the journal – just to be certain – but saw it was no longer there.

She thought little of it and sat on the edge of the bed, flattening the pages out before her.

Who are you, Emerson? Kittie asked herself and began to read.

I don't know what you've seen. But I hope you've seen enough for what follows not to sound like folly. Maybe I shouldn't wish such sights on my own son. Feels strange, that - son. Do you mind me calling you that?

We all heard stories about the hospitals. There was a time some said they'd sooner be killed than injured and taken off for curing. I caught a piece of branch blown from a tree in my left leg years before and I sure was scared. All came to nothing, though, and I could walk good as new after that. But this was different. This time they'd have to open me up proper and take those bullets out of me. Once they'd set me down in a room with a dozen others, I wished I'd died. Wished for something peaceful like death or else forgetting.

I wasn't the only one. Did your mother tell you how we met? I don't quite know what has yet reached your ears, but I for one am not in favour of sugaring the past, even for the young. She was a whore when I left her and I'm assured in thinking she may be still. For rarely do the sinful find work outside the reach of the Devil.

We all of us intended to lay with a woman before the next day's fighting. The Mexicans are a brutal people and, if a knife were about to cut your throat open, you'd hope for a sweetheart's image to flood your mind beforehand. Some men nary buttoned their pants from the moment they walked into town to the moment they walked out again. Shit, maybe I oughtn't to tell you this, but then perhaps you're just the same.

The owner of the house had overheard some of the others talk about me. 'Amos,' they'd said. 'He'll turn your mind for a fee.' The owner sought me out as I waited my turn.

'She's broken,' the man had said about your mother. 'And I was hoping you'd fix her.'

She was a beauty, your mother. But she'd been mistreated. She had been carted around the town like the other whores, but one turn down the side of a tavern led her to a group of soldiers intent on her goods, but not on paying for them. Call it a rape or what you will, but they was lucky she didn't die from it. She'd gone back, bloodied and, as the man said, broken.

'Can you help her?' he'd asked me. And so I did. I took that memory from her and put something else in its place. Nothing fancy, mind. That there's the trick, you see. Make it believable, son, otherwise it'll never take. All of this I will tell to you, anyhow.

The man of the house was so grateful he offered me a free ride from her. Either that or he wanted to test my job was done right. I slept with her and might have pretended I had to. I enjoyed it, of course. That screw didn't end there, though. We were in the town for a while longer and, knowing I'd taken something bad from her, if not exactly what, I believe it's not untrue to say she loved me.

But then we did leave. I told her I'd come back to her. Don't all men say that to their sweethearts? And what then must a man say to his whore? That I loved her? I might have done; I know not.

I talk of things I did not expect to. For we have a job at hand, my son. You must find him. Find the Devil.

He was a doctor who treated me and, just like that whorehouse owner, he'd heard of my talent. He knew what I was capable of doing. He was a curious fella. Strange accent. He wanted to forget things from just after the second Bull Run. Nothing I hadn't seen

297

before. Surgeries, and bad ones. Botched things and greenhorn doctors. He was mighty fancy, so I charged a greater fee.

I was laid for many a week in that hotel pretending it was a hospital. My wounds didn't seem to be healing and I was growing fond of the drugs. People kept dying. I saw the beds of those I might call friends empty.

There were rumours and words snatched off the lips of nurses. I suspected. And then one day I had my answer. The hospital was being vacated. All those capable of moving were to be taken elsewhere. Those who weren't were to be left to die.

The doctor came to me and told me he could get me out of there. My wounds were worsening, but still he said he could make it happen. For this, he asked that I take more from him. I assured him it was gone already, but he said more grew. This time I saw things I never care to think on. I consider them, once written here, forever forgotten.

He had killed plenty. There wasn't a doctor who couldn't say the same. And yet these memories were different. Like the light of a different room, they were shaded apart. He wasn't ashamed of these deaths, but proud. There wasn't a necessity to him pulling a man's leg from him, but a curiosity. He took delight.

There'd been talk of reb doctors torturing Union soldiers and we, to our shame, cared not a jot. But in the doctor's mind the uniforms went from blue to grey as his appetite grew. And soon I recognised the walls surrounding those acts as the ones that surrounded me.

He asked me to take those memories from him. He was reluctant, mind. Proud, too. I read it in his mind. I knew he'd prefer to keep the memories, if he wasn't so determined to start a new life. And by helping him I would save my own.

He was truly mad, Emerson. But his victims were something

298

else. They were men so acquainted with horror - tortured to the extreme at the hands of a man looking to act God. How they survived, I can't tell you. Perhaps some homespun will to carry them back to a loved one played to that man's advantage. Perhaps it carried them through what he did to them - keeping them alive when plenty others would have given in to pain and died.

What strikes me now is that they were perfect for him. They were men prepared to die, prepared to suffer. Under his knife I suppose they stuck it out for longer. But they were also men seeking to kill and whatever that man did to them didn't change that. They were animals. And, such as they were, they began to spill out from that place into the surrounding woods. I dread to think what tragedies occurred from it all.

For my shame, I began to take these things from him, each one a horror to retrieve. I found it a great struggle and then I grew too angry to carry on. I snatched at his mind in a rage. I took his past, his family, his love. I tried to distort him, convince him he was a dog or likewise something crazed. I failed to heed everything I had learned and, because of this, he shook me free.

He came to and held at his skull like I had tried to break it apart. He said he would leave me to die and I told him to go hang. I would rather die as I was than live with a monster. Yet, as you know, I did neither. The other doctors took me with them and I didn't require the help of that monster. If he'd seen me go, I don't doubt he'd have put a stop to it.

I believe I took enough from him, Emerson. He will not recall this place. He will not recall me. He will not remember the things he did. And now I ask you, from a father to a son. Hunt this man with me. Let us hunt him and kill him.

Before he shook me free, I left something for you to find. Something you will know as well as me - your mother. Your mother's

face will be there where it has no right to be. If you see it, you
know he's the one. What's more - you hand her a lime flower.
Remember that. It'll buy you time.

I appreciate you writing this down in that there journal. It'll
help some. Later, we'll talk about how best you can work your gift,
Emerson. Then, when I am better, we'll leave here.

You hear the rain? Ain't it funny? It was raining the time
before, I'm sure of it. A great storm is when the doctors

Kittie reached where the loose pages ended and her mind ran
on with those words she had read, what seemed like an age ago,
in that same shack. Those words, which had once condemned
Emerson to her mind, were now explained by others. The truth
of the situation fell into place before her and the tight grasp in
which she had held her heart eased.

Emerson wasn't the father, but the son. He had merely written
down his father's words – and, besides, he was too young to have
fought in the Mexican–American War. Kittie's heart quickened as
she traced over the last few days and thought on it again, Emerson
now free for her.

Yet her joy was short-lived. As much as she might have hoped
for Emerson to return, she knew the doctor in those pages to be
Umbründ. Despite the man's peculiarities, she couldn't find cause
to call him monster. And yet there it was, written by someone
who had no need to lie.

Her mind grew pale with fear for Emerson. She had sought
a simple answer in those pages and instead uncovered a nest of
secrets and horrors. And as much as she turned them over in
her hands, she found no answer to that question which burned
within her the most.

28

October 1879

Umbründ had told Emerson to stand and take his chair to the furthest end of the room. All the while, he held that well-polished gun pointed towards him.

'Further,' he had said as Emerson stopped short, trying his luck.

Emerson set the chair legs against the moulded skirting board and then, at the behest of a flick of the gun barrel, took his seat.

The doctor did the same, pulling his own chair back until it met the opposite wall. He kicked behind him, seeming to doubt the wall wasn't further away. He took his seat and stared across to Emerson, as though they were dining at a fine, long table.

'You can do it from there?' Umbründ called out.

'I can,' Emerson said, nodding.

He preferred to work up close, but, as far as he knew, the building was empty and there was no risk of others interrupting them. Once, a soldier he'd worked on had been unnerved by the proximity of the process. He had reluctantly agreed when Emerson explained.

'Sprays wide like a shotgun, does it?' the man had replied, only finding comparison in the tools of war. 'Up close is better, I bet.'

Emerson had disliked the analogy, but found he'd moved closer to the man, eager not to affect those in the neighbouring tents at their camp. He had often considered whether he could work on a crowd. In his younger wonderings, he'd even supposed he could have ended the war – drawing both sides together and convincing them they had little to quarrel about. He knew better now. He knew, if there was a good use for his work, he hadn't yet found it.

'Why the distance?' he called to Umbründ.

For a moment he supposed Umbründ not to have heard, and even found some misplaced humour in the possibility of repeating himself louder across the stagnant room.

'Caution,' Umbründ replied.

Behind the wooden boards, the wild night shook the window and pelted it with a scattering of snow.

'If you try to break with my mind and come at me,' Umbründ began, before setting his gun on his thigh, 'I will kill you.'

Emerson looked at the distance between them and affirmed the doctor's logic.

'So tread carefully, Emerson.'

The doctor readied himself in the chair.

'I'll begin now,' Emerson said, the two men closing their eyes as reluctantly as they had ever done.

Emerson unfolded the doctor's mind before him, being sure to keep hold of the edges. He scanned Umbründ's memories, seeing the town, the tavern, himself. A memory in a memory in a mind not his own. At once, Ora's red hair, like a beacon in the night, was urging him forward to remove a monster's conscience.

★

302

'I'm in trouble, doc,' Ora said.

'With whom?' the doctor replied knowingly, his eyes twitching in their jealousy.

'Clay.'

Umbründ's knuckles whitened on the back of her chair. His gaze roamed about the room and he settled on the mirror on his office shelf. As natural as Emerson intended the memory to be, Umbründ recalled his childhood sweetheart Lucinda's rejection of him, the mirror tumbling from her shawl in her haste to escape him. The past and present were bridged by his being spurned for another.

He did not love Ora as he had done Lucinda, but he had held faith in their phony contract, one that was written in the moments of flirtation at the tavern – a myriad of hand touches and knowing display. Now she had reneged for Clay, it seemed. And his trespass littered her womb.

'Can you help me?' Ora asked.

At once, Umbründ was afforded the opportunity to erase the past, to replace the loss of Lucinda with another, far superior prize. Ora's situation meant he was able to finally have her. By her dependence on him, he would be free to make amends with his younger, heartbroken self and assure his present pride he was as much of a man as Clay.

'For a price,' he said.

The dollar bills she offered were turned away and instead he cupped a breast through her blouse, clumsy in his hunger.

'This is how it must happen,' he insisted.

'And then you'll fix it?' she replied, not flinching from his touch.

'First, we must go somewhere else. Somewhere safe.'

★

303

Emerson had reached the beginning of what he was due to remove. He felt its weight at the edge of his toes, as though he were about to traverse a border. He readied himself and pushed forward into the memory.

'Where have you been?' Ora asked.

Umbründ set his medical bag down by the door. He looked at the floor as he unbuttoned his heavy coat. The cold from the mountain walk hung in the fabric. He was irritated at having his third appointment with Emerson end so abruptly, Kittie storming into the shack and he being drawn back to his patient, Ora.

'Where have you—'

'Away,' he rushed out. 'Tending to things.'

Ora was lying on her back, a cut of fur pulled up to her shoulders. She leaned back on the mattress beneath her, her breath escaping.

'How are you feeling?' the doctor asked.

'Slow,' Ora replied.

Umbründ noted how pale she was. Even for one so white.

'You were gone a long time,' she said.

Umbründ pulled his pocket watch from his waistcoat and checked the hands.

'Nonsense,' he said. 'I have been gone only a little while.'

'Where?' Ora asked.

'I had someone to see,' he replied.

'Who?' Ora asked.

The doctor remained silent for a minute.

'Secrets,' she said playfully, as though the doctor withheld only the trivial.

Umbründ thought how she lumbered about, like one under opium. He walked across to her and lifted a slim brown bottle from the side of her makeshift bed. The liquid had barely gone down, so it could not have been that.

'It's him, isn't it?' Ora asked.

'Do you feel pain?'

The doctor was panicked now. He had expected to return to her walking about the room or, at the least, sitting up. Yet she seemed as though the procedure had just taken place.

'The man, the stranger,' she said.

Umbründ latched onto her words.

'Who?' he asked.

'The someone you had to see. Limeflower.'

'Yes, yes, it was Limeflower,' the doctor said, feeling her pulse.

She laughed. 'Quit it, doc.'

Umbründ sat on the floor beside her and placed a hand underneath the fur and against her stomach.

'When can I leave this place? Go back to town?' she asked.

Her stomach felt bloated. He moved his hand further down and then pulled it sharply away at the touch of blood. Umbründ was far from unaccustomed to it, yet the amount shocked him. He drew the fur back and saw blood pooled about her legs, the last of it pumping irregularly from her.

Umbründ placed the fur back over her.

'What is it?' she asked.

'Nothing, nothing.'

He wiped the blood from his hand and thought back on the procedure, questioning how it could have gone wrong. His surgeon's hand carried such dark stains in the paths of its flesh that he knew not whether it was accident or otherwise. A hand skilled in death could only deliver on its trade.

Ora made her somnambulant moan while Umbründ tried to think. He had boiled the needle as he had always been taught.

The resistance and then the push, something punctured. He had drawn it from her slowly, the flow of heavy blood and eventually the half-realised fragments of a human being, like a broken china doll, impossible in its incompleteness.

'A trespasser no more in the body of an angel,' Umbründ had said. 'My angel.'

Emerson urged himself to stay with the horror. To push on into the mire of the doctor's mind.

Umbründ stood from Ora and walked to the window, eager to open it and let the stale air free. The light from the lantern threw his reflection up before him. He pressed closer still to the glass until it disappeared and he could look out into the night.

'I'd like to go home now,' Ora said.

Umbründ stepped away from the window and his own reflection came back.

'You cannot,' he replied.

Ora moaned and tried to lift herself, before dropping back down onto the mattress. 'Please, help me.'

Umbründ felt a dread in the way her words cut into him: that familiar breach, which allowed such words to land, not just in his mind, but also on his soul. He squeezed his eyes shut tight.

'Please,' Ora said again.

Umbründ could hear the pain in her voice, cracking its vessel. He walked over and sat on the floor with her once more. He took her hand and she saw the rust colour that wound its path along the creases of his skin.

'Whose blood is that?' she asked.

'It is yours,' he replied coolly.

She didn't speak, only turned her head away. Umbründ reached

over and turned her head back to face him. She was too weak
to resist.

'There is nothing that can be done,' he said.

The last of Ora's life lit up beneath her pale skin and she stared
hate through hot tears. Umbründ stood, but she refused to let
his hand go. He pulled her half from the mattress until he freed
himself, her nails drawing long cuts into his skin.

'You will not forget this!' she screamed at him. Only her scream
was a whisper.

Umbründ gathered his bag and pulled on his coat, the thick
fabric refusing to shift the chill from his bones.

'Ora,' he said, avoiding her eye. 'I will ensure I never remember
it.'

Emerson followed the doctor's memory from the room, unable to
return to Ora. He was tethered to a monster. And so he shadowed
Umbründ's mind from the hotel, down the trail and into town.

'Doc!' Kittie shouted.

'Yes, what is it?' Umbründ asked from behind his door.

'It's Blanche. She's dying. You have to come, doc. Emerson and
I found her in the woods.'

Umbründ's thoughts misted over and Emerson knew he was
trying to keep them from him. Even now, there was a part of his
mind he was steadfastly defending from Emerson's gaze.

'One moment,' he said to Kittie. 'Allow me to gather my things.'

He opened his medical bag and scanned his room for the necessary items. A slim brown bottle, a stethoscope, a gun.

★

The sight of the gun confirmed to Emerson that the doctor intended to kill him that night, regardless of any deal. Umbründ would not make the same mistake he had with Amos; he would have his mind wiped clean and then kill Emerson. The realisation almost shook Emerson free. He imagined breaking the contact and moving for the doctor. Yet he knew his movement would be sluggish so soon after the process. He would struggle to stand from his chair, let alone disarm a man.

Then he remembered words from his father about his mother: 'It'll buy you time,' he'd said. He had nothing to lose.

Emerson found his mother's image in Umbründ's mind once more. She stood there as though she cared to be no place else, unaware of her surroundings – a still image from Amos, rather than a form of any significance. Emerson acted on his father's words, passing her a single lime flower.

She took it from him and it instantly started to blossom and spread, weaving branches, fruit and finally independent trees. Emerson watched as it continued to grow unheeded, surrounding him, before he broke from the doctor's mind and hoped.

When he opened his eyes, he knew he had to act quickly. He heaved at his own consciousness, dragging it from the swamp of the doctor's mind. He shifted in his chair, his eyes creaking further open, and saw the distance between them.

Out of haste, he launched himself at Umbründ, falling from the chair, which clattered forward with him. He hit the floor hard and the air blew out from him. The noise seemed to rouse the doctor, who shifted in his own seat.

Emerson coughed into the floor, noting the stains before his face. The impact had brought him round some and he looked up, watching the gun on the doctor's leg. Umbründ's hand fell by his side and the pistol swung there. In desperation, Emerson pushed his hands into the floor and raised himself up onto all fours. His balance eluded him still and so he crawled towards Umbründ.

The doctor convulsed in his chair as though broken from a half-sleep. His awakened eyes fixed on Emerson. He looked to focus, to aim, but then moved his head about as though trying to gain a better sight of his target. He looked around the room wildly and Emerson followed his gaze, not knowing what was happening.

Umbründ wrenched at the gun too quickly, firing into the floor at his side. The sound rang out like a thunderclap and Emerson screwed his eyes shut.

With each passing moment, however, Emerson's strength returned. He drove himself forward to Umbründ and raised himself to a crouch. He began to sense his body returning to his control, feeling the extremities of his arms and legs.

The doctor cocked the gun and swung his arm up. Again, he looked for Emerson as though he was hidden. He pushed with his arms, as if moving branches aside.

'What is happening?' the doctor shouted. 'Where are we?'

He fired another round that whipped past Emerson's ear towards the window. There was the splintering of wood and glass and sunlight came pouring into the room. Emerson's mind momentarily upturned at the thought that it was day outside. He looked ahead of him, pushing towards the doctor. He was only a few feet away, unsteady on his legs and unarmed. He knew that if Umbründ had time for another shot, he would surely hit him, regardless of what was interrupting his mind.

The doctor drew back the hammer once more. At the click of the cylinder, Emerson leaped forward, flying hard into Umbründ's chest and slamming the pair of them into the wall before toppling the chair over onto its side.

The men wrestled with one another and Emerson waited for the shot, but it didn't come. He struck Umbründ under the chin and the doctor's teeth clacked together painfully. Umbründ shuffled his hands about the pistol, trying to raise it to fire. Struggling, he instead struck Emerson across the face. The fresh wooden edge of the butt cut into Emerson just below his eye and he felt the skin there grow hot. He grabbed at the doctor's arms and the two of them were locked together.

Umbründ's legs flailed about and he found a target in Emerson's knee. He kicked repeatedly, drawing yells from Emerson as the doctor tried his best to knock the kneecap clean off with his shoes.

Emerson countered and hit him hard in the groin. The doctor let out a hollow gasp and his grip loosened on the pistol. Emerson seized his chance and twisted his hands to gain a firm hold on the butt, driving the gun downwards into the doctor's right shoulder. The long thin barrel nestled just below his collarbone and Emerson screwed it into his skin, pinning him against the wall and reaching with his forefinger for the trigger.

The doctor's eyes widened and he tried to push the gun away from him. His hands heaved at the barrel, sliding down its oiled surface. A finger hooked on the trigger and a blinding pain flooded the doctor's face.

With the sound of the shot so close, Emerson turned away from the grapple and onto his back. He tried to shake the ringing from his ears and turned to see he had pushed the gun barrel through the blasted hole in the doctor's shoulder, all the way to the wall. The already stained surface there was now caked in fresh blood.

The doctor panted and opened his eyes, looking awkwardly at his wound. He let out a series of short screams, which prompted

Emerson to pull the gun free, the sticky slip of torn flesh reluctant to let the metal barrel loose. The doctor's form was frozen and he lay there, gently shaking, his eyelids dipping heavily.

Emerson stood and set his feet apart, aiming the gun at the doctor and drawing back the hammer once more. The metal was streaked with the same blood that now ran darkly from the wall and across the floor. The doctor clapped a hand to the wound and looked at Emerson.

'Please,' he said. 'Please.'

Emerson set his finger on the trigger and pulled slightly, trying to recall how much it took to send a shot free. He thought of Ora and his mind raged with what to do next. Reluctantly, he lifted his finger from the trigger, but kept the gun trained on the doctor's head.

The doctor looked at him and the agony fell from his face. He blinked several times and fell unconscious. Emerson released the breath he hadn't been aware he was holding into the now silent room.

Some hours later, when the doctor came to, Emerson had patched up the hole in his shoulder as best he could, given what had been to hand in such surroundings. Umbründ's eyes widened as he saw the rolled piece of bed sheet stuffed into the hole.

The doctor's neck ached with every movement, but he twisted his head to look around the room and took in the surroundings. Emerson had brought him to a part of the hotel that was un-familiar. There were no windows, but lanterns were spaced about the room, shining brightly.

'We are back inside,' Umbründ said.

'What?' Emerson asked, thinking him delirious from the gunshot.

'Earlier. I don't know how you did it, but you dragged me outside. Hid me amongst the trees.'

Emerson tried to discern meaning from the doctor's words. Then he remembered what his father had said about the lime flower all those years ago, how handing it to his mother would buy him time, if he needed it.

'What did you see?' he asked Umbründ.

'Trees. Everywhere. Growing quickly and crowding my eyes.'

Lime trees, Emerson thought. *They flooded the doctor's mind. Stopped him from making a clear shot.*

Emerson shook the thought aside, eager not to dwell on Amos having saved his life.

'Why did you bring me back here?' the doctor asked.

Emerson walked close to the doctor. Umbründ went to raise his hands and set about his grovelling, but found them tied behind his back. His legs were tethered to the legs of the chair he sat on. He shifted about for a moment until the pain in his shoulder throbbed intensely.

'If you free me, I will go and never return. You do not want a man's death on your conscience.'

'My conscience won't give a damn what I do with you.'

'Please,' the doctor said, searching his mind for possibilities.

'You'll die today,' Emerson said. 'Best get used to the idea.'

'Why?' the doctor exclaimed.

His question, too redundant after that morning and all that went before, seemed meant for the ears of a greater power, someone who could listen and be blamed for the longer-lasting implications of fate.

The doctor seemed to come to an understanding. His body sank and for a while the room was silent but for the crackle of the lantern wicks.

'Where am I?' he finally asked.

'Look around,' Emerson replied.

Umbründ moved in his seat, but could see nothing.

Emerson lifted one of the lanterns up to illuminate the wall's markings. 'Anything?' he asked.

The doctor shook his head.

'Do you know at all what you did?' Emerson asked. 'Can you recall a single thing? A single face?'

'What do you talk of?'

'You remember my father,' Emerson replied, 'but nothing more? Then he did a good job, after all.'

'Tell me what you speak of! Is this a lasting torture you intend for me?'

'You seem to think this tale is about one man. It's not. It's about plenty more. Let me share it with you, hold your own past before you – reacquaint you with a memory my father took.'

January 1863

'You will have to cut the leg again,' the nurse said.

Umbründ shook his head and pulled at the skin. He had already sawn at the limb twice. When he had trimmed the skin, it had reached enough to make the stitches. Now, the white gleam of bone shone out from between the folds.

'You will tear it, doctor.'

'Quiet,' he said calmly.

He was sure there had been enough skin before. Now he was convinced the body worked against him. It was as though the limb regrew, sprouting out as quickly as he tried to sew the wound shut.

The skin split and the orderly grimaced. Holding the gauze to the patient's face, he reached for more chloroform.

'You cannot,' the nurse said to him, seizing his arm. 'Doctor, you must cut more of the leg away.'

Umbründ released the skin and it receded up the leg once more. 'I will not,' he said defiantly.

'He will die.' The nurse looked at the orderly who held the gauze to the soldier's mouth. 'Please, Patrick! Are you aware of this?' she said, outstretching her arms. 'Won't you say something?'

The orderly only trembled and attempted to clear his throat. 'I'm sorry, nurse, but Doctor—'

'Leave us,' Umbründ said.

The nurse turned back to him. 'What?'

'Leave us.' He nodded too to the orderly who held the gauze. The nurse watched all before her as though it could not be happening.

'He will die, doctor.'

'Miss,' Umbründ began, 'I will call for them to take you away, if necessary. Now leave us.'

The orderly took her by the arm, but she shook him off and stormed from the room. He followed and closed the door behind him as politely as though he had intruded in the first instance.

Umbründ set his implements to one side and placed a seat next to the soldier. With his bloodied hand, the doctor turned the man's face on its side to face him.

The man's eyes had started to twitch and, after a moment longer, they opened. His pupils were flooded and Umbründ made a quiet wager in his mind as to how long it would take before he felt the pain in his leg.

The man wasn't his first. That fall previous, Umbründ had attempted to count the number of men he had lost on the operating table and in the field. The same calculations would run through his mind, faces half remembered and injuries never forgotten, until he reached the hotel made into a hospital. Here, the numbers climbed into impossibility.

'We can dispose of the bodies, sir,' one of the soldiers had told him. He brushed his bloodied hand against his plaid shirt, staring at a pair of dead friends before him.

'No,' Umbründ had replied. 'We have a system.'

The soldier had nodded and left the room, glad to be excused.

Umbründ would transport the bodies down into the bowels of the hotel. He supposed, when it had accepted guests rather than patients, the cellar had been used to house the staff. Now it housed Umbründ's fascinations.

He would spend more time on the dead during the night then he would on the living during the day. The human body would antagonise him. It would conspire to evade his attempts to save it – to stop it from bleeding, to locate a bullet – the folds of pulsing muscle giving sanctuary to the poisonous pieces of metal.

In the cellar, he would have time. The light in the bodies' eyes had long gone and so, away from the prattling nurses and untested doctors, he would be free to truly work. He was childlike in his horror, delighting in his curiosities and unhindered by conscience or remorse.

Soon after, the chests of his victims quivered still as his attention turned to the living. While he worked on them, they would stare beyond Umbründ to the ceiling, perhaps to the heavens, making rapid, shallow breaths. As he grew brazen in his practice, bed sheets were stuffed into the men's mouths to stifle their screaming. Regardless of the morphine, Umbründ's methods would flush their suffering out of its drugged stupor. Men who believed they had traversed the blackest horror of the war arrived at that hospital to find their suffering had only just begun.

In the weeks that followed, blood stained Umbründ's arms to the elbow. He would tell the nurses and doctors that he was working on a new procedure, a more accurate surgical instrument, anything to stop them from interrupting him.

He pushed his patients to the very brink of suffering, all the while keeping them leashed to life, even by the faintest tether. He asked himself what use it was for these men to return from the battlefield. What hopes might they have to travel home and pretend they hadn't seen all those horrors, they hadn't killed all those people. Instead Umbründ sought to keep them steady on the path. To push them further along the route war had set them on. To flood their lives entirely with death and pain.

October 1879

'You lie!' Umbründ shouted. 'You lie to me.'

'Why would I?' Emerson asked. 'You never wondered what was so bad that you needed it gone? Soon after you decided, once the war was done, so were you. If you were to settle elsewhere, you didn't want to be followed – even by your own conscience. So you found my father and that's where we join up.'

Umbründ shook his head all the while. Emerson wondered if, now that he had been reacquainted with his past, his memories were able to return.

'I can see the question you want to ask,' Emerson said.

Umbründ looked at him, half thinking whether to speak.

'Go on,' Emerson prompted.

'If this is true, then why would I allow him to live? Why wouldn't I kill him, like—'

'Like you planned to kill me?'

Umbründ kept Emerson's eye and nodded slowly.

'You were too late. The staff left, taking him with them to a hospital away from here. You left too, stumbling into the nearest town to make a life for yourself. As soon as you left here, you'd forgotten it – this place, what you did – all except Amos.'

Emerson walked from one side of the room to the other, lantern in hand. As he did so, the portion of darkness he vacated filled with sounds.

The doctor twisted his head towards the space. 'You have told a dark tale to frighten me.'

'I've told you the truth,' Emerson replied. 'I'm not sure if you know that now. But you'll come to realise it before they tear you apart.'

'Who?' Umbründ demanded. 'Where am I?'

'Home,' Emerson replied.

He held the lantern out and Umbründ saw a table of surgical instruments flickering back at him. They were flaked in rust and dark stains. The doctor shook his head wildly and heard the sound coming from the edge of the room again.

'Like I said,' Emerson continued, 'you found this place years ago. Not months.'

'Please,' Umbründ begged. 'End this. If you mean to kill me, do it now.'

Emerson lifted a scalpel from the table and dropped it sadly. The clatter drew more sounds from the darkness.

'This isn't a place of quick death,' he said, almost to himself.

He walked around the perimeter of the room, lantern in hand, and began to turn each of the others off. The sounds grew as darkness drew across the room – strange, soft moaning and wailing, whispered horrors misting across the floor.

The doctor struggled in his chair and toppled over sideways. He screamed at the pain in his shoulder and a scatter of similar calls came back from the darkness.

The doctor looked to the edges of the room, making out little more than movement, a blur of uniform. He writhed on the floor, trying to kick free of the rope that bound him. As much as he tried to resist thinking on what Emerson had told him, he could not. His nightmares now came alive in the room.

'This is a trick,' he shouted at Emerson.

Emerson only stared at him and shook his head.

'You fool,' Umbründ spat. 'You think this will bring you peace?'

Emerson crouched by the doctor, all the lanterns now unlit apart from his own. The light just reached Umbründ.

'What on this earth makes you think I want peace?' he said.

He picked up the lantern and walked towards the stairs leading to the door. As the light receded, so the hellish cacophony grew. Coughs and chokes; nails clawing at the walls.

'Those things,' Emerson began. 'Those men. You wanted them to survive, didn't you? Well, they did.'

He held out his arm, pointing beyond the cellar wall.

'Some escaped. Out there. Killing still. Long after the war was over.'

The doctor's face contorted.

'But they'd always come back here,' Emerson said.

The noise continued to grow and Umbründ watched as the figures moved slowly towards him. He caught the maddened eyes of one and squeezed his own tightly shut.

'I can see it on your face,' Emerson said. 'You believe what you did.'

The doctor shook his head and flinched and screamed at unseen things touching parts of him that lay in shadow.

At the top of the stairs, Emerson looked down at the doctor's face, his hand on the door.

'I'm not sorry for this,' he said. 'And that troubles me.'

29

October 1879

Emerson had little need for a lantern. The stars were somehow sharper for being those of a new night. Regardless, he decided to keep it with him, at least until he was nearer town.

He stood in the shelter of the hotel doorway. The evening was already cold and he looked down at the ground to find it covered in snow. The light fall from that morning had become a thick plume that left no ground uncovered. He contemplated how long he had been in the hotel, feeling trapped within an eternal night. The daylight had passed him and the doctor by and he felt a rising sickness in his throat, realising he had not eaten or drunk anything for almost a day.

The doctor would die alone in that room. The horrors had all been from Emerson. He had recited what Amos had taken from Umbründ back to the doctor, before turning those memories outwards to populate the room in flickering horror. As though using his device, he had fed in a ream of the doctor's nightmares and projected the show onto the inside of his mind. He had conjured memories before, but never had he used a man's own mind to kill him.

Umbründ's trauma at thinking his victims had returned and were about to tear him apart would be enough to drive the doctor mad, to cook his mind in fear and give him a slow death in the hotel cellar. A fanciful part of Emerson hoped the sentence might quell the memories in his own mind – as though the victims, now appeased, would rescind their sufferings from his nightmares. He tried not to deny the likelihood of such a thing, convincing himself the moment deserved a fantasy, if only a brief one.

Snowflakes stuck to his face on the threshold of the hotel step. He pulled his jacket tighter about him and began to walk, his feet sinking into the white with a crunch. He had come ill prepared for the weather, the snow tumbling over the tops of his boots.

He found himself unable to pull free from the hotel, taking only a few steps from the door. He halted and looked over his shoulder. The screams of the doctor had died away. Emerson was certain he was dead, and yet he was unable to leave. His mind raced to concoct reasons why he should not go back. That was, until he struck on why he had to: the girl's red hair, as free and full of life as a flame.

Emerson closed his eyes and thought back on the doctor's mind. He followed the path of Umbründ and Ora as they walked through the hotel, the blanket beneath the doctor's arm, all dark parts of the recollection inescapable.

He glimpsed the numbers on the room's door and found he was already walking back towards the hotel's entrance. As he stepped inside the building, he held the doctor's gun more pointedly than he did the lantern, knowing all too well that in this place it was better to shoot what came your way than give light to its abhorrence.

The hallways were quiet, but Emerson still felt his heart's beat thrum in his ears. By delivering such horror to the doctor, he had been forced to stand on the periphery and watch. Despite being long dead, those men, those creations of Umbründ's, were truly terrifying. What were ghouls and demons in the doctor's mind had once been husbands and sons to others. The idea chilled Emerson as he imagined them having a place beside a sweetheart or telling a story aloud to their children before the hearth. He wondered, if such things came from the ordinary, the everyday, what stopped them from happening again?

The experience had only served to pose more questions in Emerson's mind concerning his gift.

Gift, he thought. *Who am I to call it that?*

He had worked to his father's instructions and yet surpassed them. He had taken from people, but exceeded the amount Amos had ever taken. He had placed things back, adopted a role in the minds, poked around at leisure. He had spied on his father's takings. He could feel the potential to do more, to change more minds, to bewitch and to divert. He had felt it when he put on the show for the sisters, their minds all in tandem and open to his story.

He moved forward more determinedly, thinking on the peace Ora deserved. Finally, he saw the brass numbers on the door. He had, ashamedly, hoped he might be unable to find it.

He set the lantern by the door, which he opened onto the room, the gun aloft, before he raised his eyes.

August 1865

'I'm thinking that's it,' Amos said.

Emerson set down his pencil. The windows of the hospital

ward had been opened to let in the cool air, with panels put in place to keep flies from men's wounds. Emerson had been sick with their constant buzzing, but a storm had washed out the heat and he was glad to note the flies had left with it.

'You really write all that down, son?'

Emerson turned the journal over in his hands, running his thumb across the filled pages.

'That's a lot in there. A lot to remember. Best you did it after all, I suppose.'

Amos closed his eyes for a while.

'How did you find me?' he said.

'Asked around.'

'Asked around?' Amos said. 'It was that easy, huh?'

'I heard tell of a man like you who had been shot in Virginia. That, and things you saw, I saw too. A carry-over.'

'Like what?'

'Like you fighting. You getting injured.'

'You are making fun of me?' Amos supposed.

'I'm not,' Emerson insisted. 'I saw you talking to a man. A fine leather wallet. Dollar notes, not coins.'

Amos opened his eyes. They widened as much as they might between their black, swollen lids.

'Shit,' he said. 'Ain't that something. I never knew that to be a thing.'

Emerson nodded and turned the pages of the journal in his lap.

'That was him, you know,' Amos said, resting back in bed.

'Who?'

'The leather wallet – it was that son of a bitch who left me to die in that place.'

'The doctor?'

Amos nodded. 'You recall what he looked like?'

'No,' Emerson said. 'It's too hazy when I get it from you. Like reading a book under ice.'

'I wish you could see him. It'd help some with the hunt.'

'The hunt?' Emerson said.

'Yes, son, the hunt. We're gonna find that doctor and kill him.'

Emerson looked around him.

'Ain't nobody here but us, don't you worry,' Amos said. 'The nurses won't come unless I call.'

Emerson remained silent.

'Don't go green on me now, son. We just finished a war. One more dead man on the pile don't make a whole load of difference. You went and killed some in this war, didn't you?'

Emerson nodded vaguely.

'I knew it. I saw it in you.'

Emerson closed the journal, satisfied with its contents.

'I could look into your mind,' he said, holding it aloft, 'like you taught me. I could look on his face.'

Amos laughed uneasily. 'I feel queer about that, son. Plus, I thought of that, too, in case I forget his face or he changes it.'

Emerson leaned closer.

'Your mother,' Amos went on. 'You ever see her again, then you know it's him. I put her image in his mind. I knew that cocksucker might back out of our deal. I put her in there for future reference. He can't run from that, huh?'

Emerson sighed. 'You've told me this before.'

Amos seemed to doubt himself. 'I did?'

'You did,' Emerson replied.

'I am sorry, son, I am not well. Perhaps I ought to rest.'

'Tell me more about the lime flower,' Emerson said.

Amos smiled at his interest. 'The doctor – he's a tricky son of a bitch. You find yourself backed into a corner? You find your mother in that man's mind and hand her a lime flower.'

'And what will that do?' Emerson asked.

'It'll buy you time.'

Amos began to cough and Emerson lifted a glass of water to his lips.

'Besides, I'm here, ain't I?' Amos said. 'We'll find him together.'

Emerson drew the glass from his mouth. 'How are you feeling?' he asked.

Amos turned to his left arm. The skin was a queasy mixture of green and black. 'About the same, I reckon. But I'm fine to travel. Might lose the arm, but I guess it's no longer mine, anyhow.'

Emerson placed the journal and pencil on the chair and walked over to his father's side. He peered down at the arm. Amos watched him, uncomfortable with his curiosity.

'Don't stare too close, now,' Amos said.

'Why not?' Emerson asked.

Amos narrowed his eyes and made a futile attempt to shift away from his gaze. 'Because I'm telling you,' he said. 'Your father is telling you, Emerson.'

The boy's hair was limp and he pushed it back behind his ears. He raised his eyes to look at his father.

'You don't be looking at me like that, boy,' Amos said.

'I travelled all this way, I'll look at you how I want.'

Amos twitched in the bed. His face grew greyer. 'You don't plan to rescue me, do you?'

Emerson shook his head softly.

'You son of a bitch,' Amos spat.

Emerson smiled. 'I thank you for all you've said. Truly, I do. But now you've plain run out of usefulness.'

'You little shit,' Amos said. 'I don't think you can. I don't think you will.'

'Your opinion is about to change,' Emerson replied.

Amos spat at his son and landed a heavy glob on the boy's shoulder.

'You go to hell! Why, I'm your goddamn father!'

'You fucked my mother; don't make you my father.'

'Watch your goddamn mouth!'

'If I said it wrong, correct it. Didn't you screw my mother? Didn't you fuck a whore?'

'We loved each other!'

Emerson laughed a child's laugh, shrill and affected. 'I cannot abide this horseshit,' he said, packing his journal away.

'Wait!' Amos shouted. 'Please, wait.'

'Wait for what?'

'You can leave me here to die, but you gotta tell me.'

'Tell you what?' Emerson asked, buttoning his jacket.

'Are you going to find him? Are you going to kill him?'

'Who?'

Amos's face paled with rage. 'The doctor!' he hissed.

Emerson sniffed at the word. 'I'm thinking, if I meet him, I might just shake his hand.'

'You don't mean that!' Amos shouted.

Emerson turned and walked towards the door. He noted the bright sunshine outside, lifting the smell of rain from the ground and into the room.

'If not for me, then for the others! I told you what he did! You said you seen it yourself!'

Emerson tilted his head at Amos with contempt. Moods changed on his father's face as readily as clouds passing over a barley field.

326

'Please, Emerson. Don't let this be the end.'

Amos began flinging himself about on the bed. His bad arm twisted and expelled glimmering liquids of putridity. He had managed to hoist himself up and his face was ablaze with the pain of doing so.

'Why do you hate me so?' he shouted.

'I don't hate you,' Emerson replied. 'I just don't love you enough to take you away from here.'

Amos fell flat on the bed and rattled out a sigh.

'God damn you,' he said to the ceiling. 'God damn you.'

Emerson watched as Amos began to weep and, to his disappointment, pitied him. He might have promised to hunt down the doctor, even if he never would, just to give his father some peace. Yet, his mouth remained closed and he decided that was sign enough the words weren't meant to be said.

Walking down the corridor, Emerson passed nurses tending to other patients. He watched as men changed in size and shape from bed to bed – some bandaged, others missing limbs. Before he left the building, a doctor at the front desk attempted to ask him something, but Emerson ignored him and walked on.

Down the long gravel path, he thought on what Amos had said about his mother in the doctor's mind and questioned whether it was true. He didn't know what was possible, but decided he needed to find out himself, to continue his work with other people's minds, regardless of his father.

He passed beneath the thick metal arch of the hospital gate. The last time he had seen it had been in the carry-over, several weeks earlier – the thoughts from his father, more accurate than any map.

The idea of a lime flower kept recurring in Emerson's mind, as though he'd failed to wash its smell from his skin. In a moment he'd thought back on little since, he decided to keep such a trinket of information, and instead of expanding on it in his journal, he sewed it into his name so he might never forget. A boy born to a whore and a dying man was in need of a surname, and it mattered little to Emerson that his came from a grudge.

As the hospital slipped behind the crest of a hill Emerson thought how, on the way there, he had considered saving Amos. He had contemplated the outcome of their reunion with just about every variable there could ever be. Yet he knew that it was all useless. He knew that whatever would happen, would be born in the moment. For what use was anticipating what the heart might ask? Especially in the matters of love and hate.

October 1879

The grave Emerson dug was shallow. The ground was frozen solid and only by fortune had he uprooted a heft of dead tree. He swept the hollow clear and placed Ora inside. To ensure she fit, Emerson tucked her knees up to her waist and her arms in at her lap, as though she were sleeping. He replaced the roots about her and scraped at whatever surrounding soil he could move to encase her.

By the time he was done, the snow had almost completed the job and all that was visible were a few strands of hair, neither hidden nor dulled from beneath the tree.

He stood there for a while and, in the place of prayer, thought on Ora and when they had first met, how she had struck him with her beauty from the very first moment. He proceeded to the uglier passages of recollection witnessed from the doctor's mind and was glad he had left them there to die with the man.

Those remembrances would fade, but he would be sure to think on his first night in New Georgetown and to give Ora a place in time to reside. He would quash the now inappropriate attraction he had had towards her and think on her mystery and her face in the glass of the tavern door – a rare portrait of one so accustomed to being looked on, alone with only her innermost thoughts reflected back at her.

Emerson was glad to have the hotel at his back as he stopped in the mountain path. He could not say he was relieved to have killed Umbründ or even that he felt different having done so.

For a moment, he wondered what had come before with Umbründ. To Emerson's distaste, he felt a curiosity, a desire to trace that man's life, to figure what had been taken by Amos, what is was that had been replaced by Gengenbach, his parents and the silver mirror. Yet, whether he might have found more death or a man living something so common it could be called a life, Emerson decided he was best not knowing. For was it a worse fate to uncover more horror from that man, or to find someone – a man Emerson had now killed – who could be described as ordinary?

His thoughts soon turned to the town. He wondered if people would look to him because of the doctor's disappearance and whether he would be considered suspect. After all, he was the last person to be seen with him alive. He wondered if he would be able to convince people the doctor had been shot while being robbed. Or perhaps, in the dark, Umbründ had taken a rogue step and slipped from a ledge to his death. Emerson knew the town would look for him, either way. Rarely did answers go unquestioned in such a place.

No, that won't do, Emerson told himself.

He would need a story or else he might as well never walk back into town. He gave himself until the base of the mountain to have found an explanation, otherwise he would continue on the road, back in the direction from which he had first arrived.

With Umbründ gone there was little need to return to the town, and yet Emerson never questioned his need to do so. The truth was that he was returning for Kittie.

In that moment, it all became clear – a surge of unavoidable purity and power through his heart; the push of a sharp needle that pierced and let loose something he was glad to be rid of, while all the while pulling a taut, immovable thread behind it. Love.

His chest thumped and he felt all corners of his body moored to its call. He was entranced by her. He wanted to look on her for longer than was decent. He wanted to hold her and brush a fingertip across the dark freckle on her lip's edge. He wanted to possess her and answer his heart's call to be with her forever.

Emerson embraced this realisation all the more sincerely out of determination that it was his own. He tightened his grasp in an effort to assure himself that it belonged to him and not to that particular phantom who walked the hallways of his being. More than anything, he wanted his heart to feel something that wasn't a memory for someone else.

He knew that, if he lacked a plan when he came to the path's turn, his earlier resolve would mean little and he would continue on to the town to be with her regardless. These ruminations went with him at every step. Emerson was so intent on answering them that he took his gaze from the path and began down a different route. Only as the thicker branches and interrupted track troubled his steps did he notice. He continued on, though, soon arriving at a slope that overlooked the path.

It was then he heard voices coming up the road. He shrank back and lay flat on the ground, pushing into the shadows and feeling for Umbründ's pistol at the back of his belt. He set it on the ground beside him, hiding its shine from the moonlight's bite.

'And then what?' a voice asked.

'And then we shoot him.'

Emerson's heart beat against the cold earth beneath him. A stray thought fixed on what the creatures that burrowed there made of the sound. He wondered if these men had come to kill him. He peered down to the road and saw the light of a lantern approaching. He waited eagerly to see who was holding it.

'Shoot him?' came the first voice, alarmed. 'Clay, I ain't murdering nobody.'

Clay, thought Emerson. *From the tavern. The man Ora spoke of too.*

'You already done enough for a hanging,' Clay said. 'Better you help me now and we forget this whole thing.'

'I ain't never gonna be able to.'

'Well, start trying.'

Ideas flurried in Emerson's mind and he supposed the two men were there to hunt Umbründ down for what he had done to Ora. Emerson looked down at them again and saw the men carrying something between them. It looked to be a fawn or some other willowy creature, but then, as the lantern swung in Clay's hand, Emerson saw it was a boy. He shrank against the ground again, pressing his eyes closed.

Emerson wished he had not seen the boy. He cursed himself for looking on the scene and not waiting until the men had passed by before raising his head from the dirt and continuing on. The peace he'd believed himself to have that night was once again interrupted by conscience.

331

He felt for the gun at his side and, twisting his head, looked to check it was loaded. It was. Emerson cursed again at not having reason enough to stay hidden until those men passed by. He quickly sifted through the options available to him. If they planned to kill that boy, they would doubtless have a gun about them. He had the element of surprise and that was his one advantage. His disadvantage was that he had not fired a gun since the war – and even then he had left more bullets in trees and dirt than men.

Should I stop these men? Emerson thought. *For all I know, that boy could have raped someone and I might intrude on their justice.*

Emerson watched as the men walked nearer. He had started to hang the most heinous of crimes around the boy's neck, seeking escape from any responsibility, when he caught sight of more of his face. It struck him as familiar before he recognised it for certain. *The boy from the theatre. The piano player.*

The men were almost in line with the ledge and Emerson, prompted by this vague association with the boy, shouted out. The footsteps stopped and the two men looked about them. The man next to Clay dropped his side of the boy and touched at the rifle on his shoulder. Clay, meanwhile, pulled a pistol free from his side and aimed its barrel up at the ledge. Emerson could hear them exchanging hushed urgencies.

'Holster your weapon,' he shouted down. 'You're outnumbered.'

'Outnumbered?' Clay asked nobody.

The fat companion let out a stream of curses as he squirmed on the spot like he needed a piss.

'Yeah?' Clay shouted up. 'Then show yourselves.'

'Clay,' his friend said.

'Shut up, Ellsworth!' he hushed. Then, raising his voice again, 'Cos I think there's only one of you up there. A man with friends don't hide.'

Emerson pushed back from the ledge and pulled the gun into his body, his finger on the trigger.

'Yeah, now you're thinking,' Clay said, and dropped his side of the boy, the body falling in a heap. 'Now you're thinking; I can hear that, all right.'

Emerson squatted on his haunches to test how much the men below could make out. He was crouching there, but still Clay squinted against the darkness.

Emerson refused to believe the boy from the theatre could have done something that warranted an execution. He had watched from beneath the stage as the player had relished in the show, his face dancing in joy at the shootout. Yet Emerson knew horrors hid well from the outside eye, and recently passed was the age of boys killing like men.

'What's he done?' he called down.

'Ain't nothing to do with you what he's done,' Clay snapped back.

'I got my pistol trained on you and your friend, so I think it's got plenty to do with me.'

Ellsworth looked over at Clay pleadingly.

'See, I don't believe that neither,' Clay replied. 'I think you up there alone and unarmed. And you think yourself the hero.'

'That I'm not,' Emerson said. 'But I am now making whatever you're doing my business.'

'This here's a personal feud,' Clay shouted. 'And you're best out of it, friend.'

Emerson grew impatient and cocked the gun, aiming it at Clay's shoulder. Clay's ears pricked up at the sound, but he kept still.

'Now I'm your friend, huh?' Emerson shouted down.

'Well, no, I'm guessing not by the sound of it.'

A second more and Clay pointed up at the ledge, dropping the lantern in a splash of flame and firing off a round from his pistol. A patch of earth to Emerson's left kicked up in the night and he fell to his right, spilling rocks and dirt down the slope. Clay aimed anew and fired again, this time a hand's width above Emerson's crouching frame. Emerson aimed his revolver at Clay, but then saw Ellsworth swing the rifle off his shoulder, lift the gun like a man attuned to killing and pull back the hammer. Emerson adjusted his aim and fired. In the light of the flames at his feet, Emerson saw a cloud of red mist burst from someplace on the fat man. No scream, no shot. The rifle dropped from his shoulder and he fell forward like timber.

'Don't move!' Emerson shouted down to Clay, but he sped back down the path. Emerson fired twice and missed him both times. He brought his aim back to Ellsworth, whose arm lay across the rifle on the ground.

Emerson dropped from the ledge and walked towards him, gun ready. He kicked at Ellsworth's arm before heaving him over, ready to take the shot if he was only playing dead. As the man's body slumped flat on his back, Emerson saw he had shot him dead centre, in the middle of the forehead. Ellsworth looked the more surprised out of them both and a thin trail of blood ran down his face and into his thick, unkempt beard.

Emerson looked over at the boy they had dropped and saw his face was swollen and bloodied. His hands were tied together by a leather strap and wrapped in black cloth. Emerson pulled the cloth free and retched at the sight. Even in the poor light, he could see the hands were a furious red and smelled like nothing he had known. The wounds ran up to the wrists, as though the boy had grown tired of his skin and pulled it free, like gloves. The fingers were uneven in their swelling and oozed yellow. He pushed the cloth back over the wounds and stood away to gulp down the cold air.

The boy murmured and Emerson was astounded he was alive. He took Odell's head in his hand as one of his eyes creaked open. Far from relief, Emerson felt sorrow at the realisation that this boy had lived through whatever things had happened to him, his face all cut up, his hands stripped to meat – likely never to play that piano again.

He lifted the boy onto his shoulder. He was light and Emerson could carry him easily. He was trying to say something and Emerson tilted his head to listen, but only heard a stammer of the letter *K*, repeated over and over.

Odell coughed and spat a heavy wad of blood onto the ground and Emerson's boot. He failed to notice and Emerson did not care to tell him.

'New Georgetown,' he said.

'And where in New Georgetown?' Emerson asked.

'Tavern,' he said. 'Take me there.'

Emerson couldn't help but smile. 'You need a drink, huh?' he asked.

The boy stayed silent, so Emerson started to walk down the path. After a few paces, he looked back at the body of Ellsworth. At once, two murders seemed easier to explain than one and he tossed the doctor's revolver up the path. He noted, one last time, its silver glimmer and how, despite its gleam, it had seen more action in the past day than some pistols did in a lifetime.

Emerson held Odell tightly over his shoulder and felt the push of the boy's breath against his back. As the path levelled out, he saw the first sign of light from New Georgetown. The gas lamps were ablaze and Emerson quickened his step, eager, for the first time in his life, to return somewhere.

WINTER

30

December 1879

The cold hurries things along, thought Kittie.

She was looking out from the window of her parents' room, thinking how, not two months earlier, it had seemed the town might stay half-built. Now, though, the frames of houses and buildings were being filled out with solid walls, lending the place the feel of something not entirely unlike a town.

As nature hid from the cold, the town grew. It was as though the events of October had finally put an end to the war and the rebuilding could now commence. This was the fanciful idea Kittie played with. She knew as well as everyone else that the work had long overrun and, keen not to allow the damp to set into the wood any more than it had, the contractors had decided their buildings needed walls and roofs.

Not long before, it had been a place weary with time – buildings, such as the theatre, the tavern and even Horace's workshop. Now they creaked all the more unsteadily for their newer, finer cousins, which stretched out in the hitherto abandoned spaces.

Where before there had been skeletal frames, outlining what

339

a house or a place of business might look like, there was now unblemished wood and perhaps a lick of paint adding some further indication of what it might be. One hotel, named Eberdeen's, had even opened for business, its rooms ready for guests. Areas that Kittie had imagined would remain barren now saw men holding plans this way and that, pointing to how the land could be reconstituted. People swarmed the town. It seemed, to Kittie's great surprise, that New Georgetown had become a place to live.

She gained much information from Elena, who delighted in Clay's business. He was rarely up at Marianne House, which suited Kittie fine, but he had made assurances with a ring, and while he was down in the town, filling invoices out with relish, Elena could usually be found before the fire, watching the light glint off the stone, set in brass, like a pixie dancing in the flames.

Perhaps because of this newfound popularity, talk of the tragedies the town had suffered not so long ago was rare. It seemed people were determined to slot them into the past and watch them go with time. To a lot of the townsfolk, and to Kittie also, when mysteries surrounded bad things, it was best to let them remain mysteries.

When Emerson returned, he did not speak of what had happened. He carried about him the marks of secrets; a few more scars for the collection. Kittie had been the only one to see him and Umbründ disappear together, and even if Elena had had the inclination to notice, the ring on her finger was by now a far greater distraction.

On Emerson's first night back, Kittie visited the shack at the base of the yard, taking him some cornbread and water. She set it by the door when he refused to answer.

'Won't you speak with me?' she shouted.

The shack remained silent. She moved to the window and

through the gauze of the curtain saw Emerson's figure on the bed, turned against the wall.

Kittie thought about tapping on the frame but stopped short of doing so. She breathed heavily and Emerson's image disappeared in the mist of her breath on the glass.

She started to walk up towards the house before she doubled back and sat on the shack's porch. She tore off a piece of cornbread for herself.

'Emerson, I don't yet mean to know your secrets,' she called out. 'Just don't paint me a liar for supposing there are some.'

She had stayed on that porch for most of the evening, having fallen asleep in her waiting. When she awoke some time later, she had a jacket of Emerson's pulled about her, keeping out the cold.

Following the fire, the sheriff from nearby Underwood had been sent for. Kittie had heard it was one of the newcomers to the town who had sent for him. He was a stubborn old goat called Crift, and someone reluctant to pass law in one town, let alone take on the responsibilities of a second.

She had met the sheriff once before, after the deaths of Lori and Kittie's brother, George. Crift had sought an account from Clay – the son of a man he knew well enough – who told him it had been a bear that did the killing, and he had returned on the day's ride back to Underwood almost immediately.

Kittie thought him a relic from the war. Only fourteen years had passed, and yet it was enough to make a man like him seem an anachronism.

He arrived in the town as though his last visit had been just yesterday and it was nothing but an inconvenience that such a place carried an acquaintance with death.

'Are you the sheriff?' one of the new townsfolk had asked him as he stepped from his horse.

'Son, I'm *a* sheriff. This town don't have one. That's why you're in this mess.'

Crift seemed keen to employ Clay once more, asking where the Welston boy was. Clay was, however, absent this time, perhaps keen not to risk showing what part he had played in the events.

The sheriff reluctantly poked about in the wreckage of the Long Cape, declaring the fire to have been an accident and little else. It was only when he was confronted by a woman named Millicent, claiming her employer, a Dr Umbründ, had disappeared, that he was denied a swift return to Underwood.

Out of an eagerness to satisfy a worrisome woman, Crift sent for his deputy, a man named Daniels, and when he arrived they took several men and searched the surrounding area. He wondered if this foreign-sounding fellow mightn't be the reason behind the fire, having fled the town that very night.

Several days later, Crift and his party returned to town, carrying a corpse between them. They held its limbs outstretched, as though they intended to thread them through wheels and make a carriage of sorts.

'Damn thing is frozen solid,' Crift cursed as they set the body down in the doctor's old office. 'This your doctor?' he asked, brushing as much frost from the face as he could.

Millicent shook her head and began to cry out in horror.

'Then why the hell are you crying?'

'It's a man named Ellsworth,' she said.

Crift turned to anyone who might listen. 'Is she telling me someone else has died? God damn this town.'

Soon after, Daniels entered the room in haste. He held his hat to his chest, as though to cover a hole there.

'Well?' Crift asked him.

'We found a woman. Buried.'

Crift breathed a heavy sigh and removed his own hat.

'We can't get her out of the ground,' Daniels continued. 'She's frozen in there.'

'God damn this town,' Crift said again, this time every word meant.

That evening, Crift called a meeting in the centre of town. The gas lamps around them had been lit and the sheriff sat on horseback before the crowd that had gathered. It was a pose he had favoured since the war – addressing the attentive faces as though the news was still of advances and tactics. His deputy stood beside his own horse, watching with unease.

Crift delivered a short speech to the town as he leaned forward on his horse. Many people's regard for Underwood rose during his brief visit, such was his determination to return there.

He told them that, despite his best efforts, Umbründ had not been found. Owing to the fire, the doctor's hasty retreat and the bodies of Ellsworth and Ora, he supposed him to be a murderer.

'To my eyes, it seems the doctor intended that girl harm. Knowing this, Ellsworth went after him and paid for that decision.'

Daniels watched Crift and willed him to step down from his horse, if not just to deliver this news. He tightened his grip on his own horse's reins and his shoulders ached. He had helped dig a grave for Ellsworth the day previous. Unable to unfix his arms and legs from being splayed such as they were, they'd had to dig the grave no fewer than five feet across.

Crift picked something from his horse's mane and continued.

'This sure is a mess,' he said. 'And one I'll be reporting. Whether they'll send marshals here, I can't say. But that's my reckoning.'

The sheriff searched about the faces in the crowd and then along the line of the buildings. His desire to return home grew as he watched the figures moving in the lighted windows.

'Looks to me like you've got yourselves a town here,' he said. 'About time you had some law to go along with it.'

He turned his horse and urged Daniels to join him. The deputy nodded to a few people in the crowd and mounted his own horse, catching up with Crift.

The crowd began to talk among themselves, some breaking off into groups and going to discuss things someplace else, while others stood there, heads bowed solemnly. Among them, the youngest and eldest Marianne sisters comforted the other, who had lost her dear friend. To their side stood a man, glad for his anonymity, knowing there was a great deal more to the events than Crift had said. And, apart from it all, another stood outside of the light, watching the man's reactions, knowing full well his part in all that was told and glad for the shadows – the shadows that counted the remains of Umbründ among their horrifying number, and the shadow on the mountain ledge that meant he was kept alive to return to Kittie.

Always be glad for the shadows, Emerson thought. *Always.*

31

December 1879

'It is not painful?' Kyoko asked.

Odell barely felt a thing and just continued to stare into her eyes. He smiled at her and shook his head. She smiled back and then, her face turning serious, returned to removing the dressing from his hands. He shivered and she stopped immediately.

'It hurts?' she asked.

'No,' Odell said, taking one hand in another, as though concealing some playing cards. 'No, it's not that.' He put his hands down onto the table again and pushed them across to Kyoko. 'Ain't nobody touched them since, that's all. Not counting the bandages.'

Kyoko moved her hands to hold Odell's and all the while kept her eyes locked on his. She began to unwrap the muslin until she held his bare hands in hers.

He looked down and then turned away at once to avoid the sight of them.

'Jesus,' he said, starting to weep. He shook his head and tears dampened his cheeks.

Kyoko looked down and let out a slight gasp at seeing his hands. The skin was tough and yellowed, like wet paper left out in the sun. She ran a finger over the strange stiff ripples in his flesh. She noted how his hands were much improved from when she'd first seen them, how she could at least now make out the parts of a hand, where before it was all a bloodied mess. This was the first time since the night he returned that Odell had allowed her to look at them. Whenever he had needed the wound redressing, he had struggled with it himself. Soon he had become adept, one end of the fresh muslin clenched between his teeth as he wound his injuries up towards his mouth. Yet even as she noted the improvement, to look at such skin, skin so out of place on the hands of a young man, was deeply sad.

So too was the condition of the Long Cape. Although her room and the storeroom below were untouched by the fire, the front of the tavern had been coated in black by the flames. Little remained of the booths or the bar, except trails of ash where they had been. Towards the centre of the tavern, the floor opened to the emptiness below, the supporting beams the only sure way to cross. Kyoko supposed the flames had been spurred on by the bottles of alcohol and the wood that had drunk heartily from drinks spilled over the years.

Had a stranger not called out for help, Kyoko knew the flames might have reached her room. She had watched the frame of the door pulse as the flames from over the balcony grew. The floorboards had grown warmer beneath her feet and she'd felt trapped, as if in a pot over a stove.

In the days that immediately followed the fire, she decided she would no longer live in a ruin. The thought of leaving the building quickened her heart still and yet she knew she had no choice. But she wouldn't leave to become a white man's fetish in the open world once more. Odell called her Kyoko and she could not, would not return to the slurs of 'Jap' or 'the Bird'.

'You don't have to,' Odell had said.

She smiled at the remembrance, watching him now peer from the window into the street. She walked towards him and brought his hands up to her face, kissing them softly. In spite of the numbness, he could feel her lips on the skin. It was one of the very first things he had felt with these new hands of his. He turned to look at her and hesitantly ran a palm around her cheek and into her hair, his fingers moving stiffly.

'I know I love you,' he said.

His mind was suddenly staring at the blank space where those words used to be, hidden away for weeks now. He had rehearsed them and on occasion vowed never to say them, in case reciprocation never came.

Odell kept his hand on Kyoko's face. He dared not move for fear he break their contact, this moment of perfection.

She lifted her lips from his crippled palm. 'Then come with me,' she said.

Climbing the steps to his home, Horace felt the gaze of the townspeople who knew his secrets: his wife dead, his daughter dead and his son hidden away in a tavern.

Why must my grief be theirs to look upon? he asked himself.

He turned on the top step and looked down to the street. People broke away from staring and quickened their pace up and down the road. Horace unlocked the door and was confronted with the blank space of the room, and a scattering of splinters and wire he had long neglected to clear from the floor.

'We ain't getting this thing out in one piece,' Clay had said, hands on hips.

Horace remembered him climbing the steps with his workmen at his back. They had taken the saw to it and Horace had felt as though he were back in the field, having his leg taken from him. He had wanted to object, to plead with Clay that since his son and daughter were gone from him, in one way or another, could he not allow the piano to remain? He didn't say a word though, knowing Clay would not be moved.

'I'm sorry, Lori,' he said aloud to the room. 'I'm sorry I brought us here. And I'm sorry I lost you.'

Staring at the blank space before him, Horace was sure he could see his wife at the piano with Odell there next to her. Ora would come in and sing.

No, that ain't right, he thought.

She would come in and complain, more like. She would say how her friends could hear, and why not play something of the time. Horace would sit or stand in the corner, watching on. As much as he tried, standing in that empty room, he couldn't remember what it felt like to be a husband, or even a father. He had forgotten it as readily as he had forgotten being a soldier and, before that, a child.

To be ashamed of such thoughts in the company of nobody startled Horace. He went into his bedroom and pulled out the last of his trunks. He stared at Odell's bedroom door across the hall. He had not set foot in there since his boy had disappeared into the tavern six weeks earlier. Hammond had come over to collect some things and Horace had obliged him, all the while questioning why he couldn't see his boy. Hammond had just shaken his head as he lifted Odell's things into a large suitcase and carried it across the road under his arm.

Horace opened Odell's bedroom door and stepped inside. Eager to set the dust motes free, he pulled the window open.

The cold winter air rushed in and he heard the patter of conversation from outside. He imagined he caught his name as well as Ora's, and pulled the window closed again, suddenly glad for the staleness.

Horace sat on the edge of Odell's bed and thought how, even though the carriage would arrive to take him to the station in less than an hour, it might be the longest wait of his life. He felt like a caged animal in his own home. People swarmed the street discussing what the sheriff and his deputy had brought to their attention, and there wasn't a person in town that would look on him now without either pity or scorn. They were talking about him and his family, and the very idea made him shrink into his hunched body.

The bed shifted beneath him and Horace fell onto the floor with a thump. He wondered what was happening as the sheets swamped him. He fought free, realising he had fallen between the two beds, pushed together years earlier when Ora had left the house.

As he raised himself upright, his hand touched paper and he picked it from the floor, a cover of dust sliding free. Horace stood and stepped out from the wreck of his son's bed. He walked to the window and held the paper up to the light. It was sheet music.

He looked at the sketches of notes, but he could make no more sense of them than if they had been in another language. It was the writing at the top of the piece that caught his attention: *For my darling family.* Horace crumpled the edges of the paper as his grip tightened. She was reaching to him from beyond the grave.

Knowing what music had meant to his wife, this was akin to finding a love letter from her. He wondered if Odell had ever played the piece his wife had written, and if he had told him to keep the noise down, or else left the building, not realising the true intention behind those notes.

I've missed so much, he thought.

For an instant, his mind strode forward to imagine what might happen if he went over to the tavern clutching this newfound treasure. Odell might come down and, seeing his mother's composition, play the tune for his father. Horace may have had little opinion on music, but he knew his son to be capable at it.

Yes, he thought, *very capable indeed.*

Odell would play and he would rest an approving hand on his son's shoulder as his wife's composition came to life before him.

No, he thought, *that would not happen.*

Instead, Hammond would stand at the door, protecting a man from his only kin. He would hold the paper aloft and the farmer's son might snap it out of the air, tearing it in a place or two. Whatever chance Horace had had was now gone. The thought struck him and he encountered that kind of deep, boring finality that brings about longing for the new while you dwell still in the deep caverns of what is lost. You can see the light floating somewhere far off above your head, but for now you tread in the dark.

Horace folded the sheet music and put it inside his jacket pocket. Looking at the clock in the other room, he saw he had little more than half an hour now. A sudden urge overcame him. He ignored it and sat in his chair, tapping a finger on his knee to the tick of the old clock. But the urge refused to leave him and, instead, grew in his heart.

I can do this one thing, he thought, giving voice to his hope.

His eyes fixed blankly on the wall opposite. He stood from his chair and pushed open the door leading down the stairs and onto the street, snatching up his crutch as he went. By fortune, Hammond was returning to the tavern, his arms busy with fresh wood for the replacement floor. Horace hurtled down the steps and limped up the road.

'Wait!' he called out, faces turning in his direction.

Hammond turned and then, seeing Horace, pushed on.

'Please, just wait, will you?' Horace urged, hopping along on his crutch.

'I can't,' Hammond said. 'You know that by now.'

'I don't want to come in and I don't want to see him. I just want to give him something.'

Hammond's face eased and he slowed his pace. He turned to face Horace and dropped the lengths of wood at his feet. 'You're not gonna quit, are you?' he asked.

Horace just looked at him, his face red, his hand clutching desperately to something, knuckles white.

'Okay,' Hammond said. 'But you gotta give it to me out here.'

Horace held out a long slip of cloth to Hammond, pausing before setting it into his outstretched palm.

Hammond turned it over in his hand. 'What is it?' he asked, as he began to unwrap the cloth.

'Don't!' Horace snapped. 'Please, don't. It's for my boy. Nobody else.'

'Fine,' Hammond said. 'You want for me to say that to him?'

'Yes. And that I'm heading back east.'

'He won't come and see you before you go.'

Horace paused. 'I know that,' he said. 'Don't I know that already? Just tell him, though. And . . . tell him I'm sorry. I don't know how else to put it.'

Hammond nodded and picked the wooden boards up, negotiating them and the cloth in his large arms. From under the burden, he offered his hand.

'Good luck to you, Horace,' he said. 'I mean that.'

Horace shook his hand and silently nodded. He watched as Hammond walked away to the tavern and dropped the wood on the blackened porch. A man came from inside the building and nodded to Hammond, thanking him for the wood. Others followed, dragging blackened items and tossing them into a pile in the street.

Horace breathed heavily on the spot, longing, for the first time in days, at least, for the morphine he so dearly missed and was eager to seek from another town. All the while he touched a hand to his empty jacket pocket, thinking on his wife's music and likely checking to see if his heart was beating still.

'Odell!' Hammond called. 'You in there?'

Odell pulled his hands free from Kyoko's face.

'He will not enter,' Kyoko said reassuringly.

Odell nodded and opened the door. Accustomed to waiting, Hammond was sitting on the top step of the stairs, rolling a cigarette. He offered Odell a smile, and then a cigarette.

'How's the work?' Odell asked, shaking his head.

'It's getting there,' Hammond replied. 'They're patching the floor up now. Then we'll get to work on a new bar. It'll look different some.'

'I bet.'

'Clay charged me less for the wood. I've never known that man to give a discount.'

Odell's heart beat faster at the mention of Clay's name. His hands stung as though fresh in the fire once more.

'Still a son of a bitch, if you ask me,' Hammond mused, picking tobacco from his lip.

'What did you knock for?' Odell asked, keen to go back inside.

'Horace,' Hammond said, tilting his head up. 'He approached me in the street.'

Odell began to turn.

'Wait!' Hammond called out. 'He came by, but didn't say nothing about seeing you. He's run his course on that one. He wanted to give you something, is all. He says he's leaving town and that this is for you and nobody else.'

Hammond bent down and picked something up from the step. He proffered it to Odell, but, reminded of his injury, instead laid it in his cupped, outstretched hand.

'I ain't looked, if that's what you're thinking.'

Odell turned back to Kyoko's room.

'Don't mention it,' Hammond said, dropping another pinch of tobacco over himself and treading downstairs.

His feet at the door's edge, Odell folded back the cloth and pricked his fingers on something sharp. He carefully pulled whatever it was free and found it to be wrapped again in rough, old paper. This he unfolded and saw it was sheet music. *For my darling family*, it read. He looked over its notes, but failed to recognise it. It was his mother's handwriting and composition.

Has he kept it all these years? Odell thought.

From under the paper, Odell glimpsed a familiar shade of wood. He turned it over and was lifted from his feet by the past. *Lori Patch* was carved in fine letters, and he at once recognised the wood from the piano. He brushed a thumb over the name and felt a pain in his throat at recalling his mother and realising that Clay had collected on his father's debt.

Close behind that thought was the memory of the night in the workshop. Large portions of it were missing from his recollection and he was glad for that. The mind, it seemed, only went so far in its tolerance for horror.

Odell finally walked back into the room, where Kyoko was seated at a table. She looked up at him, those beautiful eyes so dark and perfect.

'What is it?' she asked.

Odell handed the parcel over to her. She studied the letters for a moment before he noted the realisation on her face.

'I'm sorry,' she said.

'Sorry?' Odell asked. 'For what?'

Kyoko stood from the table and embraced him. Only once her arms wound tightly about him did he realise how much he needed that comfort. He let his head fall into her shoulder and he began to cry, darkening the pale cloth of her dress. Kyoko comforted him and they held one another silently.

'Before we leave,' he began, 'can you play for me?'

Kyoko lifted his head from her and looked into his eyes. 'Of course,' she said.

Odell's heart beat in his chest like never before. He knew what was about to happen and wanted to scream towards it like it was the only thing he had been placed on God's earth to do. Instead, he couldn't even blink of his own accord.

Kyoko leaned forward and placed her lips on his. It was the first time Odell had kissed someone, and his head fizzed. Whether it was love or merely kindness, her affection towards him was a bulletin nailed to the frame of his heart.

She kissed him again and she moved her soft hands up onto his neck.

'You still here?' Hammond said to Horace.

'You give the package to my boy?'

Hammond nodded. Horace was gazing ahead of him at what remained of the bear.

'Sorry sight, ain't it?' Hammond said.

The head and most of the bear's left side were intact. On its right side, the fur was burned away and a wire frame below had been twisted and dipped by the heat of the fire. The clay used to pad out its bulk had melted out and set in a frozen boil.

'Sure is,' Horace said. 'Surprised there's any left of it, mind.'

Hammond laughed.

'What?'

'You know how?' Hammond asked. 'Jenkinson. He was one of the first over here. Pulled the thing from the fire, all the while shouting, "I got you, miss! I got you!"'

Horace shook his head and couldn't help but smile.

'Is he all right?'

Hammond looked at Horace.

'Odell.'

'He's fine,' Hammond said.

Horace looked up. 'I heard things. About his hands.'

Hammond nodded in confirmation. 'He'll be fine, though,' he said.

'Thank you – for looking after him.'

Hammond went to say it wasn't him who had helped, but decided not to invite more questions from Horace. He pitied the man and considered what to do, whether to betray Odell and invite his father up.

Then the music began.

It was a fine piano piece and came from the back of the tavern, where Horace supposed his son to be. Despite not knowing one piece of music from another, he was, however, certain that this was his late wife's music for her family. He felt unsteady and rested a hand on Hammond's shoulder, whose gaze remained fixed on the back of the tavern.

'That what you gave him?' Hammond asked.

'It ain't from me,' Horace replied.

Hammond turned, confused, but Horace only lifted his crutch from a nearby beam and set it underneath his arm. He stretched out a hand to Hammond.

'I know you didn't have to give that to Odell, and I thank you for that.'

'When's your ride?'

'Now, I'm thinking,' Horace said, looking back towards his home and a carriage waiting there.

'Then I find myself wishing you luck a second time,' Hammond remarked. He took Horace's hand once more. 'My mother always says, once is good manners, twice is good fortune, while three times ...? I don't recall, but it was something bad.'

Horace nodded. 'Then I'll be sure there ain't no third time.'

He looked around at the building work as the music began to play again.

'Good luck with the Long Cape.'

'You won't stay and hear the music again?' Hammond asked.

Horace smiled, his eyes glassy.

'Shit, Hammond. It's all I'll ever hear.'

32

December 1879

Emerson sat on the back porch of Marianne House. Despite the bright sun of the winter day, he suffered a cold that had refused to leave his body since the mountain. He would have much preferred to be inside, sitting before the fire or else in the kitchen, leeching off the warmth of the stove. Yet Blanche had plans for the upcoming anniversary of the town, which meant the back of the house was one of the few spaces he might reside. In anticipation of New Georgetown commemorating its birth, the house was strewn with flags and trails of bunting that climbed and dipped over the furniture, all coloured red, white and blue. By now, the inhabitants of Marianne House eagerly awaited the day itself, when the festivity might gush forth, draping anything standing upright in celebration.

Up until that winter, pride had not been something people looked to find in New Georgetown. Yet with the majority of buildings reaching completion, and businesses preparing to open soon, it seemed to be, for the first time, a town. Just as she had done with her schoolchildren, Blanche desired to celebrate the place's history as it set about its future.

'I'm thinking this town could use some cheering up,' she had said.

She had stood, hands on hips, surveying the decoration that spread across the drawing room, her sisters and Emerson lined up by the door like loyal workers.

'There's an understatement,' Elena had replied under her breath.

Blanche described to them her plans to show people about the theatre, perhaps even to restore it one day soon. With whose money, she didn't say, only speaking kindly of Clay for the first time in Elena's memory. She had even persuaded a hotel's musicians to play through the day, seeing as their bandstand was yet to be finished. Her sisters and Emerson could not help but be drawn in by her enthusiasm.

For someone who had come so close to death, Blanche had made a remarkable recovery. She could walk freely now, without a stick to lean on, and slept through the night, only on occasion waking to fevered dreams. It was the injury of her mind that seemed to impact on her the most, the trauma of travelling to the cabin to erase the presence of Shelby – so nearly killing herself in a bid to wipe the memory of someone else clear.

The back door of the house opened and Kittie stepped out, holding a pot of coffee.

'Another?' she asked, offering it.

'Please,' Emerson replied.

Kittie refilled his cup and took a seat on the porch next to him. Her very presence made his heart beat faster and he couldn't help but look on her – always for a moment longer than he should. For her part, she seemed to like it. Or at least she blushed rather than got up and left. She had spent more time with him since he had come back. Gone were the harsh rebuttals to conversation she used to issue and in their place a tender curiosity.

He had not forgotten what he had done to her that night in the kitchen. He had been a man running off the fever of his own love, breathing it down deep and giving in to its demands.

Sometimes he thought about raising the topic. He constantly sought to make an apology. Yet, by bringing it up, he worried the past would infringe on the present and he didn't want to be the one to bring this civility he had with Kittie to an end. But the impulse had not died away. Even now, he wanted to take her hand in his and tell her how he felt, always fearful his approaches would be turned away only for him to wallow in the fact that he was a man of nearly thirty, obsessed with a girl not yet eighteen.

You're some fool, he told himself, not for the first time.

'My sister intends to employ you,' Kittie said.

Emerson swallowed the hot, black coffee. 'She does?'

'She does,' Kittie answered. 'For the town anniversary.'

'What is it she would like me to do?' Emerson asked, not daring to look at her.

'Tell stories,' Kittie said, imitating a deeper, man's voice. 'Ain't that what you do?'

Emerson laughed. 'That meant to be me?'

Kittie nodded. 'I thought it a fine impression.'

They looked at one another, laughing still.

'Why was she there?' Emerson asked suddenly.

'Who?'

'Blanche. At your uncle's cabin. What happened?'

The smile left Kittie's face and she stared down at her feet.

'I don't mean to pry—'

'He hanged himself,' she said bluntly. 'Ain't no other way to say it. He had enough of this life and hanged himself.'

Emerson rubbed his face awkwardly.

'There's no cause to be silent,' Kittie said, before concluding, almost regretfully, 'It doesn't shock me anymore.'

'I'm sorry,' he said finally.

'Thank you, but there's no need to be. They fell out long ago, and she must have gone there because her memories weren't sitting right.'

'Why did they fall out?' Emerson asked.

'It's a long story, Emerson. I'll only say that it was a tragedy and nobody's fault. Someone died and Blanche isn't the type to have no one to blame. She told people Shelby, our uncle, was drunk. That he was at fault. That he could have otherwise helped. People believed her and he left the town in shame. I still visited him, mind. How could I not?'

'He didn't say otherwise?' Emerson asked.

Kittie paused for a moment. 'He accepted it as his sentence. For past wrongs.'

'Kittie, that mightn't be true.'

'Emerson, it is,' she replied smartly. 'I read it in a letter he left me.'

The front door of the house opened and closed. Emerson turned, willing for no interruption to Kittie's story.

'Blanche didn't care much for my visiting him, mind.'

'But she let you have the letter? After all that had passed?'

'She didn't even know about the letter until that night we found her,' Kittie began. 'I saw it on her bed that day. It's how I knew she had gone to the cabin.'

Emerson saw how Kittie seemed distant from her telling of the events, and he shifted back for fear of being caught in the blast of their recital.

'Then who found the letter in the first place if it wasn't Blanche?' he asked. 'Elena?'

He refused to ask who found her uncle's body, instead concentrating on the letter. He was aware of the carelessness of such a question, and yet he was keen to draw the retelling entirely from her, like poison.

'No, but Elena knows about it. Now, anyway.' Kittie nodded. 'God knows *she* has plenty, but I won't abide keeping secrets.'

Emerson nodded and then realised with a deep sadness what Kittie was saying and what, thus far, he had refused to consider.

'I found him, Emerson,' Kittie confirmed. 'I found my uncle.'

Emerson's mouth came unstuck when Blanche opened the back door of the house.

'My, you will catch your death!' she said.

Emerson stood from his chair. 'Afternoon,' he said.

'Afternoon,' Blanche replied and squeezed Kittie's shoulder.

Despite the freshness of her recollection, Kittie kissed her sister's arm affectionately.

'Where is Elena?' Blanche asked.

'With Clay,' Kittie replied drily.

'Again?' Blanche said.

'They've gone to adjust the ring,' Kittie added.

Emerson felt the air tauten. Clay and Elena had been engaged now for over a month, and despite their union having been apparent for some years, the now official nature of it did not abide well with the sisters. Nor did it with Emerson. Clay had shot at him, and intended to kill Odell. He thought him responsible for the boy's burns too, although he lacked the explanation. Emerson had grown close to all of the Marianne sisters and it pained him to think of Elena tied to such a man.

Yet what can I say, he thought, *without placing my own neck in the noose?*

He was reminded of the night when he returned to town

with the boy. How, despite the hour, people had lingered before the Long Cape, the empty pails at their feet, the blackened front of the building reluctant to cease smoking. Emerson looked to the boy's hands and wondered if he had been inside before Clay and Ellsworth had dragged him away. And yet Odell had asked Emerson to return him there.

Skirting the attentions of those still about in the street, Emerson had entered through the side of the tavern and taken Odell to the top of the stairs. He was glad to see the fire had not reached there and knocked on the first door he came to, wondering if everyone hadn't fled.

No answer came and Emerson had fixed his hand on the handle. Then, about to push it open, he noted the lantern hanging beside the door, its curious symbols like nothing he'd seen before. Without knowing why, he'd let go of the door and, leaving Odell lying there, had walked back down the stairs. His conscience made him linger by the side entrance for a while, and he heard someone come out onto the balcony. He caught only murmurs and then the boy was taken inside the room, Emerson certain he would come to no more harm.

In the weeks that followed his return to the house, he had considered telling Elena what had happened on the mountain. Yet he feared Clay would move the parts of that night to favour himself – the murders could easily be placed into Emerson's hands. While he knew Clay to be unpopular with Kittie, he was nevertheless, in the eyes of the town and Elena alike, a young man of a prosperous family, one they had known all their lives, and far more removed from the possibility of being a killer than the outsider, Emerson Limeflower.

What could they say about him, after all? That he had arrived, mysterious, and held appointments with a man who, to the knowledge of the town, was now missing? That he had disappeared and only returned when Ellsworth, Ora and Umbründ were gone? That he told stories? He would have to remain silent, or else risk everything he had returned for.

'Well, Elena was meant to help me with things,' Blanche said.

'I can help,' Kittie offered, staring down the yard.

Blanche sighed at Elena's absence, failing to acknowledge Kittie's offer. Emerson could still hear the fragile rattle in her chest. As much as she tried to pretend otherwise, she was weak and not ready to start work on the town celebrations.

'Emerson,' Blanche began. 'I was thinking . . . We could put on a show. In the town. To mark the anniversary of our time as New Georgetown. It could be for everyone, and talk of the town's history and the war.'

Emerson shifted in his seat and Kittie noted how uncomfortable he grew.

'I am uncertain,' Emerson began, 'of talking about the war.'

'But, Emerson, if we are to celebrate the town –' Blanche smiled – 'we must talk about the war.'

'Then perhaps I'd best stay apart from it,' Emerson replied.

Blanche drew a sharp intake of breath.

'But, Emerson,' she began. 'You cannot.'

'He can if he wants to, Blanche,' Kittie added.

Blanche ignored her sister.

'I'd care not to,' Emerson said, more plainly.

'The war,' said Blanche boldly. 'Isn't everyone fascinated by it?'

Emerson's reply was like a stone in water: 'There ain't no fascination in death.'

Blanche adjusted herself.

'I meant nothing by it, Emerson. I did not mean to speak so carelessly.'

363

'You did not,' Emerson replied, running a hand over his head. 'Forgive me. I am unaccustomed to discussing those years and so appear brash in my words.'

Blanche blushed, unsure where to take the conversation.

'I would be delighted to perform,' Emerson said. 'But perhaps we might tell a different story of your town.'

Blanche breathed a sigh of relief and was so bold as to take Emerson's hands.

'Wonderful!' she said. 'Just wonderful!'

Emerson smiled before Blanche dropped her hands and stepped back towards the kitchen.

'Kittie!' she called. 'I will require your help, after all. There is much planning to do.'

With that, she disappeared into the house and shut the door firmly behind her.

'You are a brave man, Emerson,' Kittie said sincerely.

'For doing the show?' he asked.

'For volunteering to help my sister.'

Emerson laughed. 'It won't be all that bad.'

Kittie looked at him knowingly and the smile fell from his face. 'Will it?'

Kittie smiled and the two laughed together.

'Can I ask you about the war?' Kittie said after a pause.

Again, Emerson shifted uneasily.

'I do not mean to interrogate you like my sister,' she said promptly. 'I only wish to ask one thing.'

'Go ahead,' Emerson said, failing to meet her eye. He concluded it was perhaps her turn to pry, after his questions about Shelby.

'Why don't you want to talk about the war? Doesn't everyone?'

Emerson ran a thumb across the rim of his coffee cup.

'I know bad things happened there, Emerson. And I know that doesn't always mean it was bad men who did them.'

'Doesn't it?' Emerson asked bluntly, turning to face her.

Kittie leaned closer to him. 'No,' she said. 'It doesn't.'

Emerson ran a finger along the scar on his palm, eager to change the subject.

'I was looking at the photo on your stairs the other morning,' he said. 'The family portrait.'

Kittie smiled at remembering it.

'Your uncle and your father were on different sides?'

Kittie nodded. 'Plenty of brothers were.'

'Still, I find myself thinking on it. On them.'

Emerson took a drink of coffee and winced from its bitter taste. The thought of those men, one in Union blue, the other in Confederate grey, was something that was familiar to him. And yet he could not shake it from his mind, the idea of two men so close, and yet in complete conflict.

'Do not think on it,' Kittie said, reaching to him.

He looked down at her hand on his jacket and was tempted to take it in his own and finally tell her how he felt about her. He had not been afforded the chance to do so since his return, always suffering interruption from her sisters, or else his own unwelcome memories of the events on the mountain.

Does she know, he wondered, *how I have fallen for her?*

Kittie returned his gaze and took his hand, as though he'd willed it.

'Some say the marshals will be here soon,' she said with a heavy breath. 'You needn't stay because of my sister. You needn't stay to help her.'

'I am not,' he said, holding her hand in reply. 'I stay for you.'

33

December 1879

'Is that all, Mr Welston?'

Clay looked up from his desk. He had the scattered remains of an old picture before him, the glass split and spider-webbed with fractures, the wooden frame broken and blooming one end in its splinters.

'Yes,' Clay said, before thinking on the matter. 'Yes, that's all.'

The man left, placing his cap back on top of his head. Clay watched him go and saw a slight shake of the head as he went. His father had taught him that they were men in whose company others would not be themselves, whether it was workers, partners, family or lovers. His father had always said, 'Look at a man leaving a room and you'll capture his true mind.'

That was what Clay did. He had called the man – Jamison, he believed him to be – into his office to question him about the deadlines the workshop had started to miss. Worse than that, some of the timber sent out had carried the wrong measurements.

'Lest you want to see a church over in Hortonville that you

366

have to get on your hands and knees to enter, I'd suggest paying more fucking attention to the scripture.'

Clay had said these words, one hand tight on the bannister leading down into the workshop, the other clutching plans for the church and flapping them about as though they were the words of a sermon. The theme was accidental, yet it captured their attention – creativity in cruelty had a knack for doing so.

When he had come back to his desk, he had found Jamison there, ready with excuses, and Clay had thrown the plan across the office at him. It had done enough to knock a picture from the wall, sending it smashing to the floor. Jamison had collected the pieces and offered them to Clay. When he refused to take them, Jamison had placed them on the desk. The photo was of Clay's father and the old theatre. He eventually picked it up, feeling the prick of broken glass in his fingertips but, rather than drop it, he gripped it tighter, twisting it as though the image might fall free, like water wrung from a cloth.

When he couldn't tolerate the pain any longer, he'd tossed the frame back onto the desk and slumped in his chair, dismissing Jamison. Clay had almost headed for the Long Cape, but then he remembered the bar was no more. Or not at that moment, anyhow. Burned throughout, dressed in ash and black, it was still standing, but was just another building Welston Timber was refurbishing. And a drink was the last thing he'd find there.

The dead crowded Clay. When he had stood listening to the sheriff, eager not to be seen by him, the tide of his insides hit hard against his ribs. Ora was dead. He had walked into town with his fiancée, worried what the two men from Underwood had to say. Far from the murder and the intent on the minds of everyone else, Clay had been worried the men were there to declare they had known about him and Ora, that they would unveil her like some carnival act and she would point accusingly at him, to tear his world apart. Instead, according to the rumours overheard, she resided up on the mountain, nestled beneath a tree root, frozen solid and curled up like an animal.

And yet, it troubled him. He had hoped to find that Ora had fled the town or else had been rendered mute. He hadn't even suspected her caught up in the ordeal.

Ora had never once threatened to tell Elena, he realised. Even when she had cause to and there was little between Clay and the Marianne sister. Even when telling her might have been the simplest thing to do.

Clay looked at his father's face in the photograph, smiling slightly as he held the waist of an actress dressed in character. They had pulled her from the troupe called in to open the theatre. She stood, with a ruffled dress and heavy make-up, amongst those suited men, like someone from another profession – one that carried no less performance in it, Clay concluded.

His father's face drew no sorrow from him. No longing. Only memories he was glad to have been forgetting at that very moment. Again, Ora's loss pricked at his heart and he realised, however inevitable and uncomfortable, that she was the first person he had been sorry to see die since he was a boy.

June 1862

After much pleading, Clay's mother was buried away from the house. His father had had to persuade the pastor she was a clean woman with a handful of money. As Clay watched, he had con- cocted a story about the woman returning from overseas, eager to be reunited with her sons. The pastor only nodded and concealed the money in the black of his clothes.

The funeral was a modest one and spoke sadly of how few friends Clay's mother had had. His father had taken him there but remained apart, sitting in the carriage by the road the whole time with Clay's older brother. Throughout the ceremony, Clay could smell his cigar smoke as it drifted down towards the grave.

Far from being perched upon a hillside, or in another such scenic spot, the grave was in a dip of ground that stood apart from the graveyard. Clay recalled how there was a tree surrounded by gravestones. They each leaned in on the bark as though placed there, about to fold inward like cards.

He remarked little about the funeral, other than that the pastor called his mother's name wrong. As the few people who were collected there – mainly gravediggers and men of the cloth – drifted away, Clay stood and felt a strange calmness come to him. He had been scared at first, stepping down towards the grave. Embarrassed, perhaps, that he still found fear in such situations, he nevertheless felt the dipped run of earth entirely accommodating of ghouls and the potential for horror. Yet, once his mother was buried and the final pat of the spade on the heaped earth had sung out, he felt at peace.

He listened to the surrounding sounds and even luxuriated in the sweet cigar smoke.

'You ready?' his father said.

Clay jumped at his voice so close. His father was standing a few feet down the slope, arm crooked around a tree for support.

'I'd like to stay a while longer,' Clay replied.

His father took a long pull on his pipe and looked at the grave uneasily. 'She ain't gonna grow back,' he said. 'So there's no point in waiting.'

Clay tried his best to ignore his father's voice, but his words had broken the surface of something. Now Clay's sadness began to seep out. He raised a hand to his mouth, but already his sobs were chugging feebly forth and he covered his face with his hand.

'I'm sorry,' he said.

He meant it for his father, but on looking upwards, saw he had left. A curious thought struck Clay. If his father was not there to receive those words, might they double back like a bird's twist in the air and, with no other place to go, find a home in the grave, his mother's ears, not long unhearing, finally plugged with them?

Clay thought how, even if he had no cause to say them, it was no bad thing that she hear them. He hoped, in some way, they might atone for his father's treatment of her. His own too. He was careful not to tread too far back in his own memories, fearing he'd trip on something he didn't care to be reminded of.

He became reacquainted with the peace and walked closer to the grave. The mounded earth was apart from the gravestone, which the men had nestled in among those by the crowded tree. Clay thought it sad how anyone who cared to visit would suppose she was buried in one place, when she resided in another.

Clay placed his hand on the soil and scraped at it, drawing the dirt beneath his fingernails. Now, if his mind failed to remember her, he would at least have the dirt for a while.

December 1879

Clay set the frame aside and lifted the photograph up from beneath the glass. He peered closer, looking at his father's face and the wry smile, as though he'd been told to place his heavy hand on the actress's waist. A partner of his father's was laughing,

370

head tilted back, and Clay wondered why another photo hadn't been taken. Perhaps it had, but this was the one August sought to have for himself.

The frame had hung in the office since August's tenure at the helm of the business and yet this was the first time Clay had looked on his father's face for more than a passing glance. The fresh reunion between Clay and his father's features gave life to words August had spoken years before.

'Do you know what a hero is?' he had said.

Clay returned to the day of his mother's funeral and how his father had stood apart from her grave.

Is that what you were? he thought, questioning August's spectre. *A hero?*

He reached for someone in his mind he might talk to about it, about his father. Someone he could perform for and watch as their eyes lit up with sycophancy. Ellsworth was whom he thought on.

As much as he fought against it, he missed his companion. Despite the imbalance of their friendship, Ellsworth was someone upon whom Clay relied. Clay recalled how, as with Ora, he hadn't been certain of his friend's death until the sheriff had said as much. He had heard the shot and seen the puff of blood scatter into the night shortly after, but he hadn't known for sure he was dead.

Relationships always became something else in hindsight, something more important, changed by the alchemy of longing and loss. In losing Ora and Ellsworth, Clay had lost a part of himself. He had lost the woman who drew something dark from him, and he had lost the man who revelled in his telling of it. Without them, he was less himself. Without them, he was alone – just as he had been by his mother's graveside that June.

Slowly Clay twisted the thick photograph until the edge tore and he could tug it in half. Something in his mind, long nested since childhood, grew in alarm at having done such a thing. He fought this by organising the pieces in line and tearing them into quarters.

'A picture you did not care for?' a voice said.

Clay broke from his tensed pose, hunched over the photograph in anger. Looking up, he saw a woman, older than himself, in fine dress. She was new to the town and walked confidently through his office, looking at the frames that remained on the walls.

Eventually she came to the vacant space and pointed a gloved finger at the lighter patch on the wall.

'You will need another,' she said. 'A new memory to hang.'

Clay thought her accent from New York, although there was a southern twang she tried hard to suppress. She was an attractive woman, yet Clay had been enjoying the solitude of his office and was prepared to tell her to leave.

'Miss, I—'

'I am looking for materials,' she said, stopping at the framed courthouse in Underwood. 'My late husband commissioned a building and I have arrived to find it incomplete and, what is done, unsatisfactory.'

Clay nodded, breathless from her busy speech. 'Miss, we are busy with work as it is—'

'And we were due to open yesterday. I have five rooms when I have promised eight. I will pay handsomely.'

He could not help but be impressed by her forthrightness. It was rare for a woman to enter such a business and he found himself rewarding her with his rarely bestowed full attention.

'And what is it you are building, Miss?'

Clay sat up in his chair. Ellsworth and Ora shrank in his mind, as though he had been administered a tonic, and his thoughts settled on the woman in his office. She turned from the photographs and walked towards his desk, taking her time with their conversation.

'My name is Clarice, Mr Welston—'

'Clay.'

'Fine. Clay.'

With Ora's death, Clay had been spared Elena ever finding out about his dalliances. He hoped, too, that the truth Odell had threatened to tell was instead encased forever within the boy's fear and torture. To his mind, he was free from the consequences of his actions. He could take his fiancée's hand and let the guilt die away with passing time and a fading conscience.

Yet he knew he wouldn't. He saw Clarice before him and knew he would strive to have her, to betray Elena again. He considered how thinking on such things lay his loss in shadow.

Clay knew that if he were to ignore Clarice, he would spare Elena another betrayal. Yet he would not be himself. And this, to such a man, was a greater tragedy.

'My wish is to finish my hotel. Eberdeen's,' Clarice said.

'Then, Clarice,' Clay replied, standing from behind his desk and offering a handshake, 'allow me to finish it for you.'

34

December 1879

Kittie watched her bedroom window for what she knew would not come. The chill from sitting outside for so long had worked its way into her bones and she pulled the blankets up to her chin. Having tried to fall asleep for some time, she blamed the cold sooner than anything that deserved more complicated thought.

She stepped from her bed and walked across to the window. She looked down to the base of the yard in the hope of seeing him or else drawing his attention.

I am a fool, she told herself, *to try and bait a man.*

Regardless, she fetched the oil lamp from the bedside table behind her and lit the flame. She held it by the window, projecting her image through the cloth curtain. She knew Emerson would see if he looked out from his shack and up at her bedroom. More than that, she willed him to – to see her humming into the night like a siren's call.

What game are we playing at? she asked herself.

Frustrated with herself, she turned the lamp off and stood in darkness once more.

She did not want to behave like this. She wanted to take action and to avoid the games others played. And yet she could not without knowing how she felt for certain. A part of her wanted Emerson to lead, to tell her he felt for her and so encourage reciprocation – a fainter action on her part, of which she was capable.

Kittie supposed she loved Emerson, but then was love something that could ever be so unsure? Was it not something people ran towards, full-blooded, and embraced? Something that dismissed all else, and was never dwelt upon for its lack of certainty?

Furthermore, her feelings were draped in a wish to atone. If she did love Emerson, this love was incomplete and in some way enmeshed with her loss of Chester.

She lifted her eyes and saw a light from the cabin. Her heart beat harder and she peered from the window, pressing her face against the thin curtain, like a veiled bride.

What is he doing? she asked herself, watching the movements of shadow.

In that instant, she built about her desire to see him the many requirements of a woman who wished to show hospitality to her guest. He might be too cold or else be hungry for having not eaten much of the supper earlier. These thoughts proved enough and, before the third reason had rooted in her mind, she had her nightgown over her nightdress and stepped from her room.

Passing Blanche's door on the landing, Kittie could hear the snore her sister had bizarrely acquired since her collapse. It was more like steam rising from a kettle – high-pitched and somewhat alarming. Kittie recalled how she and Elena had stepped out onto the landing together a week before. The sound had drawn the two of them from their rooms. It made her smile, thinking back to how they had looked at one another and then turned towards Blanche's bedroom door. The whistle had spluttered and broken, interrupted by their barely restrained laughter. Kittie struggled again now, holding a palm to her mouth as she jogged quickly down the stairs and towards the rear of the house.

Opening the back door, Kittie saw the ground was precious in the light snow. She hovered on the porch and remembered her shoes were still upstairs. She cursed herself and then saw Clay's boots pushed underneath the bench. She reluctantly slipped her feet inside. They rattled about in those muddy things like the minute feet of a porcelain doll.

The light in the cabin was still on, and now she was on the grass Kittie hurried towards it, the boots knocking her ankles uncomfortably. She raised a hand against the door and then felt her courage fall from her body.

What do I plan to say? she wondered.

She lowered her hand into her nightgown pocket and stepped back as thoughts spun in her head, all pointing towards this being a mistake.

Turning towards the house, Kittie was beginning to walk back when the door opened behind her. Her shadow reached out across the grass, almost, but not quite, reaching the porch.

'Kittie?' Emerson said.

She froze on the spot and remained silent.

'Kittie,' Emerson repeated. 'You okay?'

Kittie felt his hand on her shoulder, heavy and alive, and closer to her skin for the thinness of her nightgown.

'What is it?' he asked.

She turned at the behest of his hand, as though caught up in a dance, and faced him. Her modesty was glad to see him dressed, wearing a loose shirt he most likely slept in. He had just washed and water dripped steadily from the hair that fell over his eyes. He looked at her and his lips moved, asking unspoken questions.

'Can I come in?' she asked.

His eyes blinked in quick succession. She seemed too potent an image, too great a possibility to be there. Since he had returned, they had often spoken under the scrutiny of her sisters, only being afforded the occasional moment alone together. Whatever affection they had for one another only came forth in veiled words or looks.

So quickly were they reminded of the fragility of life, for fear of his death and loss forever, that it seemed the six weeks that followed his return had compensated for what they might have earlier had. Gone was the querying of their hearts and instead they had tentatively started on the path to love.

Yet now the time seemed to have arrived. They were before one another and, in a moment when everything might have been said, Emerson's tongue lumbered in his mouth like stone.

'I should not have come,' Kittie said, and turned.

'No,' Emerson snapped, grabbing her arm.

She spun back to face him, closer this time.

'Ask me again,' he said.

She began to smile.

'Can I come in?'

'Yes,' he said, and drew her in by the arm, as if she might not find the way.

While Kittie sat, Emerson used a towel to wipe dry his damp hair and face.

'I'm sorry if I interrupted,' Kittie said.

'Don't be,' Emerson replied from under the towel. 'I don't have much that counts as routine down here.'

Kittie smiled and pulled her nightgown tighter. It felt strange and electrifying to be in that shack with him rather than returning once more to seek out the entries in his journal. He had a fire going and she noticed pages – those from his jacket, she supposed – curling in the flames.

Emerson noticed her looking.

'You need some more wood,' Kittie said.

He made a cursory hum and looked back at her.

'You come down here to say that?' he asked.

'No,' Kittie uttered, smiling.

'Then can I ask why you are here?'

Kittie was surprised by Emerson's tone.

'Shall I fetch you some wood?'

'No,' Emerson said, turning to look over his shoulder.

'Perhaps I should leave,' Kittie said.

She stood, angry at herself for presuming his thoughts to be the same as hers. She recalled his hand on hers earlier, on the porch, and yet the assumption she had made then now seemed naïve.

'Wait,' Emerson said. 'Christ.'

'What?' Kittie asked.

He moved towards her.

'God help me for saying it, Kittie, but I love you.'

He took her hands.

'And I'll be damned if I lie to myself and say otherwise. I'll be damned if I am rude to you because I wish to hide it. I love you and that is how it should be.'

'Emerson,' she began.

He moved his hands up onto her neck. They were rough and warm against her skin. She tilted her head to rest in one of his hands, turning to kiss the palm before facing him again. His eyes were softer now and, not for the first time, she felt as though a mask had fallen away.

Is this the same man? she asked herself, thinking back on his arrival, the kitchen, his disappearance with Umbründ.

'Who are you?' she asked.

Emerson took a moment to answer, his eyes growing misty.

'I'm not sure I know anymore,' he said delicately.

Kittie placed her own hands on top of Emerson's. Her grip was assuring.

I am yours, she thought, wishing he would hear her.

Emerson bent his head and kissed her. Kittie parted her lips and she felt a surge within herself at giving everything up to this man. A warmth moved inside her like she was some vessel tossed about in the careless grip of the sea.

'Wait,' she said, pulling away. 'Wait!'

Emerson lifted his hands from her and held them in the air. He didn't want to feel incriminated like he had the last time. He wanted her like nothing else, but he would be sure to have her without having to take her.

'What is it?' he asked.

'I need to ask you something.'

Kittie laid a hand on Emerson's chest.

'Then ask it,' he said, his words genuinely encouraging.

'You ever . . . ?' Kittie stammered. 'You ever meet a young man called Chester?'

Emerson stood wordlessly and Kittie had to raise her head to see he was thinking something over.

'I don't recall,' he said eventually. 'I met plenty of folk in the war. Could have been that one of them was Chester.'

'No,' Kittie said. 'After the war. A young man about my age. He had green eyes, black hair.'

Emerson stilled her hand on his chest and cupped it in his own.

'Kittie, what is this?' he said. 'You knew this boy?'

Kittie nodded and heaved out a heavy breath.

'You think I knew him?' Emerson asked.

She nodded again.

'Where is he now?'

'I don't know,' Kittie said. 'He left here a while back.'

'What happened to him?' Emerson asked, easing each word into the air.

'I don't know,' Kittie said.

Her voice was weak and she fought against the ache in her throat.

'I don't know,' she repeated.

Emerson told her it was okay and brought her bowed head forward to rest against him. He ran a hand through her hair and it stopped there, halting by the thick curls.

'Why are you asking me about him?' Emerson said.

Kittie brought her arms around his back, where her fingers just about brushed one another.

'Something you said. It reminded me of him.'

Emerson looked up from her and across his cabin to the stove. The wood hissed and snapped there and he watched as an ember arched its way through the air to land just short of where they were standing. It died out on the wooden floor, fading to an anonymous colour in the light.

'I know it sounds foolish,' she said. 'But there are times when we're together, when I feel like I am looking at him. Speaking to him. Kissing him.'

Emerson looked at her, curious. Kittie would never say it, but, in that moment, she could have mistaken him for Chester. His eyes danced about in the untrustworthy light of the fire. Chester's green eyes lit up in the shadow of the cabin and looked at her – that same look she had seen many times before. His pleading eyes; his boisterous impatience.

'Do you see him now?' Emerson asked.

Chester went and it was Emerson's blue eyes looking at Kittie.

'I do not,' she said, moving closer to him. 'I see you, Emerson.'

He kissed her again and began to move his hand along her waist.

'This okay?' he asked.

Kittie nodded and arched her head backwards. Emerson kissed at her taut neck and over the cloth of her nightgown. She gasped as he moved his lips over her chest. She took his head in her hands and held it there, his face unshaven, his eyes pocketed by dark circles, but his handsomeness all the more wild for it.

She felt that same fire inside her well up and touch every corner of her body. All caution fell away, all hesitance pushed aside for desire.

It ain't the choice, her uncle's voice said, *it's the wondering.*

She smiled and kissed him. Emerson lifted her over onto her back and brought her legs up and around him. His eyes burned blue in the darkness of the cabin, like the heart of a flame.

35

December 1879

Elena believed Clay a fine beau, but wasn't marriage the first step in growing old? While she was impatient for a life with one man and the home they would share together, she knew she would sorely miss the attention of others and the possibility each gaze held.

Clay had bewitched Elena from the first moment. He had visited Blanche and declared himself in love with her sister. Laughing the boy away had only encouraged him and soon bouquets grew afresh at the door with each day. Eventually, Blanche approved their friendship, if only to alleviate her allergies for a day or two. In the years that followed, Clay and Elena's friendship became overgrown with courtship and affection. It went in Clay's favour that his devotion towards Elena coincided with her search for such a thing.

Since her father's death years earlier, Elena had grown increasingly distressed at her mother's solitude. She realised she had always seen her mother as a part of a whole and, without her husband by her side, she now seemed an amputee.

Her mother passed away four years after her father fell at Gettysburg and Elena saw what a considerable force love was. Even if it ultimately led to such heartache, she concluded it was something well worth having for its most luminescent moments. When once she had rarely thought about those boys who showed her favour, she now found herself calculating for a future happiness. Such was her grief at her parents' deaths that it made her vulnerable to ailments of the heart.

Any fears Elena had of Clay being promised to another soon disappeared. She was drawn to him and knew others to be too, always suspecting her friend Ora of carrying a torch for him. It was Elena who had gotten him, though. She had won him from the attentions of others and because of this felt compelled by gratitude to be with him. She told herself she loved him and was convinced of it. Not once, though, did she question her own estimation of love.

Clay had been due to accompany Elena to the jeweller's that morning, but instead had to attend to some business outside of town.

Always business, Elena mused, trying not to dwell on the elusive nature of the man she had promised to marry.

Since Ora had died, she was loath to walk about town alone. It was not so much fear that caused her reluctance as loneliness. The two of them had been friends since childhood and despite the distance that often creeps into prolonged relationships, whenever she'd seen her or the tavern, she'd felt close to her.

They had perhaps met one another's eye only once or twice in a fortnight, yet the fact that this would never happen again moved Elena deeply. It was a sadness that was compounded by the new faces that drifted into town.

This town, she thought to herself, *might as well be another*.

Wishing to neglect her duties to Blanche and failing to imagine Clay might return from his business, Elena walked out into the street. The bustle of people made her feel uncomfortable and she wished for an arm to hang on to assuredly.

Whether it was because of this or her earlier thoughts of Ora, she found herself walking up to the Long Cape. Hammond stood before a pile of blackened wreckage pulled from inside the tavern. He scratched dumbly at the back of his head, as though he hoped it might re-form there for his convenience. His neck was beaded with sweat, even in the cold December air.

'Elena,' he said, turning. 'It's good to see you.'

Elena returned his smile and stepped onto the porch.

'And you, Hammond,' she returned. 'How are you?'

'Fine,' he said. 'Happy for the work. It keeps me from the farm, at least.'

Elena nodded, remembering Hammond's father.

'When will you reopen?' she asked.

'That's a question,' Hammond replied. 'Soon, I hope. More people calls for more drinks. Clay's men say they can have the bar built by the end of the month, and then we just need the delivery of alcohol. It's all paid for, mind. The Bird has seen to that.'

He moved closer to Elena.

'She's still up there,' he said. 'But she's made little noise since. I worry if she wasn't hurt in the fire.'

Elena tilted her head up to the back of the tavern, where the joints in the frame gave way to the older structure.

'Might I see him?' she asked.

'I don't know, Elena,' Hammond replied.

She narrowed her eyes. 'Please.'

Hammond scratched the back of his head again. 'Shit,' he offered to the sky.

'Please.'

'Wait here,' Hammond said, turning and saying something to one of the men.

He walked across the newly laid boards, dipping occasionally onto the muddied ground beneath. The corridor was still there, for the most part. A few rooms had been blackened, while some had been merely whipped by flame.

After a time, Hammond came back downstairs and waved her over from the corridor. She walked through, some builders taking her arm as she trod across narrow beams and planks.

'Wait in here,' Hammond said, opening the door of the end room.

Inside, the room was bare but for a chair and a dresser. The black stain of the smoke on the floorboards stopped abruptly, showing where a bed had been. Elena took a seat at the dresser and checked her appearance, tucking a loose strand of hair behind an ear. She was adjusting her tall collar when she heard footsteps above her, which soon came down the stairs and to the door. In the mirror's reflection, she saw Odell enter the room and a strange jealousy plucked at her heart, knowing he shared a room with the Bird.

He had changed considerably since she had last seen him. His hair was longer and he had shaved the wisps that grew across his upper lip and chin. He had lost some weight too but looked better for it, the touch of gauntness suiting him. His hands were dressed in fabric and balled slightly, like a boxer's mitt.

'Odell,' Elena said, turning.

'Elena,' Odell returned, holding the door open behind him.

'You can close the door,' she said.

He obliged and pushed it shut.

'How are you?' she said, her voice cracking as she looked at his hands.

'Well,' he said, smiling.

A moment passed.

'And you?' he asked.

'Well,' she replied. 'Won't you sit?'

She stood from the chair, but Odell held up his stiff hands in refusal. Elena moved across the room to him and Odell stepped backwards, bumping into the door.

'Do I make you nervous?' she asked.

Odell nodded.

'Why is that?'

'You know why,' he said, looking at her fully for the first time.

'We have never talked about it, though,' Elena said.

'What's the use in talking about it now?' Odell asked.

Elena felt adrift in the middle of the room and wished she had remained seated at the dresser.

'Do you want me to leave?' she asked.

'No,' Odell replied, shaking his head. 'I do not.'

A smile rose and fell from Elena's face.

'I apologise,' Odell said, squinting. 'I do not like the way I am around you.'

'That's a curious thing to say,' Elena replied.

Odell nodded and met her eyes briefly. 'It is a curious thing to feel.'

Why am I here? Elena asked herself. *To give this boy peace, or else to hear his flattering words once more?*

'I loved you,' Odell said suddenly. 'I'm sorry to say that. But I don't no more, so it's all right. There ain't no need to tell anyone.'

'I wouldn't,' Elena said quickly.

'I thought on this moment,' Odell continued. 'I won't lie. Me telling you that – I thought on it a lot, but I never believed it might happen. I'm sorry to tell you that, and I'm sorry to be like

386

this, but I got to tell you it. There ain't never been something I've had to tell someone so bad.'

Elena nodded at Odell and watched as he forced himself on through the words. She was taken aback by what he said, his feelings laid so bare. Their purity undid the awkward knots she had always considered bound him. Now, in this room, there was an intimacy to him that touched her. She had to stop herself from thinking how Clay had never said such things.

'Thank you,' she said and frowned at her words.

Odell seemed relieved. 'You ain't angry?'

'Why would I be angry at hearing that?' she asked.

Odell looked down again and moved a foot back and forth on the floor, pushing the grease into a fold. The torment on his face stirred memories of the last time she'd seen him, outside Marianne House. Guilt swarmed around Elena as she now thought of these two versions of Odell as the same.

'I am sorry,' she said.

'What for?' Odell asked.

'I wish I could take those words back,' she said. 'I do. I had no right to say them. Blanche was sick . . .' She trailed off, exhausted at trying to find reasons to explain cruelty.

'It don't matter—' Odell began.

'It does,' Elena rushed in. 'It does, Odell. I didn't mean any of that. I promise you.'

Odell nodded, his eyes misting up. He smiled at her. 'Thank you for coming here to say that,' he said, and moved towards the door.

'Do you have to leave so quickly?' she asked. 'I would like to sit and talk for a while.'

'I would like that,' Odell replied. 'Please.' He gestured to the chair and walked across the room, leaning against the dresser.

'What happened to your hands?' Elena asked. 'Might I ask that?'

Odell looked down at his bandages and spread his fingers as wide as they might go. 'Burned,' he said bluntly.

Elena gasped and moved to touch them.

'How?' she asked.

'The fire,' he said.

Odell looked at her. He might have unwrapped his hands and shown her the horror of his injury, telling her how the man she loved was responsible. What hell could Clay deliver on now? What else could he do to Odell?

Clay was a man no longer able to stride about the town. He was at the mercy of two men who knew the truth of that night. Odell imagined his face when Elena confronted him, before he was led from town in the back of a barred wagon. And yet, far from joy, it brought the boy misery, as though the great fortune of his and Kyoko's survival might be undone by a long-brewing hate. It was as if his mercy towards his tormentor was complicit in his own happiness. Odell preferred not to invite the threads of revenge to entwine with a life he was eager to start living.

Elena took hold of his bandaged hands, and Odell noticed the glimmer of a stone on her finger. His heart twitched and sank a distance.

They will marry, he realised.

Elena covered her left hand in a feeble attempt to hide the ring. Odell smiled and she smiled back. He could not damn her as well as Clay, for now she was bound to him in ways outside of the frivolous heart. Odell believed his silence regarding Clay the right decision if it meant Elena was spared hurt.

'Congratulations,' he said, looking at the ring.

Elena smiled.

'Are you happy?' he asked.

Odell's words surprised her. She paused for a moment before nodding. He smiled at this and boldly took her hands in his, kissing them softly. Elena blushed and stood from her chair to say something more, but Odell mistook this for an eagerness to leave and walked past her towards the door.

'Thank you,' he said, turning, 'for coming here.'

'Odell,' she said, toeing the edge of a border she never thought to cross.

Odell looked at her, his memory massaging his heart and shortening his breath.

A part of me will love her forever, he thought.

36

December 1879

Emerson woke heavy headed, his body falling still in sleep. The curtains were open and he tilted his head up to watch the mist lifting from the lawn in the winter sun. A bright block of light was cast into the room, which warmed his bare legs. On his chest lay Kittie, her tousled hair spread out. He placed a hand on her head and brushed some hair away to better see her face. She was breathing deeply and the little finger of her left hand twitched in the hair of his chest.

Kittie Marianne, he thought.

He recalled the doctor's words when he arrived in New Georgetown – about the sisters on the hill.

How could I have known then that I would fall in love with her?

For, even after the satisfaction of lying with Kittie, those feelings remained. He was so very glad for that. Before now, he had had occasion to sleep with a woman, so keen and assured in his thinking, only for it all to fall away in those moments that followed quickly on the heels of the act. He was thankful to his heart that his love remained that morning.

He knew Blanche would soon be up and keen to begin preparations for the town anniversary. For his own part, he would have to give some thought to what show to put on. He had begun to think it over the night before, brightly alert with a keen panic in the early hours of the morning. His plans were nevertheless quashed by Kittie's arrival.

The thought of the townspeople all turning their attention his way made him feel uneasy. Up till now, he had avoided their gaze, slipping through the town's recent upheavals. Yet now he would invite them to look upon him. For the first time since his arrival – indeed, for the first time in many years – he would no longer be a stranger.

'Kittie,' he said quietly. 'Kittie, wake up.'

She stirred on his chest and then returned to sleeping. He shook her gently by the shoulder and she woke. She lifted her head and looked at him, a moment of surprise caught on her face. She pulled the sheet to hold it against her naked self.

'Mornin',' she said.

'Good morning,' Emerson smiled.

'What time is it?'

'Early still, I'm guessing.'

'Blanche will be up soon,' Kittie said, looking to the house.

'That's what I was thinking.'

Kittie seemed panicked to Emerson. He feared she regretted the night before, and placed a hand on her arm to still her. He felt embarrassed that, in covering her own modesty with the sheet, she was exposing his.

'Emerson—' Kittie began.

The back door of the house clapped in its latch. They both jumped and turned to the house.

'You sure you left them out here?' Elena asked.

'Hush, God damn it. You want to wake your sister up?'

Kittie and Emerson looked at each other and a moment later Kittie was up from the bed and pulling on her undergarments. Emerson's mind raced and he crossed to the window in a crouch and tugged the curtains shut from beneath the frame.

'I left them right here,' Clay said.

Emerson raised himself up to watch from the window and his stomach twisted with the realisation of what they were looking for. Clay's boots sat on the porch of the cabin, scattered with snow and glistening wet from the night before. He was struggling to understand how they had got there when Kittie arrived at his shoulder.

'What is happening?' she asked.

'Clay's looking for his boots,' Emerson replied.

Kittie squeezed her eyes shut tight.

'Son of a bitch!' Clay said.

Emerson looked from the window again and saw Clay turning Elena's head towards the cabin. He marched down the yard barefoot, the melting snow darkening the bottoms of his trouser legs.

'You gotta hide,' Emerson said to Kittie. 'Right now.'

Kittie nodded and smiled. Emerson couldn't help but smile back and, as she moved away, he tugged her back to him and kissed her. She placed her hands on his face and touched her forehead to his.

'You in there?' Clay called from the porch.

Still wrapped in the bed sheet, Kittie's hunched form padded across the floor, turning this way and that to try and find somewhere to hide. Emerson watched and almost laughed at her efforts.

Clay banged his fist against the door.

'Hey! You in there?' he called.

Emerson kept still, trying his best not to give voice to the old floorboards beneath him. Perhaps, in time to come, he and Kittie would tell the others about their feelings for one another. He would be proud to, in fact. But now, in this most off-colour of scenarios, he would remain as silent as the earth.

'Fine,' Clay said, slipping his boots on. 'Stay hidden. We will talk about this, Emerson.'

Clay stepped from the porch and marched back up the yard. As the sound of his his footsteps died away, Emerson boldly looked out of the window and saw him walking up to Elena, who looked as confused as he.

As Clay and Elena went back inside the house, Emerson lowered himself from the window and blew a heavy sigh of relief into the wall. Kittie collapsed into laughter.

'I thought he was going to come in,' she said.

'Me too,' Emerson said. 'And what then?'

Kittie opened her mouth to say something, but failed to find the words.

'Wouldn't that make for an interesting breakfast?' she said finally.

Emerson laughed at the idea and stood. Kittie did the same and Emerson noted how, with her hair loose about her shoulders, she was a picture of beauty. He recalled a previous thought and leaned in to her, kissing the mark on her lip.

'What was that?' she asked.

'Something I've been meaning to do,' Emerson replied.

Kittie smiled at him. She started to dress again and did so side on. Emerson turned wordlessly, amused at her modesty after such a night. When he glimpsed her over his shoulder, she was replacing her nightdress and the long drop of the open fabric across her chest made his heart ripple.

'Will you come back tonight?' he asked.

'If you want me to,' she replied.

Emerson nodded as Kittie placed her feet in his boots and opened the door a fraction to look up towards the house.

'Blanche means to have me occupied all day,' she said. 'But I will make time to find you.'

'I'd be glad for it,' Emerson replied.

Kittie opened the door wider, then stopped and closed it again. To Emerson's surprise, she reached her arms out wide and turned, as if to music, the boots still on her feet.

'What was that?' Emerson asked, as she opened the door once more.

'I turn, Emerson,' she said. 'I dance.'

Even after she had left, her spirit filled the room and Emerson wanted to languish in that moment. He had seen many things that might make a man wish he were blind, but so long as he had her to look upon, such as he did then, he would count his sight amongst the dearest things life could bestow.

37

December 1879

'Are you ready, Emerson?' Blanche asked from the cabin's porch.

Emerson straightened up. He had been slumped on the edge of the bed, thinking on Kittie.

'Come in, Blanche,' he called out.

She entered the cabin and smiled at him as he sat.

'It is a good day for a celebration, I feel,' she said, breathing in as much as her weak lungs would allow.

Emerson didn't reply, but fetched his jacket from where it hung on the back of a chair.

'I was thinking you would talk me through your presentation first,' Blanche said, 'before we walk into town.'

Emerson nodded. He laboured in his movements, his mind elsewhere, picking at the past when it might have been easier to let it set.

'If you don't mind my asking, Emerson, are you all right?'

Emerson was lost in a moment before he turned to her.

'What?' he said.

'You seem to be in another place entirely,' Blanche said, stepping towards him.

January 1878

Growing up, as he did, in a disorderly house, Emerson believed he had developed an unnatural ability to find one. As he pulled his clothes free of the snagging branches, he knew he was headed to one such place the owners were keen to keep hidden. And with that came its dangers. A sense of lawlessness had prevailed since the war's end and people were only now beginning to remember what such things as consequences were.

For most of the way he had followed a crude map, drawn for him in a hurry by a traveller in passing. The man had used Emerson's back to lean on, taking care in his directions. It denoted natural things – strange-looking rocks and cuts in trees preferred to roads and turns. Since feeling the press of the man's pencil in his back, Emerson had been worried it was all folly. Yet he had found those signs sure enough. And finally, to his relief, the woods began to thin and he stepped into a clearing and saw the building before him.

Emerson paid up front for three nights at the house. He didn't have much choice in the matter, as the man who seemed to run the place caught sight of the notes in his wallet.

'Three-night minimum,' he had said, his gaze testing and tentative.

Emerson paid, regardless, and was just glad to put his head down for a night. The room he rented was little more than a storeroom with an old mattress, stained and curdled with wear, flopped onto a weak and rusting frame. It was still the best night's sleep he had had since the war.

On the second day, a knock at the door preceded the man from the front desk entering with an eager shape behind him.

'You've got company,' the man said.

Emerson was lying back on the bed, thinking on nothing in particular. He raised his head and saw a slim boy peer over the man's shoulder. He had long black hair and his eyes were a curiously bright shade of green.

'Where's he going to sleep?' Emerson asked.

'I can fit a mattress in here, beside your bed.'

Emerson looked about the room and failed to see how anything might fit anywhere. 'I paid for the room,' he said.

'So's he,' the man replied, pointing to the boy.

'Then give me my money back,' Emerson said, sitting up.

'Now, wait just a minute.'

Emerson stared him down and watched as his courage fell away.

'Fine,' the man said.

He reached into his jacket for a fold of money. From it, he pulled two dollars, which he reluctantly dropped into Emerson's open palm before leaving the room.

Emerson watched his new roommate look around, seemingly excited by it all, until eventually their eyes met.

'Chester,' the boy said, reaching out his hand.

'Emerson.'

'Sorry to be a trouble, mister,' he said. 'You won't know I'm here.'

'I doubt that,' Emerson said, lying back on the bed.

Chester set his things down and walked over to the window. It was dirty to the point of being opaque, but he rubbed at the glass with a shirt cuff. Emerson watched him and blew out his breath with resignation.

'How old are you, Chester?' he asked.

397

Chester looked down at him, his eyes alive. It was as though he found the very prospect of conversation exciting.

'Sixteen,' he said.

Emerson raised his eyebrows. 'They let you stay in a place like this at sixteen?' he asked.

'My parents are dead,' Chester said. 'So they don't have nothing to say on the matter.' He let out a weak laugh and continued to rub at the window.

'I was talking about them,' Emerson said, pointing at the door. 'This place. They let you stay here that young?'

Chester's mouth dropped open and realisation crossed his features.

'Shit,' he said. 'I'm eighteen.'

'Don't worry,' Emerson laughed. 'I won't tell nobody. And, in this place, you keep the money coming, not many will ask.'

'Thanks, mister.'

Emerson nodded and closed his eyes once more. All he could hear was the rub of Chester's shirt on the glass, along with the murmur of conversation from the floor below.

'Say, Chester,' he said. 'You want to get something to eat?'

Chester agreed and they trod downstairs together to the kitchen.

More as a result of Chester's eagerness to follow than Emerson's willingness to lead, the two spent most of that day together. After their uneasy digestion of what the house's kitchen passed for food, they scrounged half a dozen cigarettes from around the room and took a walk through the surrounding woods.

It had been a true while since Emerson had engaged in conversation so regularly with someone, and he found himself sharing more from his own past than he had intended. Chester spoke freely also, and whatever story the boy had rehearsed before he entered the house soon fell away.

'Want another?' Chester asked, proffering another cigarette from his share.

Emerson shook his head, having grown sombre at recounting his history. He wished to return to his room and lie on the bed some more.

'I'm gonna head back,' he said.

Chester's face dropped somewhat. 'I might take a wander back with you,' he said.

His voice was cracked and dry, and Emerson felt like pulling the unlit cigarette from the grip of his lips, telling Chester it failed to impress him. He decided to allow the boy whatever missteps youth brought, though, and soon the two began to talk of where they were from. Despite the unwelcome memories, Emerson felt no reason not to talk about his past.

'My daddy ran away too,' Chester chipped in, glad for this sorrowful similarity.

Emerson trained his eyes on the path.

'He used to beat me. Sometimes bad. The town I was in tossed him out one day.'

'Yeah?' Emerson said, surprised.

Chester nodded before continuing. 'Everyone knew and then one day it was so bad I could hardly breathe. The schoolmistress gathered some people together and told him to get out. Said I could live with her for a while.'

'She turn you away too?' Emerson said. The words came out of him before he realised their indelicacy.

'No,' Chester continued, unaware. 'I left.'

'Of your own accord?' Emerson asked.

An agitation grew in Chester and he bent and split the cigarette as he twirled it between his fingers.

'I had my reasons,' he said, acting like someone else.

'And they were?'

Chester took a moment to himself, walking down that path back to the house. Something loosened in his face, as if he might have been realising there was no harm in sharing secrets with a stranger.

'The town,' he said reluctantly. 'I get that they was looking out for me. I get that, and don't think I ain't grateful for it. But things didn't feel right.'

They had come to a halt in the road and a gust of wind blew across the both of them.

'There was this girl too. And a friend like a brother. There was all sorts there to make me want to stay, and sometimes I could see a future there — all married and such.' Chester shook his head, momentarily embarrassed. 'But it weren't right. It weren't meant to be.'

'Why wasn't it?' Emerson asked.

'It weren't a place I could stay,' Chester said. 'It weren't a home.'

Emerson noted how he kept his head down, growing uncomfortable with the telling. 'And this place is?' he asked.

'Sometimes,' Chester began, 'I don't think any place is.'

The words took Emerson by surprise. He swallowed and it seemed to echo down the path.

'So you left, there and then?' he asked.

Chester nodded. 'I got up and gathered my things; plain left.' His pretence of toughness had begun to creep back into his words and he puffed out his chest.

'You ever think of going back?' Emerson asked.

He could see that town light up behind Chester's eyes, even as the boy shook his head.

'No, siree,' he replied.

They began to walk again and Chester looked at the mess of his cigarette before flicking it into the trees at the side of the path.

'And the girl?'

'Just some girl,' Chester said back immediately.

They walked on and the smoke from the house proved a welcome sight through the haze of snowfall.

'Anyway,' Chester continued, 'I need myself a woman.'

Emerson managed a laugh that broke the surface of the sadness he had just assumed from Chester's story.

'You ever . . . ?' Chester asked, filling in the gap with a vulgar hand movement.

'With a whore?' Emerson asked, Chester nodding back. 'I grew up with whores, remember?'

Chester whooped and even clapped Emerson on the back.

'Shit, I forgot. You must have hardly been off your back. And when you was, you were just on your front, I bet. Shit, what a place to grow up!'

Emerson spat a stray hair of tobacco from his lip.

'Your place sounds better,' he said.

Chester failed to hear those words as they walked into the house. They each stamped their boots and the boy seemed enlivened by what the rest of the day might hold. Down the end of the hallway, a whore was walking with her arm draped around the neck of a bearded man.

'Shit, that damn looks like Umbründ,' Chester said, mispronouncing the name.

'What's one of those?' Emerson asked, unbuttoning his coat.

Chester laughed. 'It ain't a "those", it's a "him": the doctor in that town.'

Emerson nodded disinterestedly before his past came back to him. He thought on the haze of the doctor in his father's carry-over – something he had not considered for years. He shook the fancy of such coincidence from his mind.

'Sounds foreign,' he said, eager to move the conversation along.

'Don't it just?' Chester said, staring after the whore who had since closed the door behind her. 'He sounds it, too, all curly in his speech. Fine man. Fine dress.'

Emerson's heart beat faster at the idea of fate's hand at his back. He thought of the fine wallet at home about this man's person.

This cannot be, he told himself.

After he had found his father, he had settled his dead mother's debt. He had turned Amos's bid for revenge away, refusing to settle the accounts of a man he himself despised. Was his enemy's enemy not his friend?

'He still there?'

'I guess so. Been a while since I was there, but he looked sure for staying.'

'Where's he from?'

'From? I don't know. Nowhere people know. Mysterious fella.'

Emerson willed Chester to say something that would break the likelihood. To describe him as a young man, or else colour his life with inflexible detail that would make this impossibility, once again, impossible. Yet he did not, and Emerson felt the strong prospect of being confronted with the man his father wished to hunt.

Is this not life, Emerson thought, *pushing me along its path?*

His coat off and over his arm, Chester began to walk down the hallway. Another couple of whores were talking to one another, pulling playfully at each other's straps and frills. They looked at Chester, both fixing on him teasingly. They took it in turns to whisper in one another's ear, which drew a wide smile on the boy's face.

'Wait,' Emerson said.

'I done my waiting,' Chester replied.

Emerson checked himself and tried another tack. 'This town – I want to hear more about it. This doctor sounds familiar to my ears.'

Chester's eyes stayed on the whores. 'Listen, I'll come find you later. We'll have a whisky and talk some more,' he said.

Emerson nodded. 'You do that. Come find me.'

The impatience bubbled up inside him and he watched as Chester entered the company of the two whores. One ran her hand across his head while the other pushed a thigh against his side. Emerson overheard a stray phrase from one, telling Chester how they intended to make a man of him. He was bewitched, and Emerson watched, strangely saddened by a boy so assured of the truth he garnered from burlesque.

In the hours that followed, Emerson did little else but stare at the ceiling above his bed. Faint yellow stains with specks of black made sickening constellations there and he wondered what could have happened to place such a stain on the ceiling of a tall room.

Emerson turned and felt his eyes grow heavy. It was dark outside now and the candle on his bedside flickered weakly as its wax spread flat on the wood. Chester had been with those whores all afternoon. Emerson only hoped the boy had money enough to pay them, come the end.

When they had been in the room earlier, he had glimpsed how thick the boy's wallet was. It was only now that Emerson struggled to align the boy's story with the small fortune he carried. He would forgive thievery of most men, having done it plenty himself, yet Chester seemed far from adept in such things, crucially lacking the care and attention a good thief required.

Deciding he could not afford to worry about Chester, Emerson's mind turned from the boy's money to the man he'd described. He thought himself a fool now for heeding his father's will. Why should he hunt this man? Was coincidence reason enough? He still suffered nightmares and not a day went by when he didn't think on what the doctor did in that hotel parading as a hospital. He questioned why this man had been returned to him by fate.

A knock came at his door and Emerson sat up on the bed. If it were Chester, he would have just come in, unless he had misplaced his key. Emerson blew out the candle in caution and could see the light creep underneath the door like some luminous rug. Blocks of shadow were in four patches, which told him two people stood there. His mind placed persons in those boots: Chester and an angry pimp; the proprietor and another tenant. Emerson doubted any of these combinations and instead looked about his room to arm himself. He had never had such an encounter in a disorderly house, but had heard of them and, even in his youth, had been woken in the night to hear the muffled strains of someone being robbed, or even murdered.

Why me, though? he asked himself.

He had kept his wallet close and his head down. He could only surmise it was Chester who had drawn attention to him unwillingly. Another knock came, which was soon followed by muted conversation. Emerson feared the door would be kicked down if he didn't open it soon.

'Hold on,' he called out.

More muttering followed and he saw the shadows shift

404

impatiently below the door. Emerson stood and carefully trod along the floorboards. He looked around the room for something heavy. Failing to find anything, he took up Chester's bag and dug deep within it. He felt the coarse brush of crumpled paper against his skin and then pulled his arm sharply away as it pressed onto the point of a knife. Emerson slid the blade carefully behind his back, down into the waist of his trousers. He walked across the room and stood to the side of the door, so he wouldn't be bowled over by a shove or kick, one hand on the lock and the other on his hip and close to the blade. He unlocked the door and his heart beat hard.

'You Emerson?' one of the men said.

There were two of them, both tall and unruly shapes of men. Their faces were each cast in an uneven scattering of stubble and scars: an unflattering anonymity of threat. The only thing Emerson could see to separate them was an out-of-character red flower, pushed into the lapel of the man who had just spoken.

'Who's asking?' Emerson replied.

'That means yes,' the other man said, pushing the door all the way open.

Emerson let him and stood there with his back to the wall, his hand still on his hip. Red Flower entered, closing the door behind him and blocking any escape.

'Over there,' he said, his breath stale on Emerson's face.

Emerson walked to the middle of the room and shielded his back from the men as he went.

'This about the money for the room?' he asked. 'Cos I paid it in full.'

'It ain't that,' red flower said.

'It's about the company you been keeping,' the other one said.

Emerson shook his head, nonplussed. 'What about him?' he asked.

They must have gotten his name from Chester and he wondered what could have drawn it from him. The boy was ignorant enough to confess it freely, but why would he? The only circumstance Emerson could fix on was if he had called out for help. The thought shot a shiver down his spine right to the point of the knife.

'He's downstairs, asking for you,' the other man said.

'Yep,' Red Flower confirmed. 'Wants you to take a walk down there and join him. Says he done bought you a whore to thank you for your company.'

The other man laughed.

'That so?' Emerson mused. 'Mighty grateful of someone I only met this afternoon.'

'Must be your fine company,' Red Flower said, picking at something in his teeth.

'Must be,' Emerson said.

Emerson didn't doubt that these two men intended to rob him and Chester, if they had not done so to the boy already. He knew of men like this, who supposed themselves businessmen outlaws, scouring the last refuges of the desperate, knowing their pockets were most likely filled with runaway money. Yet, in their theatrics, they were offering Emerson a way out of the room freely. He knew this to be something he should not refuse. It was dark outside and snowing so heavily his tracks would soon be gone. He would be down some dollars, but in possession of his life.

He wondered if these men's plans often worked. Perhaps their stories were never tested or rebuffed because of the type of men telling them. If Red Flower had put a hand around his throat, he might have told him Lincoln was outside to see him and Emerson would have nodded along as though he had been expecting him.

Emerson lifted a hand to pick up his bag from the side of the room.

'You don't need that,' Red Flower said.

'No, you don't,' the other chipped in. 'He's got money plenty.'

'Yep,' Red Flower chimed.

Emerson looked quickly at both men and realised they must be twins. The red flower was for little more than to tell them apart. Perhaps the one wearing it was the loser of some late-night wager, the consequence of too many employers confusing them for each other.

Emerson let his hands drop.

'Well,' he said. 'That's plenty generous.'

The two men nodded and Red Flower pulled open the door. Emerson walked slowly from the room and, for the last few blind steps over the frame, a palm at his back shielding the knife, his breath caught in his throat like a lump of ice. As he turned, he just saw Fed Flower grinning at him.

'Enjoy,' the man said.

The door closed and Emerson guessed he would have little time before the two men grew impatient at the lack of money in the room. He trod carefully before running down the stairs and along the hall where Chester had met the two whores.

'Chester!' he called in a strained hush against the doors. 'Chester!'

One of the doors opened. Out came a girl who couldn't have been much younger than Emerson.

'Who you looking for, handsome?' she asked, leaning against the frame.

'A boy named Chester,' he said.

The girl's eyebrows lifted and she smiled.

'It ain't like that. He's my –' Emerson struggled to find a word – 'partner.'

'Black hair, green eyes?' the girl asked.

Emerson nodded.

'I saw him go in there,' she said, pointing over his shoulder and to the last room on the right. 'Been in there a long time too. Seems like he worked up an appetite, your partner.'

The last word held all the significance Emerson had tried to avoid. He went to tip his hat to the whore, but realised it was up in the room with everything else he had now lost, so he merely nodded. She nodded back and pulled the door to a close once more.

Emerson knocked at the last room on the right and called Chester's name. He set his hand on the doorknob and prepared himself for the wrath of a stranger mid-act. He pushed against the door, but it wouldn't open. He thought for a moment it was locked, but felt some give and realised something on the other side was obstructing it. He pushed harder still and eventually the door gave way.

Emerson closed the door behind him and looked to see one of the two whores Chester had been speaking with, sitting on the floor there. The door had hardly disrupted her and she had been pushed a foot forward in the same loose pose – hands in her lap, legs apart. Emerson feared she was dead, but her head lolled clumsily and, when he shook her shoulder, a glass syringe bounced fraily on the floor.

Opiate, he thought.

Emerson took stock for a moment and then pushed her back against the door. She let out a weak laugh, as though it were all a game. As her head lolled the other way, Emerson noted a reddening bruise on the side of her face. He tried to piece together the sequence of events that might explain what surrounded him, but was overcome with the urgency of finding Chester and then leaving this place.

He looked around the room, but nothing led him to Chester.

As he spun back to the door, his heel slid in something and he noted a smear of red. He bent down and saw beads of blood, cloaked by the pattern of the floorboards, leading to the window. Emerson stood and pulled the curtain from the glass in a bid to see if Chester was outside. Instead, he was confronted by a handprint – the swirls that conformed to make fingers, a thumb and a palm, made up from the darkest red.

Emerson's mind rattled with panicked thoughts. He knew he had little time and that the men upstairs would soon come down to find him. He took one last look at the drug-addled whore and opened the window, pulling himself from the building.

The night was colder than he had expected and his hands felt like they had been plunged through glass as he steadied himself in the deep snow. He paused to make certain he was alone, and ran into the darkness of the woods. He wasn't sure what direction to run in, but would put it down to some fate if he found Chester on the way. If not, then he was never meant to, and the boy was on his own. Such logic only belonged to a frightened mind.

When the house was slipping from sight, Emerson heard several raised voices. He couldn't tell if they belonged to Red Flower and his twin, even suspecting for a second they might belong to the owner. He likely wasn't a man who appreciated his whores being drugged, or a customer skipping free. Emerson was quickening his pace when his foot caught on something. He fell heavily into the snow and felt the something pull at his leg. Squinting behind him into the darkness, he saw a foot hooked onto his own and that it belonged to Chester. The boy was tied to a tree, his face badly beaten. He held a hand to his side, just beneath the ropes, blood pumping freely between his fingers. What Emerson had first taken for a shadow beneath the boy was a dark pool of blood, pulsing wider.

'What happened?' Emerson asked dumbly.

'Robbed,' Chester breathed. 'Two men, one's—'

Emerson hushed him as the voices from the house grew louder. He pulled the knife from behind his back and began to cut through the rope. It was thick, like something from a dock. As he heaved at the rope, it pressed into Chester's body and drew moans from him.

'Quiet,' Emerson said.

'Go,' Chester replied. 'Leave me here.'

Emerson shook off the boy's words and continued to cut. He was working the rope furiously in the dark and his hands were half frozen. Losing his grip, the knife stuck into the tree bark and his hand slid down the blade. He cried out and pulled the knife free with his other hand, going to work again. He was even slower now and he saw the pinpricks of lantern light dispersing from the house.

'Shit,' he said.

He stopped for a moment, knowing he would not have time to cut Chester free and escape. He slowly lifted the boy's hand from the wound in his side and looked closely at the cut. Despite the weak light, he could see it ran long and deep.

'What happened?' Emerson asked, without taking his eyes from the injury, as though the torn flaps of skin might move like a mouth in reply. 'Why didn't they just rob you?'

Chester looked at him as if he could pass words within a glance. Emerson thought back on his earlier suspicions and understood.

'Or did you do the robbing?' Emerson asked.

'I'm sorry,' Chester said feebly.

Emerson winced at the cut in his hand and lifted a handful of snow, squeezing it.

'They want it all back,' Chester said.

'Then give it to them.'

'I can't. I've already spent some. Getting here. The women.'

'Jesus,' Emerson said, looking around in the hope that an answer might be hanging from a tree in the night.

'They didn't believe me,' Chester continued. 'Said I was holding out on them. One – with the flower – got angry. Cut me.'

He slumped slightly with the effort of speaking. Emerson took the knife up once more and began to tear at the rope. It was awkward in his left hand and he barely split the fibres.

Chester looked at him and rested his head back against the tree. 'Go,' he said. 'I'll tell them I can get it back. I'll convince them.'

Emerson was saddened at how the boy could remain naïve, even after suffering such hurt. The men would never let him go, especially given the nature of his wound. They'd keep what they already had and pick him apart, body and mind, searching for more.

Emerson remembered the town the boy spoke of and he thought about asking him those questions he had prepared all through the afternoon. Chester was in pain though, and, despite his ignorance, fearful of the men approaching.

'I can make things better for you,' Emerson said reluctantly.

Chester seemed puzzled and then he looked down at the knife. He shook his head, tears welling in his eyes.

'No,' he croaked feebly.

'It's not that,' Emerson said, dropping the knife.

Chester's eyes widened as Emerson came closer, more to comfort him than anything else. He began, and all went silent. The two men's souls quietened and it was as though they had both been placed on another side of the earth, far away from trouble. Emerson saw the town and the faces that lived there. He guessed at the friend and the sweetheart, but raced through, his work light and eager. He caught the edges of something, but then lost it as Chester's fear of the approaching men welled back up.

Don't ever take it all, Amos had said. *More for your sake than theirs.*

I have no choice, thought Emerson.

He knew he did not have the leisure to search in that boy's mind. The path was misted over with fear and what he imagined to be approaching death. Emerson would have to take everything if he wished to take anything at all.

He tried to justify his actions, thinking how it might be a mercy to the boy, but he knew this reason was eclipsed by his own, more selfish one. He heaved at the boy's mind and felt it pull loose. The thing was frightening to him and the monstrosity of his actions was all the worse for its newness. Chester let out a whimper, like a boy needing his mother. He had never mentioned her before and nor would he. But Emerson would know. He had the whole of him in the folds of himself.

He opened his eyes and saw the boy blink several times. He thought he might ask a question or cry out at the pain in his side, but instead he just stared at Emerson blankly, like an animal. The voices were louder and Emerson stood. His mind swam and he was sick on the ground. He felt exhausted, as though he had worked on several people at once. He swayed and shook his head. He felt the weight of Chester in his mind, unbalancing an already delicate raft.

He walked backwards in the snow, away from Chester. The boy only continued to watch, not even knowing how to be puzzled. Emerson's conscience wrenched at leaving him there, at having taken his mind. He fought it off by swearing he would find the doctor. He could no longer refuse to hunt the man down, having sacrificed the boy's life to the cause. He would draw the doctor out and search for Amos's mark – his mother, where she had no place to be.

He brought a heavy hand across his own face and took one further look at Chester, before he ran off into the night, not daring to look back again.

Soon the glow of lantern lights would gather and hum about that boy as men pulled and tore at him, searching for money he no longer had. Chester would stay silent though, even as they prodded at his wound and opened others to draw the truth from him.

He is a brave one, Red Flower would think, without knowing that, if he had the compulsion to, Chester couldn't even tell them his name.

December 1879

'Are you coming, Emerson?' Blanche asked.

Emerson stood in the middle of the yard, frozen in recollection.

'Blanche,' he said. 'I wonder if I can ask you something?'

'Of course,' Blanche said, walking back towards him.

'It's a curiosity of mine,' he said, 'that I hope you'll entertain.'

Blanche nodded, all the while slightly bemused.

Emerson only had assumptions in his mind, nothing certain, nothing yet that might deny his happiness. It could be possible that he might be able to live there and be happy.

'Before I arrived,' he asked, 'did a boy named Chester live here? With you all?'

Blanche was startled for a moment.

'He did,' she said. 'How on earth did you guess at that?'

'And he ran away?' Emerson asked.

'He did,' Blanche confirmed sadly.

Emerson nodded. That much he had been assured of already.

413

And yet its confirmation still stung him. He hoped, somehow, he had been wrong.

'Can I ask what might seem a personal question?' he said.

Blanche appeared almost hopeful in that moment, before noting the glum look on Emerson's face.

You can turn now, Emerson, he told himself, *and be none the wiser. Be assured it is only you and her, and claim your happiness.*

'Kittie. And this boy. Did they love one another?'

The question brought Emerson's words close to crossing pure coincidence, and Blanche looked at him as she had done on their first meeting. She was unsure whether to be curious or cautious – his strange behaviour prompting both in equal measure.

'I believe they did,' she said quietly.

Emerson dropped his head for a moment, wringing his hands in their skin. He would have to know for certain. And, in doing so, he would have to tell Kittie.

'I will join you in town later, Blanche,' Emerson said, fixing his hat. 'I have something to do.'

38

December 1879

'Do you love me, Clay?'

Clay was sitting up, buttoning his shirt. He looked out from the hut, across the icy Newton Lake, and breathed a heavy sigh. The spot was secluded, once used by his father to fish and hunt, and Clay's breath was about the loudest thing next to the birdcalls from the trees opposite.

Clay had removed the guns and rods his father had put in there, but kept the bed he had slept in when waking early for the next day's hunt. The only other thing that remained was the salt his father had used to keep the doors and windows unstuck from the frost. Sacks of it rested in a corner, but you couldn't take a step without its crunch underfoot.

'Did you hear me?'

Clay felt a bare leg push into his back and he seized it by the ankle. It belonged to Clarice Eberdeen. She squealed and pulled her knees towards her to protect herself. Clay smiled loosely and tossed her ankle back, like a fish he'd sooner not have caught.

Clarice seemed upset he didn't wish to play the game.

'Did you hear me?' she asked again. 'Oh, Clay?'

'I heard you,' he snapped.

He stood and tucked his shirt into his trousers.

'And I think it's a fool thing to be asking.'

He paused for a moment and turned to face her once more.

'I might,' he corrected, softening. 'One day. Love you, I mean.'

Clarice laughed and lay back against the bed. She disappeared some in the sheets, a leg dangling off the bed and pushing clumps of salt across the floorboards.

'He might,' she said to the sky. 'Well, isn't this a romance?'

Clay tried to ignore her and collected his clothes and boots, deciding he would finish dressing away from her company.

'You will try and ruin this moment,' he said, beginning to walk away.

'That's all it ever is, Clay. A moment.'

He dropped a boot and bent to pick it up, his arms full. He then dropped his clothes in the salt and cursed.

'But we all of us come back anyway, don't we?' Clarice said.

'What?' he asked her, brushing his jacket clean.

Clarice remained silent. Clay was eager to lose himself in her company, to pursue the ability to forget that her arrival had promised. Instead, in the sobering moments that tail-ended their meetings, his mind washed back towards Odell on the unrelenting tide of his fear.

After a time, though, it seemed likely this would never happen. He imagined Odell, more grotesque now than before, only sought to retreat from the world. Forgetting the horror and how it had shaken him in the workshop, Clay considered the matter a victory.

He explained to Elena how the fire had meant he was required to keep to his office and supply materials for the forthcoming

416

rebuilding effort. She accepted it as readily as everything else he said, only occasionally fearing he was suffering after Ellsworth's death.

The seduction had been simple – if, perhaps, a little too quick for Clay to have enjoyed it. Nevertheless, he found his way back to himself through his darkest acts, sidestepping the true horror of his actions and instead dwelling in his own, comparatively lighter, despicability.

'What do you mean – "we all of us come back"?' he asked her.

She sat up in the bed.

'What?' she asked him, glad to have his attention.

'Just now, you said "all of us". Who's "us"?'

'Oh, Clay,' she said, bringing a hand to her mouth as though to halt laughter.

He marched towards her and seized her by the wrist. Her games had begun to panic him and he grew impatient with her.

'You are hurting me,' she said, twisting in his grasp.

'Tell me, then.'

'Us. Me and the other women.'

'What others?'

Even in discomfort, Clarice laughed. 'You are not as clandestine as you think, Clay. We tolerate you, anyhow.'

Clay threw her wrist back at her and walked over to his boots. 'You're a fool,' he spat out.

'And you, Clay, are temporary. Handsome. But temporary. Only your orphan in town thinks otherwise.'

Clay turned to stare at her. 'Don't you call her that!' he said.

Clarice stood and walked towards him in her chemise. 'Oh, now, don't be mad at me, Clay,' she said. 'Must we fight?'

She slid her arms beneath his and embraced him, nuzzling her face into his neck. He softened somewhat. Clarice looked him in the eyes and kissed him. When she pulled away, she patted him tenderly on the chest.

'See how easy it is?' she said.

Clay pushed her away from him and picked up his boots, marching away from the hut and back towards town.

After seeing Odell, Elena walked uneasily about the town. She had left the remains of the tavern in a hurry, pushing past Hammond as he stretched out an arm, asking her something she cared not to hear.

Do not dare, she told herself, *convince yourself you care for that boy*.

She thought back to all the jokes she had made at Odell's expense, her sisters' teasing about his unreturned attentions. She considered whether it was some reciprocal punishment for having treated him so cruelly, to now find it difficult to think on anything else.

Still, her thoughts about Odell were not separate from her unease with Clay and the ring she now found too tight about her finger.

She thought how Odell's words had touched her at a time when her heart lay open and tender. She supposed it might be a symptom of such a long courtship with Clay to find fancy in other, more sudden passions.

The very idea of passions and Odell made her smile weakly. What now seemed plausible had been so recently impossible. She imagined her sisters and how they might laugh, were they able to spy on her thoughts.

My heart is a conspirator, she concluded.

Elena took the time to study the face of a building being constructed. It had seemed to appear before her that day. The construction was well into its fifth month, and yet something had recently prompted its appearance as a building, rather than

418

just upright materials – the fresh application of outward-facing walls and a newly painted sign advertising a hotel. She supposed her fiancé was responsible for such progress, such was the vigour with which he now approached his work.

The town was growing with such buildings. Their fine unblemished wood sat proudly between older, more tragic structures. Where once there had been distant scenery, now stood solid walls awaiting plush decoration. Where once stood wood, placed with crude markings etched in pencil, now were the final outward signs of construction.

A young man dressed in fine garb walked past her and tipped his hat. He lifted a woman's bags as she was handed down from a carriage, and asked the lady's name before re-entering the building. He made excuses about the exterior of the hotel, putting the woman's mind at rest by telling her that her room was, of course, finished.

Elena wondered how the hotel would affect their business up at the house, particularly when it was finished entirely. She supposed Clay's growing business would offer a balance and her heart warmed with another reason why their courtship made sense.

Elena turned from the hotel and noticed Blanche trailing bunting from one gas lamp to another. She was balancing on a wooden chair and Elena sighed at her sister's insistence on doing things herself. Children stood along the bunting, evenly spaced, watching as though the fine line and fabric might dance alive. Their parents stood about them, each in conversation with another, some asking after Blanche's health, to which, Elena imagined, she would reply nonchalantly, as though nothing had passed.

Does she care to remember? Elena wondered. *Or does she long to forget that night?*

Elena's hand was taken up.

'Well, that's a fine jewel,' Clay said, moving close behind her.

She jumped with his presence and turned to him in annoyance. She noted a sweetness to his scent.

'It does not fit still,' she said. 'And now the store will be closed until tomorrow.'

'How are you?' Clay asked, ignoring her words.

'I am well,' she returned, puzzled. 'But that is far from the point.'

'Well, I'm happy to be engaged to the prettiest woman in all of Virginia.'

Elena smiled reluctantly. She turned back to Blanche, who had stepped down from the chair and was brushing her dress down, taking a moment to catch her breath.

Elena placed her hands on Clay's jacket and felt the rub of something in her palms. She ran it between her fingers and noted it was salt.

'Where were you?' she asked curiously.

'Huh?' Clay said, distracted by the hotel.

'I asked where you were. You said you wouldn't be long.'

'I didn't think I was,' he replied.

He pulled her closer and kissed her neck.

'Clay!' she said. 'Not here.'

'Then where, Elena? Name it and let's go there.'

Elena felt the eyes of a few townsfolk drift her way. She smiled back at them, pushing away the bulk of Clay. She caught the odour on his shirt once more. Intrigued, she nuzzled her face into him, to better smell it. He took this for encouragement and continued to kiss her neck.

'Let's go someplace, Elena.'

Someplace, Elena said to herself.

420

The thoughts aligned in Elena's mind and she pictured Clay's father's hut: the salt across the floor, the bed against the wall. She willed him to explain his absence, to come up with another reason; one she had hitherto failed to think of and yet one whose truth was unwavering. Such an explanation did not come though. The grains in her palm suddenly felt as if they might set in her skin and remain there like gunpowder flash, never to be removed.

'How about the lake?' she said softly.

Clay halted a moment.

'What?' he said.

'The lake,' she said. 'How about we go there? Don't you like that spot?'

Clay stepped back a little and rubbed his face. 'Who have you . . . ?' he began, before stopping.

Elena's eyes began to grow misty. She saw guilt affirmed in his eyes and he saw it reflected back at him.

He took her by the arm and pulled her through a rabble of guests walking into the hotel. They stepped into the alleyway beside the building and he gripped her slight arms in his fists. A band was rehearsing in the hotel and they both of them heard the music through the wall, the conductor remonstrating that they should have started playing in the main street a half hour ago.

'Elena,' Clay began.

'Whose is it?' she asked.

Clay looked confused. 'Whose is what?'

'Whose perfume is that on your collar, Clay?' Elena asked, her voice unsteady in her throat. She gripped his shirt collar and pressed it to her nose.

Clay jerked backwards, tearing the fabric.

'You son of a bitch,' Elena said.

'Elena,' Clay said.

'You stop saying my name,' she said to him, her voice breaking.

Clay smelled his own collar. 'It must be yours,' he said feebly.

Elena looked away, laughing sadly. 'I know my own perfume, Clay,' she said.

Clay moved his arms sparely in the air, like a candidate short of a speech.

'Don't you dare,' Elena continued. 'I knew it, didn't I just?'

'El,' Clay said, moving nearer.

'Don't,' she said, pushing a hand into his chest.

'El,' he said again.

Elena stared at the ground, tears creeping down her reddened face.

'I don't know what you think—'

Elena stared at her feet and began to let out steady sobs. 'This isn't fair,' she said, the tears streaking her face.

The words needled into Clay's heart and he gave up. He thought of Clarice and the others and wished he could set his past alight and send its burning embers tumbling out on the wind.

'I am sorry,' he said.

'Was I not enough for you?' she asked him.

The sight of her distress brought a pain to his throat. He breathed a heavy sigh and chewed his upset like gum.

'It ain't that,' he said, looking down the alleyway, embarrassed.

'Then what is it?' she asked him, pounding his chest. 'What is it?'

Their eyes met.

'I don't know,' he said.

Elena placed a hand on her own neck and flinched as Clay reached out to touch her.

'You keep lying and now I'm done. You hear me? For once, just tell me the truth.'

Clay was chewing the inside of his mouth raw. 'El,' he said, turning once more. 'You are all to me.'

'How many?' she asked him.

'Some,' he answered softly.

'How many?' she repeated.

Clay blotted his eyes with a shirt cuff. 'Since we been engaged?' he asked.

Elena closed her eyes. 'This is not fair,' she said once more.

'Do you mean to leave me?' Clay asked.

'I am spoiled, Clay,' she said. 'Spoiled by you. Who would have me now?'

She turned to leave the alleyway and Clay snatched at her dress sleeve, tearing the frill from the cuff. Elena walked on and out in front of a carriage retreating from the hotel's front. The driver called for his horses to stop and shouted for her to be more careful.

The streets were thick with people now. Elena stormed through the crowd and up towards the house, all the while trying to pull the ring from her finger, the skin rolling and stinging, as though she meant to peel it from the bone.

39

December 1879

Kittie passed through the abandoned train cars, leisurely traversing first class, as she had when her uncle had been alive. She trod down its steps but held back from walking towards the cabin, eager to delay the disappointment of not finding him there. Or else to avoid remembering how she'd found him that abhorrent day all those years ago.

There was a time when she'd refused to recall it. Even the most far-off flicker of the memory would set her heart on edge and draw tears from her eyes. Now, when she thought on it, she felt a grasp on its sadness. She missed him intensely, but she refused to let his death eclipse his life and her part in it.

She had gently waded into the memory, bit by bit, to test her limits, remembering new things about old horrors and dwelling on them so as to strip them of their ability to shock her. She knew total absolution would never come, but she also knew that by peeling away those images she would reach a core, one small enough that she could carry it with her and not be frightened of it anymore, a stone at the heart of a fruit, all fancy gone, leaving just the toughness and the solid event of it.

She pushed the cabin door wide open and stepped inside. She had had occasion to take some winter flowers from the edge of town. Hammond's two younger sisters had travelled in from the farm and set up a makeshift stall. The flowers were nothing remarkable to look at, but in an occasional bunch was a bloom of such intensity it made those around it liven and blossom anew.

'How much are you selling for?' Kittie had asked.

'Five cents,' the older one, Mary, had said.

Kittie's eyebrows did the talking.

'Two to people we call friendly,' she corrected.

The younger sister, Lisbeth, watched Kittie from a few steps back. Kittie blushed at recognising the fascination a young person could have with those older. She recalled paying the same looks to Ora when she and Elena would play in the yard, Elena pulling her friend away from talking to Kittie, asking her to pay her little sister no heed.

I wonder if they knew, she asked herself, walking away with the flowers, *that I am a woman now?*

They would no doubt be unfamiliar with the circumstances, but perhaps it was knowingness in Kittie's eyes or a change about her person that piqued the girls' curiosity. She had crossed a line into adulthood and now looked back on them, accomplished and yet sad — sad at having trespassed on things she had not thought to experience until years later.

The flowers, Kittie lay outside her uncle's bedroom. She couldn't, even years on, bring herself to open the door. The physical sight of him hanging there would be a fiction and yet the horror would be spun in her eyes.

'I love you, Uncle,' she said, her hand hovering over the flowers. 'Forever.'

After a moment, she stepped away from the door and turned to leave, only to be confronted by Emerson on the porch.

'Emerson,' she said, her hand clapping to her chest.

Emerson remained where he was, but held out an arm in caution. 'I did not mean to scare you,' he said.

Kittie's shock turned into laughter and she waited for him to step inside. Yet he did not.

'What are you doing here?' she asked.

'I came to speak with you,' he replied.

'Can it not wait until tonight? Blanche will despair at neither of us being there.'

She smiled again, but Emerson's face remained solemn.

Something is not right, Kittie thought. *Can his mind have changed so quickly? Has he decided he no longer loves me?*

'Will you tell me what the matter is?' she said, shifting her weight uneasily.

'I don't know that I can,' Emerson replied.

'If you think it all a mistake, please say now and spare this moment further burden.'

Emerson entered the cabin and took her hand. 'Lord, no,' he said. 'Kittie, I am truly in love with you. My life has been opened by you.'

Kittie moved his hand in her own, but her heart swayed at the impression of something dark on the approach. Emerson let his head fall and squeezed his eyes tightly shut.

'I knew him,' he said. 'That is to say, I met him.'

'Who?' Kittie asked.

Emerson dug around for the name. 'Chester.'

Kittie's face opened up. Her eyes widened and her jaw dropped a fraction. She let go of his hand at once and stumbled back, sending an empty bottle rolling across the floor.

426

'You said you didn't know him,' she urged. 'You said that, Emerson.'

Emerson nodded.

'Then what?' she continued. 'Was I right to see something similar? Was I right to remember those things? This wasn't all just recollection?'

Emerson dug a thumb into his eye, searching for the answers she wanted.

'Talk to me, Emerson. I cannot now abide silence.'

'Kittie, I . . .'

Kittie had begun to pace about the cabin.

'I cannot tell what to think,' she said, feverish. 'Am I to suppose you met him and stole his manners? To what end?'

Her face was a picture of torment, the suspicions and dreaded realisations puckering there like a sickness. She twisted her hands, one in the other, before coming to a stop and staring at him.

'Did you kill him?' she asked.

The cabin grew smaller in her mind and the road to town pushed out into eternity.

'No,' Emerson stated, awoken from his shame if only for a moment.

'Then what?' Kittie pleaded. 'Is he alive?'

'I fear not,' Emerson replied.

'What?!' Kittie said. 'You speak in riddles!'

I cannot, Emerson thought to himself, *avoid telling the truth any longer.*

Emerson felt a shift below his chest. His inner voice yelled out in protest, while others from elsewhere paraded about dumbly, indifferent to their prison's torment.

'I have a gift,' he said.

Kittie waved his words away.

'Kittie, please listen. One will explain the other.'

She obliged, fighting her every instinct to question him or to doubt him or to run from the cabin for fear. So she did what any other would and listened.

'How can this be true?' Kittie asked aloud.

'I promise it is,' Emerson replied.

'Can you prove it?'

'Only by what you already know. Only by what you have already seen.'

Kittie wanted to deny herself this folly, but found she had no other explanation that tied things up so neatly. She would, she told herself, perhaps reach a saner conclusion in the weeks to come, or else tumble further into Emerson's world.

'Can I see him?' she asked.

Emerson's heart was shot.

'Chester,' she said. 'I want to see him, please.'

'You can't,' Emerson replied.

'Why not?'

'It doesn't work like that,' Emerson said.

'There are no rules,' she said glibly.

'There have to be,' Emerson rebuffed. 'This was a rule. This was something I broke. I wasn't meant to take all of him.'

'I do not believe you.'

Emerson took a deep breath and looked up to the sky through the cracks in the roof.

You owe her this, he told himself. *One last look on the dead.*

'God help me for doing this,' he breathed to the heavens.

When Emerson brought his head down his eyes were green, but Kittie refused to be swayed.

'A neat trick,' she said.

'Kittie?' Emerson said.

The word was Emerson's sound but plucked from another's soul.

'Kittie,' he continued. 'Can you hear me? Are you there, my darling?'

Kittie's face froze.

'Shh, otherwise you will wake your sisters. Will you come down? Fine then, I'll come up.'

Kittie remembered. She recalled that day, and the more she remembered, the more she realised Emerson could never have known.

'I have occasion to tell you I love you. I wish to be with you forever. Don't interrupt me, please, my darling. I know we are young, but I want to be with you. You are my soul's mate, Kittie Marianne.'

'Stop!' Kittie said, her face contorted.

She began to cry heavily and Emerson pulled back, unsteady on his feet.

'How do you know this?' she asked him.

'I'm sorry,' Emerson said, eager to comfort her. 'I am so sorry.'

'That is a cruel trick.'

'I had to convince you,' he said. 'But it is far from a trick.'

Kittie pounded a fist on her leg. 'Why is he still there?' she pleaded.

'I told you, Kittie. I had to find the doctor.'

'But you did!' she shouted. 'You did, so let him free.'

Emerson stayed silent.

'Don't you dare tell me it doesn't work like that, Emerson! Don't you dare!'

Emerson's soul stung at seeing her so upset. 'Kittie,' he said feebly.

'Why did you even want to find Umbründ?' she asked. 'Why did you have to take Chester?'

Emerson searched his own reasoning. 'I had to,' was all he could reply.

'Why did you hunt this man,' Kittie asked, 'if you didn't even know your father?'

'I knew him,' Emerson reasoned.

'You left him there, Emerson.'

Emerson's shape tightened. He grew uneasy with having someone to share his darkest secrets with like this.

'Why did you hunt Umbründ?' she asked again.

Emerson thought about hearing the whereabouts of the doctor from Chester. So long had this coincidence blazed in his heart, so long had he assumed it the intervention of a greater will, that his mind had never had reason enough to question the act.

There must be more to it than this, he told himself.

'I was compelled to,' was all he could reply.

The hunt had consumed him. The curious change he had felt when he stepped from the hotel was laid bare. What he had considered to be relief was, in fact, confusion – even guilt, perhaps. The payment of a son's debt had lifted like a veil to reveal the black pulp of murder beneath.

Kittie was angry now, her sadness drawn behind her like cavalry.

'You were not,' she said.

Emerson knew she was slipping away from him. He was now as estranged from the woman he loved as from himself.

'I love you,' Emerson said. 'And that will not change.'

Kittie looked at him coldly. 'Is this what led you here?' she asked. 'Chester?'

'No.'

'Is it even you who loves me?'

'I know myself, Kittie.'

'Why are you even telling me this?' she asked, twisting her head in exasperation.

'I have to know,' Emerson said, taking a step forward.

Kittie reached out an arm to warn him to stay back.

'I have to know,' he repeated.

'Know what?' she asked reluctantly.

'If it's me.'

Emerson tried to regain the situation in his mind. He wished for control and could not gain it. He stood there, rooted to the spot, when he wanted to do little else but take Kittie in his arms.

'I want to know if it's me you love, and not Chester.'

Kittie turned to him sharply. Her eyes were red about their edges, as though they had been ground into their sockets. She closed her mouth and looked at him hopelessly. To Emerson's horror, he saw an answer there he had hoped would never come.

He walked from her, hands lifted to his temples.

'What you should be asking is if it's you who loves me,' Kittie began, 'and not him.'

'I know it's me,' Emerson snapped, turning back. 'Chester? He didn't even want to be here!'

Kittie's eyes welled up and Emerson sought to draw the words back into his breath.

'I love you,' he said again. 'Say it back to me.'

Kittie stepped towards him and for a naïve moment he hoped she had forgiven him. Instead she searched every part of his eyes, failing to find a trace of green.

'Please,' Emerson said.

She stood up on her toes and kissed him on the lips. Her lips were dry and salty with tears. Emerson brought his arms up to hold her but she was gone already.

'I can't,' she said. 'I don't. Without him there to love, there's only you.'

Kittie's quick patter of breath filled the silence in the cabin.

'You're lying,' Emerson said.

Kittie moved across to the kitchen.

'Let me see.' Emerson went to search her mind.

Kittie flinched, disgusted and afraid. She felt him tugging at her thoughts, an implausible sensation that only now did she have the reason to explain.

She backed into the kitchen table and heard the tumble of objects there. She reached behind her and lifted a knife. She waved it in Emerson's approaching face.

'Leave!' she screamed.

Emerson's expression grew sombre.

'Leave!' she shouted again.

Her mind raced with the horror of the situation. How, one night earlier, she had been in the embrace of this man and prepared to give her life to him. Now she waved a knife in his face and begged him to leave her alone. An unbalanced war went on inside her, the soldiers' uniforms muddied and confused.

Emerson nodded and moved to the door.

Of all those that walk about me, he thought to himself, *she will be the one to never leave.*

He stood on the threshold and took one last lingering look, stowing away as much of her as he could. In that moment he didn't think things could ever fade – her lips, her hair, her hands. And yet he knew they would. Soon his memory of her would be a loose sliver that nevertheless stuck in his mind forever more. Regardless, he would sit for hours at a time to try and recall her every detail. But it would, most of it, go, like pages filled with ink in the midday sun, fading and fading until all that was left was the memory of what was written there and the everlasting torch of love.

40

December 1879

Blanche was growing uneasy at the impatience of the crowd at her back. She had told them to gather for seven o'clock and with five minutes to pass there was no sign of Emerson. She had implored Elena to help as she rushed past, but her sister only wanted to hide away from the man she was engaged to marry.

I will be shamed, then, she thought to herself, *before the whole town.*

She coughed with the thought, her chest restless, as it had been since the accident.

The accident, she confirmed in her mind.

That was what she called it. She had not dwelt on the night she travelled to her uncle's cabin. It would no doubt cause her distress to remember coming so close to death. Yet it would also mean she would return to her anger at Shelby and, inevitably, her wrongful conviction of him before the eyes of the town. For her, guilt lay deep within the snake's nest of her own hate.

'You're back,' Blanche exclaimed, seeing Kittie.

Kittie had been walking as though in a trance.

'What's the matter?' Blanche asked.

Kittie said nothing, only refusing to meet her sister's eye. Blanche failed to notice and, placing a cool palm on her own chest, began to talk about the show.

'I don't think Emerson is coming,' Kittie interrupted.

Blanche looked at her, her eyes widening. 'What do you mean?' she asked.

'I'm not sure I can explain,' Kittie began. 'He—'

Blanche pinched her sister's arm hard.

'Ow!' Kittie exclaimed, shocked.

'Now is not the time to jest with me,' Blanche said and walked past her.

She ran up to Emerson and ushered him before the crowd. As instructed, Blanche had hung the large screen from the theatre for Emerson's show. He looked over it, and only one time did he turn back to Kittie. She was horrified to see him there, supposing he would have left town. Before she could look away, he turned to Blanche.

'Is my pack here?' he asked, moving behind the screen.

'Yes,' she said. 'I brought it down from the house.'

'Good,' Emerson said.

The light was fading fast and Emerson knew that once the streetlamps were down, the conditions would be perfect. He had not performed as recently as he had hoped, but was confident he would have no problems. He considered his decision and weighed it up one final time.

Am I reaching too far? he thought to himself.

'Do you need anything?' Blanche asked.

Emerson looked at his pack to make sure everything was there.

'Blanche,' he said, taking her hand, 'I am so grateful to you for all you have done. I want to thank you for your kindness.'

434

'Emerson—' she began.

Before she could say another word, the streetlamps dimmed.

She squeezed Emerson's hand and went to the front of the screen, paying him a look – a look that said, *We will later discuss things a good deal more.* Yet there would be no later, Emerson realised. This would be his final act.

'Ladies and gentlemen,' Blanche began, standing before the screen, 'and children too. Thank you for coming out today to mark the town's anniversary.'

Blanche coughed, unused to the strain of speaking to such a large crowd.

'I have had the great fortune to meet a man called Emerson Limeflower. Many of you will not know him, for he is a quiet soul. He resides, even now, behind this screen. And yet he is capable of the most wondrous things, the most tall tales. His practice is an old-fashioned one, that is true. And yet I have no cause to be worried when I say, he will greatly enrich your minds.

'Before he begins, please join me in welcoming Limeflower!'

41

December 1879

Kittie saw the light's edge flicker on the screen. She had not been aware she was watching the show. She had been so angry at Emerson that she intended to walk straight to Marianne House, ignoring her eldest sister's pleas and having done with the day. Instead, she had watched Emerson as he arrived, shocked at his audacity.

His story still blazed in her mind and she had already begun to pick at its thread, keen to unravel it into a straight-faced lie. Yet, try as she might, she could not. She could not explain how he had been able to remind her so often of Chester. It wasn't merely a recollection of manners or a similarity in the colour of their eyes. She could have sometimes sworn it was Chester moving before her. Not in form, but in soul. The greatest mimic can replicate the sound of a voice, or the loop of a signature, but who, in truth, could impersonate the gleam of one's being?

She wanted quiet and to sit and think on his words. She moved from decrying Emerson a murderer, to a madman. If what he had said about Chester's impending torture had been true, then

436

perhaps there had been some mercy in what he had done. And yet he held selfish intent all along. If Chester had not mentioned the doctor, would Emerson have been so generous in leaving the boy blank and vague, as he had described it, to the notion of death and, perhaps, life?

Kittie had grown sick with thinking on it. She felt misplaced in a realm of fancy and her head spun as readily as if the world were upside down. Yet when the lantern grew and Emerson's contraption had begun its whirr, all faded away. Her mind stilled as though she had longed for a story and as though one might solve everything. Her eyes had not so much focused on the screen as been drawn into it. She saw past it and into another realm, eyes and mind both bewitched.

'Bravo!' a man exclaimed.

He had leaped from his chair, collapsing it beneath him. Kittie didn't recognise him, although he wore the fancy clothing of one who sought to plant business in New Georgetown.

'Bravo!' he repeated.

More people stood from their seats and began to applaud. Soon they climbed about Kittie and she struggled to stand and look towards the screen. She pulled herself up and clambered onto a seat. Others had had the same idea though, and she was pushed about for a better view.

What happened? she asked herself.

'What a truly wonderful ode,' someone said.

'A fine story,' another said. 'A fine tribute to the man, to the town.'

What man? Kittie thought.

'I thought it rich. I knew him. We served together under Forrest. He was a hell of a man, and that's the truth of it.'

Forrest, Kittie thought. The show began to focus in her mind.

437

She lost her balance on the chair as people rocked it from side to side with their shoving. She caught sight of Blanche standing before the screen, pleading for the crowd to calm down and take their seats. Over her shoulder, Kittie thought she saw a figure move from behind the screen and down a side alley. She shifted her weight to get a better look, to see if it was Emerson. She began to lose her balance though, and had to be steadied by those who surrounded her.

'Are you okay, miss?' one man asked, lowering her to the ground.

Kittie smiled politely before turning and pushing her way to the back of the crowd. People had stilled and now turned to one another in exaltation. When she had pushed through, Kittie jogged around the edge of the crowd and bumped into Elena.

'What happened?' Elena asked.

'You didn't see it?' Kittie replied.

'No. I was up at the house.'

Elena looked out over the crowd, all the while fearing Clay might be there.

'So, tell me,' she said. 'What happened?'

'I believe I can explain, ma'am,' a man said.

He was standing by them, and upon seeing Elena, had turned to address the pair. He removed his hat and swiped the pomade across his curls.

'It was a show, you see,' he continued, 'but like no other. It was a celebration.'

Elena shook her head at him and he turned, somewhat perturbed, back to the crowd. She took her sister's arm and pulled her towards the direction of the house. Not long after, they were standing in the road, halfway up the slope towards home.

'Kittie?' Elena asked.

Kittie's mind had settled. She'd remembered what the show was about and almost wept at the realisation.

'It was a wonderful tale,' she said. 'About our uncle.'

Elena's face soured. 'About Shelby?' she asked.

'Yes,' Kittie enthused. 'About him. About our uncle.'

Elena looked at Kittie, bemused. 'What about him?' she asked.

'The war,' Kittie said. 'And after. The woods. His death.'

Elena turned back towards the town and rubbed at her forehead. 'I am not sure I understand,' she said.

'El, it was a celebration. How he fought bravely. How he tried to save Lori Patch and our brother.'

'What?' Elena asked.

She studied Kittie's face for falsehood, but could see none. She recalled the show Emerson had put on for them and the strange way it had moved her and her sisters, how the events had appeared to take shape in her mind rather than before her.

'Kittie,' she said. 'How did Shelby die?'

A smile flickered across Kittie's face. 'You know,' she said, thinking it a joke.

'Yet tell me.'

'He died up at our house,' Kittie replied. 'Pneumonia took him.'

Elena looked sadly on her sister.

We reside in separate worlds, she thought.

'I know not whether to break this spell, Kittie.'

She took her sister's hand and pulled her towards the house; all the while, Kittie looked over her shoulder for Emerson.

Elena searched Kittie's room as her sister sat uneasily on the bed.

'I know it's here,' Elena said, spilling the contents from the drawers onto the floor. 'Didn't I see you get it from here?'

She moved her hands busily through the clothing until she found what Kittie had only recently shown her – a letter, yellowed and cracked with time and the labour of being a secret. She unfolded it and began to read. Kittie listened, at first perplexed. After a single passage, she slipped it from her sister's grasp and read on herself. She couldn't help but picture those falsehoods – a cabin by the railway, a man turned out by his own kin, and, finally, a rope. The last image came from her memory and not the page, breaking the surface of what she had just that moment believed. The falsehood began to waver and pull away from the truth, a single remembrance destroying the lie like wildfire.

Elena took Kittie in her arms.

'I am sorry to do this,' she said.

Kittie wept on her shoulder. She longed to be convinced of her uncle's better life once more. She longed to return to that dream world. Then she realised. She remembered Emerson's words and what he could do with a mind. She had never thought it possible to do as much with an entire town, and yet now she recalled the words of the crowd from before.

'He did this,' Kittie said. 'Emerson did this.'

'How is that possible?' Elena asked.

'I am not fooling with you,' Kittie said.

Her face convinced her sister more than her words.

'I don't doubt it. But why? Why convince them all for a moment that—'

'It's more than that,' Kittie said. 'He's convinced them for more than that.'

She thought of the town and the anniversary it was celebrating; the birth of New Georgetown, fresh from the earth; a man, a hero – the first in their history – and an uncle.

'Then how can you tell me this?' Elena asked. 'Why don't you believe it any longer?'

'Because you've told me the truth,' Kittie said, beginning to understand the impossible. 'You disturbed it in my mind.'

'Disturbed it in your mind? Slim, how you sound!'

'He explained it to me,' she implored. 'He used those words.'

Kittie thought about the people who had surrounded her in town.

'They all know,' Kittie said. She clasped her hands to her mouth. 'They all know.'

'Know what?' Elena asked.

'Shelby,' Kittie said. 'Emerson convinced the whole town he was a hero.'

'But why?' Elena asked.

Kittie was drawn from the moment and placed elsewhere. She recited his words and his actions. She watched her time with him as readily as though the show continued.

'For me,' she realised. 'He did this for me.'

Kittie ran from the house and through the crowd, which was now dispersing and moving on to further things. She noticed Blanche, tears in her eyes, talking with some of her schoolchildren.

'Was that man your uncle?' one boy asked excitedly.

'He was,' Blanche said proudly. 'He was.'

Kittie arrived at the screen, standing before it as two men unfixed the fabric from its wooden frame. She knew that Emerson wouldn't be there and yet the emptiness when the screen came down still shocked her. Only his contraption remained. She looked about at the buildings, hopeful he would be standing nearby watching her, a smile spreading on his face.

If she saw him, she wouldn't know whether to love him or hate him still for what he had done to Chester. She wouldn't know whether she'd have clarity or yet more questions. She only knew she'd have him; she'd take his hand briefly and thank him for what he had just done.

The two men began to roll up the screen, careful not to crease the material. One of them said something to Kittie, which she failed to hear.

'Miss,' he said more clearly, 'you've got something there.'

He pointed at her chest and she looked down, seeing something like sunlight on rippled water. She swatted at herself, embarrassed for having done so, seeing it was not a thing to be brushed away. The man laughed, more at his own attempt at humour than her action.

They finished rolling up the screen and walked away with the flow of the crowd. Kittie looked up and saw the light coming from Emerson's contraption. It stood there, legs set, pointing straight at her. Her heart leaped with the possibility that this meant he intended to return.

She ran towards it and noted how its light was weak and dipped in brightness. By standing on her toes, Kittie saw that the lamp inside had almost burned through its oil, the flame trying its best to breathe.

Kittie supposed Emerson had left it there after all, keen to make a getaway rather than disassemble its parts and be delayed.

She turned to walk away – where, she couldn't say. A man who she didn't recognise had his back to her and on his black jacket she saw a strange image twist and contort with his movements. She questioned whether to ask him to stand still, to become her screen for the moment.

But before she could, her head was brought back around by a mechanical clicking sound and she saw the contraption had ejected the last of a ream of paper from its peculiar parts. Beside it, in a separate pile, was the show she had just seen – her uncle and the town – an accompaniment to the thoughts Emerson had placed in all the crowd's minds.

Kittie snatched the freshly spewed ream up from the floor and found the beginning, looking at it closer than any letter. For the most part it was blank, and then she came to a fine line drawing of a girl. Her curls were wild about her head and despite the simplicity of the drawing Kittie noticed the mark on the girl's lip, just like her own, which she had often had occasion to dislike.

She followed the paper still and watched as the girl turned and danced. She felt truly touched by it and at once her heart throbbed with a love she would try her best to deny. As the girl completed another turn, the images stopped and, written in a fine hand, were the words, *I am sorry I am not him. Believe me, Kittie – while others walk about my mind, my love alone beats in my heart.*

42

December 1879

'What do you mean by this?' Hammond asked, unfolding the paperwork in his hand.

The paper was of a fine quality and stamped in a way he knew to be too important for him to be acquainted with.

'I mean, it's yours,' Odell replied.

Hammond blinked dumbly at the document before him, as though some further words might appear to help him better understand. Odell turned from him and watched as the luggage was taken from the carriage's roof and along the harbour's walkway. Every box was accounted for apart from Kyoko's violin. That she insisted on carrying herself, and he pictured her now, sitting in the carriage and reassuringly running a hand over its strings.

He had feared their leaving New Georgetown would draw attention and cause great fuss. Instead, they had slipped away with not one head raised. It seemed he had the anniversary celebrations to thank for that.

Can it be called an escape, Odell asked himself, *when it's little more than the past in pursuit?*

444

'Does the Bird know?' Hammond asked.

'Of course she does.' Odell smiled. 'It was her idea. She owned it, didn't she? Look.'

Odell pointed to the scrawl at the foot of the deeds to the tavern. It was the writing he had once thought childish or made by a deformed hand. Scratches like bird's feet padding about on the page.

'I'm not sure about this, Odell,' Hammond said.

'What ain't you sure about?'

All the while, Hammond kept his eyes on the paper.

'I'm a farmer's boy.'

'You want to be?' Odell said bluntly. 'Fine, sell it. Take your money back to the farm and buy your daddy a couple of new cows.'

Hammond thought this an over-simplified estimation of farming, but kept his eyes on the page.

'Just remember,' Odell continued, pointing at the page once more, 'the name stays. So does the piano.'

Hammond nodded slowly.

'I can't sell it,' he said. 'I'd spend the whole time thinking about what might have happened if I'd run the place.'

'Then run it,' Odell said, humoured by his indecision. 'Hammond, it's yours to do with as you please. The Bird wanted to thank you. You've looked out for me plenty. And for my sister.'

The word 'sister' still drew a look of puzzlement from Hammond before he remembered the sheriff's words.

'I'll do it,' he said finally.

He offered a hand to Odell, which he shook warmly.

'I'm glad to hear it,' Odell enthused.

And he truly was. He liked the idea of the tavern going into the care of someone he knew. His memories of that place were rich and plentiful. They would always be tethered to a feeling of sorrow, though. When he thought of the tavern, he thought of Ora.

He had dwelled on his sister when leaving the Long Cape. At first the grief had served to sour his decision, denting the hope he felt in being with Kyoko. In losing Ora, he had lost a part of himself. His mind also returned to the night he saw her climbing the road to Marianne House. Whether it was the fever of a beaten brain, he couldn't say. He only hoped that whatever it was had the legs to follow him on his journey. And to board a ship with him. The saddest thing to his mind would be forgetting her. He drew considerable happiness from knowing he never would.

But while the tavern held the pain of Ora's passing, it also held the hope of a new future. He had seen Kyoko for the first time there and played what would most likely be his first and last concert – to a paying audience, at least. In the hands of Hammond, he was assured his memories would have a home, as much a part of the furniture as that old piano he had played.

Kyoko would be happy too. If Hammond had told Odell he was going to sell, he doubted he would have told her. She had spent the last nine years in that tavern, much of it cooped up inside her room. It was a prison to her and yet she favoured it as the only world she knew. Only the fire changed that.

'I best get aboard,' Odell said.

Hammond folded the paperwork and tucked it snugly inside his jacket. 'I never know what to say, at times,' he pondered.

Odell proffered his hand again and Hammond took it, saying, 'I wish you the very best of luck.'

Odell nodded in return. 'And I you.'

Not one to wallow in the throes of sentiment, Hammond stepped back from the carriage. The driver watched him shut the door tight and in the absence of a signal, he bade his horses start their long journey.

Hammond mounted his old horse back to New Georgetown and as Odell watched him recede from view, he raised a hand in a wave to the newly crowned tavern owner. He was sad to see the last of the town slip away. He had known little else apart from it and even in the clearest remembrances of his childhood, he could only recall his mother walking him and his sister up and down the main street and returning to their father poring over the workings of clocks and watches. Stumbling across his father, he determined to think on. He didn't hate the man, but he couldn't forgive him. Not yet. He thought on whether he might write him from their new home or whether it was best to save his letters for someone else. He took in a deep breath of air unusual to his lungs and felt it reverberate off his ribs, like lightning in a jar.

While the sea disagreed with Odell, it seemed Kyoko was at home upon it. He'd worried that their voyage might return her to the horror of the past. Yet it was as though the trauma she had been through had taken place on land, and as the ship left the dock, she eased into the comfort of their cabin. There had been one bad storm during the six days they had been at sea. It had hardly troubled the ship, but shook the windows of their cabin. Odell had spent most of the night heaving onto the creaking and tilting floor, while Kyoko receded into a corner of the bed. That night had brought everything back to her in one horrid swell. Yet she survived, and Odell wondered if it wasn't a good thing to have gone through another storm and come out alive on the other side.

One aspect of seafaring Odell was grateful for was the confines they kept to. There had been a time, not more than a month earlier, when he believed all the promise life could deliver to lie in a kiss from Kyoko. Now, though, he knew much more and relished their freedom together. He believed that if his fingertips trailed ink, there might not be an inch of bare skin on her body remaining.

Their courtship wasn't a common one, yet it afforded him the opportunity to care for her and she, in kind, cared for him. On occasion Odell would seek to question whether she loved him as he loved her. Each time, though, he would be sated by the mystery of it, always thankful for her hand in his, and his love that he knew to be enough.

'I love the way you look at me,' Kyoko said, brushing Odell's hair over to one side.

He smiled at her and pulled the sheet up over their bodies. The cabin window was propped open, as Kyoko had insisted, but the sea breeze was cold and chilled his naked body. Kyoko's eyes tilted down as her mind wandered off to someplace else.

'Before we left,' she began, 'someone came to see you.'

Odell looked up at her and brushed a hand over her thigh. He enjoyed her warmth on his scars.

'Someone?' he asked.

Kyoko nodded.

'That was Elena,' he said.

Kyoko pulled a sheet corner up to cover herself. 'Who was she?' she asked.

'A friend,' Odell said vaguely, turning to look out to sea.

Kyoko reached up and pulled Odell's face towards her. He noted how beautiful she was.

'More?' she asked.

'Once.' He nodded. 'But not since I met you. She was a diffi-cult one to shake, to move on from. It took me finding someone else to realise I didn't care much for her. Not anymore, at least.'

Kyoko smiled and leaned forward, concealing her modesty against her knees. Her bare back was to the open window and the skin there prickled in the cold air. Her face was close to Odell's and she kissed the corner of his mouth.

'I do not understand,' she said.

Odell turned to kiss her again.

'But you know what I mean by "I love you"?' he asked.

Kyoko smiled and nodded.

'Then you understand,' he said, and kissed her once more.

That night, Odell returned to the deck and hung his swelling head over the side. He enjoyed the cold blast of air running through his hair and over his face. He had been sick the entire afternoon, but now felt more himself. One of the tradesmen making the journey to find work had offered him a drink from his whisky bottle.

'It stills the sea,' the man had said, tapping his head. 'Up here.'

He might have drained the whole bottle had the tradesman not watched him expectantly. He merely took a hearty glug and returned it to him with a grateful smile.

A few men stood along the deck of the ship, some taking in the air after being in their cabins and others taking exercise as they walked its perimeter. Witnessing such exertion made Odell weaken all the more and he dipped his head into the wind again.

Two men further along from him had been caught up in a conversation for some time, but only now did he begin to listen.

'Every man has a trade,' one said. 'Especially in these times.'

The conversation was thoughtful but light-hearted, such as might exist between two men sharing one another's company for a time, and then, perhaps, never again. Odell wondered how many of these conversations were carried upon the sea, alive and private in the swells of anonymity.

'I don't know what to tell you,' the other man said.

'Tell me your trade,' the first man replied. 'Maybe I can speak with someone, make it so you've got some work waiting for you when we land. Some food too.'

'I told you my trade already.'

'That's no more a trade than me smoking this tobacco.'

Odell let out a laugh that was lost to the wind. The smoking man made a frustrated groan and soon a companion of his joined them. They bade their goodbyes and left the other man to it. As they retreated, they walked past Odell.

'Who was that?' the man's companion asked.

'I didn't get his name.'

'He looked near death.'

'From his work, he says. Last job he did took its toll.'

'Well, what's he do?'

The smoking man laughed. 'That's just the thing. He tells stories, he says.'

Odell lifted his head and watched as the two men stepped back inside the ship. He then turned to look over his shoulder at the man they were talking about. Something about him struck Odell as familiar, and he moved unsteadily along the ship's deck. All was darkness but for the lanterns that swung from the rigging.

Odell had come close to the man when he turned and shifted in surprise. Odell recognised him at once. He had seen him about the town on occasion and, once, walking with the doctor. He only remembered the night of his injuries in nightmarish wisps, but he recalled the man's face and, now that he thought about it, his voice seemed familiar also.

The man's features relaxed and recognition spread across them.

'Odell,' he said, remembering the name.

'I sure wish I knew your name,' Odell replied, seizing the man's hand.

'Emerson Limeflower,' he said.

Odell was elated, but could not ignore Emerson's appearance. He would have supposed he was seasick had it not been for the men's words earlier. He almost enquired after his health, but instead chose to speak of happier things.

'What fortune this is!' Odell beamed. 'Jesus, what fortune!'

'What are you doing here?' Emerson asked.

Odell thought about Kyoko and his mouth raced to tell Emerson all about her and how they had left the town in the hope of a better life. All the while he called her Kyoko, the name 'the Bird' remaining at the tavern with so much else. At Emerson's request, Odell related how his hands were healing and moved them in demonstration.

'And you?' Odell asked, patting Emerson's arm. 'What are you doing here?'

Emerson shrugged and winced as the wind picked up, scattering them with a rain of seawater.

'You didn't think New Georgetown would make a good home?' Odell continued.

Emerson replied, but most of his words were lost to the whistle of the wind.

Odell leaned closer to hear.

'Sometimes,' Emerson concluded, 'I don't think any place would.'

Odell noticed a deep sadness in Emerson's face that might just have been the weather leaving its mark.

The ship rocked and both men held on to the side. Odell stared out to the sea and then upwards, watching the lantern at the top of the mast swing wildly.

'I best head back inside,' he shouted to Emerson, 'to check on her.'

Emerson understood and the two men shook hands once again.

Odell leaned in close. 'I never had occasion to thank you,' he said.

The two men hunched together, but met one another's eyes. Odell didn't know what to say to him that would express his gratitude for saving his life. He thought of Kyoko waiting for him back in the shelter of their cabin and it was the sweetest thought he might have in all his life. His eyes came alive at something he had not seen before.

'You know, you remind me of someone,' Odell said.

Emerson smiled like he had heard those words a hundred times or more.

'But you,' Odell said, squeezing his hand and drawing him closer against the pounding of the sea, 'you are a good man, Emerson.'

Acknowledgements

I would like to thank the following people for their help and support in writing *All Their Minds in Tandem*:

Firstly, my mum and dad. Without them, I never would have had the encouragement or the desire to think about writing. But, moreover, I would never have had a love of reading or books. To say you are the biggest inspiration in my life underplays your importance to me. This novel began with stories you both read to me, and that is something I'll forever be grateful for. You're supportive parents, but, above all, incredible friends.

Kat – there's no one who's been more patient with me than you. You encouraged the idea, the first words, the characters and the story. Your love is interwoven into the pages and you gave me the opportunity to do what I wanted to do most and take the time to write this. In a book with no small debt to love, I learned from you just what that is. You are the heart of everything.

To my wonderful and wise agent, Becky Thomas. You did everything to bring this book to a publisher. You asked me about it, sought to read it and offered such crucial advice. It changed so much for the better and I couldn't think of anyone I'd be happier to call my agent.

To everyone at Quercus who has supported the book. To Rich

Arcus, my editor, who is incredible and the finest of travel companions. Your thoroughness, imagination, humour and support have been unwavering. I'm proud to have written this book, but equally proud to have had you edit it. To Jon Riley, who took a chance on me and gave great care and guidance throughout the process. I am privileged to have been able to talk to you about this book. And to Penelope Price, whose attention and investigative mind this book couldn't have done without.

To my friend Nicci Cloke. This is an official IOU for a very good plot point, which you suggested after generously reading the book. Your own novels inspired me to take the chance and your support and kindness kept me going.

To my good friend Lucy Curzon, who said to go for it and has kept saying that ever since. The third person to read any of the words, you are someone who is there at every turn.

To my brother, Phil, and my sister, Jo, and their families. You offered me places to write, sugar for fuel and your priceless support. You taught me what family is and, even from afar, you make me feel mine couldn't be closer.

I found the following incredibly useful in writing this book:

Battle Cry for Freedom: The Civil War Era by James M. McPherson (Penguin; New Ed edition, 1990), *Race and Reunion: The Civil War in American Memory* by David W. Blight (Harvard University Press; New Ed edition, 2002), *The American Woman's Guide to the Home* by Catharine Esther Beecher (Rutgers University Press, 2002), *Collected Poems of Ella Wheeler Wilcox* (Leopold B. Hill, n.d.) and Ken Burns's staggering documentary, *The Civil War* (PBS).

And, finally, thank you also to the generous staff of the British Library, in whose Reading Rooms a good deal of this book was written, and to the authors I've had the pleasure to work with, who inspired and encouraged me in equal measure.